The past is always present: yet it is not what was,
but whatever seems to have been.

—G. K. CHESTERTON

You do yet taste
Some subtleties o' the isle

—PROSPERO

FOR
UNCLES AND AUNTS

CONTENTS

THOROFARE

WILFORD

1. Uncle Dan Arrives—1897

The cat got into the milk at the same moment that Uncle Dan
arrived from America. Naturally Barton House had been tense
all day, and probably Jue, sagacious old animal, supposed he
could do a larceny unnoticed. Also the stone milk-jars were even
fuller and creamier than usual. They stood on the cool damp-
smelling floor of the cellar, near the meat-safe—an open cupboard wired with netting where perishables were guarded. Re-
frigeration was unknown and unnecessary. "It's funny," Geoffrey said, "it's so cool down here, why does everything perspire?"

Jue had always been praised to Geoffrey as a model of dis-
creet behavior, and his black face and whiskers dripping in one
of the stone crocks was a shocking sight. The aunts were all
down in the larder to deal with this crisis when Uncle Dan gave
the Family Knock. Until then Geoff had best visualized his
uncle as an envelope floating in through the metal slot. Once
he actually saw him come: the postman banged the knocker unusually loud, the slot squeaked open, a slant of sunlight ran
down to the linoleum and the letter coasted along it. Some peo-

3

ple still remember those old blue five-cent stamps with the picture of General Grant.

"It's Dan," they cried, and in the rush up the narrow stone stair Geoff got trampled, Aunt Bee skinned her knee, and Jue escaped the punishment he would have had. Grandma came from upstairs without even touching the banisters—she had been lying down because her heart was pounding ever since midday dinner. Aunt Em stayed in the cellar to console the cat. A few black hairs in the cream wouldn't worry her, for she esteemed animals more than family.

Uncle Dan's welcome was tumultuous, but Geoff returned to the larder to watch Jue wiped and soothed. "It's a wonderful tea for him," the child said, admiring the methodical way Jue set about grooming himself. There were still beads of cream on his stiff whiskers. With whitened chaps he looked rather like Aunt Em herself, but even at that age Geoff had sense enough not to say so. Aunt Em was different and he had learned caution.

There was a coursing of footsteps overhead, to and from the little dining-room; Geoff knew that the highest of high teas was laid. The best china with its broad bands of blue, green, or pink; the Demerara sugar, the tortoise-shell tea-caddy, the knitted cozies ready for the boiled eggs, the silver spoon with holes for sifting powdered sugar on gooseberry tart; and paper-thin slices of brown Hovis bread, his own special slice perhaps sprinkled with hundreds and thousands (minute grains of colored sugar)—these were even better than the spectacle of the cat in disgrace. The first thing he asked Uncle Dan was, "Is that your picture on the American stamp?"

"That's U. S. Grant," said Uncle Dan. It was a long time before Geoffrey learned it did not mean United States Grant.

First personal knowledge of Uncle Dan was mixed with the linoleum fragrance of the floor. Uncle Dan had brought him an American toy engine, and showed him how the pattern of the hall floor would make a good track. Geoff kept explaining to the aunts that the cowcatcher took the place of buffers. Fortunately among the china animals he was collecting there was a cow. He placed the small image on the floor to justify the odd shape of the new engine. There were many questions to ask Uncle Dan. Why the bell on the locomotive, why the cylinders and pistons outside, why so large a cab when English engine-drivers had much less shelter? "We get some terrible weather in the States," Uncle Dan said proudly. "And we call them engineers, not drivers."

"Jue will like it, it says Purr," Geoffrey remarked, admiring the initials P.R.R. on the tender. This reminded them to cajole Aunt Em up from the cellar; it always took strategy to get Em to do anything you wanted her to. She pretended she had strained the cat's hairs from the milk, but of course she hadn't. She thought it would serve them right for not having put the rusty iron weights on the wooden covers of the jars. Uncle Dan made the traditional homage "There's nothing like a Wilford egg" as he lifted the knitted cozy and sliced the brown shell. "Can I have the top?" said Geoffrey. "In America they eat boiled eggs quite differently," said Uncle Dan. "Nonsense," said Aunt Em, "there's only one way to eat an egg." The sponge cake and gooseberry tart (with an eggcup, upside-down, supporting the high crust) played their share in the modest festival. There was blommonge too, but he didn't care for it, even after learning to spell it blanc-mange. But all he really remembered was the long vista of linoleum passage, the toy with a cowcatcher and cat-sounding initials. He did not even notice the traction engine rumbling by, shaking the house and filling the Thorofare from kerb to kerb.

2. Memories of a Garden

A strong palisade of aunts stood between him and the gales of the world. Within the domestic stockade the wise egotism of a child guards its own weak identity. Parents or granddams, pensioners, pets or friends may offer him all their own treasures of learning, but what does he care? Like the old folk dance, it is "Hey boys, up go *we*." Later the world is busy to beat out that singularity. But as we see him now he is the unconscious artist, riotous with self. For such pleasure two experiences are needed: sense of enclosure; sense of space.

For enclosure: there could hardly have been any pleasure-ground more suitable to his requirements. There were three regions: the red brick wall; the meadow; and "The Wilderness." Along the red wall came the first sunshines of early thaw; it was paralleled by a gravel path good for small walking. Against the washed and faded brick, pear and apricot trees were trimmed in espalier. The meadow was notable for haycocks and wasps. And below the shrubbery of The Wilderness was a hedge where Geoffrey watched the roaring passage of the Yarmouth express. No modern sentimentalist of locomotives could persuade him of any machine so glorious as those blue engines, terrible with red buffers, and flying rods that flickered like brandished fists. The engine took the S curve with a scream of defiance, the string of golden-brown carriages straightened out to rocket past the water-color meadows. Uncle Dan said someone had drawn a red herring across the track, that was why the trains were so wild. Already they smelled the bloaters of Yarmouth, forty miles away. Beyond the metals were the tidal marshes of a little river, and moist grazings wealthy with primroses. They grew there in buttered fatness; it was a joke at Geoffrey's expense that when he first saw them he flung himself into the bog and seized as many as he could clutch in both hands. Sometimes it was feared this was a character of the child.

The tanglewood of The Wilderness, damp and shadowy, was extraordinary for several stone deer with lifelike glass eyes. There was a stag with antlers, standing at a statuary alert, trailed by a stone wolf who glared hungrily from ambush. Beyond there was a winding path among spiky foliage which he heard called *pyrus japonica*, syllables he never forgot. This way led back to the stable, occupied mostly by fowls, rabbits and

6

guinea pigs. Farther to the left (looking from here) was the long warehouse with a dry smell of straw. Both warehouse and stable were semi-prohibited: the warehouse because china and glass were being unpacked, the stable because of temptation to chivvy the hens or misfeed rabbits and guinea pigs. In this back-yard space were social apparitions from which the whole age of Victoria can be construed. There was old Ellis (born in 1822), as beautiful as Father Christmas: snow-white beard, pink cheekbones, forget-me-not eyes, the perfect good servant, his delicate old hands still busy with fragile porcelain and glass, clean and kempt and winnowing the faith and kindness of seventy-five devoted years. In contrast were goblin figures, the Ghostly Demon and black-toothed Lizzie Batts. The Ghostly Demon (the child's own label for that gruesome figure) was a drooling, shamble-footed halfwit in the warehouse, abominably resembling a Messiah who had had bad luck. Indeed there was astonishing theology in that cobbled courtyard. From the dark warehouse into open sun would come alternately the sweet, patriarch figure of old Ellis and the furtive outline of the Ghostly Demon. To make suggestion irresistible, the place was fluttured and cooed over by Aunt Emma's pigeons, let out from her glittering cupola retreat, a glass belvedere on top of the house. Dismay grieved the Quaker bosoms of the family when the child stated that these three elements were God, Jesus, and Holy Ghost. But Aunt Em, white-haired, saturnine and witch-like, cackled with disreputable laughter and secretly invited the child up to her eyrie (out of bounds for any other member of the household). She seemed to reward him for impudence downstairs by giving him a withered peppermint and a glimpse of her collection of stuffed pets. In her glass cupola she had preserved by taxidermy the various cats, squirrels, magpies, iridescent pigeons, canaries, bullfinches, and even a seagull, on which she had lavished her mortal affections.

Aunt Em's life downstairs was serving as cashier of a dying business. There was a little counting-room (so-called) between the family dining-room and the shop. In the corner of this dining-room was an old horsehair settee and a mahogany cupboard in which The Games were kept—relics of the childhood of these same aunts. To keep Geoffrey amused in slack moments he was sent to this corner to explore The Games (he can still smell those old boxes and feel the cool bone counters). As he sat piling colored chips on the green felt of the dining table, he could see Aunt Em two steps up in the counting-room clanking coins. He supposed she also was playing a game. But Aunt Em's sharp profile was grim over the day's take. From this haggard employ she would draw off in her lavender print dress, muttering herself upstairs and showing a fine view of white cotton stocking and heelless black slipper. She mumbled her way to the top of the house, ascending thence by a ladder to the glass cupola which was her sanctum. Nothing in *Grimm's Fairy Tales* was more weird than his impressions of this place to which he was occasionally bidden and where Aunt Em would tell him of the champion qualities of her stuffed menagerie. He was strictly charged to say nothing downstairs of these secret visits, for the rest of the family regarded Aunt Em as a trifle cracked. There in her transparent cabin she performed the crone's magic of holding the world in trance. Her cats and birds and squirrels were still alive and she soliloquized her spells. Sometimes from the courtyard below one could see her leaning out of that lofty glass box and calling the pigeons upward in a voice of eldritch endearment.

3. *The Birthmark*

"When are we going to have tea in the meadow?" was one of Uncle Dan's first questions. In the lee of a mound of hay the picnic was set out. At that happy age Geoffrey escaped the drudgery which is part of any such outing. While the aunts bore out baskets and Uncle Dan spread straw garden-mats, Geoff had gone down through The Wilderness to show his American engine what an English train looked like. He did not often go alone to that damp and shadowy bottom of the territory, for he was privately a little frightened of the stone wolf among the dark holly trees. But beyond the palings ran the railway line. The blue locomotive went shimmering by with its long ripple of tilting carriages; sometimes also a goods engine, more humble in outline but more available for study, shunted along a siding. It was important that his P.R.R. treasure, now companion in bed and at the board, should see these things. When he returned through the field the picnic was ready. So also the wasps who had taken tenure of that particular haystack. Perhaps the cloth had even been laid right over their nest. At any rate it was the most harmless of the aunts whom they punctured from below. This was the only time he saw the famous birthmark. It was a legend in the family: it appeared once or twice in every generation, in the case of females usually modestly remote. Uncle Dan, as Geoff learned in swimming, had it on one foot, but when family talk grew reckless after three cups of tea, Aunt Bee's blemish was mentioned with bated breath as "on her thigh." Whether such oddities allure the wasp one does not know, but somewhere along that curvature came the sting.

Geoffrey was sent to the house to ask for tallow. When he got to the kitchen, the house was full of sound. In the musty drawing-room upstairs, a place of the rarest visit, was an old grand piano with yellow keys. To his astonishment Aunt Em was up there playing furiously. No one had questioned her decision to have nothing to do with the picnic: she was like that: if some casual remark had griped her, or she was bored with the harmless palaver of her kindred, she simply absented herself. But this was the first time Geoffrey had known her to resort to music. Oldest of the aunts, she was the only one who before the family income collapsed had been given a genteel education. The last flourish of that culture was an occasional outburst on the ancient piano. The tune she was playing, with the brio of rage and despair, was *The Blue Danube*. Whether in melody

9

or execution it suggested with appalling fidelity the tragic interim of summer afternoon. Unstrung by this unaccountable woe he met Lizzie and roared with tears.

Lizzie had to escort him back to the meadow where Aunt Bee was still nursing her contours and Uncle Dan appeasing her by describing how much bigger are the wasps of the States.

To Aunt Bee "bigger" was never a consolation. She was small, firmly gentle and neat, and preferred small things. When anyone else would have picked a big bundle of garden flowers Aunt Bee with tiniest buds and scraps and casuals of the field made a miniature nosegay in a mimic little vase.

4. *The Way to Deal with Aunts*

Early morning felt good in the little back bedroom upstairs. Geoffrey looked through a barred window onto the flint-cobbled courtyard; the Ghostly Demon was sweeping with a twig besom while Aunt Em's pigeons gurgled and teetered on the slopes of tile roof. A room at the front of the house would not have felt nearly so intimate. There was space between the bars to put his head through and perhaps get a glimpse of Lizzie Batts from above. With the heartless candor of childhood he called down to her, "I like looking at you from here because I can't see your teeth." Fortunately Lizzie was not sensitive and only replied, "You bath yourself, Master Geoffrey, and don't fidget about me." The bath was a round metal dish with a high back, kept in a small room of its own where splashing would not matter. As he lay comfortably in bed he could hear Lizzie panting up the steep and narrow stairs with huge cans of cold water. The social historian can hear throughout the Victorian Age the heavy breathing of housemaids trudging up and down with those innumerable vessels, painted and grained to look like wood. Even their shape has vanished from the earth: tall heavy canisters with a hinged flap, and an elbow spout so that a small tilt would start the water flowing. The chill of the bath was somewhat compensated by scraps of green vegetable frond, perhaps some sort of moss or herbage from the old stone well. These were amusing to play with as they floated in the slosh of water around his knees. Sometimes a small tissue of bath cress (so they called it) was picked off the back of his neck by an alert aunt as he sat down to breakfast.

Beyond the palisade of aunts and the rigorous little grandmother there was a further sense of protection—dimly but subtly felt, perhaps impossible to suggest to any who never knew it. The Queen. The disillusioned democrats of earth can scarcely divine what that remote figure meant to subconscious imagination. Especially so that summer, for it was her Diamond Jubilee. Her picture looking like everyone's homely old nurse was in all shop windows, the narrow streets were spanned with flags, and the climax was when Uncle Dan took him to the guild hall on Market Hill to see the first cinematograph. They stood among a dense crowd and Uncle Dan lifted Geoff to his shoulder. Amazingly, flickering and enlarging outward from the screen, came the capering shadows of helmeted lancers—he shrank back to avoid the horses' hoofs—and there was a carriage (wheels hesitating and rotating backwards) and a little old lady under a parasol fixed him with a considering shrewd eye. The memory flickers and fades, the old lady may have been smiling or weeping or waving, but the impression on a child was of the grandmother of the world.

That evening the Thorofare was full of red-coated soldiers from the barracks beyond the Seckford Hospital (euphemism for almshouse). They wore pillbox caps aside their heads and switched their trousers with bamboo swagger sticks as they passed the girls. Geoffrey noticed that on his evening off Atkins smells curiously mixed of beer and pomade. "Why do they carry those little sticks?" he asked. "Is it to switch the enemy?" When they got home there was treacle tart; the diagonal strips of pastry over the hot crumbsticky sweetness were ornamented with red, white and blue hundreds and thousands. That was Aunt Bee's idea.

The way to deal with aunts is one by one. When he had them together they squabbled or went into regions of talk from which came disconcerting suggestions. For instance Uncle Dan remembered that in their own childhood Aunt Allie (now so silent and stoic) pursued him across that same meadow whirling a murderous croquet mallet. Such revelations shake the altars of a child's conception. But each of the aunts taken singly had her own method of enchantment. With Aunt Bee there was the memorable outing to Ipswich. This involved his first ride in a train: only a few miles, but miraculous. How many children got their earliest notion of England's quiet beauty from the photographs of scenery framed in railway carriages, at exactly the right height to be studied by standing on the seat. In Ipswich, whose railway platforms seemed of incredible length, a newsboy with a tray of papers and Cadbury chocolates was shouting along the open doors. He had an illustrated paper whose front page was a wonderful picture of an exploding battleship. Aunt Bee was shocked that Geoffrey should want such a souvenir, but he had been given a copper to spend. The picture so interested him that later he used crayons (colored chalks, they called them) to rubricate the drawing. There were thrilling sheets of flame which he daubed with all shades of orange and pink, and in the blast small figures of shattered seamen flying through the air. It was a battleship called the *U.S.S. Maine*.

Adventures with Aunt Bee were likely to be sociable; with Aunt Allie evangelical; with Em they were ominous of dotage. Aunt Allie's form of frolic was a meeting of the Band of Hope, a juvenile offshoot of the Salvation Army. Children of the Lizzie Batts stratum would appear at the Bartons' front door with a vivid blue and red banner, and a bugle. A small parade would form at the front door to escort Aunt Allie to the meeting where hymns of low prosody were chanted, followed by buns and lemonade. To watch Aunt Allie, who had a way of silently

12

champing the tune with a rhythmical rotation of provincial dentures, was a great excitement. But it was somewhat embittered by the realization that some of the family thought this very low-class. Aunt Em was openly cynical and would gaze down from her bedroom window with an obvious sneer as the ragged regiment set off. But Aunt Allie was a militant puritan of the unconquerable breed. In every purlieu of Wilford she was busy with soup and succor. She knew every wastrel or victim by first name and understood the causes of their wretchedness; a drunken bargee staggering out of a pub would try to straighten up if she happened to be passing. Children's eyes are close to the ground, and Geoffrey can still see the methodical toss of her skirt hem (ballasted with little sinkers of lead) as she trudged resolutely toward some hopeless errand of mercy. It must have been Aunt Allie, watchful of his childish errors, who phrased and made statutory the bedtime prayer that shrewdly assessed his frailties. The matter of prayers was somewhat a professional jealousy between Bee and Allie. When gentle Aunt Bee heard Geoffrey's prayers he could improvise and follow whatever line of petition appealed to his mood; but supplication was formalized when Allie presided and he must say the rune she had devised as salutary for his weakness: "Help me to control my Temper, my Excitement, and my Tongue." If after the long and innocent catalogue of blessings upon kinsmen and hopes for the morrow he omitted this, Aunt Allie would sternly insist: "Don't forget your Temper, your Excitement, *and* your Tongue."

Aunt Em had long abandoned the consolations of myth and was never called upon for any contribution to divinity. It was obscurely felt that Aunt Em, if chivvied, might come out frankly for the Devil.

It seemed effective to offer bedtime prayers through the medium of Aunt Allie or Aunt Bee, because through those very simple human filters the better parts of aspiration might somehow be communicated to headquarters. To say prayers to Grandmother rarely happened: he would have felt he was getting a little too close to the ultimate itself.

Aunt Em, however, had her theological values. One day, returning from some evangelical excursion with Aunt Allie, they passed the beautiful old flint church whose great square tower dominated the town. This establishment was always mysterious to Geoffrey as the family were Dissenters, and on this occasion he noticed for the first time the stone gargoyles along the roof. He announced that one of them looked like Aunt Em, and that was one of the few times he ever heard Aunt Allie laugh.

Of course the family worshiped Uncle Dan, the boy who had broken away from the small home circle and gone to America to seek his fortune. Plenty of Wilford sons had gone to Canada or Australia, but Dan was unique in having chosen "America." It would have been interesting to get some idea of the aunts' notion of the geography of that country. One evening when Uncle Dan sat smoking in the little dining-room—it was set apart for him in case he needed "to think," a semi-mystical operation never attributed to anyone else—a question arose which involved reference to a tattered old atlas. Dan was trying to explain to them that Great Britain was about the same size as Pennsylvania, and discovered to his dismay that the aunts thought Pennsylvania was a town. He was indignant when he observed British geographers' habit of including maps of America only on a very small scale and at the tail of the book, behind the much more emphasized cartography of Afghanistan, Burma and the Malay States. Uncle Dan used to say it was only an accident that he had gone to the States instead of (as the aunts said) the other colonies. He had the impression that in New Zealand everybody herded sheep, in Canada everybody raised corn (by which he meant grain) and these didn't interest him. He said once that he was the only Englishman in the United States competing with one of America's great industries: teaching English Literature. That in itself was an accident; appar-

14

ently it had never occurred to American educators that "English" might be taught by an Englishman, just as French by a Frenchman or German by a German. It used to amuse him that Keats and Wordsworth should be "taught" by young American instructors who would be helpless to order an intelligent meal in a London restaurant. He used to speak of the Ph.D. in English from Ohio Reserve who could not answer any of the first four questions actually addressed to him in British viva voce. These were said by a steward in the Cunard dining saloon who asked the bewildered pundit would he have Thick or clear? Saddle or silverside? Sweet or savory? and White or black?

Geoffrey was allowed to sit up for a while after tea on condition that he stayed in the corner of the old horsehair sofa alongside the cabinet where The Games were kept. That inside dining-room was lit only by a skylight so one could be cozened to bed without realizing it was still daytime in the garden. But while adept in amusing himself with cards or dominoes or the old bone counters his ears were quick enough for casual remarks overheard from the elders. There was a word of special excitement, partly perhaps for the tone of its utterance by the aunts. It was the word Atlantic. When the atlas came out he used to look for it but never found its picture complete. There would be a little bit of it around the British Isles or a slice of it off the coast of America; he could never find it spread out in full. Sometimes it was divided by the fold of the book so that he had a vague notion there was an alleyway across the middle.

5. *Down to the River*

There were two ways to the River. Down the lane just below the shop was the quiet walk past the long brick side of the warehouse, where Aunt Em's pigeons balanced above on mossy ripples of tile. They looked so insolent, it was a temptation to wave and flurry them. This sent up a silky turbine of wings, which

Aunt Em probably noticed from her watch-tower. "That wicked boy," she muttered, and calmed herself with a lozenge. Sometimes a sea gull came down on the roof; then the doves huddled at the other end of the ridge and looked smaller. At the bottom of the lane was a level crossing, with a barrier, and a turnstile at one side. This way was tempting, perhaps all the more so because the aunts were doubtful of the railway crossing. Just beyond was the brewery, with a strong smell of hops and malt; so strong (they thought) it might stupefy the crossing watchman and he would forget to close the gates. When a train went by, for a few moments the smell of railway mingled with the brewery fragrance. Then a cool dusty whiff from the flour mill admired by many painters, and past wharves and a pub called The Anchor one reached the River.

But Geoffrey might have chosen the other way, along the Thorofare. It would be hard to convey such a street to any who had not seen its like. It was a narrow bending passage of macadam, three horsebellies wide (those huge rounded horses called Suffolk punches). The pavement on each side had in some places been pared down to the beam of one medium pedestrian. Some of the older houses were bracketed forward in the upper storey, over the narrow sidewalk. Of its many shops some were specially well known to him. Keeping on the left-hand side he would come first to Garble the Grocer (and "Italian Warehouse," which meant something like delicatessen). In Mr. Garble's window were those wonderful bottles and posters of Eiffel Tower Lemonade: yellow crystals which mixed with water made an elixir for the young. Just beyond was Cash Chemist with tall glass vases of dyed water; this place he associated with an opiated smell of cough medicine ("brown mixture") and sulphur that was burned in the house after measles. Then there was a shop that specialized in K-boots. These were notable for thickness of leather, and the heavy clatter of soles further armored with crescents of metal. Across the street were two neighboring entries of delight—Miss Hoo the Toyshop and

16

H. Bredfield, Bookseller and Stationer. Miss Hoo's window of many panes was full of small sailboats and model yachts, from the cheapest ha'penny dinghy to schooners of dainty rig. And at Bredfield's were all varieties of drawing books, pencils, colored crayons, paintboxes, and even more exciting, the smell of print and paper. Is it the moist English climate that makes ink and paper smell so aromatic? Surely every visitor to that island has bent his nose to the perfume of English newsprint, and Bredfield's ancient little shop was an experience to the nostril. There were sentimental reasons for making errand to Bredfield's as often as might be: the two families were friends of several generations, and bookselling, like china, was on the downgrade.

Perhaps he was towed past Miss Hoo and H. Bredfield with sidelong looks, and found himself at The Cross, the dangerous intersection in the middle of the town. At each of the two near corners was a tavern, The Cross on one side and The Crown on the other. The Crown was reputed more genteel because it had a fine bowling green tucked away behind. When a Wilford child first heard the phrase "No Cross, no Crown," he probably thought it meant a drink on both sides of the street. But to Geoffrey the crossroad was most notable for another figure of astonishment, an old white-bearded eccentric who had appointed himself voluntary traffic policeman. He wore a scarlet coat designed by himself with frogs of yellow braid and a scarlet-visored kepi. His supervision was amateur but respected by all, and he received many tips from gentry driving into town. From outlying manor houses and "gentlemen's estates" the high and glittering dog carts came trot-and-jingle and usually pulled up at that corner to visit the Post Office where the big VR pillar box shone as red as the volunteer policeman's coat. All this Geoffrey saw out of the corner of his eye as he turned left toward the two universal wonders of youth—The Station and The River.

The way down to the railway line was unimportant until the

17

iron footway bridge. There, leaning through a crisscross lattice, he saw and actually tasted the Yarmouth Express. The station was on the middle sweep of the S curve and as the blue locomotive went underneath it shook itself like a dog coming out of a shower. The stubby brass-flanged funnel whirled a hot fume of gas around his feet, frightening the aunts. The steps at the other end led down to the yellow sandy dock-side of the river. They tried to time their walks to high tide. At flood, Deben was a copious waterway; in the sandy bottom of the station dock there would be five or six feet of clear water and many crabs for easy angling. Geoffrey was early impressed by the pugnacious temper of the crab, lurking under sea-weeded rocks and braced for alarm. At bottom ebb the river was only a trickle between steely mirrors of wet mud.

If offered a river for his first delight Geoffrey would not change Deben even for Mark Twain's Mississippi. The giant river of the midlands has been sentimentalized for us by a couple of barefoot boys who knew nothing better, but it is a vast, shabby, undisciplined flood of muddy water and snags and festering bayous compared with the lucid and peaceable Deben, scoured twice daily by the salted Northern sea. For a couple of large coppers a boatman in his wherry rowed passengers across to the bathing beach on the other side of the stream. There one undressed, put on cotton striped bathing drawers and pretended to swim while one hand was still safely touching bottom. Or through another turnstile one climbed the sandy slope to Sutton Heath, a wide expanse of turf and gorse and bracken, the paradise of rabbits.

If one stayed on the town side, there was the walk down the river wall, a path of blond gravel mounded up above storm level. The path went as far as Kyson, a couple of miles downstream, but within easy reach of young legs was The Jetty, a boat-yard where one could turn back across meadows to the town. Here in a long avenue of veteran elms was the Rope Walk, leading again to a railway crossing. Tradition was that in the old days hawsers were woven here by seamen walking backward as they twisted the strands. Geoffrey had a secret imagination of pig-tailed tars weaving their way backwards in this shady alley with a chantey to speed the hard-handed work. It used to alarm him that these backward haunching seamen might have weaved themselves unawares onto the railway; this was emphasized in his mind by getting his foot caught for a moment in a switch-frog when a train was signaled and audible in the distance.

All that region was full of strange rumor for a child. Not far was the famous old coaching inn, The Red Lion at Martlesham, whose vermilion-painted sign was said to be a figurehead cast ashore from the storm-driven Armada of Spain. Years afterward he saw a painting which perfectly recorded the lonely and foreboding aspect of that elbow of the stream. It was called "Storm over Martlesham Heath," and he experienced again those cumulated purple clouds and metal sky seen in late afternoon when he was far from home. The little church at Martlesham was minutely clear in such stormy light; a blue tint of menace glittered on the obsidian leaves of an enormous holly hedge. It seemed a thorny shield to protect church and rectory from any current of wider air.

So, like the Thorofare, the River was a narrow channel leading back into something fabulously old. It runs its modest course with many windings from the primrose beds of Melton to the salt-stained shark's teeth of Bawdsey Ferry; from the lyrics of Tennyson to the barbed wire and tank traps of the pebbly coast. To be carried downstream with a fair breeze in Harry Bredfield's sailboat for a picnic at Bawdsey was a dozen miles easy sailing; if the breeze was contrary or tide miscalculated, getting back again was a long affair. The round Martello towers still stood along that shore. Faded and lichened, they were a memento of threatened invasion long ago.

There was a moment of sun and wind and high tide when Uncle Dan paused at a bend in the river wall, looked up toward the strong flint tower of Wilford church and the last of the old windmills on the ridge, and said bashfully,

> "Is this the hill, is this the kirk,
> Is this mine own countree?"

He then turned back toward the Thorofare in the apologetic silence of the Englishman who has shown his emotions.

6. *Uncle Dan's Economics*

Geoffrey once said to Uncle Dan it was unlucky that Barton House was the ugliest one on the Thorofare. It was a solid box of gray cement with moulded urns and wreaths relieving the wide show-windows filled with china.

"Don't forget," said Uncle Dan, "that concrete sent me to college."

This would make an economic essay of the kind Dan could understand—oh, he thought, if only the sociologers would mix with the caustic quicklime of their fiscal stuff the bright sand grains of human circumstance. It seems that a hundred years ago there was a local pioneer called Ramsholt who invented some new process of mixing cement and achieved a specially satisfying variety of "Portland Stone." One of Uncle Dan's best stories (to emphasize the natural ingenuity and spunk of Wilford boys) told how this young Ramsholt went scouting around the coasts of Britain in search of a particular kind of lime which could be brought to Wilford by sea. He found what he wanted near Swansea in Wales, but on his first night at a dockside inn he was so shocked and frightened by the singsong drone of the Welsh tongue that he thought they were plotting his life. In the middle of the night he got out of bed and fled from the house. Mr. Ramsholt's horror of the Welsh was a lifelong jest at his expense but it did not prevent him from making a substantial fortune out of their lime. It came in sailing barges to Lime Kiln Quay and Ramsholt publicized its merits by building a curious fortress-shaped home which was the talk of the neighborhood. It had a machicolated tower with loopholes and a flat battlemented roof and was always known as The Castle. Visitors came from far in curiosity but were startled to admiration by the qualities of this artificial stone. "My grandfather," said Uncle Dan, "was a bowling-green and taproom colleague of Mr. Ramsholt. As a result of some wager at bowls they agreed that Ramsholt should build him a new dwelling and shop of this same stuff. After Grandfather's death and the decline of the family purse I had the freakish notion that I wanted to go to the University, and borrowed the money from old Ramsholt. I haven't forgotten, he charged me six per cent."

These reminiscences were only casual from Uncle Dan and vaguer still in Geoffrey's mind. More impressive was the fact that the old contractor amused his later years by building in the back garden of The Castle an extraordinary grotto. This artificial cavern had grotesques of stone ornament, gold and silver fish, and peepholes of colored glass looking through mimic cascades and curtains of fern. It was torn down by the old man's heirs to make room for a stable, but Dan still remembered it from his childhood; it was valuable to him because it had given him a notion of Alexander Pope's famous grotto at Twickenham. Dan explained to Geoffrey that the best way to understand literature is to animate it with private analogies of one's own. Even this remote association had served to make Pope more than a textbook name to him, and he used to chuckle over Dr. Johnson's remark about the absurdities of Pope's grotto: "An Englishman has more need to solicit than exclude the sun." So old Mr. Ramsholt and his cronies, sitting at their ale and tobacco in that ossuary of rheumatism, linger as granules of human oddity in the heavy mix of Victorian economics.

Dan had a queer habit in swimming. When the tide was high on a pebble beach he used to lie in the water as close to

21

shore as gave floating depth but with his eyes open under water. Anyone coming over the brow of the hill would suppose him a corpse washed ashore, because he had learned by practice to hold his breath a long time. In some queer way, he tried bashfully to explain, that view of the green and tawny bottom was a little world of its own which could be seen and studied in the clear lens of salt water. Jewel-clean and small, estranged from our hot concerns, it is beautifully patterned with rational detail and beyond our explanation or apology. Dan sometimes felt like that looking back on Wilford.

7. *Good Morning to Miss Debbidge*

Geoffrey was surprised one morning when Lizzie Batts, after pouring out the bath water, made an extra climb and brought a jug of hot. When he asked her about it, to his embarrassment she broke into a grimace of tears. He wondered, but breakfast was on the table. Toying with his oatmeal a little later, there was the thick yellow cream. As a matter of fact cream was not as serviceable as milk for the Oatmeal Game, which was to make a relief map of the river, showing the bathing beach and the harbor, and then when the milk was filled in, this is high tide. Carefully scooping, and avoiding any of the oatmeal itself, one could then exclaim in satisfaction, "Now it is low tide!" Usually this performance caused impatience from the authorities but this morning it proceeded without comment. Powdered sugar on the upper ridges of the porridge represented the floury look of Hayward's Mill. No interference having occurred, he ventured, "Lizzie shouldn't cry. I can see her gums." He was a little startled when this caused tears from the aunts. Simultaneously all three rose from their chairs with a twirling movement and vanished into the back kitchen. Only Grandma, porcelain and unmoved as usual, remained in command. "You can play with your train on the shelf," she said. This was an unusual privilege which put any other observation out of mind.

In that room, a kind of kitchen annex, there was a long shelf below the windows which looked out on the courtyard. It was crowded with ferns, geraniums and fuchsias, but if the pots were pushed back there was space to move the locomotive along at the level of the eye. This gave intimate working view of the moving wheels and driving rods (what will small boys do when all locomotives are so streamlined and paneled that no working parts are visible?). The spaces between the plants served as stations for the train. Any volcanic action on the part of the grown-ups was easily forgotten in the progress of the engine: "We are stopping at Martlesham. You know, Grandma, that isn't a real stop, only a halt. Here's Waldringfield. Now we're getting into Bealings. I think we'll go through Bealings and just drop a slip carriage. Now we can make good time into Ipswich. The station-master will be surprised to see an American train. He'll put it on a special track."

He was expecting the usual "You better go upstairs and help Lizzie do your room," which was so much a matter of routine that when no one said it he cautiously whispered it to himself. He heard Grandma lightfooting to and fro behind him for some time and then to his astonishment, "Would you like to go into the Shop and say Good Morning to Miss Debbidge?"

Miss Debbidge was his first intimation of beauty in human form. Of course he construed beauty as a form of kindness, but Miss Debbidge (whose first name he never even knew) really did suggest something of the potter's art in her ceramic pinkness and relishable shape. Not unnaturally he associated her with the small china statuettes which inhabited a rearward shelf above juvenile reach. "Remember, you mustn't touch," was always Aunt Em's instruction when he was allowed through the private door into that world of breakables. Long afterward he began to think of a china and crockery business for its satisfying humilities. It is good to remember all those domestic vessels, jugs and basins and cups and tumblers, on their way to fulfill such simple pleasures or necessities. One cannot perform the humdrum tasks of washing and wiping and shelving away without imagining some tingle of service in the unknown bosom of maker and middleman. Old Ellis as he unpacked the crates, or Miss Debbidge with her duster among the brittle aisles, must have felt it. But to a child, under the admonition Don't Touch, all became as tenderly fragile as the ice palace of Hans Andersen. Always he found himself more shocked than most by broken glass or china, and liked to believe he could find more pieces to pick up than anyone else.

Miss Debbidge's level brows looked neatly painted and the richest brown glaze of Etruria was on her friendly china eyes. Through the long skylight above, lances of morning light skimmed upon ewers and slop basins, moved in sparks round the curves of glass. As he came cautiously down the long aisle, it was a setting for a princess, and Aunt Em the perfect beldame to guard the entrance. There was no very fulsome communication possible between Miss D. and her admirer; the most achieved was some special survey of the Staffordshire figures kept somewhere at the rear. Even in their remoteness they were not dusty, Miss Debbidge sadly had more than enough time for caretaking. There was one group, something in the nature of a coach of state with horses, that he was allowed to examine, then with the quick tedium of a child he said, "I expect it's time for my lessons. Miss Downes is coming this morning."

"What sort of lessons are you doing, Master Geoffrey?"

"The Spanish Armada. I know the first twenty lines. Attend all ye who list to hear our noble England's praise . . ."

Miss Debbidge's eyes were not just brown glaze of Etruria.

It was one of those earliest days of the world that make one suspicious of the pleasures of being dead. After arithmetic and Macaulay and the passionate pleasure that one number written on top of another creates something quite different, there was time before lunch for a walk in the garden. Frost underfoot and sun overhead were in even poise, as at certain tides and seasons the primroses of Melton and the salt gust of the North Sea would meet in delicate savor at one outpost of the River Wall; one in each nostril. On the weathered red brick of the garden enclosure there blossomed a meridian power he never forgot. The world was friendship. There was time for the circuit through The Wilderness, where even the stone wolf was, with Miss Downes massively by, only that. Beyond the hedge the steel railway metals glittered always a little farther on, a habit of theirs. "There's the low-tide smell," he announced, taking personal credit for it. Beyond the salt mud, where the river was now only a narrow gully between slopes of purple clay, a sailing barge grounded on the ebb lay over on her side.

"What do the sailors do when they're stranded?"

"They wait for the water to come back," said Miss Downes.

"They can't have tea because it would spill over."

"It's time for your dinner."

How often a meal postpones philosophy.

"I want to go down and see the mud."

"I don't know why you're so fond of low tide, it's so smelly."

"I like it because it shows the way things used to be."

Lovers of low tide will understand: to see laid bare an alien and mysterious element, which only a few hours before had been inscrutable. Students of history must know the same feeling now when the wide waters of assurance have ebbed so far, so many stained shells and broken jetsam lie clear to view.

For dinner that day they had treacle pudding. There are many other things it might have been, bullaces and custard, or gooseberry fool, or jam roll, or warden pie; but in changeable weathers treacle pudding was Suffolk's substitute for central heating. It would be a sluggish circulation that could not create its needed turnover of calories from an occasional stoking of bread and dripping or the steaming cuts of suet and hot treacle. Uncle Dan used to explain that treacle was a very old word meaning a remedy or antidote against the bite of wild beasts. Certainly it was antidote against any restlessness of

25

early afternoon; a Wilford household that had midday-dined on treacle pudding straightway repaired to its cubicles for slumber and was not heard from again until freshening breeze from the river or lengthening shadows in the Thorofare suggested the statutory walk before tea.

In the drawing-room was an old music box which unrolled *The Blue Bells of Scotland* with wiry punctures of sound; this he was allowed to wind with creaking key and turn on for one going, leaving the drawing-room door open to listen pending sleep. The uncertain timing of the melody and the fumy musk of the cloistered room came across the hall. They were equally soporific. Uncle Dan was allowed to take his nap (the family name for a stupor) on the rusty horsehair sofa behind the piano; certainly the hermetic air of that chamber gave him more complete nescience than anyone else, but when prodded up for tea he would reel and stagger and say, "No wonder Suffolk was rarely mentioned in history." Though the kettle was already singing, tea must be postponed half an hour for Uncle Dan to take a little exercise, enough to face the subsequent sausage rolls. In one of those struggles to come back to life, when he gaped wildly about, he saw Aunt Em coming downstairs from her eyrie on the roof. He said jocularly, "Emma, I'm dying. You've put the evil eye on me." This seemed to the child quite possible, for Aunt Em's birdlike orb, cold and clear as a gray pebble washed by the sea, had a casual malice all its own. She liked to stand in the gloom of the upper stair waiting for someone to transfix. Poor Bee used to say, when something went wrong in oven or saucepan, "I feel as though Em is looking at me."

8. *Another Uncle*

Geoffrey and Uncle Dan were walking off their dinner. Uncle Dan seemed to have something on his mind even beyond the exhaustion of treacle pudding because he kept to the left-hand side of the street. The Thorofare not less than Fifth Avenue

26

had its opposing rivalries; Geoffrey's preference was across the way with Miss Hoo and Harry Bredfield. But his small tentative pressures did not seem to move Uncle Dan from the lefthand pavement. It began to look as though they might be going to the Post Office. Geoff wondered if he would have the pleasure of being allowed to drop a letter in the tall red pillar box. But it was late for the River, he could see several of the old almshouse men trudging uphill on their way back for tea. These ancient pensioners wore a blue uniform with big silver buttons embossing the arms of old Sir Thomas Seckford, an Elizabethan benefactor. The emblem on their buttons was three scallop shells, as Geoffrey had admiringly noticed when he and one of these veterans took cover from rain in one of the glass shelters by the River. The shells seemed appropriate, for the old fellows spent most of their afternoons doddering on the waterside. They had a saintly aspect until you heard them talk: then you could see they had broken their teeth on the hard black bread of life. By local legend one of them had been in the Light Brigade at Balaklava; more remarkable still, Uncle Dan remembered one from *his* childhood who said he had been on guard over Boney at St. Helena. They sat leaning forward on the benches, always gazing downstream; the broadcloth trousers looked very big for their old shanks. When Geoffrey forgot about being an engine driver he had an ambition to grow old very fast and wear one of those silver-buttoned coats and stump the river walk with a cane. Perhaps it was jealousy of these blue uniforms that suggested the scarlet and yellow splendor to the old eccentric at the crossroads.

But this time they turned up Church Street. Again it seemed that Uncle Dan was choosing the less exciting side. Now he kept to the right, past the corner doorway of The Cross. The swinging doors of the taproom said "Established 1638." Geoffrey asked, "When was 1638?" a question which Dan used to quote as a perfect example of the unanswerable. On the opposite side was Bloxsome, Outfitter, a wonderful place where on

27

fine days the shop was completely covered outside with garments hanging and trouser legs jigging in the river breeze. This was always good for a pause while he prepared for the special excitement of Bessie Barritt's cakes and sweets a little farther on. But the right-hand side was mostly private dwellings and no supreme attraction until Wolsey's higher up the hill. Wolsey, though handicapped by not being an old Wilfordian (he was a foreigner from Ipswich), had large premises and enterprising ways which were too brisk competition for moody H. Bredfield. But in loyalty to the old family friend, Wolsey's was not so often visited, in spite of the entrancing display of cardboard sheets of soldiers ("The Regiments of the Queen") or Tuck's colored postcards or children's books. So interest was high this time when Uncle Dan turned in there.

The Wolsey smell was better than the Bredfield smell. The latter, as Uncle Dan explained long later, was the subtle bittersweet of unsold classics and first editions—even of Bredfield's *Terriers* which once misled Geoffrey into asking to see the dogs. Bredfield's *Terriers* was a valuable old series of land records, important in local history. But the Bredfield shelves had harbored editions more famous still. Edward FitzGerald, one of Wilford's oddities, once said, "Bredfield is a rock of ages to rely on," and old John Bredfield (Harry's father), retorted that some of the books certainly had great staying power. A few, a very few, customers on the Thorofare had seen FitzGerald's *Rubaiyat* in print as soon as anyone in the world. Truly, said Uncle Dan, that was an exotic Persian rose to bloom in a dim provincial bookshop. But Wolsey was the perfume of new magazines and the wonderful obituary sweetness of *The Times* front page (arriving by the mail train about noon). Wolsey was the honeyed redolence of Mudie and W. H. Smith (the only book jobber who ever got to be Secretary of both Navy and Army, and cartooned in music by Gilbert and Sullivan). Wolsey's was the circulating library and the bestseller (Marie Corelli and H. Rider Haggard) and Lady Collamore's dog cart waiting at the door with a groom while she explored the *Tatler* to see if her shooting party had been pictured.

Geoffrey indulged nose and eyes along the forward counters (no saleslady as lovely as Miss Debbidge), and Uncle Dan disappeared among the shelves at the back. By the time he reappeared with a package Geoffrey had found one of those little pink-covered *Books for the Bairns* which cost a penny. He was absorbed in some lively pictures of Brer Rabbit and The Tar Baby when Uncle Dan again took him in hand.

"I want a book," said Geoffrey.

"I've got a book for you," said Uncle Dan. "You can have it after tea." Then he saw what Geoff was examining. "I'm damned," he said to himself.

There was just time to go round Market Hill, point out to Geoff the tablet on FitzGerald's lodgings, and home the back way past Ramsholt's Castle. They gave the Family Knock, and the door was opened by Aunt Em.

"How are Miss Meadows and the gals?" said Uncle Dan.

"I don't know them," said Aunt Em tartly. "Did you get the hundreds and thousands?"

"I forgot."

"I *wanted* to go to Bessie Barritt's," said Geoffrey, "but you had so much on your mind."

This quotation of Uncle Dan's usual apology caused a laugh and tea began in good humor.

But Geoffrey had a way (when his immediate concerns were satisfied) of returning to an earlier topic. After the jar of Seager's potted meat, with the picture of the Ancient House, had made the round, he remembered. "Who are Miss Meadows and the gals?" Uncle Dan reached behind him for the paper parcel. "We'll find out about them after tea," he said.

It was a copy of Uncle Remus. They began reading it aloud at once.

Geoffrey dreamed that night of Brer Fox and Brer Rabbit

and "Kerblim" was added to his vocabulary. Probably he scarcely noticed at the time the question Uncle Dan asked: "How would you like to be an American?"

9. Picnic to Shinglestreet

Geoffrey fell asleep hearing the mumble of a family conclave round the table in the little dining-sitting-room. All five aunts were there for the great occasion, which Geoffrey knew only as the promised picnic. Above the murmur of talk that sent him asleep was the thrilling sound of Uncle Dan tapping the old barometer. It hung at the foot of the stairs, and Geoffrey often tapped it also, supposing this had some occult effect on rain or sunshine. Aunt Em, the skeptic, always said that if she wanted to know anything about the weather it was better to go down to Lime Kiln Quay and ask Ben, the old ferryman; in forty years, she said, she hadn't noticed that barometer register anything but "Changeable." As for "Set Fair," she said it was just a waste of lettering.

"The important thing about a barometer," said Uncle Dan, "is not what it says but the direction in which it's moving."

"Does it say 'Changeable'?" shrilled Geoffrey from upstairs.

"You go to sleep," they called, "and you won't have to bath yourself in the morning."

But there was still one more question for him to ask: "Is Aunt Em going?"

Yes, Aunt Em was going. He climbed into bed reassured. Aunt Em never went unless she was certain that everything was all right. It meant that for a few hours she had laid aside her magnificent fund of secret indignations and was prepared—with whatever prickly mutterings en route—to enter into the affair. And even Grandma was going this time, so Aunt Em would be surely under control. Even the most termagant of aunts was still privately abashed by the enduring calmness of that small silvery decider.

"I don't know why it is," Uncle Dan said one time, "that English women when they really go sour make the most unconquerable shrews in the world." He mentioned some famous examples. "Perhaps because they had been forced to live with English *men*."

"But Aunt Em never did?"

"No," said Uncle Dan, "Emma's bad temper was sheer genius."

The barometer arrow must have been moving in the right direction, for the first thing Geoffrey saw next morning was Uncle Dan out in the courtyard oiling the bicycle he had rented. It was the first bike they had ever seen with multiple gears and Uncle Dan even had a backwash of British patriotism, exclaiming that nothing like that had yet been heard of in the States. His admitted reason for going by pushbike was the pleasure of the exercise, and of course the fact that the carriage would be crowded with a hired driver, Grandma and five aunts, plus Geoffrey shifting from lap to lap. But also the bicycle would give him opportunity to pause at the Butley Oyster for a mug of beer.

There was a strong bustling skirmish by all the aunts immediately after breakfast, while Grandma was upstairs trying on various numbers of her aromatic collection of bonnets. Geoffrey in the courtyard was doing his best to unhinge the gear levers of the bike. He was aware of explosive careering up and down the passageway, the flash of a steel blade slicing Hovis loaves, and a sudden girlish chirp in the voices of the Aunts. Allie and Bee's orderly program was almost canceled by fumbling attempts to help made by the two married sisters, Gert and Millie, who had arrived from far for the event. "Turn the sand-glass three times," said Allie. They were arguing did she mean three runs of the sand, or four?

"You can't boil a hard-boiled egg too hard," said Gert.

"There's a limit to everything," said Millie.

Aunt Em had gone aloft to her eyrie to ration the doves for

31

the day and confide in her effigies and familiars. Her sepulchral warnings came floating down to Geoffrey from above. The scene was further enlivened by the enthusiasm of Miss Debbidge, Ellis and the Ghostly Demon. For just a moment it did occur to Geoffrey that it would be wonderful to stay home and spend the day counting money with Miss Debbidge in the little cashier's cupboard, but she said that wouldn't take all day. Just then the carriage arrived. In the very heave and rattle of starting came a cry of dismay. It was the special grievance of a hard-pressed Suffolk aunt thinking herself defrauded of the bloom and apex of an escapade.

"The shrimps! The shrimps have been forgotten; Lizzie Batts was to bring them. Where are the shrimps?" These were not the gross and pallid catch known to western tables (only prawns); these are the tender, minuscule rose-pink babies of the crustacean world, perhaps one inch at their most gigantic— so delicate indeed that aunts ate them whole, shells, antennae and black fly-speck eyes. As whelk or winkle to the coster, Dover sole to the Savoy, sturgeon egg to the Slav, is the sunset-colored shrimp to the East Anglian picnic.

So Uncle Dan got away first. "We won't see him again till we get to Shinglestreet?" Geoffrey suggested.

"I dessay we will," said Aunt Em. Then Lizzie arrived panting; the shrimps in some way had been delayed by the tide; and they were off.

Sitting on the front seat beside the driver Geoffrey must have learned more than he knew from the ejaculations of the family. This was one of the rare treats that happened only at long intervals. The world of the aunts was a small one and a circuit of twenty miles or so was a vast enlargement. Long years later Geoffrey could still hear and feel (rather than see) the topography of that excursion. "The Valley of Fern!" Aunt Gert exclaimed. That sylvan hollow had been rhymed as a hatchery of nightingales by a local poet, and there one of the aunts was rumored to have denied a strong proposition of marriage. So a haze of mystic and even awful beauty softened the modest perspective of that country view. Then there were strangeness and distance in the tall flat-fronded cedars on the Melton road; the old stone bridge across the river's highest navigable reach, and the marsh of primroses. So far all fairly familiar, but once on Sutton Heath, it was like Western plains to covered wagoners. The Heath has two colors, one of outbound morning, pale blue and pink spotted with the egg yellow of the gorse; the other, deepening to the mackerel and purple of the sleepy return. "It's the oldest part of England," Uncle Dan always said. He had a vague story that Boadicea herself came from Eyke, the home town of the Iceni, and Geoffrey had a dim and timorous notion that this formidable princess might still be careering in her scythed chariot across those wilds of heather. The oldest part of England, Uncle Dan believed, should be celebrated in the oldest English way; and when the carriage reached the Oyster, at a lonely crossroads where the Romans themselves had eaten shellfish until interrupted by Boadicea, he was adding a polish to the outdoor bench glossed by so many generations of corduroys, and polishing the rim of a tankard. The horses also needed a drink by this time, to say nothing of the driver.

Geoffrey accompanied the hireling and the two horses back to the Oyster, while Grandma and the aunts were marooned in the carriage. With a great flopping of skirts the aunts climbed out to pick flowers, Grandma remaining in the vehicle. When Geoffrey looked back he could see her erect little figure sitting exactly in the middle of the seat. Even relieved of the pressure of an aunt on each flank she would not sprawl. But the second-best bonnet was tilted a little in that east wind that comes (salt with marsh and honeyed with heather) across Iken Heath. Something of a small Boadicea herself, maybe; what might she have thought sitting in the last of the chariots? She must have wanted to turn for a glimpse of the child as he passed round the bend knee-high to the horses. But grandmothers with seventy years of discipline do not look round.

33

Besides the wise do not watch people going away, and a much farther going was in store.

She smiled a little at the factitious girlishness of the aunts who were scuffling for white heather.

When Uncle Dan was pleased he always called his nephew "G-offrey." When he was called "Geoff" everything was normal; when he was called "Geoffrey" it often meant sternness and rebuke; but G-offrey was the signal of hilarity and good will.

"The horses are having a drink," said Uncle Dan, "I guess G-offrey better have one. Would you like to taste my beer?" It was the boy's first whiff of that comforting sourness which no one has ever successfully described. Small flies with cold feet seemed to dance hastily up the passages of his nose. It seemed exactly in flavor with the scene: the pale sunshine on the well-rubbed bench, Michaelmas daisies breeze-bent under the windows, the splash and cream-cakes at the nostrils of the horses, and something sorrowful but not yet known under the mask of the excursion.

"I'd rather have lemonade with a marble in it," said G-offrey.

He meant one of those bottles of Ipswich lemon soda in which the impatience of the gas kept a glass marble stoppered into the neck. The publican, whose eyes also looked like wet marbles, drove a wooden prong into the neck of the bottle and with a conjurer's quickness received the jetting foam in a tall glass.

Among souvenirs of a forgotten world perhaps Geoffrey would most cherish one of those bottles empty, with the glass ball tingling inside. Like the crystal globule of youth, once the pressure was loosed the marble fell into a slot in the neck of the bottle, irretrievable.

They camped in a gully of cold pebbles above the steep beach at Shinglestreet—near enough the whitewashed coast-guard station to borrow a kettle of boiling water for tea. The success of a picnic, Aunt Em stated, is the discomforts it endures. The ravine was chosen so that Aunt Bee, after traveling all this way to see the Ocean, would not have to look at it; water in such disorderly patterns made her ill. That cavity among the ocean rubble was supposedly sheltered from the Frisian breeze, but a cold updraft rose from the stones themselves, and even a scald of hot water spilled on Em's ankle did not cancel the chill. However Uncle Dan insisted it was warm enough for "the men" to take a dip; after which, and a furious toweling, he warned the aunts not to eat G-offrey by mistake for a shrimp. The child, robust with Saxon blood stream, was too busy spreading potted meat on sponge cake to be offended by jibes. He was eager to begin hunting for amber. He did not guess why Aunt Bee looked from time to time over the ridge of pebbles and once asked, "Does the Atlantic look like that?"

"It's quite different," said Uncle Dan; "as soon as you get away from England it turns dark blue; like the violets on a pretty hat," he said gallantly, since Grandma's festival bunch of imitation violets had been loosened by the wind.

"That's not a hat, that's a bonnet," said Aunt Allie. "Virtuous women don't wear hats."

"Allie, that's the only time I ever heard you deliver an epigram," said Uncle Dan.

"I thought of an epigram," said Aunt Gert, "but my teeth were chattering so I couldn't say it."

Grandma saw a dispute rising like one of those looms of North Sea fog, and showed her genius. As so often happens, while others beat the slopes in vain for carnelian and amber, she herself, sitting placidly alert, found one close to hand. She had discovered a beautiful smooth chunk half an hour earlier but said nothing until it could be used to change the conversation.

"This is for you, Bee," she said, "you must take it to America for luck."

"I hope it's a talisman against seasickness," said Bee.

Ankle-deep in the hard, sliding shingle Geoffrey was more

interested in the search for treasure. What a sounding board is that harsh tilted shore for the boom and rasp of cold reverberating sea. The bell of some reeling fog-buoy in Hollesley Bay might have been the drowned abbeys and cloisters of Dunwich, a city of chilblained monks long swallowed by the sea. It needs flashes of afternoon sun to brighten bits of amber among so many fish-colored pebbles. No wonder the trove was rare. No wonder that when found it compensated sneezes and contusions. Earned by plodding and stooping and fatigue it was the only jewelry approved by a stubborn generation—with perhaps a necklace of the pink carnelian chips, the tender corals of that Puritan shore.

The Heath had deepened blue to purple and purple to black before they drove back down the Thorofare. Uncle Dan's imperfect echo of Uncle Remus kept them amused in the long drive, for he said he was too tired to bicycle home and tied the Humber at the tail of the carriage. It must have been Saturday night for the shops were open and lit and as they came through Melton there was the butcher with all his corpse meats gutted open and hanging outdoors on steel hooks. Bundles of game feathers shone green under the gas flares, and rows of gray furry bodies were cleft in gore. They swayed and stiffened, such nimble hurdlers in the bracken. Geoffrey burst into tears. It took some struggle before the Family learned he was thinking of Brer Rabbit.

10. A Game of Bowls

It wasn't always cold. In the sheltered bowling green at The Crown, Harry Bredfield and Dan Barton were sweating fluently. Harry paused to mop his large head with a red bandanna, then bent in earnest poise to calculate his aim. The high rearward flaps of his thick British trousers were braced up almost to his shoulder blades. "No wonder you Englishmen perspire," said Uncle Dan, "the clothes you wear."

36

Harry only grunted. Dan had cunningly tossed the ivory jack toward the rise of turf that surrounded the green. It was protected from direct approach by three kissing bowls. Harry studied the pattern. He stooped, leaning forward, hefting the heavy wood in his palm; he did not need to look at it to judge its balance, he held it extended behind his thigh and Dan said, "If you put a strain like that on a pair of American pants you'd have to go home in a sedan chair."

Harry's comment was not oral. He had been holding it ever since lunch, out of respect for his "American" friend.

The moment was happy with sensitive delay. Sunny air loitered in the domed trees overhead. The boy from the tap-room carrying two pewters of gin-and-ginger stopped under the spikes of the monkey-puzzler to watch. Bowls was a ritual at The Crown; respected like a kind of outdoor chess. Even the hostler coming through from the stable yard stood by as connoisseur.

The biased wood rolled with deceptive slowness across the perfect sod, trailing a crescent of blue shadow. Just to the right of the clustered bowls it miraculously seemed to regain momentum, slipped neatly upgrade, made three little balancing curves against the slope, hesitated, then slid sharp downward and clicked the jack. It chased the white ball tenderly a couple of feet. They lay side by side on the grass.

Tension abated. "Happen the old country yn't licked yet," said the hostler. The waiter with the gin-and-ginger was tempted to clap but his hands were in service. Dan still had a turn but he didn't take it. "I wouldn't try to spoil it by anything of mine." They sat for their drink on the iron bench by the monkey-puzzler. "An assay of bias," said Dan.

"Shakespeare?"

"Yes, *Hamlet.*—Shakespeare must have enjoyed the game, he mentions it so often."

"I expect he threw a cunning wood."

"There's a wonderful bit in *King John* about Commodity, the bias of the world."

37

"What did he mean exactly? I can feel the meaning, but how would you translate?"

"Expedience, maybe; or Advantage, or just Business.—I'd have to look up the passage. *King John* made a great impression on me as a boy because it had both a Bastard and a Bigot."

"I always wanted to read Shakespeare seriously."

"It's practically an industry in the States. They can't understand how an Englishman got to be as smart as that."

"Englishmen *were* smart in those days, they were all going overseas. You don't know how lucky you were, Dan. You got away from a dead town and you're a college professor and an American—treated like a gentleman. I'm still the village stationer—and worse than stationary."

Dan was embarrassed. Sensible people when embarrassed take a drink.

"I used to wonder," Harry continued, "why is it so damned genteel to have a monkey-puzzler in the garden? You remember old Ramsholt when he set out to build The Castle, he bought one from the Priory and moved it down to his front door. That's our whole social landscape. The family tree has all its prickles at just the right slant so you can slide down from the top but no one can climb up from the bottom—not even a monkey. That's the reason why my little business is going down like a bride's loaf—I just won't run out on the pavement and curtsey to Lady Collamore and hand her parcels up to the footman. Naturally she goes to Wolsey."

"There's no mischief in being polite," said Uncle Dan, rather troubled.

"Oh, I'm not blaming her," Harry admitted. "One reason I won't bow them in at the door is I need time to get my quid of tobacco out of the way. When I was at sea I learned to chew because it was the only way not to answer back to the mates. If I'd stayed at sea I'd have been a shipmaster by now, but Brother Tom had all the luck. He went out to Australia, and I had to come back and look after the old people. And what

38

happens now? Here I am with a wife who's got diabetes and a daughter with knock-knees. Dan, in anything that matters it don't take a measuring stick to see your wood lies closer to the jack than mine. For God's sake, take that kid out to the States with you. I wish you could take mine too."

Uncle Dan had not known that the ceremonial game of bowls would come to this. There was too much savage truth in what Harry was saying for any comment to be useful. He rang the little bell that would summon another gin-and-ginger.

"Funny thing when you look back," Harry said. "Remember when you and I were both at the grammar school and we used to play football—didn't even have a boughten football, went down to the slaughterhouse and begged a bullock's bladder and blew it up."

"And you did the blowing, you had stronger lungs."

"More wind than brains, dessay."

"You were always a little better than anyone else. Quicker on your feet, longer on a kick, harder in a scrum. When you had the ball you always looked so fierce you frightened me."

"Don't get much chance to frighten people in a bookshop. Except by chewing tobacco, and then they think you're spitting on the floor because they can't see the spit-jar behind the counter. If I'd stayed at sea I'd have been a good bucko for a Yankee Clipper. By God, no matter where I went I never got anywhere."

Dan was silent.

"I'm not clever at telling it, but I'm troubled. And it's not just for myself, neither. Don't you think I have the horrors when I look out of my window on the Thorofare and see those good sisters of yours trudging along, they've been well drilled but they know it's hopeless. There was a lot of spunk in them when we were youngsters together. Nice little Bee, I remember when she clouted me with a broom because I tried to kiss her."

"Good for Bee. I never knew that."

"I guess I wasn't saucy enough. I feel that sort of way when

Lady Collamore talks to me off the top of her palate and expects me to crook the knee for a quire of cream laid notepaper. The skin's stretched so tight on her beaked-up nose, she must look comical at the dentist's."

"Accipitrine," Dan murmured.

"Like a guinea hen drinking. Those people need a hot bath and a rubdown with Turkish towels."

11. Becalmed in Troublesome

Scandal II lay in a twilight calm, between fallen air and turning tide. It was what Harry Bredfield called the Stag Picnic; he said that just once, before they went away, Geoff must go down river without benefit of aunts.

The rickety old *Scandal II*—the first one was named, Edward FitzGerald said, for Wilford's chief traffic—was Harry's last symbol of the life he had intended. Like himself she was scarcely fit for a sudden squall. Canvas, sheets and halliards were eaten by weather and her opening seams trailed whiskers of oakum. Harry said she leaked like the book trade, but he liked her that way.

They had their lunch above the chain Ferry, where the child was impressed by a new turreted mansion, a sort of vertical brickyard which Uncle Dan called imitation Otranto. This, Geoffrey gathered, was the home of the nabob Sir Rafe Collamore, M.P. With a child's acuteness for social distinctions he knew that clerks and tellers bustled when Sir Rafe and his aquiline dame drove to town for shopping. Harry remarked that no stamping machine had been invented that would emboss notepaper heavily enough to satisfy Lady Collamore.

"Is she in trade?" asked Geoffrey. He had learned this was the prime factor of social arithmetic.

"You might think so," said Harry. "They've just ordered some new stationery with a telephone number engraved on it. I never heard of *that* before.—What's the world coming to," he added, burlesquing one of the Thorofare's favorite sayings.

The wind dropped as they slid upstream. Now they were at hook in the reach called Troublesome, above the gulf of Martlesham Creek, waiting for the upward flow. "Betwixt wind and water," said Dan. The nautical phrase recalled the knockout bellypunch by Harry in their famous Fight at the grammar school, nearly thirty years before. Like many boyhood encounters it was the beginning of good friendship. This and other memories were revived. In the crystal shimmer of dusk, air and water suffused together, and after hard exercise Harry was cheerful. But Dan was a little apprehensive. Once a year or so these two confided rather desperately, but Dan's confessions were done comfortably by letter from far away. Harry, no hand for letter writing, had the more agitating habit of getting his victim aboard the *Scandal* in a calm and then unburdening his entrails. All afternoon Dan was anxious as he felt the breeze soften in his beard; he knew what a lull might mean. He tried to keep Geoffrey in the cockpit for safeguard, but after tea (bread and dripping, shrimps, and black cherry jam) Geoff fell asleep in the cabin. There is a wonderful sense of snugness in the berth of a boat in calm. Under the low shine of the paraffin lamp he lay on the sofa listening to the voices above him. But there was much more of one voice than the other. He was puzzled by Harry so often saying something about E. F. G. (FitzGerald was Harry's great hero). The boy wanted to continue the alphabet and kept trying to say "H," but that is a difficult letter. It requires effort of breath, and the mouldy savor of those rotten old cushions was soporific. He was already adrift.

Dan was trying to keep the conversation on impersonal generalities. "It's queer," he was saying about the *Rubaiyat*, "a Puritan town like Wilford begetting the great epicurean credo."

"Not so queer, maybe. I could tell you things about Wilford you never suspected; you went away to college before you'd begun to notice. Anyhow I reckon you were too busy with your studies. There's things I could tell you here aboard the *Scandal* I wouldn't care to mention anywhere else."

"Don't you spoil my idea of the old place," said Dan uneasily. "When I get back to the States I like to think of Wilford as a sort of idyll—always high tide, no smells in the W. C. and no wasps in the jam."

Harry knocked out his pipe against the sloop's battered counter. He watched the tobacco cinders drift on glassy water. "She fare to tarn," he said. "It's getting chilly, let's have another Bass." He went below, fetched bottles from his little galley, and threw a shawl over the boy. Long later Geoffrey half remembered that moment; the stuffy cabin smelling of mildew, lamps and shrimps, and the rumble of talk above the hatch. He remembered that he had tried to stay awake; he knew by youth's shrewd guess that they were talking over his head in more senses than one, the cryptic dialect of age. He also was swinging between tides.

"Old Fitz tried to make an intellectual out of *me*," said Harry gruffly. "He took a fancy to me as a lad because I was born just when the *Rubaiyat* was first published. He nicknamed me Omar. 'How's Little Omar?' he used to ask the governor when he came into the shop. When I was about fourteen he hired me as one of his reading boys; you remember his eyes went bad and he got various youngsters to read aloud to him. I used to go to the back parlor at The Bull, he liked sitting there because he could overhear the talk of the farmers in the bar. He'd be there with a glass of port and a plum cake on the table, wearing dark goggles and that old shawl round his neck. I was a miserable bad reader but I dessay he was amused by the way I mispronounced the long words. He had me read him all the testimony in the Tichborne Trials. He'd never interrupt me except to say 'Nose, Harry, nose!' when I got into my Suffolk twang. Between the dark glasses and the shawl you couldn't see much of him but bald pate, but somehow I could tell by his attitude when he thought anything was comical. There were some mighty difficult words in the Tichborne Case."

"Of course I saw him around," said Dan, "in that funny old cape and his hat tied on with a scarf, but I wouldn't dare speak to him."

"Most people thought he was dotty. They thought it was strange for a man like him to spend most of his time with fishermen at Lowestoft or picking up Suffolk slang in a bar parlor. He always encouraged my notion about running away to sea. I told him I thought I better clear out, there was no chance at home because I wasn't a gentleman. He said, 'Harry, you're fourth generation in the book trade, that's real nobility.' "

This was the kind of gossiping Dan enjoyed. He drank his ale and visualized an intimate footnote about FitzGerald in the textbook he would some day write.

"I see they planted a Persian rose over the old fellow's grave," he said.

"Yes, and the poor thing hasn't bloomed yet. There's an irony for you, he'd have enjoyed it. He was a limb for irony."

There was the faintest ripple or tremor against the hull, and a lisping sprinkle of sound. It was the moment of balance: daylight and marshy air moving out overhead, the cold ocean stream pushing upward from below. The smallest seem to know it first. Before any flutter of evening breeze or swing of craft at her hawser the minnows guess the oncome of new power and skip absurdly on the surface. A patter of dancing trifles was capering alongside, and Harry, fish- and weather-wise, knew it as a sign. He broke off his confidences and went forward to set lights and get up the anchor.

"Geoff, ahoy," he called. "Minnows dance on a turning tide. Come-look-see." But when the drowsy child reached the cockpit darkness had thickened and the miniature ballet was over.

Scandal II slipped gently up the reach from Kyson and the lights of Wilford came in view: green on the railway sema-

43

phores, domestic yellow in the streets, the blue-white of the arcs at the station.

"Quite a feather in its cap, for a little town," Harry said. "To have had a real big person and in our own memory. Somehow it sweetens things."

12. The Guard's Van

"I am monstrous full of fleas this morning," said Geoffrey. He knew Uncle Dan would understand the quotation from Brer Rabbit.

This morning he was definitely G-offrey: they had changed trains at Ipswich and were on their way for a visit to The Relatives. But it was even more exciting than that: Uncle Dan was going to stay in Cambridge to do some studying (it seemed odd that an old man with a beard should still have lessons to learn) and Geoff was to make his first railway journey alone, from Cambridge to Kneesworth. They were in a smoking carriage, on a stopping train trundling up the Stour Valley. Uncle Dan's bicycle was in the van and Uncle Dan studied his road map. He murmured names to himself in a way that showed they meant much. *"Sudbury, Melford, Cavendish, Clare."*

"Is that a poem?" Geoffrey asked.

"It might well be. We'll make it a poem:—*Pushbike and I would like to be there.* Some day when you're old enough we'll bike around here together. Don't tell the aunts, but the best beer in Suffolk is at The Bull in Long Melford. I wish we could have seen Flatford Mill from the train."

He went on to say something about Constable but Geoffrey thought he was talking about a policeman.

"This is more in your line," said Uncle Dan, still map reading. "Here's Foxearth. What would Brer Rabbit say about that? I think he'd prefer Larks in the Wood, it's only a few miles away. You can live at Larks in the Wood and I'll live at Claret Hall." No one could watch Uncle Dan reading a map

44

without getting some idea of the dignity of words. A lady asked him long afterward, how did the English get so "whimsical" in their names of villages? "Madam," said Uncle Dan (suddenly feeling like Dr. Johnson), "it was stark realism."

What Geoffrey noticed without noticing was the thick and plushy trees in those water meadows, oaks thickened with rheumatism and no wonder, with their feet in a swamp; ancient willows pollarded and trimmed so many generations that they grew tough and twisted like the yeomen themselves. More obvious to his taste was the hansom cab in Cambridge. This at one jingling lift raised him to a social plateau unimaginable in Wilford.

How wonderful if every child at that age could have his first glimpse of those colleges and gardens; and exactly at meridian noon. When that symphony of bells (jingle-go-jangle, my boy, my boy, said Uncle Remus) comes down from sky like the Cataract of Lodore. First sight of stone walls in scales of silver mackerel gray or velveted with soot, and flower boxes blue and scarlet. "What's that?" asked Geoffrey as the cab slowed down where traffic thickens into King's Parade.

"That's one of the colleges," said Uncle Dan. "Cats."

Geoffrey, when it became necessary, knew it as St. Catherine's, but he never quite outgrew his momentary thought of a little tabby-gray cloister and surrounding dormitories entirely inhabited by small good-humored animals. In mimic caps and gowns they trotted out to lectures, and came back at dusk to their studious firesides to purr. Not even the pinnacles of Kings nor the great court of Trinity nor the Backs at John's went so straight to the quick of his mind.

They had lunch in lodgings which Uncle Dan had taken for a few days, but the child's mind was already busy with the coming journey. From an outlying spur of the railway station a toy train—miraculously enlarged to accommodate—sets off to divide the afternoon. Its engine of green and brass has a

45

well-bred sense of timing, it arrives at King's Cross so that one may comfortably dress for dinner. More magical still, tea baskets are put aboard (if bespoke) so that parsons and scholars need not even lack the Bath bun and Lipton en route. For that gentle train Kneesworth Downs is the first stop and Uncle Dan, who seemed to rise to great strokes of power on reaching Cambridge, entrusted Geoffrey to the care of the guard for this short transit. "No 'ardship at all, Sir," said the official, putting his hand in his pocket. " 'E can travel with me in the van, it's only twenty minutes."

To watch from the guard's van is like being on the podium when the conductor ignites an orchestra with his wand. The platform is at the floor level of the car and seems perfectly a stage. What sounds of tuning up: the chuckle of luggage trucks, hollow dinning boom of the tall milk cans, the rub-rub of porters' corduroy thighs, conscientious clatter of their heavy boot soles, then the long crescendo drum-roll of carriage doors closing in sequence from the far end of the train. The latching twist of brass handles, slidder of windows let down on leather straps. The pooping whistle, the clear wrangling bell, and now the maestro-guard is standing at his door, one foot aboard, one hand on the rail, the other hand unrolls the flag. Gently, oh so softly, motion begins to begin. There is no need to start with a hysteria of shock. Hear the buffers chiming in wider contact, the small vinculated tea-cup jingle as coupling chains link tight. It can't be really far, let's be gentle about it. Introduction to an ancient rhythm, the old and easy leisure of that way of life. "The Permanent Way," the rails were called. The guard composes the mood, but he doesn't think about it. He takes three or five ritual paces (adagio) with the train in his hand. Then looking behind with a last flourish of his banner he twirls backward in and the valedictory passenger notices at that moment the tracery of moss in a crack of the sloped platform end. Or the taunting fatness of a crossing-watchman's marigolds; and knows and quickly puts in safe parenthesis that what we leave is always as beautiful as anything ahead. Spongy and deep must be those blue upholstered head-rests of the first-class carriage to cushion such ideas.

But what a prelude to symphony, what an opening routine for a national pattern. What dancers those guards must be.

Twenty minutes can spread over a lifetime. Geoffrey in the guard's little cabin looking through the narrow forward window was allowed to hold the green flag. "Do you wave that at every station?"

"Supposed to," said the guard. "I'm a bit flustered abaht it today. You see we got another very special passenger besides yourself, it's Mr. A. J. Balfour, 'e's been 'aving so much trouble in Ireland hit don't seem tactful-like to wive that banner in 'is fice."

"He won't notice it," said Geoffrey, "he'll be having his tea." He had seen the label on the tea-hamper in the van.

"You're a smart lad," said the guard, "you're quite right, there's always a tackful way out of a dylemma. After I give 'im the 'amper I'll wive the flag partickler for you. You can see 'im as you go by. 'E's in the first-class kerridge next ahead of the van."

And so he was. In the moment before Geoffrey was engulfed by The Relatives he had a vision of long thin legs and a dark-eyed face looking (tea-expectant) from behind *The Times*. " 'Ang onto your ticket," said the guard, "that looks like your hescort on the other side of the barrier."

So much to watch all at once, Geoffrey was a little bewildered. Mr. Balfour—the porter in green corduroys clanging the bell —the tea-basket hoisted in and Mr. Balfour's graceful hand holding—could it be?—a shilling; the guard waving the flag, but not in view of the first-class passenger; the high scream of the brass cone-shaped whistle—the emissary Relatives may have

47

ıght him an urchin without manners. As he was hugged and
led away he tried hard to say what was on his mind: "Mr.
ıour had his feet on the cushion."

13. The Invention of Geoffland

Tea at The Drift was very different from the Thorofare. It
was in the drawing-room, and it was not a meal but a performance; served by a parlor-maid in uniform, as primly stylized as
one of Aubrey Beardsley's drawings in black and white.

Geoffrey and an older cousin were given their refreshment
at a sewing table set by the French window which opened on
the garden. A tender drizzle, so fine that it seemed to have
been vaporized in some huge atomizer, had interrupted their
pastimes outdoors. Cousin Cecil (pronounced Sissle) had probably been invited to influence Geoffrey, before he went away
into the prairies, by an exhibition of how a little gentleman
behaves. It was not wholly successful; it was never known how
Master Sissle could distribute jam so widely. There were spots
of strawberry on his Eton collar and pink suffusions spread in
the most unexpected regions; Auntie Kneesworth said he looked
like the map of the Empire. The grown-ups, whom Geoffrey
regarded with great awe as The Other Side of the Family, took
their decorous tea and Sandringham cake beside the coal fire
which makes a summer drizzle endurable. Sissle and Geoff were
fortunately obscured by a tall Indian screen. This had a double
purpose, for that afternoon Great Uncle ffolliot, the tiger
hunter, was there. Crawling through coverts and dripping
jungles after the man-eating tiger of Bengal he had taken an
ague which decades of brandy and soda had not mollified.
Consequently when he called for a "dish" of tea he meant exactly that; he drank it quaveringly from a large saucer. If one
considered this habit in the perspective of manly vigor sacri-
ficed to Indian Civil Service and the global spread of British
raj, it could be condoned and admired; but it was thought pru-

dent to screen the operation from irreverent parody. Uncle Dan always specially admired Uncle Double-Eff for his classic remark: "You live in Chesapeake, what? Many buffalo there? Very fine shooting."

It was odd to see in that dim sandalwood-scented room such a crowd of bric-a-brac from far away. There were cabinets of ivory mosaic and tortoise shell, brass gongs from Benares, cartridges fired at Lucknow, and the great vase of purple plumes, last relic of an older time when The Relatives had their own peacocks on the lawn. By the hearth was a cheetah skin, and eastern prayer rugs patterned the floor. It was well to approach them with prayer, they slid suddenly on the polished wood. Uncle ffolliot thought the cheetah a sad comedown from the great tiger skin in the old drawing-room in Hants, but here there wasn't space for it. So he never apologized for spilling tea on the cheetah: it was sometimes doubtful which were the leopard's natural spots and which were ffolliot's palsy. A taboret inlaid with false pearl carried a set of mem-sahib porcelain, and shelves and whatnots were loaded with fragile souvenirs of empire which testified the dexterity of P & O coolies. An active child could scarcely cross that room without causing perilous jingle and tremolo among so much delicacy. Even old Mary, so solid of tread that they called her Auntie's footmaid, rose instinctively on long-suffering toes when she entered, and the bread sliced for a drawing-room tea was transparent like lace.

Uncle Kneesworth himself, poor soul, was hardly less fragile. Any severe vibration caused him networks of pelvic misery and children were taught to follow a safe and narrow track from the door to the window. But the disgraceful explosion of mirth behind the screen was really Geoffrey's fault. As they made their politeness to the elders he was astonished to notice the teaspoons. Each had a little carved figure on the haft. He remarked on this when he and Sissle were at their own guarded collation. Sissle, condescending from the supremacy of an Eton

49

collar (however speckled with jam), said, "Those are the Apostle spoons."

"That's wicked," said Geoffrey, "that's graven images."

This, since Sissle's mouth was full of tea, caused the disaster which rattled against the silken barrier. They were put into mackintoshes and sent to the bottom of the garden to hunt snails. This could hardly be thought punishment, for the winding path behind dense privet had the enchantments of a potting shed, a mulch pile or midden, and a savory perfume of decay. There was also the water tank on wheels which collected rainfall from a spout. Its depths were improved by liberal contributions of snails dropped in by visiting children. One leaned over the murky water watching the snail sink. It was then a question whether the creature would have sense enough to climb up the side of the tank and reach the top before perishing. If the snail made his way back to open air it was honorable to grant him his freedom, or even a bonus by putting him back among the rose bushes. But the true historian would report that about half of them mouldered at the bottom of the tank. A dancing haze of gnats or midges, attracted by the post-mortem flavor of this dank retreat, hovered on the surface of the water, and the open mouths of inquisitive boys studying the situation must have imbibed them in scores.

In those latitudes the supply of snails and midges is unlimited; larger, very likely, than the supply of inquisitive youth. The Drift had been recommended for the dryness and elevation of its chalky soil, but even in midsummer when Auntie spent happy afternoons slicing weeds from her beautiful turf, she always put the *Standard* newspaper under her knees.

So it was all most curiously different. Instead of the narrow and bending Thorofare here was the straight wide swath of the Great North Road. Ermine Street, they told Geoffrey, was its ancient name, and the Romans had built it. It was natural to associate the white of ermine fur with the dazzling chalk of the Hertfordshire Downs; when he and Sissle walked up the white cutting where the road carved through the hill, hunting vetch and poppies to paste in their botany notebooks, he imagined the Roman legions wearing ermine capes over bronze armor. There were all sorts of queerness to set up polarity in a boy's mind. At Kneesworth he found himself unaccountably upper-class. It gave him, when he thought about it afterward, a keen sense of some of the comedies of Victorian social geology. The garden at The Drift adjoined the pleasure ground of a neighboring family. But Sissle and Geoff must play or bicker by themselves while alluring shouts of children's frolic were heard over the high ivied wall—because the people next door (who bore the deplorable name of Jones) were In Trade. They were a numerous tribe of amusing urchins, but they had never been introduced. Perhaps this restriction had its value, for Sissle and Geoff had to invent envious games of their own instead of joining the shouts of mirth next door. Geoffrey can still remember the pang with which he saw some bright-faced Jones rise momentarily into view at the topmost flight of a garden swing.

But the child who was never hemmed in knows little of the joy of release. From the limitation of the garden the boys could go under escort through a green byway that tunneled below thick trees and hedges; it was delightfully called The Drift and gave the house its name. This brought them to the Downs, a range of open hills where there was usually a wind. The short crisp turf was underlaid with pure chalk. The natural delight of those broad slopes was flying kites. Everything was purged and breezy, designed for speed; strings of nervous race horses, blinkered and blanketed and their slender hocks guarded in leather, were there training for Newmarket. Far away he could see them sprinkled in gallop across the ranges like figures in a print. The Downs gave the uplifting sense of space, and if kites or horses grew tedious there was the railway below the hills. Trains ran like toys, visible in their course for miles, with Great Northern locomotives as green as the fields. From the crest of the Downs one saw, thirteen miles away, the profile of the colleges of Cambridge where Uncle Dan was studying. Lines of poplars marched along the Great North Road, straight in file as the imagined Roman infantry. He had been told that England was only a small country, but it did not look so from there. It even seemed to reach a long way overhead, for from invisible sky came the continuing twitter of larks. Sissle was pleased to find the whiteness of chalk, known elsewhere for schoolroom chores, spread here in miles of playground.

In the garden one might say "Let's play with our Countries." Then it was easy to forget the gaiety of the Joneses next door.

It was Sissle's game to begin with. It was often prefaced by the trumpet of an enormous sneeze and the flourish of a large handkerchief above a large white beard. Uncle Kneesworth had a habit of beginning the day with furious sneezing as he came downstairs; he used to say they should really call him Uncle Sneezeworth. He was bravely humorous about it, but the sneeze was likely to displace a surgical drain he had to wear, and cause much torment. During the period of readjustment and returning tranquility, until he could settle down to his scrapbooks to paste in clippings about Mr. Gladstone, the boys were sent outdoors. The sewing table was put under the biggest lime-tree. There with pencils and crayons and water colors they drew maps of their imaginary countries. Uncle Dan had a mysterious phrase he mentioned when he saw them there, "This lime-tree bower my prison." It meant nothing but it became familiar and Geoffrey was much astonished to meet it in print long later.

If intended as prison or exile it was a happy one. Sissle's country, more elaborately delineated, was Cecilia, of which he was Emperor absolute. Geoffrey, not by political anticipation but only to be different, was the head of a democracy, Geoffland. Each of its divisions was named for an aunt, a stroke of tact which had not occurred to the Emperor Cecil I. The Empire of Cecilia, however, achieved a shrewd diplomatic stroke by creating an outlying island named for the cook; its chief towns were insinuatingly christened Trifle (a favorite dessert) and Second Helping. Geoffrey retaliated with a mountain range (higher than the Himalayas) of which the topmost pinnacle was called Uncle Dan. The rivalry of these maps, which grew until two tables were necessary to avoid quarrel, involved stroke and counterstroke of invention: armies, navies, government departments, railway timetables, and a wealth of competitive statistics recorded in exercise books. The game of Countries became almost a frenzy. Cecilia was a warlike state and Geoffrey was frequently interrupted in his peaceful development of agriculture or shipping by the Emperor Cecil's sudden declaration of hostilities. Uncle Kneesworth made the useful suggestion that war should not be declared unless for some quite unexpected incident—such as the fall of a drop of lime honey or any other garden casualty. The rose bed in the middle of the lawn was appointed a mutual chancellery to which the rulers would retire for a cabinet meeting to decide whether the honor of the country required a declaration of war. If there was an even number of bees in the roses the affair was smoothed over and peace continued. If the number was odd, war was inevitable. And of course a shower of rain meant war; the boys then retired to the playroom at the top of the house to cut out paper soldiers.

"I had no idea," said Uncle Dan one day when he bicycled over from Cambridge for tea, "that the game would get to be so competitive. They can't even go out on the Downs to fly kites without visualizing each flutter as a national triumph or disaster."

"I suppose they're human," said Uncle Kneesworth. The old gentleman himself had seen in Prussia the first rise and shine of the most dangerous patriotism in the world; he might have had much good counsel to offer the governments of Cecilia and Geoffland, but certainly it never occurred to those rulers to ask. Uncle Kneesworth in age and suffering had retired to a paradise of his own, his series of enormous and beautifully kept scrapbooks. He was impatient with any world event until he could get it safely indexed and pasted down. It was quite a problem whether Mr. Gladstone would hang on so long that he couldn't be bedded in the current album, or would he need some of those clean shiny linen pages in the new volume? Nothing was more memorable than to see sometimes three tables set out under the lime-trees: the squabbles of Geoffland and Cecilia at one side, and their host with his clippings at the other. His beard was tucked inside his waistcoat for safety from paste and scissors. Occasionally a roaring sneeze would send his cuttings adrift, followed by a waft of eau de cologne from his flourished handkerchief. The mixed smell of cologne, lime blossoms, and paste was the attar of those mornings.

14. *An Archway to Geography*

Yes, it's true (Uncle Dan thought), minnows dance on a turning tide. The morning they left Wilford, Geoffrey himself was the minnow, wriggling with the joy of futurity. Not even the hot clothy smell of a suet pudding on the stove (which gave Uncle Dan the ache of nostalgia) disturbed the boy. In the horrid prevision of such hours Uncle Dan could foresee the old house on the Thorofare going about its simple routine: lifting the green tea-cozy, finishing last night's shepherd's pie, taking out the smaller jug for the milkman's curving pour, reproaching the hypocrite cat.

Everything had been done to conceal from Geoffrey the indignities of parting. Probably he noticed nothing in the way of emotion except that Grandma's unconscious chewing was a shade quicker. It was a way to satisfy the sensitive muscles of speech without actually saying anything when there was little that could be said. Perhaps the weight and glitter of his new K-boots kept Geoffrey's attention toward his feet. Lizzie Batts had polished them with her tough old hands, and tears mixed with blacking lend extraordinary luster. A child's precarious balance is quite altered by new footgear and any youth newly shod by K stumbles on clubbed hoofs. An idea struck him as he stood at the top of the stairs. "I know what we are," he cried, "we're the Traveling Bartons," and in the joy of this phrase he fell headlong. He left for the New World with forehead patched by vinegar and brown paper. This suggested to Aunt Bee that among the innumerable precautions in the Emergency Bag she had forgotten wrapping paper, the Victorian palliative for any concussion.

The Emergency Bag, so named by Uncle Dan, was an important feature. Aunt Bee's notions of an Atlantic voyage were comfortably vague; probably influenced by an excursion made years ago from London to Herne Bay. She imagined a wide deck with campstools and picnic baskets, and paddlewheels beating an endless spread of blue. To all her inquiries Uncle Dan had steadfastly replied, "It's a ten-day boat," which was the traditional report among optimists. So she prepared a series of ten surprises for the child, each wrapped and marked for its date, to ward off boredom or mischief. These might be card games, colored crayons, a bag of marbles or a china animal, but there was one allotted to each day of the journey. They had been carefully kept secret. The rest of the bag was crowded with all kinds of innocent preventatives from the green bottle of smelling salts to innumerable small rolls of string. It is possible that Aunt Bee imagined herself bound for some dangerous frontier where civilized string was unobtainable and its function would be performed by rawhides and lianas. In spite of Uncle Dan the aunts' ideas of America were still based on the old copies of Mayne Reid at Barton House.

It was thought that the American engine would serve as sufficient talisman to keep Geoffrey amused until they got aboard ship.

It was precisely the American engine that seemed the final touch of severance to those who stayed behind. The Ghostly Demon, with the finer sensitiveness of dementia, praised it heartily but it caused breakdown in old Ellis and Miss Debbidge and Lizzie Batts. The top button of Geoffrey's coat was undone and refastened by each of the home guard; each wished to say to herself she had performed the final rite. Aunt Allie certainly visualized the child as stepping at once into a small galleon or North Sea lugger, climbing mountainous seas. Grandma, wisest of all, returned promptly to the healing aroma of the steaming suet. Getting out Lyle's Golden Syrup, to sweeten the pudding, her eyes were uncertain: Geoff had so loved the trademark picture on the tin—Samson's dead lion and the bees hiving in the carcase. "Out of the strong came forth sweetness," she said.

Aunt Em gave the doves an extra feeding, in some mystic belief that sorrow in one domain is canceled by indigestion in another.

Uncle Dan would not allow any of the Family to go to the station. Harry Bredfield turned up there and helped them by his gruff matter-of-fact behavior. He gave Geoff a very small package. "From Miss Hoo's," he said, "in case you have any trouble on the way over." Aunt Bee was mercifully busy rechecking her inventory of the Emergency Bag and Geoffrey discarded his coat. As the train gathered speed toward Bealings Aunt Bee suddenly realized they were gone. She could see down that reach of the River that it was half tide. "I wish it had been either full or empty," she said. She didn't know quite what she meant but that was often one of her charms. Uncle Dan, long accustomed to leavings, took them as they went. It was not a moment for saying things, there were other passengers in the carriage, but he did remark to Geoffrey, "Take a good look at Martlesham Heath." He meant, of course, what a look *I* am taking. How much there is to say good-by to. God, I didn't know those hills of earth, those tough-rooted spiky gorse and heather coverts, were so curlicued in my guts. Well indeed did the terrified passenger in Shakespeare's sea-disaster cry for one dry acre of ling, heath, broom, furze. Why had he not cast himself upon them in two-handed clutch like Geoffrey among the primroses?

G-offrey, at some inconvenience to the other passengers, was running his engine along the floor. "This is the Pennsylvania Railroad," he said, "we are just getting to Chesapeake."

"What did Harry give you?" Uncle Dan asked. Geoff produced it from his pocket, a toy bronze anchor. Aunt Bee felt symbolism in this, and kept looking out of the other side of the carriage.

At Ipswich, by a tip to the guard, they got the compartment reserved for themselves. It was time for lunch, as it always is at the beginning of any journey. They had brought sandwiches because the supreme treat of a dinner basket had been promised for the long ride from Euston to Liverpool, but for Geoffrey there was a special small parcel done up in secrecy by Lizzie Batts. It was the topknot of a cottage loaf, sliced across and the section richly buttered. And in the butter a colorful spread of hundreds and thousands.

In all the splendid confusion of porters, traffic, streets, a four-wheeler, he kept hearing those magnificent words: LONDON AND NORTHWESTERN—one of the great proclamations of the world. Geoffrey never forgot the dark templed façade where the word EUSTON stood above grimy pillars. The long deluge of Victorian rainfall, the sweet-smelling reek of Victorian soot, had charcoaled the portal, and between the parallel columns hung a blue scrim of illusion. The echoing vault of the train shed was sounding board for a vaster orchestra of movement than he had ever dreamed. Long dwindles of track suggested what distance looks like. There was a comfort in the giant scarlet bumpers at the end of each line. "Will there be things like that," he asked, "to stop us at the other end?" Gas and smoke had given Aunt Bee a frog in her throat—not anticipated in the Emergency Bag—and while Uncle Dan went to buy pastilles Geoffrey believed he could see the actual frog climbing inside her neck. He did

57

not believe it could get past her amber brooch, but the idea was confused with some fairy tale of Grimm. "There was an old witch," he said (trying to be helpful), "who put toads in people's mouths." Aunt Bee, always embarrassed by any personal scrutiny, made an inspired suggestion. "Why don't you go and read the luggage labels?" It was his first anthology of that most exciting of all literature. He trotted behind the porter to the van. He saw their own boxes, marked with big red and black pasters that said NOT WANTED ON VOYAGE.

"Do I have to have a label?" he asked.

"Not one like that," said the porter. "They'll be wanting you." He tagged the boy LIVERPOOL LIME STREET.

Lime Street . . . lime-trees in the garden at The Drift . . . blobs of lime honey falling on the map. . . . Lime Street was an archway to geography.

WESTERNLAND

15. *Equinoctial*

Sea-change came upon Aunt Bee even before they rounded Holyhead and slid between gray curtains of rain. Something suddenly went hollow underfoot. This was not the ocean of the steamer booklet, this was backstage. "I thought you said it was blue," she said after one look. In a small ship one never gets very far from the smell of cooking and as Aunt Bee tottered down a creaking white alleyway she seemed pursued by a whole regiment of cabbage. "Take it away," she exclaimed, innocently supposing her brother was carrying her lunch behind her on a tray.

Dan was glad to turn her over to the starched and capable rondures of Mrs. Bootle, the stewardess. So shiny a collar, such laundered girth, assured confidence. Already Mrs. Bootle, knowing what was coming, had planted her campstool at the end of the corridor where she could command her field of duty. She bulged matronly in all dimensions; Geoffrey's first thought was, She's wearing a life preserver underneath.

"Nice little bit of a chop," she said soothingly. It was her standardized understatement for the diagonal between the Skerries and the Tuskar; she had other phrases of comfort for later.

"Oh, nothing to eat, *please*," murmured Aunt Bee as she fell into her berth. Geoffrey with the cold eye of childhood was speculating his aunt's peculiar change of complexion when a loud clear voice in an adjoining room said: "I say, stewardess, haven't you got a larger basin?"

"Why does she want a larger basin?" he asked, but the sounds overheard made answer unnecessary.

Mrs. Bootle was calm. Her voice rang down the corridor to some colleague. "Tell Boxer to come over 'ere and lend me a 'and. Bring a mop."

Uncle Dan took the boy on deck to show him what a ship looks like.

"Is this the Atlantic Ocean?" was the natural inquiry.

"Not really. This is only the Irish Channel."

"No wonder the Irish are so difficult," said Professor Friedeck, the philologist. He was feeling peevish already, the purser had spelled his name wrong. A typical example of British inaccuracy, he was thinking.

Whether channel or ocean it was not far away as they balanced on that narrow walk humorously called the promenade deck. There may be some who still remember those slender and yachtlike little ships of the '90s—the "ten-day boats" that always took at least eleven. There was only the spar-deck for saloon passengers; in wet weather it was sheltered by tarpaulins stretched overhead. The canny traveler tried to be sure that his chair was not beneath the join of two strips of canvas. One of Geoffrey's pleasures was to watch rain or spray collect in a deepening sag until suddenly the slosh would descend, probably upon Professor Friedeck.

A foundering at sea on the Liverpool-Philadelphia run, if it happened in June or September, would have caused serious dislocation in American college schedules. The social and well-to-do traveled probably from Southampton, or in the famous *Campania* and *Lucania*, names that were lyrical across the longitudes.

But professors and other unpretentious people frequented the good old Red Star. To them the names *Pennland, Waesland, Westernland, Belgenland, Friesland* must still have smell and color. Have they forgotten the harmless embarrassment of being asked, "When did you get to New York?" Why was it uncouth to explain that one had landed in Philadelphia?

There is no human traffic without some snobbishness of its own. An eavesdropper under those spouting shelters might have discerned patterns of specialized self-esteem. The *Westernland* rolls and swings her narrow hull into the parallel muddle of a low-pressure area; the awnings thunder and flap overhead and the southwest drizzle slopes in crinkling mirrors on the deck. She puts her lean bow into a broad valley and the single screw drums nausea astern. Her two thin black funnels are like sticks of charcoal, drawing zigzags on the gray ceiling of the squall. In the many blended voices of her fabric, pound, gurgle, squeak, hiss, throb and rattle, and crash of china, the soft moan of Aunt Bee rises from her galloping berth. The good sailors sit in line cocooned in rugs, and since Aunt Bee's steamer chair is empty, a succession of friendly passengers borrow it to talk with Uncle Dan and amuse the child. Meanwhile Uncle Dan smokes his pipe and hopes to discuss philology with Dr. Friedeck.

It was really a word as much as the weather that kept Aunt Bee in her cabin. Uncle Dan had often spoken respectfully of September gales. When Geoffrey reported with great satisfaction, "Uncle Dan says it's an equinockshul," his aunt collapsed without shame. Good-natured Mrs. Bootle suggested that Miss Barton and Geoffrey have breakfast served in their room, which the boy thought would be much fun. With the best intentions a steward pulled out their cabin trunk from under the berth for them to sit on; but just as he was handing a tureen of porridge the *Westernland* met the first of the deep-water surges. She sashayed to it with the dip and slide of an old partner. Plumbing yammered in the pipes, the bed curtains floated wide with a click of brass rings and the emergency lamp leaned over far enough to drip a little paraffin on Geoffrey's toothbrush. The trunk shot out from under Aunt Bee and Geoffrey, they rolled on the floor beneath steward and porridge. After that Aunt Bee returned to her berth. They were on the starboard or northward side and the port over the upper bunk was of course screwed fast. When on rare occasions Aunt Bee tottered to a stand all she could see through thick glass was the green underside of despair. It was bad luck that one of the engine-room ventilators led downward past the wall of that cabin. When Uncle Dan occasionally came in to assure her that the weather was brightening, the constant sough of wind down the big pipe seemed an ironic contradiction.

"What is that dreadful moaning?" she asked. She had a secret notion that helpless immigrants were battened down below and pleading for escape from disaster.

"That's the stokehold ventilator," said Uncle Dan with the irritating confidence of one who is enjoying every minute. "You want the stokers to get some fresh air, don't you?"

It was worse when Geoffrey, his cheeks very damp and pink, would come below and innocently report remarks overheard.

"We're going to have beef tea at 11 o'clock," he said. "We won't need salt in it, there's so much drips from the awning."

Aunt Bee reckoned that an awning must be somewhere near the roof, and how would salt water be coming through it unless they were sinking? Her lips tried to frame this thought but they seemed not flexible enough for speech. She remembered her view of this detestable element from the pebbles of Shingle-street and knew that she had then been warned. Those pebbles were cold and bumpy, but oh how secure! A damp washrag, which Geoffrey had carelessly tossed on one corner of the wash-hand-stand, slid off and fell cold and adhesive on her face. A remark came into her mind which, after hours of sick brooding, she was able to deliver at Uncle Dan with surprising vivacity. "I don't mind being drowned, but do I have to be humiliated?"

62

In a subtle way, partly because Geoffrey had to be escorted to bath and toilet by his Uncle, he now seemed admitted to the freemasonry of men. "You and I both have invalids to live with," said Uncle Dan as they stood side by side among plumbing and camphor balls. "Dr. Friedeck in my cabin feels so badly he has forgotten his English."

It would have been wise not to be quite so confidential with Geoffrey, who was likely to pass on anything said, and usually at the least felicitous moment. But Uncle Dan was enjoying the innocent illusion of bachelors that children treated as adults will behave as such.

Aunt Bee's disability allowed Geoffrey to rummage the Emergency Bag; Uncle Dan found him sitting on the cabin floor surrounded by all the carefully planned amusements supposed to be spread over ten days. A small bag of marbles was perhaps the least successful for they rolled elusive to and fro and one was usually waiting for Aunt Bee's foot if she attempted to rise. The serial value of the toys was lost, but Uncle Dan did his best to pack them up again, marked in their proper order. They took the first of the series, a picture-puzzle map of the world, up to their camping site on deck.

The reclining chairs were lashed in line against the deckhouse on the starboard side where there was some shelter from the wet southwester. For Geoffrey the pleasure of occupying Aunt Bee's chair more than compensated his dismay at her illness. There were plenty of empty chairs and though the spot Uncle Dan had found was comforted by warmth from the funnel casing it also was in the very axis of an upward draught. The fragments of the map kept jumping about. Uncle Dan, who had been hoping for a snooze, endeavored to give the geography game as much glamour as possible. "Start with something you know," he said. "See, this green piece is Ireland. Now you must look for bits that will fit. All these blue shapes are parts of the ocean."

Geoffrey tried but the breeze was too strong. "I can't make the ocean stay flat," he said reasonably.

Uncle Dan's excellent idea was to arrange a couple of rugs in the form of a tent over the back of the chair. This would perhaps keep the child amused and also absorb occasional gouts of water that rolled down from the fiddley above. But while trying to fasten the coverings with safety pins (the most useful utensils in any Emergency Bag) his legs projected farther than he realized across the glassy deck. At that moment the *Westernland* made one of her deepest curtseys and Miss Shaugraun tripped over his feet. Left to their native impulses neither of them might have spoken for several days, but formality never lasted very long in those leaping vessels. With a wide flash of Celtic eyes—eyes that like Ireland herself changed color with the weather—she sprawled into the adjoining chair. Uncle Dan admitted afterward that if they had known that Kilda Shaugraun was going to be in the next chair they wouldn't have needed the ten-day surprises. Geoffrey was completely absorbed in admiring her enormous clumps of jewelry or her equally emphatic temperament. Her skill with safety pins was no better than Uncle Dan's. They tried to settle Geoffrey in an igloo of blanket but he kept emerging to relish the conversation. It was many years before anyone realized his efficiency as eavesdropper.

There was some conversation as to the proper ownership of the empty chairs adjoining. These belonged, said Uncle Dan, reading the cards, to Dr. and Madame DuQuesne. But it didn't seem likely, according to the deck steward, that the DuQuesnes would occupy them for some days.

"They're not really ill," said Miss Shaugraun, "they're just brooding about Fashoda."

"Or maybe Dreyfus," said Uncle Dan.

The groans of Dr. Friedeck were specially trying to his two roommates. Dan, before retiring to his berth with the latest Anthony Hope, tried to encourage the stricken student of tongues. He and the third roommate, one Chrisdie, were trying to undress simultaneously in the lurching cabin. "There's not much room for the three of us," said Chrisdie.

"An indefensible construction," said Dr. Friedeck. "If the English language were rational, *of* should be a partitive. It should not be allowable to say the three *of* us, since three is all we are."

"I suppose it's a kind of appositive," said Dan.

"Very true; strictly speaking, we should say *The three who are we*. It is curious that the English dialect considers a prepositional group equivalent to a true genitive," said Friedeck sadly. "Once I crossed the ocean in the *City of Rome*, I reflected how irrational was that *of*; it should have been *The City Which Is Rome*. I told the Captain so, but you English are not sensitive to the finer distinctions of syntax."

Chrisdie, a history teacher from Ohio, felt a bit nettled. "It sounds to me like pedantry," he said.

"The English, when they don't know about a thing, always call it pedantry."

"Damn it, I'm *not* English. What business is it of yours?"

"You mean, what of my business is it." Dr. Friedeck sat up, tying a knot in his handkerchief. "To remind me to argue these matters with you when I feel stronger."

The others drew their curtains.

16. Geoffrey Acquires More Aunts

"The deck steward says the glass is going down very fast," said Miss Shaugraun with the elation of one raised in the west of Ireland and therefore a connoisseur of foul weather.

"That doesn't necessarily mean disaster," said Uncle Dan. "Going west the barometer always drops quicker. We're approaching the area of low pressure and it's hastened by the speed of the ship."

"If you can call it that. Ha-haugh!"

65

Geoffrey looked out from his tent and gazed carefully at her. Miss Shaugraun had a precautionary habit of concluding any remark of humor with a kind of warbling falsetto whoop. She had learned that among strangers it is wise to signal an irony. Geoff was interested by the musical boom in her voice. The vowels of Kerry are quite different from East Anglia's. They seemed amplified from within. "Some of your voice stays inside" was his way of thinking it. He was about to say so, but his attention was diverted by the flutter of a strip of cloth in the jamb of the heavy door a few yards away. For the first time in his life he was seeing unusual phenomena so rapidly he could not catch up with them in questions. But there was something peculiarly wrong about what he saw now. It went home to the instinctive suspicion of youth. Children, like Frenchmen, are always morbidly alert to remark accident or crisis.

"Somebody's caught in the door," he said with placid relish.

"Fishwives!" exclaimed Miss Shaugraun. "It's my roommate. I know that underskirt."

It was true enough. Miss Bristol, the mathematician, had been caught by a volleying squall as she strove to swing the heavy door. It banged shut and a wide fold of tweed brightened by an undertow of scarlet wool flapped in the crack. Uncle Dan hurried to aid and Geoffrey's first impression of Blanche Bristol was her flushed face and cropped curly hair darting through the opening as Uncle Dan struggled to hold the door. She was small and scudded toward them like a cork from a popgun.

"I suppose I should introduce you," said Miss Shaugraun. "Miss Bristol, Mr. Barton." Geoffrey studied Miss Bristol as Uncle Dan politely tucked her in a blanket and pretended not to notice the red fringe. She had a sharp little face, clear hazel eyes, a round tippet of fur under her chin. "You had your tail caught, like Brer Possum."

That was how Miss Bristol got the nickname Possum. It spread through many friendships and generations, her students

66

at college were calling her that years afterward with no guess of its origin. Miss Shaugraun and Miss Bristol were immediately adopted as aunts.

Service as an aunt involved many miles of touring around the quadrangle of deck, varied by paper and pencil games in the chairs, or readings from Uncle Remus. Geoffrey did not suspect that the Chair of Greek on one side and the Chair of Mathematics on the other made an audience which spurred Uncle Dan to such dramatic renderings. The language of the Old Plantation may have sounded a bit Suffolk but it was even more fascinating when attempted by Aunt Kilda. Miss Bristol refused to read aloud but after a good deal of listening made the remark that Uncle Remus is as good as Aesop. Geoff asked them: "Is literature all about animals?"

Nothing is happier than a sudden unpredictable intimacy among the naturally shy. The little democracy of a tumbling ship is a civilization complete; and it has its prayer book and its god. The prayer book (Uncle Dan was suggesting) is the framed chart: there the Collect for the Day is penciled after the meridian salute to the Great Circle. His tentative parables of nautical theology were swiftly developed by Miss Shaugraun, who had learned at Girton not to be afraid of her mind. Even the genuflected tilting approach of Stretch, the deck steward, with forenoon beef tea, became a benefit of clergy. Above the rumble of wind-drummed awnings and the hiss of latitude fifty arose volleys of mirth audible on the bridge where God in the guise of Captain Bompjes grinned in spite of himself. Even Geoffrey, at that moment under the rugs impersonating Brer Fox, laughed without knowing why—a kind of laughter so easy to outgrow. It was the last indignity of Aunt Bee's distress that sometimes these carefree sopranos came magnified down the ventilator. Captain Bompjes, taking a good offing from the battered ledges of Cape Clear, could look down from the bridge and see this gay quartet laughing against deluge in their alley of wet canvas. Well-salted Fleming, he had no special affection for passengers, but of these he remarked to himself his best verdict of approval, "It's vot I call civilized." He did not even bother to have the outboard curtains lowered—as he sometimes did for the complaining sort—when he saw *Lucania* creaming up on them from astern. The profile of the smart Cunarder passed them like leapfrog, going two to their one, and Uncle Dan explained to the ladies that the *Westernland* did not somersault like that.

"But we're practically standing still," said Kilda.

Stretch, unwrapping them from their soggy blankets, knew what to say. "The Old Man 'as slowed 'er down to fifty-three so you can enjoy your lunch."

"He's an optimist," said the Chair of Greek. "Ha-haugh!"

"Fifty-three!" cried the Chair of Mathematics. "We can't go as fast as that?"

"Har-Pee-Hemm," said the steward.

"Revolutions per minute," explained Uncle Dan.

"How do you get to know all these things?" said Kilda.

As Dan leaned over to hand them up from their chairs a button burst off his overcoat. "Let me sew it on for you," said the Chair of Greek.

Uncle Dan was a little disturbed; he knew that Aunt Bee, when she regained consciousness, would remember that button, whose tenacity had already been doubted.

"Please don't bother," he said, "I'm quite a good needleman myself. Bachelors have to be."

Miss Shaugraun had a retort for this but just then the *Westernland* rolled them all together against the lee railing. They stumbled warily down to the dining-saloon. Miss Shaugraun thought the chart, on which no runs had yet been posted, looked very wide and empty. "I feel more jubious when I get below," she said, embracing the newel post.

The pea soup was just coming on the table, and Captain

Bompjes—for his own convenience as much as anyone's—*had* slowed her to fifty-three. He took the barometer more seriously than Uncle Dan did.

Pea soup was even more fun than the oatmeal game. The steward, Boxer, before setting it in front of Geoffrey, poured water on the slippery tablecloth to improve adhesion. "That's the first time I ever saw anyone spill something on purpose," the boy said. He watched the thick fluid creep slowly to the brim of the plate and lip over. The *Westernland* had found a hill really worth climbing. A complicated glass crash sounded somewhere in the pantry, and Boxer linked an elbow round a stanchion, holding his tray on his palm like a juggler. Captain Bompjes came up the slope with very short steps. He reached his seat at the head of the long table just as the ship poised for the slide. With seaman's instinct he balanced cautiously and lowered his solid torso in time with the plunge. "Like sitting on ze air," he said cheerfully.

Bad weather, if one can enjoy it, gives a wonderful fellowship to its congregation. Miss Shaugraun and Miss Bristol sat right and left of the Captain. Geoffrey was allotted the seat next to Aunt Kilda, and Uncle Dan next again. So he was monitored from both sides. In the empty chair opposite hovered faintly the ghost of Aunt Bee, who was actually contemplating mortality a hundred feet away.

"Always serve thick soup on weathers like this," said the Captain. "It don't schloop over so quick."

Geoffrey was having a notable time. Upon the movement of the ship the twirl of his swivel-chair described secondary curvatures; even after scooping a spoonful, when it approached its destination his mouth was somewhere else. Near the trough of that valley *Westernland* discovered an oblique hillside that had slipped sideways up the hundred-fathom curve from Biscay. She dodged it politely, and Geoffrey was suddenly surprised to see Aunt Blanche down below him. In spite of the fiddles his knife and fork hedgehopped across into Miss Bristol's compartment, preceded by Blanche's own cutlery which rattled into her lap. "Is this rough?" Geoffrey piped. They laughed, and a couple of passengers tobogganing toward their cabins wondered why. Even Captain Bompjes opened his square maroon face with a grin; a little too soon, for a bubble of pea soup escaped from the starboard corner of his mouth. Geoffrey saw it fall on the striped braid of his cuff, but it did no harm, the gilt had already been oxidized to similar green by years on his open bridge.

Geoffrey found too much going on between the table and his face to enter very usefully into the conversation, but at least one statement was helpful to Aunt Kilda. "I've got soup in my pocket. Is this why sailors call it a mess?" Kilda was truly feeling jubious; she didn't reply. Geoffrey, having dominated or dispersed his soup, then inquired, "When do we get to America?" Boxer, pinning a Southdown chop onto the plate until the boy could take over, murmured, "You yn't off soundings yet." From his revolving perch at the top of a momentary pyramid Geoffrey saw the line of portholes boiling in liquid green and a passenger's hands fielding a baked potato which had leapt in air. "It doesn't seem to want us to get there," he said.

"It's really tremenjus," said Aunt Kilda.

"She'd roll a purser out of bed," admitted Captain Bompjes.

"That's why they cut the cabbage in cubes," said Uncle Dan, returning Geoffrey's attention to his meal.

The saloon was living-room as well as dinner table. The mainmast rose through the floor and (especially when it creaked) gave a feeling of nautical realism. The rake of its thick trunk, iron painted to imitate rare wood, was troublesome to eyes that craved rectangles. The tactful stewards' department tried to mitigate suggestion by building a sideboard round the bole of the mast. This was the high altar of Mr. McScoon, chief steward; when the bugle blew for meals he stood there on reception, with a fixed smile between sandy sidewhiskers and swaying tenderly on a harvest of well-earned bunions.

A vase of mixed flowers, their stems sealed with boiling water and a quinine tablet for preservation, was riveted to the shelf. This was flanked, when weather permitted, by museum pieces of cold joint and mosaic galantines of which the chef was pardonably proud; though the pale and crackled haunch of pork returned more than one client to his stateroom. The tongue jellies quaked in tremolo with the racing screw; Mr. McScoon watched them carefully and removed them if they fell apart. Mr. Murk the engineer maintained he could tell the r.p.m. by watching the vibration of the jelly. When the weather was so violent that these showpieces had to be removed they were replaced by a haggard Stilton cheese and pyramids of napkins in curly shapes. These blossoms in linen were the work of Boxer, the captain's steward, the artist of the ship and also barber between meals.

Geoff was greatly impressed by Uncle Dan's easy command of shipboard life: sometimes before taking his chair at the table Dan would pick out a clove from the sideboard ham and with a wink to Mr. McScoon chew it as appetizer. Indeed this was a more lively Uncle Dan than the one at Wilford.

On either side of the central tabernacle was an alcove with blue upholstered settees. The corner on the port side had an upright piano where both C and D of the middle octave had flattened with tremors of distress. Aunt Kilda begged Geoffrey not to strike them so often, they quavered like the jelly. Opposite the piano stood a glass-windowed case of books; the top shelf was hymnals and prayer books for Divine Service. On the other side of the saloon the starboard alcove was a refuge for ladies who felt strong enough to leave their cabins but not ambitious to climb the stairs. While the weather continued wet and steep these two recesses of the saloon played the part of library and lounge. For smoking there was a small dark barroom on deck, aft.

Geoffrey soon accepted, or created, a satisfying routine. After breakfast a canter round the deck with Aunt Kilda or Aunt

Blanche. If the wind in the narrow crossing under the bridge was too sudden they fell flat on the wet deck, and so much the merrier. From that end of their circuit they could look down on the forward hatch where an occasional comber poured green across the lower deck. Captain Bompjes endeared himself by joining them one morning but to everyone's chagrin he almost went sprawling at that starboard corner. Fortunately he grabbed the rail of the bridge ladder just in time. For two or three days thereafter, the deck was said to be too dangerous for passengers and all social life had to keep below. "Are we battened down?" Geoffrey asked with excitement. By an innocent misunderstanding he informed Aunt Bee that she had better get up because the rats were going to scuttle the ship.

Uncle Dan enjoyed the important morning pipe in the fortress of the smoke-room. He assured the ladies that they did not miss much in not visiting that gloomy lazarette. No swab or squeegee had ever deleted the dregs of Liverpool beer from under the black leather sofas. But this flavor did not seem to dishearten a trio of persistent poker players who spent most of the voyage there. The instinctive classification that arises on shipboard seemed to draw a line around these mysterious people, but they were extremely polite and touched their tweed caps every time they passed a lady on deck.

Geoffrey of course wanted to know where Captain Bompjes's short thick legs went when he vanished up his brass-treaded ladder. He was excited to learn there were other countries above with the tremendous names Hurricane Deck and Flying Bridge. He was hastily assured no one was allowed up there. But as deck of any kind was soon forbidden, the dining-saloon became more important. Sitting on the settee alongside the piano he could hear the jarring thunder of the sea against the bulkhead. Even such simple games as drawing the blind pig had extra charm when the pencil made such unexpected twirls on a slanting table. From that upper corner of the room he could see down the long tables all the revolving chairs turning one way together as though an invisible company of diners swung round to greet some guest of honor. Buttressed among cushions he admired the mannerly rotation: they all turned toward him as though Geoff-land should make some announcement. On every chink and edge of gear, pressure was sharpening its teeth in a hurry. Drops of moisture oozed mysteriously round brass rims and painted bolts. Above all other sound the tuning-fork of the equinox keened its high wave-band. "Why is somebody whistling?" Geoffrey asked.

17. Listening Under Water

"I gied ye a chap at the dure," said the bath-steward as he escorted Geoffrey to the little thwartship corridor. "All I got was a lamentation frae yer mither."

"That's not my mother," said Geoffrey. "I never had any."

"Weel, they're often an embarrassment," said the bath-steward tactfully. "Should I stand by or can ye handle yourself? You see they put the bath in the middle of the ship so's it won't flit aboot sae lively. It dinna really mak much deeference," he admitted as the greenish hot water rose in a wedge at one end of Shanks's deep china. "Shanks & Company, Barrheed," he said proudly, pointing to the maker's name on the heavy fixtures. "When ye see that ye're in a Mersey-built ship. I drew it salt, ye can fancy ye're marooned in the Gulf Stream. It's too tepid, mebbe." He paddled a well-bleached hand in the tub, turned a big brass cock which bubbled a jet of steam into the water. "Straight frae the biler, that's the stuff that makes us go. But dinna fiddle wi' the tap, laddie, it'll scald your hide."

He stood by to guard against accidents. But Geoffrey, after some flotsam to and fro in the long tub, seemed perfectly amused. He clung as instructed to the crossways shelf which held an enormous sponge and a cake of salt-water soap. When the call bell sounded the steward did not hesitate to leave the child to himself. A gigantic swing of the ship completely buried

73

Geoffrey's head under water. At first he was frightened, then suddenly he heard, as one hears only under water, the deep inward drone and rumble of the faithful screw. Rhythm, rumble, and pause. Rhythm, rumble, and pause; then a longer blank while some unseen acolyte turned a wheel and slowed the great fans racing in thin water. It was only the briefest apprehension of a strangling child, but the instant calmed him and taught him to listen. Rhythm, rumble, and pause—he forgot to be frightened—and swung in wet, humming symphony. The reverberating screw pushed its leaping silver spiral up the green curve of the world. The steward returning was horrified to find him completely immersed in the downslope of the bath.

"Gorblimey, he's a derelick! I thought you was foundered. Did you have a good scrub? You didn't. The soap's dry. No matter, we'll have to come ashore now. You didn't swallow a lot o' ocean, did you?"

"I liked it," said Geoffrey.

"I can see you'll be a good customer. Regular Leviathan. It's a privilege to bath a gent like you. I'll give you a nice curry with this 'ere rough towel. You're all complexion from head to foot."

18. Making Friends with Boxer

Since they were locked off the decks Uncle Dan and the adopted aunts had less anxiety about Geoff. They supposed hopefully that in the safety of below nothing serious could happen. They hadn't noticed the slippery steel ladder that descended to the engine room. Through the opening came a hot billow of oily sweetness, flashes of greasy light from great arms and fists of steel. Luckily the doorway was under observation by Boxer, whose barbershop was opposite. He caught Geoffrey's ankle.

"Just in time, or born in the vestry," he remarked cheerfully,

74

hauling the boy back. "That there slide valve 'ud mince yer into collops, not 'arf."

The resources of a sea-going barber are various. From some storage of his own he produced a small lattice gate which he spread across the danger. Evidently it had been used before as it fitted into hooks.

"Up tails all, and a louse for the 'angman. Step in 'ere an' see the Demon Barber."

In the chair was an aproned figure under a mask of towel. A metallic voice exclaimed: "Listen, blokes, it's bloody 'ot in 'ere. Ginger, you're barmy. Lovaduck, lovaduck, lovaduck."

"Is that an American accent?" Geoffrey asked, recognizing the customer's trousers and pointed shoes as Dr. Chrisdie.

"That's Marie Lloyd," said Boxer. "Oh, she's a lovely bird, she's my ole Dutch." It was the ship's parrot, hanging in a cage behind the door.

"You should 'ear 'er sing *Come an' mike eyes at me, dahn at the ole Bull an' Bush.* Set yerself on the sofa. This is a slow ship, maybe you'll need a shive before we reach the Delaware."

"They don't shave in his family," murmured Dr. Chrisdie.

With a child's genius for living in the moment, Geoffrey had already forgotten the alluring blast from the engines. Here was more sensuous perfume: a riot of chemical verbena that exhaled from Dr. Chrisdie's lean cheeks, overlaid by an effusion of parrot. There was so much to admire all at once, he was prudently observant.

"All eyes and no mouth," said Boxer.

"You don't know him yet," said Chrisdie. The towels were removed but the barber, pretending to sway with the ship, kept between his customer and the mirror until he had sprinkled more powder on the chin.

"A kipper for the nipper," squawked the parrot. "Bloody 'ot in 'ere." She beaked from wire to wire, fixing Geoffrey with a suspicious eye. The boy was fascinated; he was saying the forbidden adjective to himself to hear how it sounded inside his mouth. Barbers are good lip-readers (they have to be). "Sorry abaht that bloody. She's only a bird, she don't know no better," was his apology. Hastily he put a strip of plaster on the gash.

"It's the right word in here," said Dr. Chrisdie. Boxer swung up the chair in time with a heave of the ship. Dr. Chrisdie rode the impulse with a leap to the floor. Boxer kept him so busy putting on coats and muffler he forgot to feel his chin until he was half way along the passage.

Geoff was wondering whether good manners compelled him to go too. As a stratagem to stay in this exciting place he said, "Perhaps I'll have my hair cut?"

"Just a little witch 'azel," cried the parrot. "Dirty ole man!"

" 'Op in," said Boxer. "Marie's thinkin' of a rhyme wot we sung in cockney:

> Sam, Sam, dirty ole man,
> Washes 'is fice in a fryin' pan,
> Combs 'is 'air
> Wiv the leg of a chair—

You don't want to model yerself on that there bird. She was rised east o' the Menshun 'Ouse. Yn't a haitch in 'er 'ole vocabulary."

Geoffrey put his mind on the problem. "You could try breathing on her."

"It only puts 'er in mind of a drink."

Marie opened her beak wide, showing a curved and lumpy tongue, and astonished Geoffrey by making a noise like pulling corks—fifteen or twenty of them in quick succession. Then she exclaimed, "Blimey, I'm drunk," and pretended to collapse in the bottom of the cage. She lay on her side with closed eyes.

"Don't pay no attention, she's only flirting. She's an old basket. Besides, conversation in barbershops is always 'eld confidential as among gents. 'Old up your napper good an' steady. I 'ope your ma won't mind if these golden ringulets gets trimmed? They're a bit Fontleroy by American standards."

76

Geoffrey was too much interested in watching the bird to feel conversational. She had just given him a ribald wink.

"That professor and me been 'aving a good Hanglo-american argument. 'E kept asking for an 'ot towel which I couldn't reely give 'im, I'd never stop the 'emorrhage. 'E says in Britain he couldn't never get a towel proper 'ot, nor 'e couldn't get cold ice in 'is drinking water. Runs to extremes, 'e do, like all them Yanks. But 'e certainly 'as a deliberate taste in scenery. 'E come from Ashtabuler or somewheres far West and 'ow 'e talks about the Cathedral country, it's a fair treat. I'm telling you strite. They must be starving for a thatch roof and a cathedral out in Ashtabuler? It must be a mountain canyon with buffaloes and helks. I notice Chrisdie don't say much in the saloon, but like all Yanks 'e likes to talk to the 'airdresser. I tells 'im what I've taken to 'eart, an American is only a Henglishman what's been starved for scenery, and 'e says a Henglishman is only a Yank what's been starved for plumbing. That yn't so bad, not 'arf. I like this 'ere weather, it's good for trade, the gents is leery of shivin' theirselves. Now if your old man is afride 'e might cut 'imself, tell 'im to come 'ere, I'll do it for 'im."

"My Uncle has a beard," said Geoffrey proudly.

"Oh, then 'e's the one what they're getting up 'is birfday party. You better not tell I told you but when there yn't 'airdressing to be done I does double shift as confectioner and pystry cook. Just look at 'ere."

This versatile of trades lifted a napkin from a large, partly iced cake carefully lodged among cushions at one end of the settee. Trails and scallops of pink sugar were in process on its ornamented surface. A Union Jack was already outlined in confectionery kalsomine and evidently the stars and stripes were to come. The traditional words were also sketched but not yet dribbled in sugar.

"Yn't finished yet," said the artist. "It don't look right some wye?"

"That's not the way to spell Birthday," said Geoffrey.

"Gord, you're right," said the barber. "It ought to be t-haitch." He leaned over to make a proof correction with the scissors. "You got to be careful not to get lather and sugar mixed up," he remarked.

"Bloody 'ot in 'ere," announced the single-minded parrot.

"That there bird ought to've been a professor," said Boxer. "Now, just let me douse you wiv that 'eliotrope essence, you'll smell as sweet as 'Ampstead 'Eaf."

Aunt Bee was not feeling strong enough to take much notice, but presently Geoff was rummaging under the berth to look for the P.R.R. engine.

"Has somebody sent me flowers?" she asked faintly. "Goodness, child, you look like a convict."

"It's an American haircut. Dr. Chrisdie says it looks slick."

She subsided into another spell of weakness, not really caring what happened. Geoff tried to help by letting her have the toy engine in bed with her. This was uncomfortable, she kept rolling on it, but didn't have energy to remove it until later when the boy was going to bed.

"What on earth have you been doing? You're black and blue all over."

He was climbing into the upper berth; the inside one, as Aunt Bee thought the bunk by the porthole was too close to the enemy outside. As he shinned up the ladder and wriggled over the leeboard he showed a fine panorama of bruises. He was mostly unaware of them; he had concluded that falling about was a natural part of going to America. Uncle Dan and the adopted aunts had remarked a little peevishly that they never saw a child tumble like that. Whether on the stairs or straddling the high brass sills or turning passage corners he was constantly in a sprawl.

"Honestly," Dr. Chrisdie wrote in his journal, "I felt sorry for the poor kid. I could grind my teeth at those people for letting him bash himself a/c of those terrible shoes. You never

78

saw anything like them, soles an inch thick and the conscientious boot-boy probably puts polish on the bottoms too. Of course every time the kid tries to balance himself, over he goes. I said to him, 'You're getting a lot of bumps, haven't you any lighter shoes?'

" 'Those are K-boots,' he said very proudly. Well, I guess the British are a heavy-footed race. The problem was solved by the barber (hairdresser, he calls it). I was having a shave when I heard young Jeff take a crash just outside. This time he blubbered a bit and I said, 'That kid's going to kill himself.'

" 'I don't want that to 'appen,' said Boxer. ' 'E's a good customer. We can fix it.' He rummaged in one of his drawers and brought out a pair of child's tennis shoes. 'Somebody left 'em be'ind last vyage,' he said. 'Wot's left in staterooms is steward's perks.' (Perquisites?) So I bought them from him for a shilling and we put them on the kid. Maybe it was a mistake because now he gets around a lot quicker. I heard him telling his folks that now he had a pair of sneakers, a word he didn't know before. They looked at me as though I had taken a liberty, but I guess that's only the English way when you try to be decent. We really had a laugh when poor old Dr. Friedeck got out as far as the saloon. Everybody gave him a cordial reception (though of course I'm still a bit sore the way the German navy behaved at Manila) but we couldn't help noticing his being so sick had hurt his pronunciation. No wonder, he lay in bed for about three days muttering to himself in German. He's sensitive about that sort of thing because he wrote a book on English philology and we were talking about the difficulty of the English language. I said, the words the English themselves find hardest to pronounce are 'Thank you.' I got quite a look from Shaugraun on that one, but by God she'd earned it. Dr. Friedeck laughed long and loud and called for a glass of beer, so I guess he's all right again. Prof. Barton said the time he was in Germany he gave up trying to learn the genders; whenever he said a noun he gave it all three, if he wanted to say 'Where is the railroad station?' he would ask 'Wo ist der, die, oder das Bahnhof?' He said that always got a laugh, but it didn't from Dr. Friedeck who doesn't like anything German to be joked about. He said, 'Of course you English cannot appreciate any language which has scientific rules and paradigms. The English language has no rational structure at all. It is simply emotional helter-skelter.'

"Naturally that started a sort of imperial argument. I don't remember how it got military but Dr. Friedeck was an Unteroffizier in 1870 and he still has a bit of ramrod in his backbone. He said, 'The British Tommies wear red coats and the French Zouaves wear red trousers, but we Prussians have the red in our blood.' Just as well Dr. DuQuesne wasn't there."

19. Captain Bompjes on the Bridge

Slop-an-slidder, said Captain Bompjes as he watched the *Westernland's* narrow prow climb, tilt, and then reel slantways into a long furrow of broken sea. It was one of the private phrases of a man who talked mostly to himself; his label for this kind of weather. On the port wing of the bridge, his left shoulder dented into the dripping weather-cloth, he was taking the gale just abaft the upper flange of a thick red ear. His hearing was better to port than to starboard, and he had learned in years on that corner that a certain cock of the left ear (in itself a fleshy weather-cloth) caused a small vacuum, helpful for listening. There are latitudes and seasons when the ear is as useful a navigator as the eye.

He leaned heavily against the damp shove of the canvas windbreak and canted his head a bit to looard. From under the dripping brim of the rubber hat the long plunging shape of his command was in view clear to the wet yellow slopes of her turtle stern. He was happy in his own stubborn way. Holy Roller (his nickname for the ship; and why not, with a length ten times her beam) had made a good offing, she was alive and at work. From the tops of her two thin stacks the reek was whipped flat by the squall. Sometimes those twin funnels seemed the livest things about her, and a kind of message to him from the competent Mr. Murk down below. A small plume from the bell-mouthed escape pipe was like a white flower on her lapel. Scoured to cleanness and patience Captain Bompjes was content. In years on that bridge, in the chartroom or his little cabin adjoining, he had come to terms with his ship, knowing she would give him back as much as he gave her. He held her taut and controlled in his mind, stoic against the temperamental sea— temperamental but fair. It washes all lands alike, he had observed, and behaves as it must. Both ear and eye had taught him that it tries to warn you when it can. He often thought (but did not so often say, it sounded too fanciful) you can't blame the sea for what the sky does to it.

Catacornered to the smoking slopes she seesawed and quivered. The funnel stays will give a bit under the strain, he thought in one of her delirium wallows; take up on the turnbuckles. Looking aft as her bows towered dizzily he could see her tail dip until a great flattened mound seethed at the very base of the flagstaff. Even through rain and scud he noted something amiss. He beckoned the watch officer. "Mister, send a man to unreeve those taffrail halliards. They'll flog themselves into yarn." It was a small detail but characteristic of a shipmaster's eye. From his working vantage he knew every inch of her microcosm, whether visible or concealed he saw it in a honeycomb section. With wary prospect he scanned the wrinkled hollow ahead. It looked seamed and whitened with immortal age. As the ship cascaded into it he knew by clairvoyance how everything was between decks. He could see (and grinned a little) a couple of hundred passengers staring or holding on with sagging faces; cooks securing saucepans on the stoves with both hands, elbow and knee; Mr. Murk casting a dour look of suspicion at the pendulum that marked the angle of roll; stokers on slippery steel clanging the firedoors shut, and the barber's parrot interrupting an oath to grab the wires of her cage. He admired passengers civilized enough to sit in the saloon talking about books while even the stewards were playing human crokinole from stanchion to stanchion. But the fantasies of practical life had slackened his capacity for fiction. He had listened a while to the discussion in the library alcove; in heavy weather he made a point of joining the passengers now and then to relieve their anxieties, but when they appealed to him to arbitrate he refused to take sides. "Belgium," he said, "is always neutral." He added one of his favorite sayings, "I was born exactly in the middle of this century, I am every way a middling man."

He enjoyed his little visits to the passengers, but they seemed unreal, only a parenthesis in the solid text of his concerns. He never felt entirely comfortable except topside. Even his home in Antwerp, which he rarely saw, had now become a sort of mirage. In a freak of affection he had pet-named the two funnels for his twin daughters, Alma and Sophie; when they leaned and swayed against a racing sky he imagined two pretty girls in a dancing lesson. It was only to a very understanding kind of passenger that he ever confided this. He told it later to Aunt Bee.

The passenger-palaver about literature made him think of what he considered the greatest book in the world—but he didn't mention it; it would mean nothing to them. He could visualize it now, in its worn black binding on the shelf above the chart table. He had carried thousands of English and American travelers, many of them of high intelligence, but not one had ever heard the title of that great breviary of the northern ocean. His copy, a relic of old sailing ship days, was almost as tattered as that wind-whipped flag halliard. Passages which he esteemed perfect writing had woven themselves as the sticks and strings of his mind. He knew by heart what Findlay's *North Atlantic Memoir* (the 1878 edition) said about a south-west gale and a falling glass. He had bought it in a seafaring bookshop on Darnley Street, Glasgow, soon after he passed for master. He took his pipe out of his mouth to repeat to himself a favorite passage—even while doing so he automatically held the stem north-south so as to judge the wind by the stream of smoke. *Ze unsinking commander* (Findlay had written *unthinking*) *who places his ship's keel on a course as if it were a groove wizout taking account of numerous causes which will horse him off, such as bad steerage, leeway, heave of sea and set of tides.*

"Civilized writing," he thought, and crossed over to look at the binnacle. The self-conscious attitude of the quartermaster showed he was not proud of the swing of the card, and the Captain's scrutiny made him extra nervous. Captain Bompjes made no comment, he knew that his presence alone was sufficient, but he did remark to the officer on the other end of the bridge: "She's bound to vobble, but I like her to vobble the same both ways."

"Very heavy sea, sir," said the mate with a note of apology. "Difficult steering."

"That quartermaster holds her too tight. She has her natural swing, must get the feel of it. It's like dancing a lady in a valse."

"That's right, sir; I'll speak to him," said the officer respectfully, also wondering with amusement what Captain Bompjes would look like as a dancing partner. "Uncomfortable weather for the saloon, I'm afraid."

"Can't be helped. Shakes them together, they'll be more sociable."

He retired to his cabin to dry out, and rang for his favorite refreshment, hot milk with brown sugar.

Dan missed the solitude of previous passages when he had crossed the runway to the turtleback and leaned over the taffrail to watch sunset light on the Skerries or the Old Head of Kinsale. At such times he wondered what he was thinking as granite reefs or green bluffs dipped lower in the lilac dusk.

What does one think, saying good-by? In easy weather the stern of a ship is a tremulous and dreamy outlook. The drum of the screw, green and white boil of braided water sluicing swiftly away, even the occasional bucket of scraps and potato peel from the galley chute, all suggest the sense of fatal movement onward. The wake of a ship, widening and fading, is better to dream about than to study. That sallow trail behind, widening across the grape-colored blue, reaches far. It smooths and is forgotten. But how many had traveled it; that was a Thorofare too. Only once in backward gaze did Dan discover any articulate idea: Does an island ringed with cliffs seem to say Keep Off? Does a continent approached by flats of sand seem to say Come On?

But now, with sea-swept decks locked off, sociability was unavoidable. The long narrow passages were too depressing: even the jostling rumble of Mr. Murk's engines could not dominate the creak of panels and the distress of passengers. It was choice between the draughty little lounge upstairs, where the sudden shaking rattle of steering cables oppressed the nerves, or the dining-saloon alcove where the lift and sag of the settee seemed emphasized by strong salutes of cabbage from the galley. "Sometimes I am a little jubious," said Kilda, "whether *Jude the Obscure* is just the right book for reading here. Too much pig chitterlings, ha-haugh!"

In spite of these difficulties Uncle Dan was discovering himself not so shy as he had always supposed. He enjoyed the reading but perhaps conversation was just as much fun. His own particular kind of shyness, which men later called inferiority complex, was left behind on the Liverpool Landing Stage. It faded in the wake of the *Westernland* like those green terraces of earth, but in the to and fro (a little more to than fro) of an argument with the ladies, Dan felt guilty. Perhaps *Jude the Obscure* made him think of Bee the obscure in her suffering. It was hard to go just then, for they were taking Dr. Chrisdie over a Grand National steeplechase in the matter of literature.

84

"Who ever reads an American book?" quoted Kilda Shaugraun, who had grown a trifle vehement. "Not even the Americans." This was too much for Uncle Dan's enthusiasm. All sorts of contradictions shone in his mind, but he postponed them. "I better take this brandy to my sister before it spills."

The brandy was partly selfish, for Aunt Bee's small cabin was undeniably stuffy, a dreadful blend of damp plush, fresh paint, beef tea, lavender, and carbolic soap. Before unhooking the door he always inhaled a whiff of the cognac and held it in his mind. But this time Aunt Bee was evidently feeling better. She was sitting up in bed and actually asked for the Emergency Bag. "There's a looking-glass in there," she said, "I want to see if I can recognize myself. I feel as though I had been right out of the world. What's going on? Is Geoffrey all right? Has he been swept overboard? I hear such terrible noises. I tried to put on a life-belt."

"Geoff's fine. I think he's keeping away on account of his unauthorized haircut. You mustn't scold him, he says he looks like an American. As a matter of fact just now he's making friends with our three men of sin."

"Only three?" said Aunt Bee faintly. "The boat must be full of them to make us suffer so. I tried hard to get up, I looked out of that window and just for a moment I saw a little round picture of another ship standing right up on end. It was awful. I could see the water dripping off her keel. Do it always keep muddling about like that?"

This was a quotation from an old Wilford saying; so Dan knew she was in better spirits and complimented her.

"I believe I considered death seriously for the first time," she said. "Also my morality is gone. What would they say at home if they saw me drinking brandy? I hope Geoffrey is wearing his warm jersey. I see you've sewed that button on your greatcoat, or maybe the stewardess did it for you, she's very kind, isn't she? Who are the men of sin?"

"That's just Miss Shaugraun's name for them, I dare say

85

they're not so terribly sinful but they play poker all day long in the smoke-room and I don't think they lose money by it. It's a recognized way of crossing the Atlantic, in spite of the notice they always put up warning people to look out for gamblers."

"Everyone is a gambler taking a trip like this."

"Like most gamblers they are probably kind-hearted," said Uncle Dan. "One of the crew has made a most wonderful model yacht, really beautiful, and the men of sin are getting up a raffle for it. The proceeds will go to seamen's charity and Geoff says the smoke-room gentlemen are all going to give him their chances. He's having a grand time making friends, I haven't seen any other children his age and the grown-ups are all spoiling him. His special ambition at the moment is to blow the bugle for meals but I think that's a bit beyond his powers."

"I don't know why the steward always starts it just outside this room," said Bee. "It gives me a dreadful fright. I admit it sounds cheerful but the food itself when they bring it is rather disappointing. I spilled soup on the life-belt, do you think you could wash it off without Mrs. Bootle noticing?"

"You forget about life-belts," said Uncle Dan. "You'll be getting up soon, we've made some very good friends and I want you to meet them. Now I'm going to try to cheer up my roommate, Dr. Friedeck."

"Tell the steward I think I could manage a cutlet for supper."

20. Saloon and Barbershop

"It always takes the printed word a little time to catch up," said Uncle Dan. They were discussing the Saloon Passenger List which was at their places on the dinner table. It was a foolscap sheet of about sixty names, mimeographed pale blue in the Purser's handwriting. "Usually they put it out as soon as they see who actually comes aboard at Queenstown."

"That's where the steerage passengers get on," said Geoffrey.

"Are they as nice as us?" He had been much impressed by the tender in Queenstown Harbor and the old women who came up the ladder to sell lace and blackthorn sticks.

"The Purser dassn't make up the list sooner," said Dr. Chrisdie. "So many of the Irish change their minds at the last minute." He didn't notice that Miss Shaugraun was weaving her way to her chair, which turned round as if to receive her.

"Well, at least my chair's polite," she said, challenging the historian with a resentful blue flash.

"I know why it's late," chirped Geoffrey. "Boxer said the printer fell into the hutch and beggared his wrist."

"It's nice to know people's names," said Miss Bristol hastily. "It always seems such a liberty to ask them. I hope Dr. Friedeck got spelled right this time."

"How perfectly infuriating," said Miss Shaugraun, putting on the ribboned pince-nez with a heavy crossbar; they made her gaze even more menacing. "Why is Barton Professor, and Monsieur DuQuesne is Doctor, and Friedeck is Professor Doctor, whilst Blanche and I are just Miss? Fishwives! It's discrimination against women. I shall complain to the Captain."

Perhaps the Captain had been complained to about so many things, he was taking that meal in his own quarters, but his empty chair at the head of the table oscillated nervously.

"Captain Bumpus is like me," said Geoffrey, "he has a pillow under his chair so his legs can fit."

"It's the chivalry of the sea," Uncle Dan suggested. "I mean pretending that you and Miss Bristol are ladies when you're really professors."

To Dr. Chrisdie's astonishment Miss Shaugraun accepted this with a smile. "Suppose I had said that," he meditated.

"Kilda and I have been spoiled," said Miss Bristol. "Where we teach, at Radnor, it isn't thought odd for women to be intellectual. Even my short hair didn't frighten them."

"How did they know you were ladies?" asked Geoffrey.

"Boxer says . . ." But Boxer, who was serving them, came down from behind and muffled him with a napkin.

"Now I know why Professor Doctor Friedeck is so militant," said Miss Shaugraun. "I see his name is Arminius. Wasn't that the guerilla who chased the Romans through the woods?"

Geoffrey made a mental note of that word "gorilla" but the wary Boxer stopped his mouth with an Eccles cake. "That there kid is a bit of orlright," he told the wounded printer afterwards. "Strewth, it's a fair treat to over'ear his commentaries, not 'arf. Blimey, dunno wot 'e might sye if I don't belay 'im with vittles."

"Whatever you do, don't chaff the Professor about his name," said Uncle Dan. "Everything I've said to him seems to go the wrong way. When he was feeling so ill I really did try to play up to him. I said, 'What a pity Beethoven never had a sea voyage, he was the only composer who could do justice to it in a symphony.' That was all right but then I went on and said, 'What strikes me most about Beethoven is his sense of humor.' Friedeck was very annoyed."

Geoffrey seized the opportunity of Boxer's absence to twirl round and take a good view of the unconscious Dr. Friedeck at the other long table. He really did look a little like what Aunt Kilda said, but with less hair. (So many of the Wehrmacht of 1870 went bald afterward; it was the Pickelhaube.)

"Try to get some of that soup inside as well as outside," said Uncle Dan, spinning him back.

"Friedeck's all right if you handle him with care," said Dr. Chrisdie. "We were talking about the Franco-Prussian War. He says it was that campaign started him on philology. He got interested in place names in Alsace. So many of them had some old Roman significance. He says every time they captured a French village he learned some new etymology, the only trouble was they went through them so fast he couldn't learn as much as he wanted to. He told me about a place in the Vosges Mountains, of some strategic value, called Saverne or Zabern. He was so excited to learn that this was a corruption of the Roman soldier name Tres Tabernae, originally three taverns at a crossroads, that he forgot to take cover and nearly got shot by a franc-tireur. He's convinced now that the Germans invaded France in pure educational zeal, for the good of philology."

"How is your sister?" fluted Mrs. Lotus Bannister from farther down the table. "The stewardess says she has been very sick."

Dan was sufficiently Americanized to endure the word "sick" but still he wished it had not been said just then. "Yes, she's been sadly," he said, reverting to an old Suffolk phrase, "but I think she'll be out soon."

"What are we going to play after dinner?" asked hopeful Geoffrey.

"Something exhausting, so you'll be good and sleepy," Aunt Kilda suggested.

"I'll do Tit-tat-toe with you," offered Dr. Chrisdie.

"He means Noughts and Crosses," Geoffrey explained. "He's a derrydownderry, he likes to see little folks merry." A suspicion bothered him. "Do you play games after I've gone to bed?"

Uncle Dan was reassuring. "No indeed, nothing happens at all. We just sit, very solemn."

"Maybe a little *Jude* later?" said Kilda. "I'm anxious to learn what happened to that idiotic woman."

"I was reading ahead," said Chrisdie. "No wonder people were bewildered. What do you suppose Hardy calls a cash register? A 'mechanical tell-tale of moneys received.' Try that on John Wanamaker."

Boxer was stropping a razor when Geoffrey took the usual header over the sill and sprawled on the floor. "Kerblim!" he said. The barber's chair (a new American invention of which Boxer was very proud) looked interesting from underneath and he crawled over to examine it.

89

"You better come out from under there," said Boxer. "Tell you wot, 'op up in the chair and I'll trim that napper a little better. Looks like I left some ragged edges the other dye."

"Is this a hurricane?" Geoffrey asked.

"It y'nt far short of it, I 'eard Bosun say 10 on the Beaufort scale. That's what they call an 'ole gale. On the 'airdressing scale we reckons it 10 slices a dye."

"Then you should sing Old Dan Tucker," said Geoffrey.

"I don't know that one," said Boxer. "I know Tommy Tucker, 'e sang for 'is supper, but 'ow does Dan Tucker go?"

"Uncle Remus sang it to a hurricane."

Boxer misunderstood. "Is your uncle a good singer? Maybe 'e'll do something at the Ship's Concert?"

A wise child never attempts to explain anything complicated but follows his own thought. "When you almost tromped on me it was like the elephant tromped on the crawfishes. That's American shrimps."

"It sounds like 'ard luck for the shrimps."

The parrot Marie leered between the wires and uttered the preliminary clucks which to Boxer's occult ear foreboded the language of the focsle.

"She's as sassy as a jaybird," said Geoffrey.

"She is that." The barber hung a towel over the cage. "She's in a wicked 'umor this morning, she don't fancy the weather. Where she come from it's tropical like those elephants you was pleased to mention."

"They tromped on the crawfishes," Geoffrey continued, for the picture was very fresh in his mind.

" 'Eartless thing to do," said Boxer.

"The animals were all there, but the crawfishes kept on getting tromped. They got up a perambulator with some whaffoes in it but nobody paid any attention."

Boxer made several tours with the scissors, then he gathered from Geoffrey's silence that he was expected to inquire further.

"Wot were those whaffoes doing in the pram?"

This had puzzled Geoffrey, too, but he liked the sound of it. "Maybe the whaffoes are the baby crawfishes?" said Boxer.

"The elephant and the lion and the unicorn were there, and the hyena was laughing to himself. But they kept tromping on the crawfishes and the whaffoes. Aunt Bee was reading it to me but it interfered with her being sick."

"Why didn't them crawfishes clear out of there? It y'nt reasonable to 'ang round and let people walk on you."

"They did, they got together with the mud turkle and they burrowed out of sight, down to the fountains of the earth. That's what caused the flood. Then they were all drowned, elephants and everybody, because they didn't pay any attention to the crawfishes."

Uncle Dan came along just then. "I say, you don't need a haircut every day."

"This y'nt a professional engagement," said Boxer. "I was just giving 'im a bit of a trim where we was interrupted the larst sitting."

"Bloody 'ot in 'ere," said the parrot feebly.

"The parrot's right," said Uncle Dan. "You come along with me, Geoff, the weather's clearing and they're going to let us on deck."

Boxer released his client, standing sideways so that if Prof. Barton should feel impelled to pass a small tip, hand and pocket would be tactfully close. "Yes sir, thank you sir. It's a good thing for a nipper to 'ave uncles wot can tell stories. That there fairy tyle sounds to me like double intender."

On their way forward they found Mrs. Bootle on her camp-stool, commanding the corridor. "I think you should get Miss Barton on deck," she said. "If she stays down 'ere much longer that stateroom gets 'abitual, like a bunny in a nutch. Just keep a shawl round 'er 'ead when she goes past the chart, it always depresses 'em when they see the dyly run marked down, it looks like they y'nt neither 'ere nor there. She keeps sayin' it's all too big, that's wye she 'ankers to settle down in that there cabin. She was arskin' me to 'elp find 'er scrapbook."

Uncle Dan knew the scrapbook. It was an old sales album from some crockery wholesaler; in the prosperity of the Barton china business photographs of fine Staffordshire or Lowestoft ware—too precious to be consigned on chance—were pasted in for the merchant to study. But the fat volume, with only a few such pictures inserted, had been turned over to Bee as her private thesaurus. Through many years she had filled it with clippings and photographs of special meaning to herself, and those small lithograph cutouts of pets and flowers, redbreasts, butterflies and holly dear to the lingering childhood of the Victorian spinster. It had Framlingham Castle, and the Valley of Fern; Lord Kitchener at Khartoum and Albert Edward in a frock coat with Plenipotentiary (a horse). It was her way of trying to make life stand still.

"You're quite right, Stewardess," he said. "I'm afraid I've been thoughtless. See if you can get her dressed and I'll encourage her upstairs."

21. Change of Weather

The deck chairs had been moved to the port side where morning sun glittered and slid on wet planks. The world was one perimeter of sapphire ridged and laced with liquid snow. The spin of Mr. Murk's bronze petals astern lifted white as a gardenia, then sank mumbling into a wealth of shove; the long fishbodied 4000 tons came rioting upward surge, chasing the rainbow beyond her stem. She was pushing hard but making little. The screw wove behind her a bubbling burrowing rope of twisted effort, like a submarine wormcast of lime and green.

Captain Bompjes took his elevens of hot milk and crackers, he felt the joy of command when the horizon is clean and far, sharp as a sill. His admired funnels looked proud and fast, trailing long banners of combustion like gypsies with flying hair, though he knew thrifty Mr. Murk would say sadly, "Long black smoke, short white wake." No one has ever analyzed exactly why that special angle of thin striped funnels shows such gallant profile against roaring space. But Captain Bompjes knew it. He felt by the sideways flattening of his feet, consciously varying stance, what oblique and looping curves Alma and Sophie measured on the cyclorama sky. After such a washing his men were out with rag and polish. Every join and brightwork glittered, curly davits and monkhood cowls of ventilator shone flat white. The iris over her bow lifted its middle color from the charging onset of the sea. The perfect convex circle was like one huge lens on whose upmost enormous curve the ship twinkled, an accident of light.

"Easy with her," he said to the quartermaster; "don't lace her too tight, she likes to feel soople." The unequal push of sea and wind, not yet readjusted to each other, was giving the *Westernland* a shocking stagger—not quite civilized perhaps. The skipper noticed that one of the outboard seams of his boots was beginning to part under the strain of his broad balancing feet. Uncomfortable for the passengers, he thought, and went down the lee ladder to see how they were taking it.

A little row of chairs was neatly established abaft the cabin doorway and most of them were occupied with blanketed figures. With one exception they seemed in good spirits, and Geoffrey was capering to and fro with the slant of the deck. But nothing of passengers' behavior was alien to the Captain's watchful eye and he saw that Aunt Bee, though apparently reclining at ease, kept her eye on the white rails. The others were talking gaily across her, but Captain Bompjes saw the fixed anxiety of her expression and how on the downward roll she unconsciously drew in her feet. From that position in a deck chair, as he well knew, it looked as if the seething blue would actually slop over. He seated himself squarely on the end of her chair, shutting off the view, and made his tactful comment for that quarter of the compass. "Now you know what Labrador smells like. Good clean air, straight from Hudson's Bay."

"She doesn't mind the air," said Geoffrey, sprawling across the patient's knees. "It's the water she doesn't like. It makes her stomach feel cross-eyed."

"We can fix that," said the Captain. He beckoned a deck man who was overhauling the canvas cover of one of the life boats a few yards away. "Turn this lady's chair facing inboard."

Uncle Dan and Dr. Chrisdie lent a hand and Aunt Bee found herself turned the opposite way so that the nauseating seesaw of the railing was not visible. Now if she opened her eyes she saw only the brass rim of a port with two domestic little chintz curtains inside. This was much better. "We can hang the Emergency Bag where you can see it," said Geoffrey, looping its tether over the guard-rail of the deckhouse.

"No, please," she said, "don't hang anything where I can see it swing."

She noticed that Uncle Dan and Miss Shaugraun seemed pleased: now they could talk across her feet instead of leaning over her lap. She stopped struggling, closed her eyes to shut out the band of sunlight moving up and down the blanket. "She's asleep," said Kilda Shaugraun.

"No I'm not," Aunt Bee murmured, "but if you go on talking I will be, I always can go to sleep when people talk."

"A very sensible woman," said Captain Bompjes.

They heard a thump farther down the deck where Dr. Chrisdie and Geoff had taken a tumble into the scuppers. Geoffrey came racing back to reassure them. "It was only a prairie dog hole. Dr. Chrisdie says cowponies often trip in them."

"Gosh, it's really wonderful," said Dr. Chrisdie, "a regular American sky. I haven't seen anything like this since last June. You don't get silver air and silver clouds like that in Europe."

"What Mr. Jennings Bryan calls Free Silver," said Aunt Kilda.

"When can I have some peanut butter?" Geoff asked the

Captain. "He says it's better than marmalade. Peanuts is the American for monkey nuts."

"Unpalatable stuff," said Aunt Kilda. "Don't remind me of it."

"I don't believe we have any in the pantry," said the Captain, "but I'll ask the Chief Steward."

"You can always tell when the ship gets half way over," said Uncle Dan, "because they begin to serve hot cakes for breakfast."

"What they call flannel cakes," said Aunt Kilda. "It's the right name."

"You're awfully down on your adopted country, aren't you?" said Dr. Chrisdie. "Do you remember the story of the child on the farm who heard they were going to slaughter a pig?"

"What is slaughter?" piped Geoffrey.

"What they do in Chicago," said Aunt Kilda.

"Also in Wessex," retorted Chrisdie.

"Touchée, ha-haugh!—Well, what about the child on the farm?"

"The child said, 'What, kill the nice pig that gives us such good bacon?' "

"Dr. Chrisdie's right," said Uncle Dan. "The clouds and sky *are* different. Now take Constable's paintings. . . ."

22. *A Letter to H. Bredfield*

S.S. *Westernland*
Approx. 51 North, 30 West

DEAR HARRY:

I'm quite surprised to find myself in this dingy little smoke-room with a chance to write a letter, this voyage has been so chatty. Being a sort of Family Man is of course a new experience. Poor Bee, like most others, went down with maladie de mer as soon as we turned Holyhead. Maladies unheard are sweeter; even the creaking of the narrow little corridors couldn't muffle the groans (and worse) of the sufferers. That put Geoff entirely on my hands; sometimes I almost wished he'd succumb too. But I hadn't realized what a good stalking-horse a child makes, usually I'm too reserved to strike up friendships easily, but as Geoff immediately adopted every un-prostrated female as a substitute aunt I found myself in all sorts of unexpected intimacies. There's an amusing Irish lady, Miss Shaugraun, a remarkable creature and undeniably an orig-inal. She's a teacher of Greek and there's something quite Hom-eric about her, a sort of bosun's voice (makes me think of Mrs. Pat Campbell), but sometimes I'd like to hear what her friend Miss Bristol has to say.

I wish you were here as you are the real seaman and I only an onlooker. After some very horrible weather (locked below decks three whole days) I have got myself into the easy routine of a slow ship. Today the wind has shifted and we have gor-geous cold NW gale. "It makes my teeth ache," said Miss Shaugraun, putting a bleak red and blue profile into the weather. Geoffrey said, "You should keep them covered." I overheard Dr. Friedeck, an aggressive little German, say to himself, "Kinder sprechen immer die Wahrheit," children al-ways say the truth. Friedeck (eminent philologist at Chesapeake Univ., but I'd never met him before) has been rather wretched surrounded by British weather and British passengers; he's very critical of both and makes a difficult cabin-mate. Even though I explained that I'm an American citizen he still resents me. I fear he realizes it's going to be a long struggle to drill the world into Prussian efficiency. The most unfortunate things do happen: Miss Shaugraun was showing me a letter from a friend in Montreal and Geoff asked if he could have the stamp. She tore it off and the wind blew it into Friedeck's lap. Of course it had to be that new imperial stamp the Canadians have lately issued with all the British colonies marked in red and the motto (a bit jingo, you'll admit) *We hold a vaster Empire than has been*. Maybe only coincidence, but after studying it the Herr Professor Doktor staggered up and went to the lee rail.

This time the crossing seems more permanent than ever before; perhaps because I'm going to have a home of my own, not just living in lodgings. I think I told you, I've rented a little brick house not far from the college and with some of the old furniture Bee is taking over there'll be at least one corner of it that will feel like the Thorofare.

My other roommate is a very worthy chap from Ohio, his American patriotism has been a little inflamed by a summer in England. I think he feels almost guilty because a phantom fleet of Spanish ironclads might have bombarded Atlantic City in his absence. We chaff him about always looking off to the left, as he calls it, for Admiral Cervera. Miss Shaugraun is almost too lively in twitting him, when we saw some floating rubbish or wreckage this morning the good Chrisdie was sure it must be from a defeated Spaniard, but Shaugraun said, "How embarrassing if it should be a crate of deviled beef from Cuba." You remember the scandal about embalmed rations.

Don't say I never write, though I admit this is partly selfish—I wanted to find out what I myself am thinking about.

DAN

P.S. Rather a good saying of Bee's apropos that floating wreckage. Some of the ladies were asking, is it flotsam or jetsam, and I explained the distinction between the two. Probably I was a bit longwinded about it, Bee said, "Dessay the ocean doesn't care."

23. Mr. Murk Answers Questions

After his midday visit to the bridge Mr. Murk enjoyed stopping by the row of blanketed figures on the sunward side. Miss Shaugraun concealed a paper-bound Seaside Library and made room for him on the foot of her chair.

97

"What I like about Dr. Chrisdie," said the engineer, "he really reads his book, doesn't just carry it round with him like the rest of you."

"He's afraid to look up," said Miss Shaugraun. "If he shows the least sign of weakening Geoffrey will pounce upon him for a game."

"Geoffrey's found a playmate, young Chester Marple, the boy that's been sick up to now. I saw the deck steward marking out shuffleboard for them. Chips will have to cut out some more discs, two of them have gone to Davy Jones already."

Dr. Chrisdie, hearing this, felt safe to lay down his substantial volume. Mr. Murk looked at it.

"Och aye, *History of England in the Eighteenth Century*, William Edward Hartpole Lecky. They tell me that's good rational stuff."

"By an Irishman, I'll remind you," said Shaugraun. "He's M.P. for Dublin University."

"Aye? It's risky for historians to meddle in pragmatical politics. It's an odd thing, I notice the Americans all have a morbid interest in the eighteenth century. Sometimes in Philadelphia I get to thinking they're still homesick for it. The Old Country wasn't really at its best just then."

"Two terrible things happened," said Dr. Chrisdie. "She took in Scotland and she lost the Colonies."

"She'll recuperate. She has a verra enduring constitution."

"And how is the barometer behaving, Mr. Murk?" asked Mrs. Lotus Bannister. She was sitting to windward and the engineer had guessed by a waft of saccharine lotions that she was leaning in his direction.

"It's holding its own, Ma'am."

"I'm always so interested in technical details," said Mrs. Bannister. "I've promised to read a paper on my trip abroad to our literary sorosis and I think it's so much more instructive to give them an idea of all your wonderful devices. I haven't been the least bit nervous in this dreadful weather. That first night when it was so turbulent I really bruised myself in bed, but I kept thinking, 'Lotus, this sort of thing must happen all the time to the men who go down to the sea in ships, and if they can stand it you can.' "

"Verra courageous thought," said Mr. Murk, "but mebbe you bruise easier than they do."

"I left a blank in my diary," said Mrs. Bannister, producing a hefty morocco-bound album from under her blankets. "This is what I call my Treasure Book, the sorosis gave me a Bonvoyage Shower before I left home, things that would be useful for traveling, so naturally I feel obligated to do justice to it. I was writing up the storm and I wanted to say how big the waves were, I wasn't going to guess at it, I said to myself, 'Now you ask that nice Mr. Murk and then you'll be sure to be correct.' "

Mr. Murk, not daring to catch the eyes of the others, was glad of a question to which he could apply his endangered gravity. "There's an awful lot o' nonsense talked about waves. It a' depends on how far they've traveled frae where they start. You see they get bigger as they go, each helping the ither like heaving a bairn in a swing. Ye'll no can reckon very good just now because we've had a shift of wund and the undulation's confused, but if ye've got yer motive power operating uniform and continuous ye ken reckon it one-point-five by the square root of the fetch."

Mrs. Bannister did not seem satisfied, but Miss Bristol was obviously interested. "The fetch?" she said. "You mean the distance from the first impulse?"

"Precisely. Let's say wind and wave have been moving 900 miles, like that sou'wester we had, then you'd figure 1.5 times the root of 900."

"Goodness," said Miss Bristol, "waves forty-five feet high?"

Mrs. Bannister wrote "over forty-five" in the blank in her notes.

"Come to think of it that formula was projeckit by a reputable

99

old Scotsman, his name was Thomas Stevenson. Most of the passengers know him by his son."

"Who wrote *Treasure Island?*" said Miss Bristol.

"Ye're right. It might be a lesson to you college folks, there's ither kinds of literature besides bit story books."

"Well now I must ask another question while I have my pen working," said Mrs. Bannister. "I'm so intrigued by those lines on the chart, where you put down how many miles we have gone every day."

"I'd be mair cheery if they were a little longer. There's a big coal consumption."

"Dear me, that's something I never thought of, I must leave room for that." Mrs. Bannister made a note. "But I mean, the lines look so straight on the map, do you know beforehand you're going in the right direction or do you make a little turn every now and then?"

"It's just a form of fantasy," he said dourly. "Ye'll maybe have noticed the watter is no actually flat. Anyhow that's not my department, I'll be keeping my mind on gauges and bunkers."

"If you found you didn't have enough coal, I suppose you'd have to go faster? Well, I fear I must leave you good people."

They helped her out of her chair, picked up the notes for the literary club before they blew overboard, and smiled companionably among themselves.

"I could bruise her a bit myself," said Mr. Murk. "Yon's a teepical Yankee idea, ye can solve your problem by going faster. What would be the use telling her fuel consumption varies as the cube of r.p.m.?"

"Naturally," said Miss Bristol. "To double your speed you'd have to use eight times as much coal."

The engineer looked at Miss Bristol with admiration. "Well, Goad be thanked for a lass wi' brains. And we're talking about speed of engines, not speed of vessel. Dinna forget percentage of slip."

"What would that be, in weather like this?" asked Miss Bristol.

"I'll hide nothing from a scientist," said Mr. Murk. "More than ten per cent."

"I'll buy you a grog," said Dr. Chrisdie to Mr. Murk after the others had also gone below. The chief had given Miss Bristol a hand as far as the door.

"Yon's a lassie wi' wits in her head. She's got what engineers would call congenital magnetism.—Come awa' to the smoke-room. There's just time before old Triton blows his wreathèd horn."

24. The Egg

Geoffrey noticed when it was put before him that the egg-shell had a pale lilac tinge. "It looks like an Easter egg," he said. Boxer of course had ready excuses.

"Oh, they all looks like that, don't you worry. It's some kind of chemicals they puts in the cold storage. Mr. McScoon, 'e's very deliberate about 'is heggs. If there's any question at all they goes right aft to the steerage."

"It looks jubious to me," said Aunt Kilda.

"Oh no indeed, Miss, you don't need to 'ave no 'orrors, this 'ere's a pedigree hegg." Boxer, in pendulum stance with the swing of the ship, smartly sliced the shell. At once all adjoining chairs spun outward and the party fled from the table. Even Geoffrey, though fascinated by the blue-green embryo, fell backward in an eddy of gas. "Fishwives, it's a foetus," said Aunt Kilda.

"McScoon was certainly too deliberate with that one," said Uncle Dan.

Boxer for one of the few times in his service was stopped at the source. Hastily he smothered the offense with a napkin and started for the door. It was an upgrade at that moment, he had to pause for support at one of the stanchions so the other table got a whiff too, but Boxer's discomfiture proved a social solvent. Passengers hitherto aloof came over to occupy the vacant chairs beside Geoffrey and Uncle Dan and rival anecdotes were told. Dr. Friedeck said it reminded him of Paris after the siege, and gave the details (delightful to Geoffrey) of a memorable fricassee of rats. Geoffrey was so much interested that the little German quite warmed to him. "We had a saying when I was a child, *Hast du Eier gerne frisch, Setz das Huhn gleich auf den Tisch.*" He was surprised that the boy repeated it at once with substantial accuracy, evidently delighting in mere sound.

"You have an ear for speech," he said, "very unusual among the English."

"What does it mean?" Geoffrey asked.

"To have fresh eggs you'll not be able, unless the hen lays on the table," suggested Uncle Dan. Mr. McScoon came in to make apologies. Even Boxer was a little subdued; the best he could say was it must have been one of a shipment intended for the Cunard.

"Let us change the topic," said Dr. Friedeck. "Speaking of words, here's an English paradox: if for a ship it's meant, you call it *cargo*; if in a car it goes, you call it *shipment*. What can science do with such anomalies?"

"I like the way you talk," said Geoffrey. "Tell me some more."

When the group gathered a little later for *Jude the Obscure* they were amused to find Dr. Friedeck and Geoffrey sitting together at the piano. Picking out the tunes with one finger, the professor was humming the student songs of his youth. Geoff had never known that words could sound so comically and deliciously different.

"We'll make a philologian out of this child," said the professor. "He has instinctive Sprachgefuehl—don't worry about the meanings, just enjoy the sound."

"Do the one with a bugle in it!"

"Again? *Gott, wie er freut sich*," said Dr. Friedeck. "He makes a good audience." In an undertone of luscious sentiment he warbled:

> *"Morgenrot, morgenrot,*
> *Leuchtest mir zum fruehen Tod.*
> *Bald wird die Trompeten blasen. . . ."*

and followed by an imitation of a trumpet call.

"It doesn't sound like the lunch bugle, it sounds sad," said Geoff.

"English doesn't do it justice. English is imperfect for its own sentiments. How could it be adequate to ours?"

"Oh morning red, oh morning red, Tomorrow morning I'll be dead," Uncle Dan translated.

"English doesn't do it justice," repeated Dr. Friedeck, angrily.

25. Mid-ocean

The weather softened, people not seen before appeared on deck, including the DuQuesnes, Mr. and Mrs. Marple and their scion Master Chester Marple. The latter seemed to Uncle Dan an unattractive child, pallid and oppressed by nasal obstructions, but he was just enough older to arouse admiration in Geoffrey. Chester's exaggerated deference in public gave Uncle Dan a suspicion that he was at mischief around corners, but when he tracked the boys he usually found them gaping at the yacht model displayed outside the saloon. The sheltered side of the promenade was now well filled, and the readings of *Jude* were slowed down by miscellaneous conversation. Dan felt a little self-conscious about the reading since Aunt Bee had joined them. Even when she seemed asleep she was often alert to more than one might suppose.

Mr. Snead, one of the poker players, was particularly awed by the conversation of their learned group, which he called The Faculty. He would lean against the rail, looking quizzically from under his pancake tweed cap. "I guess the future of American education is O.K.," he would say; or "I wouldn't understand, I'm just a lowbrow." Uncle Dan was tickled by this coinage. "Wonderful!" he exclaimed. "A perfect example of instinctive genius for wordmaking. Good Elizabethan too: there's something in *The Tempest* about 'foreheads villainous low.'" Mr. Snead winked to Mr. Marple and drew him away to the smoke-room.

More difficult was Mrs. Lotus Bannister who sat simmering with enthusiasm on the edge of the party. She had little control and vented sugary or irrelevant ejaculations. Dr. DuQuesne was telling them how much Shakespeare had cribbed from Montaigne when Mrs. Bannister burst in with "Do you think Dreyfus was really guilty?" Friedeck and Miss Shaugraun were at it hammer and tongs about Gildersleeve versus Von Wilamowitz-Moellendorff and Mrs. Bannister asked, "Would you spell that wonderful name for me, Professor, so I can write it down?" Dr. Friedeck excused himself and brusquely pulled his chair to a windy but secluded spot.

"I say to myself this is really my college education," Lotus confided, after several struggles with the German name. "It was so good of Mr. Bannister to let me come, poor him, he gets so unsociable when he's left alone, but I'd always set my heart on my literary pilgrimage. You don't know what England does to an American, so much history and intellect, it hardly seems fair in such a small island, it just shows that size isn't everything. I was thinking when I was up in that darling Lake Country, really quite small ponds and yet all that marvelous poetry, now look at our Great Lakes, why shouldn't we have some Great Lake Poets? Of course there's Chautauqua—"

There was silence for a while.

"I remember a cryptic remark of Gildersleeve's," said Miss Shaugraun, "how he spent an Atlantic voyage reading Pindar in the smoke-room. That's where you men have such an advantage."

"I got one of the best tips from Gildersleeve that a student ever had," Dan said. "He was talking about the use of the summer vacation; he said take away with you a clean copy of the text you're working on, so your previous notes don't interfere with freshness of vision."

The memory of this wise advice gave him a sharp need for movement and silence.

Aft of the midship deckhouse a long narrow gangway spanned the orlop and led to the fenced platform of the poop. This passageway had been barred during the gale; the plunge of the sloping stern was terror and vertigo for the landsman. But now in the soft curve of afternoon Dan found the gate unfastened. White iron gates usually lead into gardens, he thought, remembering one between the Meadow and The Wilderness. This was very different, but in the acceptance of the hour he blamed nothing for being itself. Perhaps with falling wind and gentling sea the mind was slackened too. For the first time since Queenstown Harbor conscious attention did not have to apply itself to mere equilibrium. The wide parallel ridges of ocean were no longer hostile, only a surly habit. The imaginative barber, taking his off hour on the hatch below, shouted up a friendly hail. "We yn't gettin' kicked abaht so, more like swingin' a babby in yer arms." Crumbling blue profiles spread in acres of snow, but now it seemed melting snow in a softening thaw. Yes, like February afternoons under the old garden wall in the beginning of Dan's world; the crocus time. He envied his shipmates who seemed all at once to have disappeared into siesta. The weather had relaxed and they with it, subconsciously assured that the storm had not intended anything personal. Even Geoffrey and Chester had been lured by the deck steward into a diversion of quoits. Uncle Dan knew this was going well for he had seen one of the rope rings tossed wildly overboard and spinning in the green riot below him.

His emotions were always tardy. Why did he seem only now

saying his real good-by, reviewing with wretched clearness the innocent and stoic life of the Thorofare, and all humanity frozen in poor attitudes of parting? Residual magnetism, I suppose, he thought. Mr. Murk had interested him by expounding three different kinds of polarity that bedevil the compass at sea. There was the ship's own congenital magnetism born into her in the builder's yard; and the induced or momentary magnetism of the course being steered; and the retained or residual polarity that lingered in the binnacle as a result of any protracted voyage. "It's no deeferent frae a boozer's hangover," said Mr. Murk. "I'm tellin' ye when we turrn the Delaware Capes and steer norrard we'll have to set a course twelve degrees eastward of actual for compensation. Ye'll no can run east and west like this wi'out giein' the needle a wryneck. The magnetic pole is an unco pheenomenon. There was a vessel I traveled in once, her compass was so flighty we maun put in a Flinders Bar six feet lang. It cam doun into the second mate's bunk and he sleepit wi' a shaft o' cold iron in his oxter. He was a romantic-minded laddie, like all they second mates, and he tried to imagine it was companionship. The Iron Maiden he ca'd her, but she was no verra comforting shape."

It was news to Dan that the compass was so temperamental. Like any organism of keen and subtle temper it had loyalties or memories of its own. He remembered having felt secretly disturbed when he acquired his citizenship in the United States. He had to "renounce allegiance" to any previous affiliation; yet there are allegiances or residual magnetisms which words do not annul. So there was consolation in Mr. Murk's jocularity about the grievances of the wheelhouse.

No one need be reproached for mixing latitudes and longitudes in the hypnotic lull of sea-solitude. He tried to visualize them, lines of geometry stretched like lace over the arched breast of the world. The run of the waves lifted them against clear distance, through pale scallops of hollowed foam he could see them, string-taut on the imagined perfect sphere. He chose one far ahead, marked it off with his eye, felt accomplishment as he rode over it and the flailing screw tore it apart. Solitude is never embarrassed and he mumbled to himself phrases that seemed of great wisdom. Mid-ocean, he said, mid-ocean! This must be just about it. But each phantom meridian—he could see them exquisitely black as hair strokes of India ink—drew his mind forward to sketch and covet a new one. His eyes were tired of switching to and fro. I must choose one and stick to it. There it is in that long purple valley. Mid-ocean. Worse than that, the fortieth meridian, maybe. Unpleasing coincidence, for he knew from Geoffrey how secret the fortieth-birthday cake was being kept. Even the word mid-ocean was a quotation from Geoffrey. "I'm monstrous full of fleas, this is mid-ocean, Boxer says so. He says we'll have Mother Carey's chickens for dinner." Association with children makes an artist of the most literal. Even in a few days aboard ship Dan had drawn more pictures, invented more games, told more fables, exercised whatever in himself was poet more than in a decade of teaching literature. Horrible, he exclaimed, and hammered the vibrant rail. Here he was nauseated by the sickness of the skull—infinitely worse than any sickness of the sea—the mystery of transition and impermanence, while a child, the monkey of the moment, nimble and insensible, is at home everywhere, even when surrounded by visible infinity.

Mid-ocean: it would look well at the heading of a letter, what I'm really doing now is writing to Harry, good old Harry, a letter that will never be put on paper. Harry was the only person with whom he had ever been able to communicate. The heroic figures of his mother and sisters were like seated marbles; one lowered one's voice, spoke with the anguish of love or homage, but it was unreal. Had the stony reticence of so many generations broken down in himself? Harry, it's a good thing they keep the stern railed off if this is the kind of thinking it starts. I guess (I can say "I guess" now because we just passed the dividing line, I saw it very clear), I guess what's the matter is just the homesickness of a poor damned prof, that's what they call us in the States, for the only thing a student is ever homesick for, his books. I suppose you imagine a teacher leads a gay impulsive life of scholarly conjecture; the fact is he's frightened, hasn't guts enough to tackle people his own size and wants to get back to the safety of classroom and curriculum. No, that isn't quite fair but I'm not *really* writing to Harry so I can say what I feel. I had a funny twinge of envy when I saw Chrisdie asleep with Lecky in his deck chair. No wonder he's keen about the eighteenth century. It looks so neat and orderly from this distance. (I'd be distrustful of anything that looks so museum-piece as that?) It must have had the fires of hell inside it when it was happening. I was telling Chrisdie about the jokes Alexander Pope used to play on the booksellers and he said that it wasn't important because he wouldn't dare mention it to his students. For that matter I wouldn't either. I remember your old father telling me the yokel tradition in Silly Suffolk that if you hang a dead dried-up woodpecker on a string it always points its bill in the direction of the wind. I guess that's what we teachers are, just dead woodpeckers. He looks rather like one too, I mean Chrisdie, he's got the most comical long nose and he's going bald very young (most middle-westerners do, I don't know why, but even the country out there hasn't much foliage) but I like him better as I get used to him. He was a bit shocked at first by our little group, he thought us all very flippant and I'll admit Kilda, I mean Miss Shaugraun, is a bit of a termagant. One of the difficulties about English and Americans is they don't have their talkative spells at the same time so whichever one happens to be talking infuriates the other, but I could see after two or three days Chrisdie decided (after thinking it over in his diary) that he needn't take us too seriously. You could see him racked with resolution as he sat down with us, saying to himself, "I must be more playful." But imagine that temperament dealing with Swift or Pope! I guess one of the things that happens to the English mind as it moves westward is, it gets more solemn. But you'll see when you come over (I'm still talking to you, Harry) something does happen. It always seemed to me very odd, on the coasts of the British Isles you see the ocean rolling in—then you go three thousand miles and you see it rolling quite obviously and regularly the other way. But nobody notices where is the dividing line, like a parting in one's hair. Certainly there's a division of some sort, where the combers are neatly combed in opposite directions. That's what we just crossed.

Dan heard a clang as the gate was opened and closed at the other end of the footway. He was surprised to see a figure with brightened color and whipping skirts leaning her way across. It was Miss Bristol.

Still a bit dazed with his rocking solitude he gaped at the surprising picture. Centered on the long swing of the ship in such a panorama of movement and color the small figure clung to the rail with one hand. Two were needed, but her red knitted cap was about to blow off. Even in the moment of hesitation before he realized she needed help, Dan decided that the jersey cap was woven of the same fabric as the fluttering petticoat and wondered if this was economy or art. He hastened forward and grabbed her elbow.

"You shouldn't come out here."

"I won't again until I have four hands," she said, trying to manage cap, skirt and railing simultaneously. "But ever since we came on board people have been telling me what I can't do."

"Now you're here, come all the way, it's really marvelous on the turtleback."

"The right place for Brer Tarrypin," she said, but the wind blew it away.

"You can feel the screw fighting with the sea, I never saw such colors, like beating green eggs."

"I've got news for you, that's why I came."

Dan had never supposed a woman disheveled could look so pretty. He couldn't really hear what she was saying but he helped her back to the lee of the deckhouse. She shouted in his ear, which had not been so closely approached since it was scoured in youth.

"I hated to bother you," she said, "but I am afraid you'll have to do something about Dr. Friedeck. He was asleep in his chair and Geoffrey and that nasty little Chester tied him with a skipping-rope. They said he was General Custer tortured by Indians. It must have been Chester's idea. Anyway when he woke he was startled and thought he was drowning and struggled to escape. His chair fell over, he hit his eye and he's very angry. He says it's an outrage after he's been so kind to Geoffrey, and he must have an apology."

26. Dr. Chrisdie's Diary

I always imagined, wrote Dr. Chrisdie, that aboard ship one would have leisure to settle down and think, but honest to God, this 10 P.M. supper when they put watery cocoa and pilot crackers on the saloon table and you help yourself is the only chance one gets. All day long we get shaken together like liniment in a bottle. There wouldn't be room here to put down a fraction of what goes on. It never struck me before what a small portion of actual events historians can describe. (N.B. That would make a good start for my talk at the seminar on Historical Method?)

Most absurd thing I ever witnessed, I was having a lovely nap, I guess everybody was. We were stretched out in our chairs, Miss Shaugraun with her horse profile looked like a crusader's tomb, Dr. Friedeck had pulled his chair out of the way behind the ventilator. I thought I heard the kids whispering. It seems they took a piece of rope and tied Friedeck into his chair while he was asleep. He must have had a nightmare or something, everybody has a theory about it. Dr. DuQuesne thinks Dr. F. was tied up and frightened by a French firing squad in 1870, anyhow when he woke he made a fearful jump, the chair went over and he cracked his eye on a big iron ring-bolt on the deck. There was hell to pay. He said that everybody had been insulting him for days and he must have "satisfaction." Shaugraun said, "What does he want to do, fight a duel with the two children? Tell him I'll meet him with one of McScoon's eggs at ten paces." What made it worse, in his tumble his china teeth got dislodged, he couldn't speak until he rearranged them and the two kids were yelling with laughter. Naturally we were all as sorry as could be, we bandaged his eye right away with a towel and cold salt water, of which there's plenty. I figure the stunt was young Chester's idea because he hastened to make himself scarce. Geoffrey stood by, I'll say that for him, but his comments weren't exactly tactful.

When Barton got there Dr. Friedeck stood up very stiff and said he wanted a formal apology. He put it in such a nasty way no one knew what to do. We all stood around trying to pacify him and a weird windy echo kept coming from nowhere, "Oh, *please* apologize!" Friedeck got madder still, I guess he thought it was somebody kidding. It was poor little Miss Barton down in her cabin. She heard the fuss through the ventilator, it acts like a magnified speaking tube, she kept calling plaintively up the pipe but the ferocious little man was terribly sore. The ship's doctor came up from the steerage where he's been busy most of the voyage. Barton took me aside to consult. "I can't give him a written apology," he said, "it's too ridiculous. I dare say Geoffrey ought to be put in the brig on bread and water but after all it was only a child's prank."

"I don't see how those franc-tireurs could have missed him," said Dr. DuQuesne, "that would have solved everything."

The stiff little man was really very childish himself, standing with one hand on his eye, the other holding the ventilator handle, waiting for someone to satisfy his pride. "He's so excessively Prussian," whispered Miss Shaugraun, or she thought it was a whisper. Everything looked very bad, for how could Barton and I get along with a cabin-mate in this mood, and tomorrow is the get-together of the Ship's Concert, to say nothing of Barton's secret birthday cake? The rest of the afternoon everyone was in dismay but I suppose the deck steward must have told Captain Bompjes about it. Wonderful man, I never realized how smart a captain has to be. I guess he knows the importance of a uniform, anyway he sent the first officer to see Dr. Friedeck where he was sulking in the cabin, with a written apology on behalf of the ship herself. Captain Bompjes explained (what I'm sure he just made up) that there had been a terrible billow, a sort of tidal wave, extraordinary and unexpected, which must have upset the chair, so it was the fault of the ship and she humbly asked his pardon—signed by the Captain himself and with Barton and me as witnesses. He had the first officer add verbally that the barber was very skillful in painting shiners and would Dr. Friedeck accept a treatment with the compliments of the company?

I wish I could have seen the patient receiving this document but Barton and I thought it well not to visit our cabin until he had been mollified. The officer described him sitting up in his bunk with a slice of fresh beef—well anyway, beef—over his eye. He made a dignified little speech and put the paper in his wallet, probably alongside the letter he cherishes from the President of Harvard.

27. Advantages of Mathematics

Uncle Dan found them in the library alcove. Under instruction from the President of Geoffland, Aunt Blanche was drawing a map of that country; Aunt Kilda was knitting and enjoying the boy's communicative mood.

"Geoffland is a long narrow country," its ruler explained. "There's a street that runs right through the middle, that's the Thorofare. Up at this end is a big part that's very jolly, it's for the sociable people, it's called Saloon. There's a through train on the P.R.R. goes all the way to Seckford City. It drops a slip carriage at Boxerville."

"I can see that Geoffland is a great resource," Kilda said to Dan. "It reflects whatever the President is thinking about at the time."

"I was amused the other day," Dan whispered. "It was confided to me that some of the ladies in Geoffland were allowed to cut their hair short."

"Seckford, that's the capital of County Steerage," continued the geographer. "They wear shawls and dance outdoors when it isn't infectious. Now we can color the different places."

"Such a lot of counties, I don't believe there are enough crayons left," said Uncle Dan. "The best colors seem to have disappeared. It's a way they have."

"How many have you got?" asked Aunt Blanche.

Uncle Dan looked through the Emergency Bag. "Only four, rather tame. Yellow, brown, pink, and a sort of gray."

"That's plenty. You can color any map, no matter how many subdivisions it has, with only four colors."

"What, without having the same colors touch along the boundaries? Surely not! Think of the United States, forty-four of them—no, forty-five, they brought in another since I became a citizen—you'd certainly need more colors than that to mark off all the boundaries."

"I don't care if it was Germany in the Middle Ages, any map at all can be done in four colors without any two contiguous divisions using the same tint. It's a famous curiosity in geometry. It makes atlas printing commercially possible."

"I thought I knew something about maps," said Dan. "Can you prove it?"

"I don't think it can be formulated, it's just so. Take the crayons and try it."

"While you do the colors I'll be the train to Boxerville," said Geoff and choo-chooed off. Dan experimented with the crayons.

"I guess you're right," he admitted. "I'll never need to buy so many different colors after this. I had no idea geometry penetrated even into Geoffland."

"Wait until she tells you about spiders," said Kilda. "I always disliked them, nasty things, but when I learned they spin by logarithms they horrify me, cold-blooded, ha-haugh!"

"I never met mathematics socially before," said Dan. "Speaking of that, if I had an ideal country it would never have any social fixtures. Tonight I've got to be chairman at the Concert, and now the Captain asks me to read the lessons or something at the church service tomorrow. He says we'll be on soundings, he can't leave the bridge, too busy with the blue pigeon."

"That sounds very High-Church," said Kilda.

"It's what they call the sounding lead.—I tried to beg off, the Church of England ritual is quite out of character for a Quaker, but there aren't any parsons on board. It seems to disprove the old superstition that you only get bad weather when there's a clergyman in the ship."

"Quite a change from Jude the Obscene. I shall look forward to the service for the first time in years."

"Very kind of you, I'm sure, but here's the point: nobody, not even Mrs. Bannister, seems to know which particular Sunday it is. I mean, how many Sundays after Trinity, which is the way you take soundings in the prayer book."

"Why not ask Mr. Murk? He knows everything. Trinity is eight Sundays after Easter; somebody must know when Easter was?"

"I'm afraid she's a godless ship," said Dan. "Neither Mr. Murk nor Mr. Huskisson remember the date of Easter because they were ashore that week."

"Perhaps I could work it out for you," said Blanche. "There's a formula for finding Easter, invented by Gauss. Have you a pencil? I'll show you."

Aunt Bee came into the saloon and sat down beside them. "What on earth are you doing?" she asked.

114

"We're trying to compute the date of Easter, but I ha got room for the figures."

"Last Easter? It was April tenth. I remember perfectly because Lizzie Batts went to Framlingham."

"Splendid," said Dan. "How much more useful is the simple domestic mind than all the sophisticated sciolism of science. Good alliteration, what?"

"You ought to finish working it out, just for discipline."

"No thank you. Things are difficult enough without that. Now we know when Easter was, we can find the right place. Hand me the prayer book, please—I want to read over the collects and things beforehand."

"A man of letters should be more familiar with the book of common prayer," said Kilda severely. "If you look at the back of the book, you'll find a special section for use at sea. There's that wonderful psalm for thanksgiving after a storm."

"Yes, but there's a verse there that Bee won't like, 'their soul abhorred all manner of meat.' We'll take the other one, about turning the sea into dry land."

"You're always so squeamish about what you think will startle other people," Bee said. "I overheard you all talking together about the terrible things in *Jude the Obscure*. You were so dreadfully shocked and couldn't believe people behave like that —why there isn't anything in the story that I haven't seen right at home in Wilford. You should ask Allie if you want to know the seamy side of a country town. It's a good thing you never heard the family history of the Ghostly Demon."

Dan looked at his sister in amazement. She had taken out her knitting and was reckoning stitches.

"When Dan went away to college," she said to the others, "we all made up our minds to conceal from him anything that would distract him from his literature. Students have to lead such a sheltered life."

Blanche was amused to notice a dim flush of annoyance creeping under Dan's beard. Bee must have noticed it too for she said briskly, "You better go to the hairdresser and get trimmed before the Concert."

"Damn it all," he said, "literature isn't sheltered. It deals with the actual matter of human trouble."

"It never catches up with it, though," said Bee.

Dan went for a stroll on deck. Mr. Huskisson, the purser, out for one of his seldom gulps of air, came round the corner. "Extraordinary thing," said Dan, "just happened to me for the first time. I'm homesick for the States. It suddenly felt like God's Country."

Even in his outing the purser was consumed with affairs. He was studying a memorandum, reckoning his resources for the Concert.

"There seems a shortage of talent," he said, "even in spite of Mrs. Bannister. It's risky, but I think you'll have to call on Boxer for his song about the sparrow. That old cockney piece about 'The blasted, blooming sparrow flew up the bloody spout.' I'll tell him to say blooming instead of bloody, but when he gets excited he forgets and then somebody always complains."

"He catches it from the parrot," said Uncle Dan. "Geoffrey did too.—Couldn't you invite someone from the steerage, they always have wonderful performers."

"Wouldn't dare, they've had some kind of a little epidemic down there, probably only chicken pox, but somebody would be sure to worry about germs. You should have been with us in '93, the cholera scare. The purser gets all the bad news from every quarter of the ship. This year it seems to be broken shafts. Happened twice in the Cunard, cost them five thousand quid in salvage. You should have seen old Murk this voyage, down in the tunnel with a lamp, nursing his bearings."

"You'd never guess it, to talk with him."

"Certainly not, never lose face in front of the customers. Well, give us a good speech tonight. The tickets for the raffle have sold very well."

"The Men of Sin said they would do something, they ought to be amusing."

"Within reason, I hope. Dr. Chrisdie is rehearsing them in a quartet, they're at it in the smoke-room now. I think I better tell the bar-man not to serve them anything more before dinner. I heard them just now as I went by the door, something about 'pale in the amber west.'"

"It *is* amber. I was just noticing what a peculiar light."

"Fog," said Mr. Huskisson. "We're coming right onto it. The good old corner, about 47-47, between Flemish Cap and the Virgins."

A canvas bucket swung down past them on a line, and was hauled up slopping sea water.

"I see he's taking temperatures, that means we're on the Banks?" Dan noticed then how close the horizon had come. It was like walking into a great wall of wet gray blanket.

"You'll be getting a nice little obbligato from the ship herself."

Above them the *Westernland* lifted her first bellow of indignation, beginning with a fumbling sputter and then the full deep roar of the horn. The railing quivered with the escape of boiling steam. "I hope Dr. Friedeck has his teeth in tight," Dan thought. The bell on the foremast rang two pairs of quick strokes, they sounded muffled and flattened in thick air.

"I'll go and dress, I suppose it's noblesse oblige for the chairman."

"Don't miss my little party," said Mr. Huskisson, "a glass of wine in the engineers' mess-room for the good of the ship." Dan was turning toward the companion entrance when a clatter of feet came down the bridge ladder. One of the quartermasters going off watch saluted him politely, and brushed a glittering fringe of fog-drops from his pink eyebrows.

"Captain's compliments, Sir, he's sorry he won't be able to come below for the Concert. He says he hopes the siren won't interfere with the music."

Dan began to feel victimized. Evidently the evening was going to rest heavily on him, he had a silly twinge of envy for the seaman in oilskins retiring to the simplicity of the focsle. But if the social responsibility was to be his, the first thing to do was to pacify Dr. Friedeck.

Dr. Friedeck's mind had also been busy. It was undignified to hold an uncle responsible for the errors of a nephew. Also he had a genuine respect for Professor Barton who had at any rate struggled to escape his provincial origin and in spite of imperfect scholarship was plainly a person of sensibility. After all, was not that the extraordinary thing about the British race, under their haphazard manners and their complacent Inselbeschränktheit, they have imagination. A Prussian scholar need not fear to admit the truth, and the astonishing truth is (he thought, laying out his dinner clothes) that those fantastic people, undisciplined and boorish, are poets; even the undrilled and impromptu character of their verse has its bucolic charm. A German Gelehrter would not fall into the absurdity of Voltaire who could not esteem the English genius because it disobeyed all rules. It would be pleasant to say something of this sort to his roommate Barton. With just the correct rigor to suggest that though one knows there has been offense one is gracious enough to overlook it. Standing erect to push the studs into his glossy shirtfront he unconsciously practiced a small authoritative bend of reconciliation. At that moment the foghorn blasted his tight nerves and the studs flew in all directions. Much sharper angles of flex were required in search. He prostrated under the berths, but still two buttons were unfound. His ardent blood stream was intolerant of such postures, the arteries of ears and neck drummed pressure, and the newly enameled eye rubbed brusquely on the edge of the washstand. He rang for Stretch, but the steward was busy elsewhere. He was making a last furious grope behind a trunk when Dan tapped gently at the door.

Grunting disgust he drew his legs out of the way and shouted through the opening, "Damnation, blue fire, why didn't you come sooner?" By the time Stretch arrived, the situation was beyond repair. Dr. Friedeck had locked the door shouting, "I don't care how many people want to dress, there's only room for one. Who do you think you are, Cecil Rhodes?"

28. When the Foghorn Blew

"What was that Word you said?" Geoff asked as Uncle Dan came downstairs. But Uncle Dan's mind was on other concerns, he shook his head vaguely and replied, "I didn't say anything. That was the foghorn."

Geoff thought he knew the Word, he had overheard Uncle Dan use it several times in conversation on deck; and in so special a tone that it sounded important. But he wanted to be more sure before saying it aloud himself. A strange word, magical perhaps; laughable-sounding yet always uttered by Uncle Dan with a tinge of gravity. The first blast of the foghorn had sounded a little like it, beginning with a hiss, then lung-deep from within. He stood in the passage holding the handrail, happy and absorbed. He was admiring his miscellaneous panorama of America. Perhaps it was something like Geoffland, with a prairie, an endless Sutton Heath where Indians chased the buffalo—or vice versa. Or a very small *U.S.S. Maine* bursting in flame and fragments; or the vast, cloudy, benignant outline of Uncle Remus, with Brer Fox saddled and bridled for Miss Meadows and the gals.

It was that hour of late afternoon when the sea had leveled to a broad greasy swell and all had retired to their quarters to make ready for the Captain's Dinner and the Concert. The saloon doors were closed while Mr. McScoon and his stewards dressed the tables, and there was emptiness in the lobby. Perhaps Geoffrey could even feel it as a threatening or impending empti-

119

ness: the dangerous world of larger people had mysteriously re-tracted its forces in preparation for some new absurdity.

Nothing is more queer than the exact record of what people were doing at any moment of crisis. Mrs. Bootle, for instance. When the fog shut down she was rushing from Bootle Junction to the aid of Mrs. Bannister. That lady, preparing herself with art to inflict her Selections at the Concert, was carefully balanced before a quite incommensurate mirror. But a given bulk which has trained itself to a certain latitude of swing is sure to over-compensate when the roll does not go so far. Accordingly as the obedient *Westernland* adjusted herself to a new rhythm the opulent Lotus leaned too wide. She fell heavily upon her settee and burst a number of necessary fraps. She bore down on the stewardess's bell with a well-padded thumb, and in that instant heard the ship make speech for the first time.

Mr. Huskisson in his cabin wrestling into his mess jacket, was in no danger of falling; his room was so narrow he could wedge his feet from side to side. He was calculating how many guests he should invite to take a glass of sherry as a warm-up for the celebration. He had instructed McScoon to serve wine and hors d'oeuvres in the engineers' mess-room as he felt the evening was going to need stimulus. Every purser has a small allowance from the company for necessary strokes of tact, but the allow-ance is moderate and obviously had better not include the smoke-room quartet. Mr. Murk always resented the use of his officers' mess for such receptions, it necessitated the removal of certain Parisian lithographs cherished by the junior engineers, but there was no other space for the requisite privacy. These and other intricate concerns were busy in the purser's mind when he heard the opening blast. As usual, he thought, the Captain won't come down for the Captain's Dinner, and murmured to himself his commander's habitual epigram about the Grand Banks: "Dirty per cent dirty weather."

Boxer, having finished Dr. Friedeck's eye, was due for service in decorating the saloon. It had been a difficult session because the parrot, who always knew when anything unusual was toward, was very talkative. Dr. Friedeck, morbidly alert for personal reference, had been offended by her innocent repetition, "Dirty old man. Lost my drawers, lend me yours." Boxer wondered if he ought to cover the cage but felt it was not quite fair to do so on Marie's evening of riot. Trouble is, he meditated, she and the Prof got such different senses of 'umor. If any. As barbers and gods may do, looking down from above, he was curious to consider what kind of peculiar traffic was moving just beneath that armored pate. 'E's got a 'igh pressure temperament, not 'arf, he thought as he saw occasional flushes of circulation redden and fade on the customer's skull. A sprinkle of witch 'azel for 'is 'ot box, he thought in philosophic detachment, and didn't even charge for it. He was startled when Dr. Friedeck, instead of buying only one ticket for the raffle, took a dozen, which even at a low percentage yielded more than the tip Boxer had faintly hoped. He often knew what Marie was going to say before she said it, and he saw her beak already open for her special blasphemy when the foghorn roared. The parrot drew in every quill and shuffled to the far corner of the cage. Loyally he apologized for her. "Gor, she don't relish a fog."

"I think I shall wear my fascinator," Blanche was saying, "it gets so draughty in the saloon."

"Also it's very becoming," said Kilda, enjoying a cigarette on their stateroom sofa. "I'm glad to see the Square Root of Minus One perking up a bit."

"Barton, poor fellow, takes this evening very seriously."

Blanche did not admit that Dan had confided to her that afternoon the gist of the terse and witty little speech he hoped to make. They had met accidentally at the after end of the promenade, and in the lee of the ventilator he told her how really significant the Concert might be made. But he was rather distracted by the small curly head and knitted cap so becomingly framed in the circle of the ventilator rim.

"I wouldn't make too many international comparisons," Blanche suggested.

"I dare say you're right."

"Your sister is a very wise creature," said Blanche. "We were speaking of Professor Friedeck and she said, 'Poor man, he's terribly unhappy.' I said, 'He doesn't look it, the way he struts about.' 'Oh yes he is,' said Miss Barton, 'it's pride. People who are so full of that stubborn morbid sensitiveness need all sorts of help. Anything stiff breaks so easily.'"

"Perhaps I'd better go back to the stern and think over my speech again," said Dan humbly.

This dialogue was repeating itself in Blanche's mind as she excavated the fascinator and her evening gown from the trunk. She had not expected they would be worn during the voyage. If I had known, she thought, I would have used more tissue paper. At that moment came the foghorn. The vibration shook apart one of Kilda's smoke rings. "Fishwives! How's that for an appetizer?" She clambered to her knees to look out of the port. "Real Newfoundland fog," she said. "Maybe some of the fishwives won't be getting their fish."

"Oh, poor Mr. Barton," said Blanche. "Will that be going on all through his speech?"

Geoffrey, coming back to the lobby, found it still empty. The foghorn, which seemed to him just one more novelty for his enjoyment, had evidently frightened everyone out of sight. He was alone with the model yacht.

There were several things about it he would like to discuss with Uncle Dan but there had always been someone in the way —often the domineering Chester. The two boys had coveted it together, and Geoffrey described sailing on Wilford River, but Chester was contemptuous. Who ever heard of sailing on a river, he said. Sailing was done on lakes. Geoffrey felt different about Chester since the accident with Dr. Friedeck. Chester had first crossed his heart and hoped to die that he only participated in the trick to please Geoffrey, and then instead of saying he was sorry he shammed sick. There were things about the model yacht that Geoff would not care to express to anyone like Chester. It was a little ship inside a big ship, and that seemed to mean something.

He did not know exactly what happened at a raffle, but he felt that the yacht was almost his already. He even had in his pocket the anchor for it. It was more wonderful than anything in Miss Hoo's window, more perfect than Harry Bredfield's *Scandal*. No smell in the cabin, no mildew on her snowy sails, he could feel her trembling alive where tide and air were equal partners. Even her name, who knows what music it meant to the focsle artificer: those exquisite letters in green, ELLEN ARKINS. The varnish of her three-foot deck, the cockpit with a little brass wheel, the coil of mimic halliards, tiny reef-points, sweet groining of her stern—how exquisite a retreat into the understandable from surrounding bedlams of space. Where everything jostled she was fixed, where everything rioted she was steady, where everything was huge she was minute. He wanted to say to Uncle Dan: If I were small enough I could sail her.

29. *The Purser's Party*

The retrussing of Mrs. Bannister made Mrs. Bootle a little late in her own private schedule. A well-trained ship's company leaps to automatic alert when the foghorn blows; they know that melancholy cry causes an immediate droop in the morale of passengers and it is inadvisable to let them brood. The stewardess hastened to the staterooms of the other ladies under her charge, either to offer assistance in equipment or to urge dinner dress upon any who seemed languid. Fog and the curdling drone of the whistle break down even professional reticences. When she met Stretch in the bathroom passage she rebuked him for

123

not goading his gentlemen into boiled shirts. "If it's fog," she said, "I allus gets ladies into a decoltay. It keeps up their pecker, and if there's going to be wallering in cold water they might as well look their best."

"A wonderful comfort you are, old nannie. 'Ow long does yer think a dress shirt will 'old starch inside a life-preserver?"

Mr. Huskisson's guests were comfortably seated in the engineers' mess. They were in excellent spirits, and to outward seeming the worthy purser had no care in the world. In spite of competition from pistons below and foghorn above he was delighting the party with some verses from sea chanteys.

> "We was sick of the beach and our money was gone,
> Away, down Rye-O,
> We signed in this packet to drive her along,
> An' we're bound to the Ri-i-o Grand!"

"Oh, that's wonderful, and such *melody*," warbled Mrs. Bannister. "I wish you'd sing some of those at the Concert."

"I might forget myself and sing the real capstan words."

"Music and the ocean seem to go together, don't they? I've been crooning to myself all afternoon, 'Speed, bonny boat, like a bird on the wing,' my mother used to sing it to me when I was a tiny girl. She was from Tidewater Virginia, you know they have so much *soul*."

Miss Shaugraun was always roused to perversity by the mooings of Mrs. Bannister. "I suppose the genuine sea songs are always bawdy," she said. "Probably that was why Ulysses made his sailors put wax in their ears while the sirens were chanting. Most lyric poetry is so beastly sentimental. It's really only a biological gesture, a form of rut, ha-haugh! Like the wail of the tomcat or the nuptial dance of the bustard."

Dr. Chrisdie entered just then, raising his eyebrows; the purser hastened to pour sherry. He had planned his little group with care, so he was surprised when the three Men of Sin also appeared. They had a keen intuition for any sociability, and after their rehearsal they had followed Dr. Chrisdie. He dodged around various passageways, but they stuck to his trail; and Geoffrey followed theirs.

"What's a bustard?" asked Geoff, just as he looked cheerfully through the doorway.

"Not me," said Mr. Snead. He was carrying a small silk American flag, which he handed to the boy.

"Here you are, bub, stick that in your Yorkshire pudding." He dazzled Geoffrey with a direct gaze brightened by smoke-room harmony. "Bring you luck for the raffle."

"Why do you call it 'Old Glory'?" asked Geoffrey.

"God's Country!" ejaculated Mr. Snead's two colleagues.

"Sit down, gentlemen," said Mr. Huskisson, attempting to resume command.

Miss Bristol remarked to herself that the quartic, as she called them, were in good form. Even Dr. Chrisdie's sallow cheek showed a spot of enthusiasm.

"Where's Brother Murk?" said Mr. Snead. "I miss the rumble of his R's—." He stopped suddenly as one of his friends jabbed him with a pointed elbow.

Mrs. Bannister, holding herself very erect (the belaying by Mrs. Bootle was rather taut), said, "I don't suppose he'll leave the machine shop in this fog, poor him, but it's a comfort to know he's in charge of all those wheels and things."

"I'll tell you another comfort," said Mr. Snead. "I just noticed, there's a lookout on the back stoop as well as up front. I said to myself, 'Buckingham, that's a good idea, on this boat there's more danger of somebody crowding us from behind.'"

"Let's not be morbid," said the purser. "This is a social occasion, I invited you to drink the health of the ship—also Professor Barton's. We understand he is crossing his fortieth longitude."

"Bottoms up," said Miss Shaugraun.

"Not very well chosen as a nautical toast," said Mr. Snead.

At that moment Boxer carried in the birthday cake beaming with small candles.

"I thought you would like to cut the cake in here," said Mr. Huskisson. "Save embarrassment in the saloon."

Geoffrey was busy with his forefinger. "Why is it so hard to count things in a circle?" he asked.

"What a wonderful purser you are, you are!" said Aunt Kilda. "Even the correct number of wax-lights."

Boxer as usual was very alert. He produced a bottle of stone ginger for Geoffrey, and while setting down the cake indicated a small plimsoll mark on the load-line of the confection. "The lucky bit's in 'ere," he whispered.

"Thank you, Boxer," said Mr. Huskisson. "Remember, go easy on the sparrow tonight. Now we'll cut a slice for Captain Bompjes and you can take it up to the bridge."

" 'E can use them candles up there too," said Boxer. "It's a rare old peasouper, not 'arf."

Uncle Dan expressed a well-simulated surprise, the cake was cut and enjoyed. Geoffrey noticed that the marked piece went to unsuspecting Aunt Blanche. "Don't bite too hard, Possum," he suggested just in time.

These ceremonies made Mr. Snead realize that the poker-game trio were crashing a private party. But after a musical hour in the smoke-room he had comfortably relaxed his usual canny wits. Perhaps as a gesture of courtesy he should offer to do a few card tricks?

"I guess the boys and I didn't realize this was an invitation affair," he said. "I never was properly introduced to these ladies. In God's Country we're very punctilious about introductions, I always like to exchange cards with fellow passengers bearing their load on the rough roads of life. I just got one from Mr. Chrisdie, let me introduce Mr. Elihu Van Sweringen Chrisdie, 118 Buckeye Street and pleased to meet him. Someday about dusk the Sweringen Van Chrisdie homestead will enjoy a re-union, old friends of the hurricane."

"We seem to have struck a rich pocket of humor," whispered Miss Shaugraun to Miss Bristol.

"Rich, the very word," continued Mr. Snead. "A most successful trip, ladies; in Manchester alone I sold enough leather belting to go round the waist of the world. As for the traveling expenses, Mr. F. X. Marple has helped."

The purser was gently urging him to resume his seat. Mr. Snead bowed politely to them all, took from a neat leather folder a card engraved *Mr. Buckingham L. Snead, Genesee Valley Belting Company*, and laid it very carefully on the table. "You may fire when ready, Gridley," he murmured, sank against Dr. Chrisdie's shoulder, and went peacefully asleep.

"A hot time in the old town tonight," said the patient Mr. Huskisson.

The Concert was Geoffrey's first formal public occasion and he was congested by the number of askable questions. "Why did Mr. Snead go to sleep? Are those Uncle Dan's best clothes? Do you feel jubious? Will the parrot be here? Do they have thrippenny bits in America? If Aunt Blanche couldn't spend the lucky coin, she might give it to him? Perhaps it was unlucky that sitting to enjoy the Concert he was next to Aunt Kilda. Her replies were so much more audible than anyone else's. "The chosen symbol of a congregation's devotion. Ha-haugh!" she announced apropos the thrippenny bit.

"You'll have to do better than that," said Mr. Marple, to whom a red velvet bag had been entrusted for taking up the collection. Only Mr. Huskisson knew the history of that receptacle. He had hooked it from a chapel in Wallasey; privately he didn't think it was lucky because the inside smelt like copper. However he had explained to Uncle Dan that when the collection was announced the Chairman must mention that the *Westernland* held a record for high contributions among ships of her class. In token of this she had a flag with the emblem of the Shipwrecked Mariners Society. It was displayed in Boxer's dec-

orations over the sideboard, flanked of course by the Union Jack
and the Stars and Stripes. It was as well that Mr. Snead was
asleep in his berth when Geoffrey, puzzled by the unfamiliar
banner of the S. M. S., asked, "Is that another Old Glory?"

The revolving seats had been lubricated to avoid squeaks;
they moved easily to the long heave of the Grand Banks and
Geoffrey chaired in comfortable arcs was astonished to see so
large an audience. Indeed the whole passenger list had rallied
themselves or been chivvied out by Stretch and Mrs. Bootle.
At least, they thought hopefully, the Concert will be better than
staying in one's room to shudder at the foghorn. People whom
Geoffrey had only seen as blanketed mummies on deck or bath-
robed invalids tottering toward Shanks's porcelain were now
rotating passively behind him. A small stage had been set abaft
the sideboard, Mr. McScoon had spiked down the ship's two
potted palms on each side. The flags were draped to conceal the
shelf of condiments but Geoffrey kept an eye on the bottle of
Major Grey's Chutney, the regular vibration of the foghorn
had jarred it loose and it was slipping gently in front of a ripple
of bunting.

Neither the Thorofare nor The Drift had prepared him for
the splendors of evening display. Perhaps not even the maddening howl of the siren every ninety seconds was as startling as
Mrs. Lotus Bannister in the slithering rustle of her froufrou.
"Who is that hissing?" he trebled but they had scarcely hushed
him before the sibilant expanse of shot silk, green and peacock,
wafted down the aisle.

Why doesn't it go all the way up? Geoffrey wondered, but
the foghorn intervened. Uncle Dan, after final instructions from
Mr. Huskisson, now took the platform. Even his all-forgiving
sister thought he might not have looked quite so defeatist. Perhaps it was partly the batter pudding which the chef had served
at dinner as a birthday surprise. He had put on his dinner coat
in last-minute haste (after Dr. Friedeck vacated the cabin) but
discovered too late that his only dress linen had been worn once

too often at the high table in Cambridge. "What is that on Uncle Dan's shirt?" Geoffrey asked.

"That's a varsity education," said Aunt Kilda. "Port wine, ha-haugh!"

Uncle Dan balanced himself as nearly as possible abeam the potted palms. There was a smatter of applause, for everyone knew it was a birthday. Accidentally he seized one of the fronds and cut his finger. He said, "I have a message from the Captain," and on that instant the foghorn drowned everything. "Even if he can't be with us we can hear him," he said. That pleased everyone and the Concert was off to a good start.

30. Ship's Concert

Everybody else is at church, wrote Dr. Chrisdie, and likely they need it after last night but this darned foghorn has got me too jumpy. I can hear them singing *Those in Peril on the Sea*, at least I can hear Shaugraun. The worst peril of the sea is social, as I figure it. Shaugraun was as audible as the foghorn last night, maybe that sherry the Purser set up. What with her and young Geoff, I really felt sorry for Miss Barton and Miss Bristol. Shaugraun was talking it all over in her stateroom afterward. I don't see why nobody tips her off that the ventilating system which circulates bad air from one room to another also circulates Shaugraun. Anyhow, she has taken such a scunner against Friedeck and Marple she has laid off me. Of Marple (maybe of me too) she said, "Typical American face, my dear, something tight and skinny about the jaw which however never prevents it from opening. Ha-haugh!" Nutz!

Barton won't forget his birthday in a hurry. When we tried to get into our room to dress Friedeck was in his Meinself und Gott mood and locked the door. I suspect B. had planned a nice little speech about hands across the scuppers and the gallantry of seamen, but something certainly put him off his stride. He shouldn't have introduced Lotus as "our representative of the Gibson Girl." It only inflamed her. Among other things she recited that old chestnut about *The Barber Kept on Shaving,* which probably excited Boxer. He got pretty fresh in his Cockney way, began by alluding to the chairman's beard and then did a couple of limey songs very cleverly but caused much British agitation by saying "bloody." Something about "The blarsted bloomin' sparrow flew up the bloody spout." Madame Du-Quesne had very kindly offered to sing a couple of French ballades and I was to accompany, but after the introduction nothing happened, I looked round and she had collapsed. Her husband said the foghorn made her so nervous her "gorge" had closed up. Here was where Barton showed bad judgment. I'm sure he meant well, he called on Dr. Friedeck. I guess Friedeck was sore at being considered a pinch-hitter. He shouted, "I put my contribution in the bag. I have nothing to say." The foghorn blew just then and Barton didn't catch it. He politely again invited Dr. Friedeck, who repeated, "I have nothing to say."

I thought maybe we could pull things together with our smoke-room minstrels—Snead had gone to bed but we could get by with three of us, that good old glee club harmony about the Merry Men in the Greenwood:

> One had a sword, Ta-ran-tara—
> One had a shield, Ta-ran-tara—
> And one had a twanging bow.

I gave the boys the chord and we were all set to let fly when I saw Snead teetering down the aisle. With the usual instinct of anyone in his cups he had put on his tuxedo, thinking that would conceal his condition, but his necktie was way round to starboard and he was grinning with idiotic good humor. He handed out his business cards to several people and when he climbed up on the platform we had to rescue him from capsizing. The Purser was riding herd, trying to persuade him out, but of course this only made him stubborn. The best thing to do was start the singing, which I did. Snead was full of brio and did all right until the twang of the last bow string, which he followed with a magnificently timed hiccup—such a *whang* to it you could almost see the arrow leave the string. Half the audience were disgusted. The others applauded heartily and I heard Shaugraun say, "Fishwives, the man's an artist!" I thought so myself but *Pale in the Amber West* wasn't so good. In that one there was no way of using hiccups as part of the illusion and as the west got paler so did Snead. "She sleeps, my lady sleeps" was followed by a notable gulp and he interrupted to say, "She snores." They gave us a charitable hand afterward, but Snead insisted on making a speech of apology. "I owe it to myself as an artist," he said (and almost bowed himself into Shaugraun's lap), "to say a word of explanation." At this instant, with the uncanny quickness of the partly stewed, he saw that a sauce bottle was just falling off the sideboard. He reached out and grabbed it in midair like a conjurer, pretended to think it was a bouquet someone had thrown, really it was funny and everybody roared. "A word of explanation," he repeated. "I thought I could temper the wind to the shorn lamb, I mean time it to the music. I see—glup—I was mistaken."

He offered to do *Casey at the Bat* as a forfeit, and I'd love to have heard him, but we thought it wiser to play safe. His two silent friends escorted him to a seat at the back of the saloon, still nursing the bottle.

Everybody was relieved when it came time for the raffle, which had been the subject of a good deal of harmless conspiracy. The stewards carried round the collection bag, everyone put in their tickets and Mrs. Bannister was nominated the Queen of Love and Beauty to draw the winning number. Our bunch all hoped the Barton kid would win the draw; he had spent about half his time admiring the model in its glass case—

The service upstairs must be about over. I hear them singing *Sun of My Soul*, that's the kind of hymn that comes near the end. It's about the only sunshine there is at this moment. I just looked out and it's certainly thick. Maybe we needn't have been sore about the raffle except for Snead making a scandal of it. Barton said a nice little spiel about this beautiful example of patient craftsmanship and the collection for a noble cause and we all hoped this Lilliputian vessel (meaning the *Ellen Arkins,* not the *Westernland*) would sail halcyon seas of make-believe. I think Geoffrey supposed because his uncle was chairman the boat was already his, when the stewards carried it in with great applause the poor kid stood up as if to receive it. Anyway Lotus was blindfolded and tenderly supported while she drew the ticket. Maybe that's why she took such a long time groping in the bag. "Number 76," Barton announced. "Who holds Number 76?" "I do," stated Mr. Marple. Young Chester shouted "Hot dog!" and was up at the platform even before Mrs. Bannister was unbandaged. Most of us were disappointed but all would have been O.K. except for B. L. Snead. I think the Purser had been trying to coax him out of the saloon and likely he lost his temper. He shouted, "It's a plant! Ladies and Gentlemen, the cards were stacked. I saw that gentleman (pointing to Dr. Friedeck) hand a bunch of tickets to Mr. Marple. I demand a fresh deal." It was a painful scene, the two kids were both bawling and Dr. Friedeck didn't help by saying, "I suppose we should accept Mr. Snead as an expert in tricks with cards—"

Dr. Chrisdie never completed his conscientious report of the Concert. There was a series of short quick blasts from the siren (its timbre rising more shrill in emphasis). This and a hurry of feet above suggested that Divine Service had ended in an outburst of praise and relief by the congregation. But no assembly of worship would disband quite so fast. Just outside he heard a thin squealing tin horn, strangely childish and absurd. He leaped on the settee and looked through the round window. Lifted on a wrinkled gray slope only a few yards away the fishermen seemed looking straight at him. What startled him most was that the man at the wheel of the little schooner calmly ran his finger along the brim of his sou'wester and flicked the drops of fog casually toward the liner. Then he spat overside and turned to look at the leech of his canvas.

The historian's record was much briefer than his notes of less serious matters. "Nearly ran down a fisherman," he wrote.

"It came very pat after those prayers you read," said Kilda. They were looking over the rail as the schooner faded astern.

"I'll never complain again about the price of fish," said Mrs. Marple.

"It's playing blindman's buff for pretty high stakes," said Mr. Marple angrily.

Dan, though tempted, did not speak. He was guarding a secret.

He had been restless during the night, whether from the fatigues of the Concert or the nerve-shaking boom of the whistle. The snores of Dr. Friedeck were almost equally trying. Before the earliest sifting of gray light Dan put on his dressing-gown and went to smoke a pipe in one of the laboratories of Shanks. He had not noticed before that in the middle watch kerosene lanterns replaced the electric bulbs at certain duty-points in the corridors. He could tell by a softer rhythm from below that the ship was slowed. Woodwork sighed to a slow and yielding refrain; the dim light, the easy onward slopes were drowsy and comforting, even the repeated steam blast was becoming a sound of courage, not anxiety. He was sitting half asleep when his pipe fell clatter on the tiles. The whistle was immediately followed by another in a little different tone—an echo? But what out here would throw an echo? He waited for the next blast, and suddenly was clear awake. The engines had stopped. The sagging retard of the hull was heavy in his feet.

He wondered, tingled, stood alert in the opening of the lavatory door. There was a porthole only a few feet away, and though the glass was clouded with vapor he could see a glow of brightness. He ran swiftly a few yards down the passage where the door opened on the steerage deck aft. A great shape, leaking fuzzy shafts of light from her upper works, was moving slowly by. Whistle sounded to whistle—the other even deeper in tone. The *Westernland* slid so quiet he thought he could even hear the plates of the other hull crisping through slaps of water. Magnified in pale luminous glow she looked enormous; and even while he stared she dimmed, was gone. He heard her bass whistle. Already it sounded miles away.

An officer in oilskins came forward from the poop.

"I say," said Dan. "That wasn't much fun."

The other held up a lantern. "Oh, hullo, Professor. Sounded like the *Teutonic*. What the newspapers call a greyhound. Think they're ruined if they don't log their 500 a day. She and the *New York*, cutting each other's throats." He started up the ladder, then paused.

"I wouldn't mention it to the other passengers, Professor. What they don't know won't worry them."

31. Channel Fever

"It's almost like breaking through a kind of membrane—that sounds silly, but one does feel changed. As though we'd slipped into another dimension—do you remember the wonderful drawings of Alice going through the looking-glass?"

"*Two* wonderful drawings," said Uncle Dan.

"Back to back on two pages," she exclaimed. "—you turn over and see Alice coming through on the other side. How that used to thrill me!"

They were standing in mid-afternoon, forward of the deckhouse. Geoffrey leaned between the rails, wriggling because Uncle Dan kept a firm grip on the back of his coat collar. "It's very humiliating to be held like that," he observed. He was watching a sailor who stood on a grating slung over the side and twirled a weighted line. "What's he fishing for?"

134

"For the bottom," said Uncle Dan. "You have to feel your way across the Banks like a blind man with a stick."

"Like Pew in *Treasure Island*," said Aunt Blanche.

"What was that fishing-boat fishing for?"

"Codfish. You can remember that when you have to take cod-liver oil. That's what makes American boys so big and strong."

"Chester is big but he isn't strong," said Geoffrey. "His mother says he has to be humored because he has a pulp in his nose."

"Why don't you trot along and see what he's doing?" suggested Uncle Dan.

"I can't bear to, he's so deliberate about that yacht."

"Aunt Bee still has a surprise in the Emergency Bag."

"She's asleep. Mrs. Bootle got her some earstops to cure the foghorn and she's sleeping very fast. I know it's good sleep because she's drooling."

Blanche was looking the other way, but Uncle Dan could see a small tremor in her attitude.

"If you don't talk too much perhaps Captain Bompjes will give you a pebble from the bottom of the ocean. Sometimes they bring them up on the blue pigeon."

"How do they get there?"

Patiently Uncle Dan opened his mouth to reply, then realized that this time it was Blanche mimicking Geoffrey's habit. They all laughed, even Geoffrey without quite knowing why.

"Do you realize the foghorn has stopped?" she said. "I wondered why I felt so relieved."

There was a pale blue shimmer ahead, the fog sifting apart in clots and shreds. "Yes, this is better," said Dan. "I was monstrous full of fleas all last night. When you get across the Banks one always wants to come up forward and look ahead. The early part of the voyage I find myself gravitating toward the stern."

Blanche waited for what seemed the inevitable query, "What's *gravitating*?" but it didn't come. The boy had suddenly cantered off. The space he had occupied between them narrowed a little from both sides.

"We could gravitate to the bow," Dan said. "I didn't want to take Geoff out there."

He unlatched the gate and they went across the trestle to the long spearhead of the focsle. Dan was a little sheepish about this liberty, but looking up he saw the Captain make a friendly salute from his vantage on the bridge and took this as permission. Before them they could see the haze thinning to pink and opal, breaking away into blue tunnels and long vague avenues of calm.

"This is nicer than that seesaw at the stern," said Blanche.

"That was where I had my big disappointment. I saw you coming and thought we'd have a good talk. It was only to tell me about Dr. Friedeck's mishap. Then I thought I'd have a chance after that awful Concert, but nobody could say anything with the horn going."

"It did seem a very big voice for a small ship."

Just as well, too, he thought. He remembered the looming shape of danger that shimmered in the night. With a high leaning scend the questing prow carried them forward into opening space. He wanted to say "Do you read Whitman?" but was tightened with shyness. The pause continued until he got frightened.

"It's going to be plane geometry now," he said feebly. "I was getting tired of three dimensions."

The hiss of the dividing bow-wave sounded a little louder; leaning over the concave wedge of the stem they could see a nostril-curve of broken water lift higher along the black plates. Mr. Murk, turning a valve two hundred feet away, sent them a little encouraging quiver, almost like a friendly hand behind the shoulders. But after all a ship is only a ship and not endless as a topic.

"Do you ever read Whitman?" he asked firmly.

"Not much, I'm afraid. I tried to, one time, but I got so out of breath."

That seemed to conclude the subject. He had felt communicative a few minutes ago, he wondered why he was so dumb.

"I hope Dr. Friedeck has simmered down," she said presently. "It must be very awkward for you, in the same cabin."

"Yes, most embarrassing. I've had so little experience in that sort of foolishness, I don't quite know how to behave. You see, usually I only quarrel with people I love."

Blanche was so pleased by this remark she said nothing. She thought, it's splendid when you hear someone you like say a perfectly charming thing.

"I was all prepared to ask the Purser to put me in another room, and then to my amazement, this morning the little man suddenly offered me first go at the wash basin. He bowed very stiff, you can't imagine how he looks in his green pajamas, like a bullfrog, and said, 'I know how you feel, please don't agitate yourself by any further explanations. We will speak no more about it.' Was he apologizing to me or the other way around? I think the foghorn had just about driven him crazy, he tried to sleep in his life-belt."

"The last few days were enough to get on anyone's nerves. Even Kilda and I had the most ridiculous spat."

"I dare say it was good for her. She does ride a pretty high horse. What about?"

"Well, it was too absurd. I don't know why I mentioned it." But having done so, it would be worse still not to go on. She invented hastily, determined not to admit the real argument. "Oh, it was something about flannel cakes for breakfast. I said it was nice to have them again and she said it was just one more reminder that we were getting back to the wilds."

She found that she was staring at the overcoat button which had been the cause of the argument; and hastily looked elsewhere.

"I rather like getting back to the wilds."

"So do I," she exclaimed. "How gorgeous when you break through and come out on this side. Just look at the sunshine, and even the water is a different color. I get the queerest feeling now that we're going downhill."

"In a sense we are, we parallel what they call the hundred-fathom curve all the way down to the Delaware Capes."

"Look," said Blanche, "they're taking down those curtains on the bridge and Captain Bompjes is grinning."

"Yes, he ought to feel pretty good. You wouldn't realize what he goes through unless you studied his charts. He let me look at them the other day. Just the names along the New-foundland Coast are poetry, every one has in it the doom or sal-vation of some old mariner—Funk Island and Occasional Har-bor were two I noticed, and all those nasty little rings of dotted lines, shoals with the initials E. D., Existence Doubtful."

"That's how I felt." She drew a long breath of brightening air and leaned forward over the rail. "We're going quite fast, for us."

"Can't go too fast for me," Dan said. "I'm so eager to get back to work."

"You're an American citizen, you have a right to feel that way. I'm eager too but I'm always a bit upset on landing, herded apart and classified as an alien. It was a shock the first time I came over, made me feel like an immigrant. That's what I was, but it's hard for the English to think of themselves that way. They are so accustomed to take things for granted."

"With everyone else doing the granting. Don't I know. Im-migrants are only servant girls with shawls on their heads, or Dago laborers. You and Kilda and I, and DuQuesne and Fried-eck, are immigrants too: we don't cook soup and lay railroad tracks but maybe we do something just as important. I don't like the word, but doesn't anyone ever think about the intellec-tual immigration?"

"I thought of becoming a citizen myself," Blanche said, "but what held me back was my Father. He couldn't possibly understand it. He's puzzled enough just by mathematics and short hair—he thinks they're both phases of the same unaccountable eccentricity."

"I can't help saying one is perhaps more attractive than the other," Dan ventured.

"Well, the hair was only typhoid fever. When it's once cut off you realize how it simplifies life."

"I suppose mathematics is a kind of fever too?"

"You tutor me in Whitman, I'll talk to you about mathematics. If you have the feeling for it, it's an art of its own, and maybe it's better than literature because you really touch perfection."

Dan was rather wishing he might.

"If you ever saw a country rectory in Shropshire, you'd understand it would be inconceivable to have a daughter who thought of being an American citizen. Just outside the vestry door there's an enormous old yew tree, it overhangs one of those ancient table-top gravestones, quite illegible, I mean the stone. Well, my Father is like that yew, he's put his roots so far down he can't even imagine any other kind of earth. Maybe roots oughtn't to be roots, only tendrils."

Dan was trying to visualize the Shropshire rectory. He saw the church square-towered of cut flint—like black poached eggs, but of course he was thinking of Suffolk. Damn, he thought, that's roots. We all come from such different kinds of places. How could we ever explain them to each other? Suppose Captain Bompjes were to try to tell about his ship to someone far inland?

"The best kind of roots are imaginary, like that square root of minus one you mentioned." But as he said this he realized he was only talking, this was just a mannerly parenthesis to keep conversation going. He was really thinking such simple things he was ashamed; and they were harder and harder to say because he hadn't said them the instant they came to mind.

There was a sudden grinding rattle behind them. With the

return of fair weather the bosun was trying out steam in his winches. "Goodness," said Blanche, "we are getting on. That's always a sign of something, isn't it?"

"The donkey engine," said Uncle Dan, "that'll mean more questions from Geoff. It's almost the only thing he hasn't asked about yet."

"And here comes the donkey," she murmured. Mr. Snead was approaching on the gangway.

"I was going to tell you, " Dan said hastily, "how impatient I am to get back to the extraordinary comedy of the U.S.A., I mean things like Happy Hooligan and Mr. Bowser and street-car conductors, but here it is on top of us before I could say it."

"Hope I'm not Buttinsky," said Mr. Snead. "I know how it is, you folks have got Channel Fever. It's the first symptom, when everybody hustles up to the bow. It's an English saying, the way sailors feel when they get into the Channel after a long voyage. When you know you're that near Swanee River you just can't settle down to anything, not even drinking. However, that isn't what I've got on my mind. I've got humiliation fever. I've been going around telling everybody I'm sorry I broke up the cakewalk last night. All the drinking I've done in a mis-spent life, I ought to be able to handle it better than that."

Dan and Blanche were somewhat embarrassed and made no intelligible reply.

"It wasn't even very sportsmanlike to get crabby about the little Dutchman," Mr. Snead continued. "The other boys and I had been trying to stack the cards for young Geoff, the only thing was Friedeck was so crude about it. When I saw him hand that fistful of tickets to F. X. Marple I just got sore. We had fifteen chances for Geoff out of a hundred tickets sold, but the Dutchman must have rounded up twice as many."

"If Geoff's chances were only one in seven I am sure we had no right to complain," said Blanche. "Mathematics is very honorable about such things."

"Darned if you ain't right," said Mr. Snead. "As far as games

in the smoke-room go I know better than leave mathematics decide it. But naturally down in the social saloon and working for
charity, a man feels sensitive about loading dice. I reckon we
could have squared the Lotus-lady, but she's so dumb it would
have been risky. All I'm trying to do is beg pardon for raising
a scene. What do you think I ought to say to the little Dutchman? Maybe it's better to leave him stew in his own juice?"

"I think you're right," Dan said. "He's had one apology already, that ought to see him through."

"Well then I won't horn in on you folks any longer. I'll go
on with my tour of penance. I notice the mathematics of chance
did well by Miss Bristol, you got the dividend from the Doc's
birthday cake. That ought to mean good luck, whatsay?—That
roommate of yours is quite a card, she has a powerful way of
putting things. I was trying to make a sort of special apology
to her because I know she riles easy. I said, 'It's a pity we don't
land in little old New York, the other boys and I could take
your bunch out to splash a little red paint, Delmonico's or somewhere's. Of course in Philly it's different, they put the town to
bed at sunset.' But Sister Shaugraun came right back at me. She
says, 'I'm glad we don't land at New York. It's so painful going
by that Statue of Irony.' That really tickles me, you sort of
realize she's been turning things around in her mind and they
fly out irregardless. I guess she makes an amusing roommate—
well, I better vamoose, I'm talking too much."

"What an enchanting person," Blanche said. "If all his apologies are so delightful he'll put the whole ship in a good
humor."

"I do admire that quality in Americans," Dan said. "They
have a way of meeting you head on without so much preliminary sparring and precaution. I can't tell you how lucky I've
been in the friends who were so kind to me when I first came
over. It's extraordinary how they accept you without asking any
questions and if you just behave decently there isn't anything
they won't do to help. There are some people called Warren in

Chesapeake, they've been so incredibly generous and as far as I could ever make out only because I had read Coleridge. They live out in the country in a remarkable old place where they used to keep slaves before the War. Now they make slaves out of literary people by their excessive kindness. If you should ever come down our way I'd love to have you meet them."

"The Mathematical Society meets at Chesapeake next Christmas holidays. I'm rather worried about it. I have to read a paper on 'The Functions of a Complex Variable.'"

"That sounds very sinister," Dan said. "An essay on the New Woman? But seriously, if you do come I'm sure Bee would be delighted to put you up."

She did not reply for a moment, and Dan wondered if he had spoken too fast. "Wonderful sunset light," he said innocently.

"It's very kind of you. Your sister was good enough to suggest it already."

32. God's Country

Free of fog, the *Westernland* mended her pace. Skirting the blue bend of the Gulf current she laid white riffle behind her, pushed her southing close to her supreme 14½. Mr. Murk, with oil-bags over her bearings, turned up a 350-mile run. Now that it was almost too late her patrons remembered what a smart little ship she was. Mr. McScoon surprised them with delicious kedgeree and kromeskies, zested with curry powder and mushrooms and cuttings of lemon; only housekeepers realized these were the cleverest way of merchandising broken meats. For the Chief Steward not less than the Purser has his Day Book. He was flattered to copy out his kedgeree recipe for Aunt Bee.

As they neared the Capes they met their oldest sister *Waesland*, outward bound, the dean of women in that modest fleet. By Captain Bompjes' courtesy they watched her from the bridge through the glasses, and Mr. Murk spared a curt plume of steam for company salute. They could see her elderly bowsprit and figurehead creaming the sparkling heave. "Fine old lady," said the Captain. "Civilized; clipper bow and figurehead, like real ships. Built in '67 as the Cunarder *Russia*."

Geoffrey wasn't much impressed; *Waesland* had only one funnel. Aunt Bee thought: She has a terrible lot of ocean ahead of her, poor thing. Dan focused the glasses for Blanche.

As Mr. Snead had said, their minds were forward; it was Channel Fever. It could be felt in every pulse of her metal veins. As she comes toward port from a long voyage it is true of every craft, clipper or cargo-wagon, liner or tank. With gear trimmed taut and even the idlers at lookout—Geoffrey could see the chef's white hat poked outside the galley scuttle— she foots the paling water. That unease, anxious edge between past and future, blend of eagerness and regret, is Channel Fever. It is a sense of destination—and destiny.

In a glamour of September noon she swung far suthard to avoid the Five Fathom Shoals and turned to the right past Cape Henlopen. Why is September sunshine the most perfect of all: has the sun also got Channel Fever, over the hill and on his downward slope? They passed the great octagonal lighthouse, flags were up and the ship's own personal signal, M.B.V.S. In such exhilaration none would have suspected she was indulging herself the twelve degrees of correction to compensate past errors.

They were in front of the deckhouse, each with specialized excitement. Mr. Snead, apologies accomplished and forgotten, was high with pleasure to see Old Glory at the fore. He insisted on explaining to Miss Shaugraun: "First the flag of the country you're coming to, then the house flag, then the U.S. Mail signal, then the ship's own pennant, and the Union Jack way down at the tail. Nothing invidious, just marine etiquette."

"I dare say you're right," said Miss Shaugraun, "but I'm not going to spoil my day by admitting it."

"What *is* invidious," said Dr. Chrisdie, "is that gunboat over there—gosh, that gives me a thrill. One of the White Squadron. I bet those Dons will think twice before they come up this way. Look, that's a United States warship, see the guns, those big bumps are what they call barbettes."

"If the bullets don't work," said Aunt Kilda, "they throw the beef at the Spaniards."

Geoffrey was a little bewildered, the first view of America was so different from anything preconceived: no Rocky Mountains, no Indians, not even any cowcatchers, just this wide spread of yellow water. It even occurred to him they had got to China by mistake, but he was distracted by the extreme geniality of Mr. Snead who suddenly took to referring to himself as "Your Uncle Dudley." "Say!" he pointed. "There's the customs boat, look at those caps with the eagle on them, that sure looks good to your Uncle Dudley. Tarara Boomdeay!"

Mrs. Bannister realized that her literary pilgrimage was coming to an end and there were so many details not yet recorded in the Treasure Book. When Uncle Dan told her that the four code flags were the ship's initials, "her autograph, you might say," Mrs. Bannister exclaimed, "Oh, I'm so glad you reminded me. I want you all to sign your names in my Treasure Book, I thought of it last night, I know it's a nuisance and I argued with myself without prevail. All you good people must write your names so I'll have something to remember you by."

"I'll remember this voyage even without an autograph, ha-haugh!" said Miss Shaugraun.

"Oh, but you must do it now before we get split up into citizens and aliens. Once those inspectors get hold of us everything is so governmental. I always say they're much harder on the citizens. When I got that lace at Queenstown I forgot I already had my hundred dollars' worth so I said to myself, Lotus, you tack it onto your underthings and if they're gentlemen they couldn't possibly know. Just basted it on, you understand, I can rip it off in the train, it'll give me something to do in those terrible sleepers. Do you suppose we'll get to Philadelphia in time to catch the train to Cincinnati?"

"Broad Street Station," said one of the Men of Sin, triumphant at last to contribute information.

"Just take a surface car up from the docks," said Mr. Snead. In his high spirits he began whistling *Daisy, Daisy, Give Me Your Answer, Do* through his teeth.

"They're all surface cars in Philly," said Mr. Marple.

"You're right. I keep forgetting we're not landing on the sidewalks of New York. Gee whiz, I bet it's a hundred miles up this river."

"Will you go on to Chesapeake tonight," Aunt Kilda asked Uncle Dan, "or will you go to an hotel?"

Geoffrey was listening but his greater attention was on the surprising cavern that had opened below them into the hold of the ship. Already the chattering winches were swinging up masses of luggage. Far down he saw the black rounded top of a familiar object. How many days it had stood in the little hallway on the Thorofare while Aunt Bee trotted up and down with armfuls of miscellany, or had consulted Grandma: "Do you think I'll need this?" and Grandma, perhaps concealing the tremor of her chin with her handkerchief: "Dan says the winters are very bitter." Was it really only twelve days ago?

"I can see your box," said Geoffrey. "Not wanted on voyage. I bet everything in it got seasick down in the cellar."

"That's not a box, that's a Saratoga trunk," said Chester Marple. Geoffrey had been avoiding him because he so exultantly carried the *Ellen Arkins* round the deck in his arms. The boys now created a diversion by leaning over to look down the funnel of the revenue cutter coming alongside. A whiff of coal-gas nearly strangled them, and put an end to their sociability for a while.

A bundle of papers, thrown up from the tug, landed on deck with a thump, and Mr. Snead pounced upon it. "Hot dog, here's the news! New York *Herald* too; say, that's smart. Good old

Gordon Bennett, always first aboard. Yon can have the *Ledger*, Professor; me for the *Herald*. Now we can find out what's happened. American Flag Hoisted in Havana—hey, Chrisdie, listen to this; that makes you feel good, how about it— Gather round, girls, here's the latest—Roosevelt Forging Ahead for Governor. Hurray for the Rough Riders! Colonel Hay home from London to begin duty as Secretary of State, arrived yesterday on the *Teutonic*—"

"That's John Hay," Dan explained to Aunt Bee. "He was ambassador in London, the one who made that fine speech about Omar. He always wanted to go down to Wilford to see the rose on FitzGerald's grave."

Aunt Bee could see the little Thorofare, curving its kindly business past the old houses; the quiet byway up to a country churchyard; and the famous important man who didn't have time to go there. She could even smell treacle pudding—

"I'm going over on the shady side, this coal-gas gets in my eyes."

"Look at here," said Mr. Snead, showing a headline to Uncle Dan. "*Teutonic* in Peril. Almost a collision in mid-ocean, the steamer's machinery stopped in time to avoid crash. Narrow escape from going to the bottom early Sunday morning. During a dense fog—unable to ascertain the name of the steamship which ran across her bow.—That must have been the same fog we were in."

"We didn't run across her bow, she came up on us from behind" . . . Dan blurted it out before he remembered.

Mr. Snead looked at him sharply. "You saw it too, did you? Same here. You mightn't think it, but there's times when I know how to keep my mouth shut.—There's times for opening it, too. You recollect what the Governor of North Carolina said to the Governor of South Carolina?"

Dan had learned this phrase in the works of R. L. Stevenson. He knew it was an invitation not to be declined without offense. It was likely to imply Bourbon, for which he had no taste, so

146

he said apologetically, "I'll join you in a small Bass. But first I better see my sister and Geoff past the immigration officers."

"Glad we got a moment to ourselves," said Mr. Snead when they were settled later in the smoke-room. "I didn't mean to get gabby, but when the Irish countess does her high-tiddley-hi-tye on me it sure rubs my fur. You should have threw a dornick at me the other evening and put me in my place. Silly to get peeved just because folks talk different—what part of her palate does that voice come from?—you know how it is, it's darn difficult to be polite when you're being patronized.—Here's How.—What I'm trying to say, in spite of her ladyship, I know the U.S.A. has got a lot to learn from folks like you and I'm glad you're such a good mixer. I admire the idea of a few of your cultivated subjects coming over to fly their kites in our sky. If we had a few teachers like that in Genesee Valley I'd not have been so crude myself. I always say there's really nothing too good for God's Country, I can even swallow Shaugraun if you tell me she teaches her kids Simon-Pure Greek.—Here's to you, Professor.—I was scared you might be sore because I was kidding the Faculty sitting on deck. I was honestly doing a kindness taking F. X. Marple away to the smoke-room so he wouldn't presume on your beanfeasts. I roused up notions of my own scouting round some of the best pubs in the old country. There's often time to think between North and South Carolina. I put it this way, Great Britain looks to me like art and the States is energy and I'll bet each of them could give the other a hand. I know you're a U.S. citizen so I'm talking to a consort. If you're ever up Genesee Valley, or Miss Barton or the kid, be sure to come slide on my cellar door. In case you mislaid my card, here's another. You mustn't think the other boys are unfriendly if they don't hand out their cards too. They used them all up making friends in London. That's why they've been so sheepish. They tried to get the ship's printer to run some off in a hurry, but you know how it was, he fell down the glory-hole and crippled himself."

147

"It's been a very pleasant voyage," said poor Uncle Dan. He was always dismayed in such circumstances by his lack of small-talk.

"You bet, here's jackpots. Gee, we're near up to Wilmington already. Now there's an industrial center that this war won't do any harm. I wish we had deep water like that up our way, the biggest common carriers right alongside the dock. Even going into New York you don't see a line of chimneys like that. Just look out of the window, Professor. How's that for industrial scenery?"

As they did so a clear voice was heard from the deck. "How gruesome to spoil the landscape with all those gaso*meters*."

It was a tribute to Mr. Snead that though he shuddered slightly he made no retort. He winked at Prof. Barton, finished his highball and only said gently, "What a word for gas tanks."

Uncle Dan knew what Geoffrey had in mind when he asked "How do you go to bed at thirteen?" This was because he had once been told, incautiously, you go to bed at eight because you're eight years old. So Uncle Dan replied elliptically, "It'll be long past bedtime when we get to the pier."

"Perhaps people go to bed later in America," said Geoff hopefully.

By the time the ship docked, and the good-bys and tips and Mrs. Bootle's embrace had all been performed, he was too weary to notice or care. There was a moment on the gang-plank when he remembered with protest that he hadn't said farewell to the parrot, but this was soon forgotten by the curious behavior of the pier itself. After so many days of the *Westernland* now the solid footing rolled and hummocked beneath him. He stood a moment swaying solemnly to study this phenomenon, and when someone jostled past, he fell flat. Aunt Kilda consoled him with history: "That's William the Conqueror at Hastings. When he jumped ashore he stumbled, but

148

he turned it to a good omen. He grabbed two handfuls of earth and said, 'So I take seizin of English ground.' "

Geoffrey looked about for a chance to repeat this notable gesture, but remarked with unusual restraint: "I don't want to take seizin of horse-dirt."

He was asleep in the carriage by the time they reached the old Continental. "Is this an hotel?" he asked, with unconscious echo of Aunt Kilda's accent.

"You bet it is," said Uncle Dan, who seemed to be talking in a different tone of voice ever since they landed. "A very famous hotel. This is where Charles Dickens and Abraham Lincoln both stayed."

"They needed a larger room than this," said Geoff.

"Now you're just going to have a nice dish of tapioca and go right to bed," was Aunt Bee's comment.

"They don't have tapioca when you're abroad."

He was relieved when he found that they didn't. Aunt Bee baffled the chambermaid by asking for French plums, and what finally arrived was French toast. It was served to Geoff in bed by a colored waiter, and he fell asleep in the happy assurance that he had met Uncle Remus at last.

Dan was on fire to give Aunt Bee a glimpse of the new world. She did not like to leave the child alone in such savage surroundings, but Geoff was very sound asleep and she was persuaded to take a brief stroll up Market Street.

They walked as far as Broad Street Station, to buy their railroad tickets for the next day, but Dan would not let her see a cowcatcher. "I'm saving that for Geoff. Did I tell you the story of my first American train? I had only a minute to catch it. I rushed up to the gate and asked the man: 'Can I take this train to Chesapeake?' He said, 'That's all right, brother, the engine'll take it.' "

"I think that was very saucy of him."

In spite of her reluctance to commit herself, he could see that Bee was interested in the lighted windows. "They wear very complicated hats, don't they? How much is $4.95? Goodness, more than a pound? It would be eight shillings in Ipswich."

"The shops are wonderful, wait till you learn your way around."

"Everything does look very bright, but just a little bit shoddy?"

They were very gay in the daycoach next morning; as Geoff said, his P.R.R. engine knew the way already. Dan didn't even go into the smoking-car or read his copy of *Puck*, he was too interested in showing them everything. The conductor, reading the labels on their bags, said "Welcome home!" and entered into a friendly conversation. Bee was enchanted; Dan had never seen her show such unconscious coquetries before. "What a handsome guard," she said. "And all those brass buttons! I thought at first he was an Admiral who had mistaken us for old friends of his." Geoffrey asked, "Do you have to buy a ticket for your hat?"

After an hour or so they came to a noble river which they crossed slowly on a long bridge. Dan waited until they could see the view of woods and hills upstream.

"What do you think of that?"

"Wonderful," said Bee. "It must be a very high tide. What is it, the Mississippi?"

"The Susquehanna," said Uncle Dan proudly.

Geoffrey, who had been amusing himself in the aisle with the toy engine, looked up quickly. He flattened his nose against the windowpane, and murmured the syllables to himself. Susquehanna. That was it. That was the Word.

CHESAPEAKE

33. Geoff Becomes Jeff

Skinny Granger was late for the meeting but it wasn't fair to accuse him as the other members were doing. "I bet he's finishing his homework first," said Star. "That's a stinking way to do, that's punko."

"Anybody who does homework first is a horse's horse," said Bert. "Aw gee, keep that paint out of my hair."

Jeff had the post of vantage on top of the ladder so any drippings from the brush fell on the others. They were in such a hurry to get the new name up in front of the club-house that the previous initials could still be discerned. The mixture of the old G.C.C. and the new T.S.O. 4 made a muddled anagram but one they viewed with satisfaction.

"It's a good thing he's late," said Jeff. "He'll be extremely surprised. The Game Cocks Club turned into The Sign of Four all of a sudden."

"Shucks, we had a quorum, didn't we?"

"Do you think he'll cry?" said Star, whose own personal vanity was that he never did. But even that could be made a chance for torture. Bert's father was a doctor and Bert had invented the rhythmical cry "Yay, yay, he hasn't any tear ducts" —and the harder Star struggled to summon up moisture the more arid his eyes became.

"If he cries," said Bert, "we'll have to go back to the old name. It's discipline."

The most important rule in the Constitution of the Game Cocks Club had been the penalty of reversion to Old Names. Each member, in the maturity of approaching teens, was earnestly trying to live down an earlier nickname which suggested some highly personal reproach.

This was a matter of some concern to Jeff. He had suffered so much from ironical cries about Thomas G-offerson and G-offerson Davis that any suggested return to the unmanly spelling was horrible. Prudently he tried to forestall.

"Just the same," he said, "it isn't fair to call him Baby. It's that brace on his teeth that makes his eyes get wet. He had to go to the dentist after school, that's why he's late."

"I know what we'll do," said Bert, "we'll hang our handkerchiefs on the gate, then if he gets here with his eyes running he can wipe them before we have to notice it." This seemed a good idea but it failed in effect because even Skinny did not recognize those three atrocious rags as handkerchiefs.

"Dentist or not, there's got to be Penalty," said Star. "It's in the Constitution." Jeff painted busily; this was a critical moment. It had become a depressing ritual that when club meetings developed into physical shindy (as they always did) he was usually the scapegoat. If it was Bunker Hill or Fort McHenry he had to storm it, if a naval engagement it was someone else who cried "Don't give up the ship," in Indian warfare he usually represented the unfortunate Braddock, and how many times he had given up his cutlass at Yorktown. "Didn't anybody but Cornwallis ever give up his sword?" he once asked Uncle Dan. "Try Robert E. Lee," Uncle Dan suggested. Jeff did so and alas, that was what started the rebel yell, "Yay G-offerson Davis!" I thought people came to America to get away from History, he brooded. He was finishing the 4 in T.S.O. 4, and his hand shook. A large gob of green fell on Bert's nape but in the flush of a great idea Bert was too excited to object. "He'll have to be Moriarty!" he exclaimed.

They amended it into the Constitution at once before Skinny could arrive and enter protest. That accounted for the stains of paint on the document and additional blotches when they tried to force Skinny to sign: "Skinny to be Moriarty, unannimus." Skinny managed to scratch out unannimus but he had to sign. Fortunately he did not know how many humiliations the role of Moriarty would involve. He had not accompanied the other boys to see *Sherlock Holmes*. Worse still, he had been taken instead to Sothern and Marlowe and was under the hateful suspicion of having enjoyed it. Poor soul, as he trudged up from dentistry, his mouth a large warm ache where the wires had been tightened on his rabbity teeth, he even meditated suggesting to the G.C.C. a production of Shakespeare in the coachhouse loft. It was a shock when he found that the club and all its rites had transformed overnight. He didn't even know what T.S.O. 4 meant and very unfairly he had to promise to be Moriarty before they would tell him.

"I'm Holmes," shouted Bert.

"Fen Dr. Watson." This was Star.

"Dibbies on Lestrade," Jeff said hurriedly.

"Put him in the gas chamber," cried all three and they hustled Skinny to the odorous old henhouse. There was enough ammonia there to warrant anyone except Star weeping a little, but when the members retired exhausted to the hayloft the quorum showed some compunction. There were no handkerchiefs left but some of the hay was fairly clean.

"Stinkers, darned old stinkers," moaned Skinny—which was by now even truer than he realized.

"Let's make a concession," said Jeff, "he can be Mrs. Hudson."

This really was generous, for Jeff had rather thought of that performance for himself. It turned the ground of argument. Skinny saw his chance. "Yay G-offerson, Long-Word G-offerson!" he screeched and this time it was Jeff at the bottom of the scrimmage.

34. Paper Soldiers

Uncle Dan said it was a pity that the houses in the 1900 block were neither really new nor really old. Jeff's comment was that 1910 was getting old very quickly. This was particularly true on rainy afternoons when Jeff and Skinny played Paper Soldiers. Spontoon's stationery store down on North Avenue kept a wonderful stock of those sweet-smelling cardboard sheets on which the armies of a bellicose planet were lithographed as romance. There were Rough Riders, Cuban patriots, Zouaves, U.S. regulars, Scots Highlanders (kilts and busbies), bearded Boers, and even British redcoats of high shootability. Ten or a dozen to the sheet in their bright colors they were an immediate temptation for scissors and glue; Uncle Dan was kept smoking more than was good for him to supply empty matchboxes on which the figures were pasted to stand upright. One of Aunt Bee's grievances was to find a little pile of loose matches where Jeff had emptied them out in order to use the box. Skinny was in worse plight, his father was a clergyman who did not smoke, and he had to cadge empty matchboxes from the neighbors.

These armies were enlivened by other figures too: the cardboard sheets representing Buffalo Bill and his herd of bison, or the Deadwood Coach attacked by Indians. When the forces of Jeffland and LaGrange faced each other with pea-shooting artillery their battle lines were variegated with cut-out Indian chiefs, buffaloes, the pony express and galloping Wells Fargo coaches. It was a technical understanding that an Indian chief must fall twice before being put out of action; this because his feathers were so arduous to scissor.

One characteristic of a house neither new nor old, Uncle

Dan learned, is the transfusion of sound. His study at the back of the second floor was at the end of the passage which gave good scope to pea-cannon and marbles. He had discovered in Aunt Bee's provisions for the wilderness one of the old Wilford sandbags to stop draughts on a doorsill. This laid at the foot of his study door slightly cushioned the impact of rolling marbles, but the political dialogue of the warring nations was perfectly audible. Sometimes he remembered that his idol Coleridge had also been beset by children as well as Persons from Porlock; though he growled yet also there were times when he eavesdropped with profit. The adoptive parent is often more patient than the actual and he tried to believe that every child is Kubla Khan or the Ode on Intimations.

It was only with Skinny that Jeff played Paper Soldiers to the full reach of fancy. One knows by instinct with whom one may confide; with Bert or Star the game was Paper Soldiers only, but Skinny entered with perfect understanding into the conception of Countries. During the reconnaissance, the actual engagement, or the calculus of gains and losses, both commanders carried on what were two soliloquies rather than conversation, two imaginations independent but mutually stimulated. On this occasion LaGrange had won a considerable victory. Because Skinny had traveled from Patapsco Street carrying his armies in a crackerbox through the rain he was allowed the advantage of a fortified position. It was called Martello Tower; it bore a disconcerting resemblance to the chamber pot from under Jeff's bed, but they had pasted paper around it as disguise. The light musketry of the pea, the heavy artillery of the marble, were equally thwarted by this porcelain cliff, and then a sudden rush of Colonel Cody's bisons had overwhelmed the old guard of Jeffland. The Battle of Martello was a famous victory for LaGrange.

"Jeffland is in a turmoil," said the President. "The citizens are thronging into the streets in unprecedented numbers."

155

(Uncle Dan grinned, recognizing the phrase from some historical chapter he had been reading aloud not long before.)

"The LaGrangers are ecstatic," said the Governor of that country. "This great victory encourages them to something the Powkeepsie has had in mind for some time."

(The "Powkeepsie," the name of the governing council of LaGrange, was a term that Jeff really envied.)

"They're having a secret session," continued the Governor, "to consider changing the name of their country.—What's different from a virgin?"

In the glorious lucidity of a young mind the President of Jeffland knew precisely what was worrying the Governor of LaGrange. Allusions at school—the Virgin Queen—the death of Queen Victoria—the great commonwealths of Virginia and Maryland—the oppression of older sisters—

"The people of LaGrange are extremely romantic," mused the Governor. "They want a Queen, but she's too old to be a virgin."

"They could have a matron, that's older than a virgin," suggested the President. "There isn't anything else." He was not very certain but neither was the Governor. "Is Aunt Bee a matron?"

"Of course she is," said the Governor. "A matron is anybody who does the marketing. She's too grown up to be a virgin.—How would Matronia do for a name?"

"It isn't fair to upset the populace just because you want to have a coronation. Nothing disturbs the citizens so much as changing the name of the country."

"It's very serious," said the Governor, "but if they do we can draw the maps all over again. That would be fun. My father's given me some new paints. He says he's going to have a country called Afterthought, where they can have some really good government."

"You could pacify them by just changing the name of the administration. You can be Mugwump—or there's Rajahs. Keep

156

it LaGrange and be Rajah. There's too many matrons anyhow. Patapsco College is full of them."

"That's good, Rajah of LaGrange. Slick! That's hunky-dory, and they can have a vice-Rajah who's an Amazoon."

"Dibbies on Amazoon," exclaimed the President. "In the humiliation of defeat the Congress of Jeffland impeaches itself into the Amazoon. They're very querulous about the result of this campaign, there's going to be a great civil war testing whether the nation can survive."

The Rajah was so much interested he forgot his own political troubles. "You've got to have an issue," he said gravely.

"They've got a wonderful issue. They can't make up their minds whether to keep on the right-hand side or the left. It's practically strangled their commerce, the common carriers keep bumping into each other, they're going to have a tremendous highway right through the middle of the country called Thorofare Extended, and everybody's got to keep to the right."

"Except Virgins!" shouted the Rajah. "That's how you can tell."

"Let's go down in the dining-room and use the table," said the President, rubbing abraded knees. "I've got a name for a new town, it's called Kneepad."

"Dibbies on Splinter," said the Rajah.

Uncle Dan had overhead this game often enough to understand the allusions to that scurfy floor in the passage. Thinking of mending-baskets he hoped that the chivalry of LaGrange and Jeffland were wearing the pads. Physical accidents during play were faithfully reflected in cartography. Not without reason did LaGrange's picturesque island of Corduroy have a town called Split.

35. The 1900 Block

Dan was so happy in the prospect of escape from lodgings that when he went househunting he would have chosen almost anything. But very likely the numerals of the 1900 block appealed to him as a kind of symbolism. Carroll Street was near Patapsco College, the rent was within his means, and the first time he studied the two facing rows of small brick homes was one of those sultry spring twilights when Chesapeake digests its fried chicken and hominy sitting on the stoop. The earliest fireflies of the year were blinking Morse code in the scaly sycamore trees and along the series of little white marble steps sat pretty girls in ruffled dresses. Frequently they rearranged their overlapping draperies, gathering them about ankles that seemed too fragile for the mileage they would undoubtedly incur. Young men suitable for the purpose sat in homage at respectful gradations. The Life Force had produced them with punctual prodigality. The dialogue, alternating hoarse cackles and gurgling mush, was not less vapid because in the adjoining parlor windows sires lurked in shirtsleeves behind the evening paper. Student and lover of speech, Uncle Dan eavesdropped as he prowled along. In his early days at Patapsco he thought the Chesapeake patois was simply an unconscious biological chuckle, like the cooing of doves, until he learned that it was actually an articulated language. But all consonants were submerged in a syrup of vowels. It sounded like American marmalade, too sweet. No word ever came crisply to an end but fondly impeded the next one. Among Dan's burdens was a course called *Declamation and Forensics*. He startled his pupils one day by writing on the blackboard:

> I beg you, not so mum the word:
> Your diction, like your mind, is blurred.

But now, in evening languor, the soft slopping talk was provocative and kind, like a mulled sweet wine. It sounded somehow like Omar Khayyam: Edward FitzGerald would have loved it. Barton, don't be such a prickly Puritan, he said to himself, smiling to consider what the Thorofare would think of its young sitting out to collogue on doorsteps. And how delightful to see that the Chesapeake belles, even bracketed by papa at the window and swains at their ankles, were so entirely in command of the situation. Woman, he thought, is a deponent verb: passive in form but active in function. That would be a good epigram for English VII. . . . Perhaps Carroll Street is the kind of place that puts ideas in one's head?

The more strident small boys of the neighborhood could be heard, mercifully remote, from a bushy vacant lot a couple of blocks away, along Division Road. In the after-supper drowse there were no wheels on the cobbles and Carroll Street gave an illusion of quiet. Then at number 1910 Uncle Dan saw the sign FOR RENT, and even one of those telltale mirrors called "busybodies" projecting from a three-sided bay upstairs. His decision was prompt. He knew it would never be possible to lure Aunt Bee into the sociability of the front steps, but surely she might enjoy watching it reflected above.

When he inspected the premises later with the agent his observation was superficial. The little back room upstairs, overlooking the yard and the alley, appealed to him as a study. He visualized his books along the wall and a couch for siesta with Rider Haggard and Anthony Hope. A colored man on a wagon went bumping down the alley crying the seasonal chantey "Strawbe-e-y, Nice Fresh Strawbe-e-y," and this seemed an additional picturesque. The dreamer did not then conceive how often the cries and clamors of the alley would come between him and his dream. He did say vaguely, "I wish there were a third floor, it would be so useful for working," but the agent, that ready debater, replied (in the drawl which is so dangerous because it sounds so innocent), "You wouldn't cherish another trudge of stairs for yo' good lady to climb?" So Uncle Dan accused himself of deficient chivalry and easily agreed.

It may have been the numbers of the 1900's that prevailed. Who remembers now with what hopeful anticipation men of good will looked forward to that mystic date. Perhaps Uncle Dan specially, for he was often happy in small private fetishes, omens, and computations. For example the Hazlitt necktie, which for some chancy reason he associated with the ulcerated essayist; he always wore it when the season came round for his lecture on Hazlitt, and one of his rare quarrels with Aunt Bee was when, not realizing its inspiration, she cut up the tawny silk for a quilt. And so he philosophized the even numbers of the 1900 block as an orderly vista of fortunes to come. He foresaw himself returning in afternoon peace from the task work of the classroom and like a rider on Mr. Wells's Time-Machine collapsing the momentum of the years, at any rate as far as 1910. How far away that looked. And by 1910 perhaps the Professorship at Chesapeake would have been achieved and perhaps even a house in real country.

In his usual route from the college Dan passed all the dates on Carroll Street from 1700 to the new century, and reflected cheerfully that these were also the limits of his literary duty. When going downtown he crossed North Avenue into the 1600's he felt like a boy at recess. Here were centuries of escapade with which he had no professorial concern.

Some of his students got into embarrassment by following his methods. He told them if they had difficulty with dates to visualize them by house numbers on their own streets. No wonder, he said, Alexander Pope (the greatest virtuoso who ever lived) was good at couplets: his "dates" were 1688 to 1744. One of the girls, taking him too seriously, prepared herself for an examination by staring so earnestly at 1744 Patapsco Street that she was insulted by one of the boarders.

36. First Visit to Greenaway

Memory is careless of chronology. Afterthought of what one loves, as Jeff learned and loved Chesapeake in those years Before the Fire, is casual to and fro. But very early in the Carroll Street days came a loud scream which he could not choose but hear. It was the Ma and Pa. That mimic railroad hiding in the gorge below the North Avenue Bridge sent two leisurely trains a day winding the valleys toward Harford County. It was a Book of Genesis railroad, Uncle Dan said, created on Sixth Day with the other creeping things. When Jeff hankered for a toy train like Star Lanvale's, Uncle Dan reminded him that they had one practically in the back yard. The MARYLAND & PENNSYLVANIA (so the cars were labeled in wide-spaced railroad lettering) had no false vanity. It would stop anywhere, all you needed to do was build a little scaffold and put out a milk can. Patrons had an almost protective affection for it. The cowcatcher was sharper, the smokestack taller, the whistle shriller, the conductor more benevolent than anywhere else. Even the conductor's gold watch was bigger, because (he told Jeff) we have more time on this road. It was said to have one spare locomotive, whether Ma or Pa; Bert Eutaw maintained that he had seen them both and could tell their sexes apart. Ma, he said, always ran backward; he had even formed some erroneous biological theory about this. Though there were two engines the train was always the same: a flat car, a box car jingling with milk cans, a blind baggage, and one passenger coach. Ma and Pa traveled with domestic fidelity to and from rural Pennsylvania; they did not look as if they had any wider yearnings. Few people ever learned where the two met and passed; the single track must somewhere be supplemented by a siding, but it wouldn't need to be a big one. Even a Wilford train would look large compared to Ma and Pa. That was one reason why Aunt Bee enjoyed it so much.

It was one of those unexpectedly hot days early in October when Uncle Dan took them out to Greenaway. Jeff was naturally much excited by his first glimpse of the small railroad, of which Uncle Dan had given almost too much preliminary description. There was time to study the engine before they mounted the train; Jeff asked the engineer, "Is this Ma or Pa?"

"This is Ma," he said, adding confidentially to Uncle Dan, "You can always tell, she's got two humps on the boiler."

Aunt Bee, who was often subject to minute annoyances, was more concerned by a mosquito bite on the tip of her nose. It was her own fault. Their first night at 1910 she found all the windows carefully screened. To a Wilford eye this was merely a wanton blockade to keep out fresh air. So without asking anyone's advice she removed her bedroom screens, and lay awake with Puritan grimness while beset by all sorts of methodical biters and buzzers. She supposed this was a part of frontier life, and was well speckled by morning. Something in her untainted Suffolk blood must have appealed to the creatures. "What terrible midges you have here," she said. Uncle Dan warned her not to scratch, but of course she did. She felt it unfortunate that she should be so spotty on her first visit to Uncle Dan's important friends.

But the novelty of the trip soon distracted her from small troubles. The valley of the stripling Jones, though the name seemed odd to her, is no less beautiful than the Valley of Fern, but the latter has nothing like a stand of gum trees in their purple climax, or maples catching fire from hill to hill. "How far is it?" she asked.

"About as far as Bealings."

"I thought it must be farther than that because the trees look so tall," she said mysteriously.

"How can you tell if it's the right hand or the left hand?" Jeff asked, "because there's only one track."

"Everything is such a queer mixture of familiar and strange," said Aunt Bee.

"What is a cotton duck?" asked Geoffrey. "Is that a toy for small children?" They were passing a large mill beside the stream and he noticed the sign "Woodbury Cotton Duck."

"It's a sort of canvas," said Uncle Dan. "I'll tell you something that will surprise you. One time when we were in Harry Bredfield's *Scandal* I noticed his sailcloth was Woodbury. So you see we're not really so far away."

"I bet it's always high tide in America," said Jeff, pursuing

162

his own thoughts. "I saw something in a book about High Tide at Gettysburg."

"That was a different kind of tide. Don't say too much about Gettysburg when we meet Major Warren."

The magic of Greenaway always had a special effect upon Uncle Dan. He tried to explain to Aunt Bee: "Nothing could be more American and yet in the queerest way I always feel so close there to the best of England. Perhaps it's because it's so George the Third. A great deal of Chesapeake is pure eighteenth-century."

"I don't know about pure," said Aunt Bee. "I must say I'm questionable about the cobblestones and the drainage running down the gutters. In some ways it seems more behind-the-times than Ipswich." Her noticing spirit had been surprised by the rich exhalation of Jones's Falls in autumn sun. And she had already had glimpses of some of the famous alleys inhabited by what she called darkies. Aunt A. and the Band of Hope would not have accepted them without a struggle.

Uncle Dan had not grieved much about the sociology of his adopted town. He was disturbed that his sister's eye had been so alert. It was a contradiction of Jeff's enthusiastic but premature remark: "America is large and clean and new, England is small and old and dirty." To the scholar it was rather an amusing paradox that a great American city should still be living almost in the sanitation of Queen Anne. "Wait till you see our great beauty spot," he said. "Jones's Falls at sunset on Wash Day. All the rinsing water from this side of the city flows into the stream and by afternoon it's the most beautiful copper blue. People hang over the North Avenue Bridge to admire it, like the Arno at Florence."

"Very jubious," said Aunt Bee.

It was a different phase of the eighteenth century that Uncle Dan relished at Greenaway. "This is one of Major Warren's Sunday breakfasts," he told her. "There may be other people

163

there too" (Aunt Bee cautiously dabbed her nose), "or it may be just us, so you needn't be frightened. He told me one time how the breakfast parties started. His father, Tullius Teackle Warren, such a gorgeous name, was really a devotee of the arts and escaped from business as much as he could. It's quite a story, Tullius Teackle spent some time in England as a young man and made all sorts of sentimental pilgrimages. His great ambition was to meet Coleridge but by the time he got there old Sam was too ill or too queer to be seen. But the young Warren prowled around and made an acquaintance with Hartley Coleridge up in the Lake District. He even met Daddy Wordsworth, they were all very kind to him: they were astonished that a young American should be interested in their doings. The Major pretends to think that all this was partly because his father was born in 1809 when there was such a tidal wave of literary progeny. He says if anybody is planning to have babies nowadays he recommends waiting until 1909, that might be a lucky year too. But you can imagine what his friendship has meant to me; on account of his father he knows more about the Wordsworths and Coleridges and all that period than most college professors."

"I shall feel very shy if they talk about nothing but literature."

"Don't worry, that's only when the Major and I get off by ourselves. He has a marvelous library of his father's books. You try Mrs. Warren on cooking. She wants to know how to make treacle tart, only she says they'll call it Teackle, that's the name of her son. It's a family name round here. But about the breakfasts, when the old Mr. Warren was in London as a youngster he got invited to one of Crabb Robinson's famous breakfast parties and when he came home he started the same sort of thing for himself. Several times a year he would ask people who enjoyed ideas to come out and spend Sunday morning sitting round the table. Then everybody takes a nap until tea time. You must be sure to drink some of his Madeira because it's a tradition. His grandfather owned privateer clippers and they either stole the wine on the high seas or else used it as ballast, I don't remember."

Aunt Bee was a little confused as to the different generations of the Warrens but she decided to be her own wary self and accept things as they came.

Major Warren and young Teackle met them with an old shiny barouche at the tiny shed which was Greenaway's own flag-station on the Ma and Pa. By happy coincidence their host himself had what he called a sty on his nose—perhaps Madeira rather than mosquito. Even Jeff's private sensibilities were assuaged when one of the Major's first remarks was, "I'm glad you wore good solid boots. Teackle wants to take you for a scramble." This made Jeff feel better about the K-boots. He explained to Major Warren, who had a courteous air of attention that made one feel important.

"I've been embarrassed," Jeff said formally, "because American boys don't wear K-boots, but they can be very valuable. They have a trick at school, they ask you if you know about the Stamp Act and suddenly they jump on your feet. If you've got K-boots you don't feel it."

Aunt Bee was relieved by Major Warren's weathered and countrified look, his old-fashioned brown frock-coat and riding breeches reminded her of Wilford on market day. He limped a little too, which softened her. "I'm glad you-all came out with Ma," he said, saluting the train crew. "She doesn't seem to throw as much soot as Pa. I'm afraid our toy railway is a shock to you after those beautiful trains on the Great Eastern. I've never forgotten a hamper of tea I had on the Yarmouth Express. I wish we could paint Ma and Pa bright blue like those engines of yours but it would be only a burlesque of a great work of art."

"Then you must have been through Wilford," said Aunt Bee, quite excited.

"Yes indeed. I got tired of hearing about the Lakes, I wanted to see the Norfolk Broads. I think Wilford was where my tea spilled in my lap, that wonderful curve at the bottom of your garden. You see your good brother has told me all about it."

The cautious Aunt Bee cottoned at once to the Major, and Dan was happy. He had the adoring affection of a naturally awkward man for the one who always says the right thing.

"You-all must forgive Mrs. Warren for not having come down to make her curtsey. She takes these breakfasts right serious, and she's up to her ears in the kitchen trying to explain to the cook how to make sausage rolls. Must have sausage rolls, your brother has talked so much about them, but we can't seem to get the right formula."

"And Teackle tart," said Teackle. "Come on, Jeff, get up on the driver's seat with me."

"It's like the captain's bridge," said Jeff. "Can I help you steer?"

Aunt Bee also had a way of saying the right thing. "It's like Rendlesham Hall," she said, as they arrived under the long façade of rose-colored brick. "Even holly trees!"

Major Warren was much pleased but politely deprecated his pleasure. "One of your old Suffolk manors? But I'm sure Rendlesham Esquire would have too much sense to build a big portico he couldn't afford to paint."

"What a funny smell," said Geoffrey, relishing the exquisite sour-and-sweet which is a secret of that region.

"Goodness, is it box?" asked Aunt Bee. "It never smells as strong as that in England. And the way there's a sniff of roses mixed up in it."

"Toasted box, we call it," said Major Warren. "It always surprises visitors in hot weather. These hedges have been toasting a long time. Squire Rendlesham would probably have cut his down to make lawn bowls. We have a measly time in winter wrapping them up. I can't afford to buy so much burlap any more. There's one tree I was worried about in an ice storm. I tied it up in my long woolen underwear. I'm afraid Mrs. Warren didn't approve."

Aunt Bee's anxieties were well relieved when she noticed the antique endearing shabbiness of Greenaway. An old colored man in a white coat helped her out of the carriage as if she had been Queen Victoria. The top of his head had such crisp gray nap she would have liked to stroke it; and his coat had been mended. Mrs. Warren was plump and cordial: her confession that the sausage rolls had somehow miscarried seemed a subtle compliment. There were no other guests and it was impossible to be formal in such a spell of warm laziness. Jeff found much to study and said little. He kept looking up at a huge bamboo fan rotating fitfully over the dining-table. "What is that propeller?" he asked as the long slender blades came to a pause.

"The motor is very primitive," said Mrs. Warren.

"Is Jeff interested in motors?" said their host. "Would he like to see it?" The Major led him out into the hall and opened the door of a cupboard under one curve of the big double staircase. A small colored boy was sitting on a stool holding a cord which passed over a spindle and revolved the fan by hand. He started with surprise and his eyes and teeth looked like china in the shadow. "Try to give us a little more elbow-grease, Mutual," said the Major. "We're showing off for company."

"Yassuh, Major, I got sleepy. It's this mystical weather."

Aunt Bee had been afraid she might be sleepy too, but in spite of Madeira and fried chicken, she enjoyed the conversation. Evidently there was something in the relation between the Major and Uncle Dan which put them both at their best. "He doesn't always talk so biggity," whispered Mrs. Warren, "but he says your brother is the best listener he ever gets. I didn't know the treacle tart was going to set him off on smells."

"Remember George Fox's remark when he got religion," said Uncle Dan. "He said the whole creation had a different smell."

"If I could write the history of this house," the Major continued, "it would be an essay on that subject. Your nose, Miss

Barton, is in for some interesting surprises if you ever explore downtown. Chesapeake smelled so bad in the eighteenth century that everybody who could tried to build a house in the country. As a matter of fact the family fortune, when there was one, came through the nose. That old fellow in the picture over the mantel, holding the ship-model in his hand, that was Great-great-grandfather Zeb. He was smart enough to see that the tobacco fields around here were all smoked out (tobacco's a right greedy crop for soil) and he went into the grain trade. Built himself a trading schooner to carry wheat to Bristol. He had to build a pier to lay her up at but most of the shipping was going to the other side of the basin. Smart fellow, Old Zeb, what does he do, builds an oven on the end of the pier and gets some good colored cooks to bake spoon bread and punkin pie and cinnamon bun right where the sailors could smell it. Yes, Ma'am, they come in starvin' from a long voyage and they smell that hoe-cake and cinnamon pie and they make straight for Zeb Warren's dock. One thing and another and likely a little free-booting in the West Indies, he did powerful well for himself. That schooner he's holding, the *Mermaid*, had her masts raked back so far everybody said they'd fall over. They said he stepped 'em that way because he had a squint and couldn't see perpendicular, but it made the vessel mighty sweet on the wind. Other folks took to imitating her. Likely she was one of the first of the Chesapeake clippers. Old Zeb filled her full of wheat and he'd bring back Bristol Milk."

"Would the milk keep all that time?" asked Aunt Bee.

"It's a sherry," Dan explained.

"It is indeed," said the Major. "The nut brown maiden of all sherries, a real brunette. He built this house about 1760. Doesn't seem so old in Wilford but we feel it's right creditable."

"That was before the American Rebellion?" asked Aunt Bee.

"It always tickles me when the British call it a Rebellion instead of a Revolution," said the Major. "No, Miss Bee, in this neck of the woods Rebellion signifies different. The old place

168

had its troubles. In the Revolution somebody burned down the kitchen wing but they never rightly knew who did it, whether the Liberty Boys or the British."

"They've been burning things there ever since," said Mrs. Warren, thinking of her sausage rolls.

"Are we British?" Jeff asked innocently. He had already been puzzled by this word, rare in Wilford.

"British is really a kind of a swear-word, like Yankee," said the Major. "Let's have some more Madeira. Lightfoot, fill up the glasses. It's a good eighteenth-century drink, Miss Bee. What was really comical about Greenaway, the poor old place never quite knew what side it was on. They used to say that was why Old Zeb built that double stairway out there, one branch for Tories and one for patriots. It came in handy in '61 too. I tippytoed down one side to join the Confed'racy while my old man was pretending to look up the other."

"Zeb Warren was loyalist, wasn't he?" Uncle Dan asked.

"Yes, not any theocratic enthusiasm for the Crown, just hard-headed merchant, knew he had everything to lose by any kind of trouble. He was busy exporting barrel-staves to the West Indies for their molasses casks—probably to satisfy your British, I mean English, passion for treacle tart. But he must have used one of the barrel-staves a little too often on his son. That was poor old Scurvy."

"You shouldn't call him that unpleasant name without explaining," said Mrs. Warren.

"May as well rattle all the family skeletons at once," said the Major, "let Miss Bee know the worst. His real name was Purvy. Anyhow, stinging with barrel-staves he run away to sea and went privateering with Whipple. He was captured by the British, I mean English, and put in the calaboose in Charleston. That's where he got scurvy, the only kind of rhyme he was capable of."

Uncle Dan anticipated Geoffrey. "Put in jail," he murmured.

"G-a-o-l?" said Geoffrey.

"Good boy," said the Major. "G-a-o-l sounds much more uncomfortable than jail; like John Bunyan."

"Daddy was in jail himself," said Teackle.

This is a very exciting family, Geoffrey thought.

"Yes, Lightfoot and I spent two years in Indiana. That was Lew Wallace's fault. No wonder he did so well with that chariot race in *Ben-Hur*. That cavalry of his rode too fast for us, didn't they, Lightfoot? We dug our way out of that prison once, but after a look at that Indiana landscape I figured we might as well be back in jail."

"If you're going to fight Secession all over again," said Mrs. Warren, "I'm going to take Miss Barton away for a siesta."

Aunt Bee agreed happily. The fan overhead had ceased again, the Madeira was strong, the browse of velveteen bees in the roses outside filled the great mahogany dining-room with meridian weight. She thought she saw the colored butler waver on his feet and she felt that way too.

"Take her up to Betsy Patterson's room," said the Major. "When Betsy was going to marry a Bonaparte she figured she better have a real soaping bath. She came out here to Greenaway where they had a china tub and a boiler of hot water."

"What wonderful furniture polish you must have," said Aunt Bee as she paused with Mrs. Warren in the great hall. Long curves of banister on each side rose shining into the shuttered dimness. "What is it, lemon oil?" At that moment Teackle and Jeff slid down from above, one on each side.

"I'm afraid you can see what it is," said Mrs. Warren. "Five generations of young breeches."

"What I call backside oil," said the Major. "Tell her your story about shining up the highboy."

"I declare, Major, you'll have her all worn out with fatigue. It's just that we had a green colored wench and I told her to shine up this old highboy." Aunt Bee had a half-asleep vision of a sea-green maiden rubbing the smooth wood.

"I came back and found it just as dusty as ever, so I told her,

'Mandy, you never polished the old highboy.' She insisted, 'Yes, Ma'am, yes indeedy, I sholy did.' I asked her to show me how she did it, and she took me to admire the portrait of Great-grandpa Zeb. The way it hangs over the chimney, she thought he must be Old Highboy."

I might have done the same, thought Aunt Bee; *I'd* call this a sideboard or a chiffonier.—She was glad to be led away for the promised siesta.

"It's awful hot. Can I take Jeff down to the Branch for a swim?" asked Teackle.

"Yes, after you've shaken down that fried chicken. Take him out and show him the slave quarters. Come on, Sir, you and I will go in the Apery while the ladies take their forty winks. It will be mo'n forty if I know Mrs. Warren. She can sleep any time. It's a wonderful trait in a woman. Lightfoot, *Gens Inimica Mihi.*"

"Yassuh, Major, yassuh. *Navigat Aequor.*"

"Lightfoot and I have a little code of our own," the Major explained. "Maybe I never told you how we studied Virgil in that Yankee prison camp? We translate that line, 'I don't care for folks that navigates on water.' It means 'Open another bottle.' " He led the way through a corridor hung with guns and sporting prints into the wing of the house known as the Apery. The Major was always pleased when this name for his library puzzled visitors. Over the wide battered fireplace the mantel-beam was carved *Sic Vos Non Vobis Mellificatis Apes.*

"A library is a kind of honeycomb," he said, sinking into a chair. "It sure tickles me when folks think it means something about monkeys. Have another glass of Madeira and we'll talk."

Dan knew perfectly well what would happen. After apologizing for everyone else being so drowsy the Major would soliloquize for twenty minutes or so and then fall asleep in his chair.

"Yes, Sir, Virgil has been a great influence around this plantation. When I first put up that verse my brother Randy, the old scalawag, he named a couple of bird dogs Vos and Vobis. He thought Sic had something to do with hounds. A spirited fellow, but lacking in culture, Sir. When he passed on I moved all his fowling pieces and sporting prints into the passage. I only kept that picture of Lightfoot to remind me not to bet on horses. Horses' necks pretty near sunk this family."

The warm midday aroma of bees and box, the rump-sprung leather chair ("Make yourself easy, Sir, you got to set your cheeks just so in that chair"), the colored butler muttering to himself as he uncorked another bottle, caused Uncle Dan to wonder whether he himself might drift off before the Major. "Horses' necks?" he asked vaguely.

"Yes, Sir, the necks of other horses that Randy didn't bet on. That's Lightfoot, that chestnut gelding over there. Not the same as *this* Lightfoot."

"No, Suh, Mr. Barton," said the butler, "my name comes from the Lees of Virginia, Suh. My folks lived with them in the old days."

"That's one of Lightfoot's fantasies. Says he's one of the Lees of Virginia. I tell him he's one of the dregs. Don't you shake that wine, you rascal, your old limbs getting mighty tremulous. Some time when you want fun, get Lightfoot to construe some Virgil for you."

Evidently this was a sentimental topic between the Major and his servant. Lightfoot's gnarled hand quivered with restraint as he tried not to speak until the wine was poured. He breathed heavily with relief. "Ah never was no good at that scansion," he admitted.

"He didn't know arsis from thesis," said the Major. "None of us did until the Commandant got interested. You see, we were all perishing of boredom, Clara Barton or the Sanitary Commission sent a box of books for us Johnny Rebs and by the time Lightfoot and I got around to it there was nothing left but a textbook of Virgil. I was always ashamed because I never had any university education. I went off to ride cavalry with

172

Mosby. Well, Sir, there was quite a number of Confed'rate officers in that prison that wanted to read Virgil, we-all got together a group of us, we'd read it aloud and try to figure out what it meant. Lightfoot couldn't read but you'd be surprised what a lot of tags he picked up. We didn't any of us know how to read hexameter so it sounded like po'try, but then the Commandant of the prison got a curiosity about what we were doing, and he showed us how to elide. I reckon we sort of took advantage of his classical education. He got to thinking we were just a lot of innocent students. We got permission to set out evenings in an old laundry they had, so we could do our construing. It was right comical because while we had a crowd in front talking loud about datives and genitives, Lightfoot and some of the others was diggin' a hole under the washtubs."

"Yassuh," said Lightfoot, "we mighty near elided right out of that old jailhouse." He doddered about with the tray of wine, prolonging the pleasure of reminiscence. "Recollect that Commandant act a bit irksome. He say ef we try it again he give us a different kind of hexameter, six foot underground."

"You can be excused now, Lightfoot," said the Major. "Go and take a nap, give your legs an armistice."

"What a pity Dr. Gildersleeve wasn't captured with you," Uncle Dan suggested.

"Yes, Sir, I've often thought of that. But maybe it was more fun because none of us were real scholars. There was a kind of false pride about it too. We were hell-bent to remind some of those Yankees that it was really a war between gentlemen and tradesmen. I guess the tradesmen always win. But everything was all mixed up in the Warren family. My father, for instance: every time there was a war he went abroad and stayed until it was over. Damn sensible too, that's how he bought all those pictures; worth a fortune and he gave 'em to a museum. His brother, Uncle Coalbox, was managing the railroad and fixing to get himself shot at by both sides. We called him Coalbox because he run the line through to the coal mines, did as much as anybody to win the war for Old Abe. Remarkable man, Uncle Colfax. We cut his railroad three-four times around Harper's Ferry, but he always had the cars running again the next day. One time we got driven off when we'd only torn up one rail going around a bend, we made the mistake to cut the inside rail and the story was Uncle Coalbox figured out just the right speed and run the train round the bend on the outside rail alone. What they used to call centrifugal force. Just a fairy tale, I reckon, but Uncle Colfax was a fool for luck. I hope I don't weary you but I like to think this room is the home of lost causes. Your very good health, Sir."

Uncle Dan knew his cue. He raised the glass, they exchanged glances and toasted "The Northeast Trades." His host had often explained that the old Chesapeake clippers profited by the happy coincidence of prevailing fair winds from Madeira to the Virginia Capes.

"You're real unselfish, Sir, but I think we have a relish for the same things. Ever since my Governor was captured by the British at Winander there's been a streak of literary poison around this place."

Uncle Dan's mind had wandered a little. "The Battle of Winander?"

"When he was captured, I mean captivated, by those Lake Poets. 'There was a boy, ye knew him well Winander.' I suppose it was old Daddy Wordsworth's name for Windermere. I used to hear my Governor say that so often, I never worry much about what it meant. We had a private car on the railroad called Winander."

"That would have shocked Wordsworth. He wrote some sonnets complaining about railways."

"Did he so? Well the old hypocrite! He was always wanting to buy some Blue Ridge shares. I always mean to read more of old Daddy but it's so much easier to go over the bits I know than to break fresh print. *The Prelude* was my favorite for putting myself to sleep. I often wonder how you teach poetry,

Dan. Do you have to explain it to the students? I never wanted it explained. Sometimes the less I understood it the more I liked it. What I wanted was pictures in my mind, like the boy rowing a boat on the lake and the mountain rising up steeper and steeper till it cuts off the moon and scares him; or the time he goes in the woods and whistles at the owls."

The sun of early afternoon slid through an aperture of the slatted cane blinds, slowly feeling its way along a shelf, like a hesitating golden finger. Dan was curious to see what book it had reached. He rose to look and suddenly was interrupted by his own thoughts. "Do you remember, Major, Coleridge as a boy was so frightened by the *Arabian Nights*, an old black copy in his father's rectory, he never dared take it from the shelf until the sunlight struck it? I wonder if Hartley still had that copy?"

The Major did not reply and Dan turning saw that he was blissfully asleep. The shadow of the mountain had blotted out the boy in the boat.

37. *The Album*

It's too bad, Uncle Dan thought, seeing anyone else asleep always makes me wide awake. He tiptoed out of the library by the back door and wandered in the box-garden, a rectangle of paths hedged about a central plot. The Major liked to call it a maze but it was a very simple one. Too simple, perhaps, to symbolize any actual human patterns. But college "English" was also a kind of formal evergreen garden? He was sorry the Major had evaporated just then because for an instant—like the yellow sunshine on those books—he had felt the answer to the question about teaching. For the students' advantage (he wanted to say) you must try to explain a little, even if only to show there can be all sorts of explanations; even if the children don't take in a word you say. You better warn them that much of what you suggest will sound like desolating nonsense, but let them make notes anyhow: maybe ten or twenty years later some of those suggestions will begin to penetrate. Let them take time out from the proud certainties of youth to prepare themselves for the possibility of blissful doubt in middle age. . . . He laughed aloud at the absurdity of trying to convince a group of girls in their teens that middle age could have any merits whatever. Strolling the gravel paths between tart-savored shrubs he reached the dial in the center of the garden. The sunlight yawned, open wide in clear vacancy. Somewhere toward the stables he could hear the jocular mumble of the colored servants, a comfortably idle sound. III o'clock said the shadow: III sharp, he thought, the edge cut so black. In color, in smell, in slope of afternoon the most relentless beauty of the day—the day that was itself already middle-aged. And yet an hour later, and later still, they would say to themselves, Now it is perfect. Marvelous that no one can ever guess beforehand how the mind compensates, finds its balance-point in every tension. He thought with delight of his attractive young pupils reveling in their harmless assurance that no one before had ever tasted the peculiar flavor of living. Politely, humorously, even respectfully, they filled their notebooks, but how impossible for them really to believe that Wordsworth or Coleridge or Hazlitt—or even Dan Barton—were still really younger than themselves in everything that mattered. It was the sun-dial that made him think of Hazlitt, connoisseur of shadows and evasives; or maybe the warm bitterness of the boxwood smell. If he only had his class sitting here among the green alleys he could almost describe to them how literature and all the arts are woven (*implex* was the word that came to mind) into the whole stuff of looking and growing and feeling; so that the smell of a garden parterre can be the equivalent of a page of pollened prose. Extraordinary, he said to himself, testing the different warmths of the bronze dial with his palm, I was never so happy. It's the Major does that to me; he got through his resentments a long

176

time ago, he just drifts with the tide hoping his guts will hold out. It's humiliating though, I most approve the Major where his tastes or ideas confirm my own. Damme, can't a man ever be philosophically detached?

Dan was probably thinking of the time the Major (in the full shove of a trade wind from Madeira) sat by this same sun-dial and uttered a soliloquy about marriage. "I never discuss these things in the house," he said. "It's not prudent, married men and soldiers better hadn't boast. No, Sir. But I reckon Miz Beuly and I made a success of it because we didn't marry too young. Everybody in Chezpeake was overcome to astonishment when I took to myself a wife. I was supposed to be a natural bachelor; just what they thought they meant by that, I'm too delicate to inquire. I declare it's risky when folks marry young—this is another thing you can tell your gals, Dan. They won't give no heed so it won't make any difference,—because young people try to adapt themselves to each other and of cose that's fatal. You set about adapting yo'self to someone else and you just naturally succumb. Maybe yo' private character has no chance to develop itself a-tall. No, Sir, you make friends with yourself before you start to homage some gallivantin' gal. There's another feature about this here middle-aged nuptial: it offers all kinds of surprises. I thought I was past child-bearing when I married and we-all supposed young Teackle was the last fig-leaf on the tree and then, Sir, by God, ten years later along comes baby Trundle."

"You'll have to get out of the habit of calling her that nickname," Dan said. "It's amusing while she's crawling around, but she won't like it when she gets older."

"You're quite right, Sir; it's not mannerly to take advantage of a lady, no matter how young she is. The colored folks always give her full entitles, Serena Lavinia, they love long names. I reckon I've told you why we call her Lavinia, another quotation from Virgil. Like Aeneas, after all his campaigning, Laviniaque venit, Along came Lavinia. Just a kind of enclitic at the tail of the whole biological series."

The first good *sprawl* since the Meadow at Wilford, Dan said to himself; but not even midsummer on the Thorofare gave such a stupor, drugged and flooded with sun. He was lying out in the open pasture beyond the box-garden while Greenaway took its afternoon doze. Perhaps it was one of the same fields that the Major said had had the jizzum leached out of it by tobacco. There seemed still plenty of vitality in red earth and stubble under that heavy glow. A counterpointed symphony of insect hosannas shook the warm slope with vibration. The weathered snake-fence cast zigzag lines of shadow like fractured staves of music. Every cricket fluting like Sidney Lanier. Dan was letting his mind soak, stew, simmer—faintly acrid, like toasted box—spread, dream, relax—sluggish and easy, like sleep that starts in the ankles and seeps upward. He checked it with a kind of tourniquet at the knee. Sleep begins: In the shins: Upward seep: Mind at neap: I'm asleep— The rhyme startled him with pleasure. The mind floats from a word to an idea, then back to some associated word, which in turn signals a new thought and another kindred word—that wonderful saying of Coleridge about *the streamy nature of association*—how staggered S. T. C. would have been by the insect music of America— Insect fiddlers that forebode the frost, Dan said happily, laying his ear among the grassroots to listen— Sounds like the last line of a sonnet— A cornfield hosanna—a rhyme for Susquehanna! My unwritten sonnet!—But sonnets are not written by lazy men.

He sat up, scratched straws from his beard, sat in comfortable slump. He was feeling his way back into America. Colors of earth, shapes of trees, touch of air, tone of voices, every sense was different, and he reveled in his perception of the change. Down toward the creek was a grove of huge tulip and chestnut trees; some of them with storm-scarred limbs. American woods

178

look so much more ragged and impulsive, he thought; more vehement somehow, more emphatic, more beset. He could hear shouts from the swimming-hole. Time for Jeff to come out. He strolled over the ridge of the field, the boys saw him coming and three naked figures, one black and two white, scrambled across the soggy meadow to meet him.

"I felt like the *Westernland* as I came over the hill," Dan said. "Grasshoppers jumping up under my bow like spray."

Jeff visualized the picture with a polite smile, but he wasn't thinking about the *Westernland*. "The water's funny," he panted, "they forgot to put salt in it. There's crawfishes, big as prawns."

"Ah'll make real spray for you!" cried Mutual. He and Teackle sped back to a waterside stump to show off their diving. Jeff, who could not really swim yet, watched enviously.

"I like to see Mutual dive," he said, "the bottoms of his feet are white."

"He's much livelier here than he is in that cupboard under the stairs."

"That's only profession, workin' that ole fan," Mutual agreed. "Anything goes round and round the same way is natural sleepy."

"Better get your clothes on," said Uncle Dan. "I think they're going to have tea in the garden."

"Cheese it, Mutual," said Teackle, "if the Major's going to have tea outdoors you better hustle and sweep that sod. If he finds it all littered up Lightfoot'll tan your rump."

"My rumps is tan already," said Mutual, bending in impudent illustration. "Got frenzy in mah feet, watch me bu'n up dat grass." He leaped into his faded overalls and streaked off uphill.

It was Aunt Bee's first experience of tea in tall glasses with ice. In first experience of so many phenomena all at once she was content to watch and listen as they sat on the lawn (swept just in time) near the sun-dial. The baby, Serena Lavinia, looked whiter and more scalloped with lace than any child she had ever seen, but perhaps it was by contrast with the black mammy who carried her out and set her on a blanket for the admiration of the elders. Dan had heard rumors about this famous child, but had never seen her before. Her father lifted her up for an exhibition dandle and remarked proudly that she was solid. "I declare she weighs as much as Dr. Johnson's Dictionary," he said.

"I am afraid the Major feels about her just the way he does about some of his old books," said Mrs. Warren, "something to take down from the shelf and show off now and then, just for curiosity."

"And no wonder, at my age," said the Major. "Confound it, I think it's remarkable. And to propagate a woman-child too; that seems to me to suggest the recuperative splendor of the human race. You're quite right, Beuly, infants of this age should be on display only so long as they're amusing."

Serena retaliated by clutching his neat Confederate goatee, and he replaced her on all fours with an appropriate pat on her center of suavity. The child estimated the available resources of fresh admiration and crawled over to make friends with Aunt Bee.

"Don't let her be a nuisance," said Beulah Warren.

"Dat honeychile, she sure thrive on attentions," beamed the Negro nurse.

"The Warren womenfolks always been spoiled," the Major admitted. "Seems like they make a cynosure out of 'em even befo' they wear smallclothes."

"Major, you hush yo' mouth," said Mrs. Warren amiably, dropping into the family dialect which Aunt Bee found so puzzling.

"Maybe I don't mean cynosure, I mean sinecure." Siesta and a slug of rum in his iced tea had made the Major specially genial. "It's what they call Suthren chivalry, Miz Bee. We put the ladies on a pedestal until they likely to take sunstroke. Admiration's like juleps. Breakfast time you don't want to hear of 'em again, but come sundown you start to hanker."

With the alertness of a watchful host he could see that this Dixie talk was bewildering to Miss Barton. "Push Baby Trundle away," he said, and reached under his chair. "I've got a surprise for you. Here's the famous Album."

"You brought it outdoors?" exclaimed Mrs. Warren. "Gracious, don't spill anything on it. Usually he keeps it locked up in the safe," she explained to Aunt Bee. "It used to be on the drawing-room desk but a terrible thing happened, we had a wild Western poet staying here, he was lecturing at the University, and he wrote in the book without being asked. After that the Major always keeps it hidden."

The Major carefully removed glasses of tea and the decanter of rum, jam pots, sandwiches and other hazards. He spread a napkin on the iron table and laid the faded green and gold volume open to the sun. "I thought the old book would like a breath of fresh air. I don't suppose it's been outdoors since Grasmere, if then." Affectionately he turned over pages of elderly hairline script. "You see, Miss Bee, Hartley Coleridge gave it to Tullius Teackle, my father, way back in '35. Those were the great days of albums."

"Bee's a connoisseur of albums and scrapbooks," said Dan. "She has one of her own that she studies more than she ever did Fox's *Journal*."

Bee was never quick to show her inward light: she remained placid, but a peculiar ghost of distant things seemed to rise to her from the handwritten pages. Uncle Dan pointed to important familiar names but these were not what impressed her. The sloping gray curve of the Thorofare was in mirage before her; a familiar dark green door just beyond the bend; an iron knocker and the polished brass letter-slot—the Family Knock, the door opening to the dearly remembered vista, a passageway of shadow, and geraniums and sunlight in the back kitchen.

"Do you mind if I smell it?" she said.

"Good for you," the Major assented. "That's what I always do."

"It smells just like those fresh-water poets," said Uncle Dan, "a little musty." He did not really mean this, he was just excited.

"I think it's Dorothy Wordsworth's homemade paste that savors so queer," said Mrs. Warren.

Aunt Bee bent her face to the pages. It took a moment to get over her homesickness. "She used too much flour," she said. "Or else she was in a hurry and didn't stir out the lumps. Unless you mix well it gets mouldy."

"Dorothy was always in a hurry," said the Major, "but God, Ma'am, you're right smart to deduce that from the smell of her stickum. They had a wonderful time fixing up this album for the young American. Is yours the same kind of thing? If all your Wilford Wits wrote in it, it must be quite a collection?"

"Oh, no, mine's quite different," she said. "Mine isn't an Album at all, it's a Commonplace Book."

"Magnificent!" cried the Major. "Most girls of your generation don't know the difference." Aunt Bee sat up very straight and drank some iced tea (which she didn't like) to conceal her pleasure. "Of co'se technically this isn't quite an Album. Some of the morsels had to be pasted in. Poor Tullius Teackle was so grieved not to be able to pay his respects to old Sam and some of the others, Uncle Hartley got Miss Dorothy to paste in a lot of scraps they had. But don't you love Hartley's dedication? What I like about it is he marks his triple rhyme with a bracket, the way they always did." He read the lines aloud:

> "When this fair volume, like an honour'd fane,⎫
> Or holy tomb of Saint, or Martyr slain ⎬
> In Truth's defense, or virgin void of stain, ⎭
> With gems of verse from many a region brought
> Shall gleam effulgent with untainted thought,

Then my wild words, that like bewilder'd chimes
Limp into tune, and stumble upon rhymes
May prompt some voice in tones acute to ask
To whom was given, or who usurp'd the task
To set, 'mid other Bards' melodious strains,
This product of his own fantastic brains?

HARTLEY COLERIDGE,
Grasmere, 1835

Everybody was supposed to write poetry, but I think Miss Dorothy was getting a bit queer in her head by then. She put in her recipe for Statesman's Pudding."

"Statesman's Pudding?" asked Aunt Bee. "Is that the same as Cabinet Pudding?"

"That's a cute guess," said the Major. "No, statesman was a Lakers' word for the farmers or dalesmen, people who had their own small estates."

"It's what we call Shepherd's Pie," said Aunt Bee, looking at the recipe.

"Daddy Wordsworth played a low trick on Tullius Teackle," said the Major. "He used to tell me how the old man sat down and spouted him a poem right out of his head, and then years later we found it in one of his books. He was a bit of an old fraud by that time. What a great poet he'd have been if he died at the age of thirty. Poor Tullius Teackle, he was an idolater. He was terribly disappointed when they took him for a picnic, ginger beer and bannocks, up on the hillside near Kirkstone Pass. My poor Governor tagged along with old Daddy thinking he was going to hear some literature. The old fellow sat down on a rock and studied the landscape long enough to trail some pretty good clouds of glory, but all he did was rumble up ginger beer and then say, 'Don't forget about those railway shares.' "

"He must have been a dreadful old man, and you're another," said Mrs. Warren. Even Baby Trundle on the rug gurgled a little and they wiped off her bubbles with a napkin.

"Uncle Hartley said Dorothy shouldn't have used Sam Coleridge's recipe for ginger beer. It was sure to be too gassy."

"Perhaps he forgot the tartar emetic?"

Uncle Dan felt that perhaps Aunt Bee was not showing the Album its due reverence. "I dare say Hartley was really the best of the lot," he said.

"I wonder where the boys are?" asked Mrs. Warren.

"Their tea will get cold if they don't come soon," said Aunt Bee. Uncle Dan realized from this touch of irony that his sister was beginning to feel at home.

"Likely they don't care for any tea," said the Major. "I suspect they're off somewhere smoking co'nsilk cigarettes. I reckon young Geoffrey might as well learn his deviltry now as later. You're right, Sir, about Hartley. Sometimes I think he was the finest gentleman I ever knew, except maybe Robert E. Lee. Did I ever tell you I took a message to General Lee one time? We didn't exactly meet on sociable terms because he was on horseback and I was in the slough. He was so much concerned about that message he didn't even look at me, but I stroked Traveler's nose. I calculate Traveler could read, too, because he tried to bite me."

There was a yell of laughter from behind the hedge and the two boys burst upon them. "Why did you stroke the traveler on the nose?" asked Geoffrey.

"Traveler was a horse," said the Major. "How long have you rascals been eavesdropping?"

"Fruit cake!" Teackle exclaimed. "With frosting!"

"Plum cake!" said Geoffrey. "With icing!"

"We've been getting an education," said Teackle through a mouthful.

"It doesn't seem to have done you much good," said his mother. "Don't turn your back on the guests."

"I beg your pardon, Ma'am," said Teackle politely, "but if everybody sits in a circle, how can I help it?"

184

"You better make up your minds are you laughing or eating cake," said the Major. "Keep away from that Album."

"Teackle said you told him the best way to get educated was to listen to grown-ups talking," cried Geoffrey, wriggling with glee. "We listened carefully."

"It sounded like a lot of darned old nonsense," said Teackle.

"Fantastic brains," quoted Geoffrey with a yell of laughter, and they were dismissed just in time.

"I was afraid Teackle would be a bad influence," said Mrs. Warren. "He's just like his father, if anything strikes him comical he loses all sense of decency."

"On the contrary," said the Major, "I think it's a great tribute to my theory of education by accident. It's the first time anything I've said ever made any impression. I was telling him that Uncle Hartley said the best education he ever got was listening to those poets talking."

"About railway shares," said Mrs. Warren.

The Major winked at Uncle Dan. "No, he was remembering afternoons at Southey's house in Keswick. They'd all turn up there for a good meal, then poor old Southey would retire to his study to work, while the rest of them sat out in the garden and cut the pages of his books with butter knives."

"I always like black currant jelly better because Keats spilled some of it on a copy of Ben Jonson, when he was ill and taking his meals in bed. He said he tried to lick it off but it still left a stain."

"You're making me very nervous about the Album," said Aunt Bee. She carefully brushed cake crumbs away from it.

"I think Dorothy Wordsworth's recipe for pudding is more touching than most of the poetry," said Mrs. Warren. "And so many interesting autographs. It's hard to realize famous people sit down and do handwriting like anyone else."

Bee was turning the pages. "Here's one that looks familiar," she exclaimed. "Why, it's Dan's."

185

"Sure enough," said the Major. "That's why I brought it out. We're very proud of it. Read it aloud."

But Bee was too shy, and she could see at a glance that the lines would trouble her. Major Warren, unconsciously waving time with his cigar, read out in his best voice what Dan had inscribed some years before:

"AN ANGLO-AMERICAN SONNET

We cross the ocean from the well-loved land
Whose glory makes her meanest son feel great
To this vast future, even now elate
With vast achievement: this united band
Of States, each with uplifted youthful hand
To grapple human ills and mend our fate.
We are not suffered to be desolate
Through alien ideals, for there stand
Fair homes whose high delightful courtesies
Outstretch Atlantics and from either shore
Cull what is rarest. Souls refreshed arise
From earnest art and literary lore
And chivalry. Hence larger sympathies
And lives more beautiful for evermore.

"Signed by D. BARTON, *Greenaway*, 1893," continued the Major, who had delivered the lines with such gravity that his own eyes felt hot. "Yes, Sir, a very handsome sentiment; it would have tickled old Hartley. If you ladies give us leave, I'll put the book back in the house, and I want to show Dan something out in the paddock. You remember that spirited little mare Dido? She's coming with foal; she was joined in stable marriage, *connubio stabili*, like the goddess said to Aeolus."

"I wish you didn't have to go," said the Major as they waited at the little Greenaway station for the evening train.

"Will it be Pa or Ma?" asked Geoffrey.

"It'll be Ma on her way home," said the Major. "They don't

think it's wise for her to stay out all night. Teackle, show Geoffrey how we flag the train. It's too bad this is the only way to get back to town, I was just beginning to feel communicative. Sometimes I think we should start our breakfasts at midnight. That's when elderly people like me begin to get loquacious."

"Like De Quincey," said Uncle Dan. "When they gave him a dinner party, one of Christopher North's *noctes ambrosianae,* they timed it so the dessert would come on about 3 A.M. because that was when the Opium Eater's conversation began to flourish. By the way, Major, I noticed in the Apery one of your volumes of De Quincey is missing."

"Well, I should say so," said the Major, "Tullius Teackle destroyed that volume. He said no gentleman would have it in his library, all the unmannerly things De Quincey wrote about the Lake Poets. I give you my word, Sir, that story about old Parson Coleridge and the shirt-tail was a humiliation to Uncle Hartley all his life. Of co'se I laugh like a fool when I think about it, but as Mrs. Warren has told you, I'm not a gentleman in the old-fashioned sense."

"What was funny about the shirt-tail?" asked Teackle, but just then Ma blew for the forest curve and her headlight dazzled down the track.

Geoffrey was lively with notions on the way home. "What happens to a sun-dial at night?" But Uncle Dan and Aunt Bee were in a meditative mood. It was never urgent to answer Jeff's inquiries, he could always find another one. "They didn't have any apostle spoons," he said. "Why did they have a picture of Brer Rabbit on the spoons?"

"That's what they call a crest," said Uncle Dan. "You see the name Warren has something to do with rabbits. Probably in the beginning Major Warren's family took care of the King's rabbits, what they used to call a warrener."

"He didn't take care of them very well. There was a dog biting the rabbit. I saw it on the ladle."

There was silence for a while as Ma rumbled down the valley, but Geoffrey was still reviewing the observations of the day.

"I claimed most of Greenaway for Jeffland," he said. "I think there'd be room enough to put it in that new state I invented, the one called Westernland. I could do like Washington, D. C., and make it a district, the District of Greenaway."

"You can write a nice long letter to the aunts in Wilford and tell them all about it," said Aunt Bee. "What part didn't you claim?"

"The slave quarters, they're full of bad ventilation. Mutual showed me where one of his fathers lived. They use it now to smoke hams. Why did Mutual carry a rabbit's foot in his pocket? Was he one of the warreners?"

"It sounds to me you got a young catechism on your hands," remarked an amused stranger from the seat behind them. "I can answer that one, Bud. In the old times when the slaves ran away and hid out in the woods they used to throw the dogs off the scent by rubbing fresh rabbit on their feet. That's why they superstition rabbit's foot means luck."

Geoffrey pondered this. "It wasn't very lucky for the rabbit," he said.

The long and many-colored strangeness of the day was now enclosing Geoffrey in secrecies of his own. After all the world is too rich for continuous comment. Draughts of air like warm milk sprinkled with soot rippled his sailor blouse as he tried to look out of the window. There were strange gigantic shapes of freight cars on the Northern Central sidings, men with lanterns in the dark, a large gauze-winged locust, big as a Wilford wren, squashed in the corner of the sill (not even his fingernails could unglue it) and as they slowed into the city the humble exhalation of Jones's Falls.

"When you used to talk about Jones's Falls," said Aunt Bee sadly, "I imagined something like Niagara. Come, Geoffrey, this is where we get out— Geoffrey! Don't tell me you've gone to sleep hanging out of the window."

But Geoffrey wasn't asleep, he was thinking that rabbits have a hard time. "Is George Fox the same as Brer Fox?" he asked.

Aunt Bee was weary and perhaps a little cross. "Certainly not," she replied, hauling him down the aisle.

"I think I shall write to Aunt Blanche," said Geoffrey.

He made just one more remark as he was pushed into bed. "Let's go to the greengrocer and buy a pumpkin—I mean punkin. Teackle told me about jack-o'-lanterns. I think Americans have some very good ideas."

38. "Ya-a-y, English!"

It was a long walk from 1910 down to Mr. Bolton's school. "In Jeffland," Jeff said one morning at the breakfast table, "boys get to school without walking. There's a kind of dirgable balloon picks them up and takes them there in the twinkling of an eye. It works with pedals like a Columbia bicycle, a hundred and twenty-five plunks."

Not Uncle Dan, not even Aunt Bee, could properly gloss this tightly condensed statement. It was said in the early days before Jeff and Skinny had learned to walk down to school together for mutual defense.

The direct route to Bolton's led past P.S. 16, whose hostile tribes gathered in great numbers just at the time when the President of Jeffland was on his way. Was it the still-enduring K-boots that annoyed them? was it the Wilford Norfolk jacket (with the Eton collars which Aunt Bee thought must be worn out)? was it the pink cheeks of East Anglia? Not even imagining those tribes as Indians, Boers or Spaniards softened the humiliation of their onset. Sometimes the traveler took a long detour (thinking that at least the added mileage would wear down the soles of K) but even so, at some apparently peaceful corner rose the shrill two-fingered whistle, the patter of pursuing feet (so lightly, swiftly shod), the mocking hateful cry, "Ya-a-y, English! C'mon, kids." Stones or snowballs filled the air, and even flight was vain. Evidently to Spike McMechan and his gang of "Mount Royals" there seemed something peculiarly offensive about the bare knees of Jeffland or the drizzling brown eyes of LaGrange. Unconsciously the roving Mount Royals carried on the ancient traditions of Chesapeake hooligans. They were only once thoroughly routed. Aunt Bee was shopping at the North Avenue market when she saw Jeff and Skinny, unarmed, chivvied to despair by a group with hockey sticks. Rushing forth with umbrella and a head of cabbage, she hurled the vegetable like a grenade, and laid about fiercely with the other weapon. The enemy dispersed in shocked amazement. Even her Quaker conscience never reproached Aunt Bee for this militarism; what startled her most was that the widowed mother of the smitten McMechan called on her later and thanked her for what she had done.

Perhaps this was one of Jeff's first realizations of rich social irony: he and Skinny were persecuted in the outside world for being mollycoddles; and reproached at home for being rough.

If one were morbid to analyze grievance in its private multiples one might report the episode of the lunch box. Rulers of imaginary countries are keenly sensitive to carry the particular model of equipment fashionable in their own era. No matter how beautifully Aunt Bee packed a lunch in wrapping paper, the sturdy package was an embarrassment. So after many pleadings and suggestions the collapsible lunch box was acquired, a folding case of plaid-pattern tin. It gave a faintly metallic taste to the strongest pickles or peanut butter; after recess it was folded flat and fitted easily into the bundle of books noosed in a strap. Then one day the President came home without it. "I lost it," was his only explanation. That was a lie, but like any gallant falsehood it was worth sticking to. Only by watching the

Mount Royals of P.S. 16 at their lunch would the fate of the tartan box have been known.

Everything looked terribly big in those days. A citizen of I Class (so it was always written), the lowest grade at Mr. Bolton's, would notice it specially in the black-stockinged legs of schoolmates thundering upstairs in the changes from room to room. The tough Shawbuck brothers, for instance: how bulging and muscular their balustrade calves looked in the tight breeches of that time. A President or a Rajah took only small consolation in the existence of the primary department, pitiful Lilliputians whose existence was ignored; they carried on a dwarfish career in a room of their own presided upon (humiliation indeed!) by women; their shrill voices were overheard in unison chanting, the walls of their classroom embellished with pictures of lamentable childishness, birds and flowers and infantile blears in color. They might as well have been girls.

But on the stairs of the main school or on the pebbly playground beside the gym were larger creatures of atrocious vigor: voices that suddenly slipped from shrill to bass, and even swarthy cheeks overdue for the razor. The marble (striped, or milky agate) sped with brio from those hard and grimy thumbs, the football spiraled off the saddle of the foot with the tight boom that means mastery. The Shawbucks had a catcher's mask and mitt of their own; they were a battery in themselves and made signals. If the spectators were young enough Bill Shawbuck could throw a perceptible curve. It thudded into the hollow of the mitt, and admiring whisper said, "Gee, an Out Drop!" If such powerful persons occasionally faltered in class, prudent small fry did not too quickly raise the responsive hand.

There were even more Olympian profiles on higher levels, giants of V and VI who got off early for track practice. They were seen hairy in the showers or with ribbons of the school colors on their white running pants. Strange diagrams left on blackboards showed that Mr. Bolton was harrying them for a far-off mystery called College Entrance. One was even seen in the candy store on Cardinal Street smoking a pipe—and entered for the Interscholastic pole vault too. What a pity, Jeff thought, there was no system of fagging as in *Tom Brown:* it would be glorious to run errands for such heroes. But these were of another world entirely.

Though wise as anyone is likely to be (within the limit of individual wisdom) even Aunt Bee could not guess all the overtones of that remark about the dirgable balloon. Uncle Dan sidestepped the allusion to the costly Columbia bicycle (advertised in *Puck* every week) by explaining the adjective *dirigible*. It didn't take long for the correction to travel from Jeff to Skinny. "Not dirgable, you chump; it's dirigible; means you can steer it."

It was nice, Bee thought, that uncle and nephew set off for work together. Dan used to groan because he had an 8:30 class five mornings a week, but really he enjoyed it. In the clarity of the early hour it was satisfying to walk a few easy blocks arranging in mind the familiar, sometimes too familiar, précis of the lecture which docile nymphs will take down in ill-favored script. Their unquestioning minds would receive as gospel such lucid simplification of literature's complex woe. God forgive the teacher (poor Uncle Dan would mumble in his safety valves) who thinks to triumph in (a) and (b) and (c) over the blood stream and anguish of art. And thinking so he would hear Aunt Bee on the steps of morning marble: "Now hold up your heads, both of you." She smiled with a Thorofare grimness to see her two children set off down Carroll Street with chin on breast. But Uncle Dan was rehearsing English VIII, Jeff perhaps plotting a new detour to avoid P.S. 16. As they approached North Avenue Jeff would say, "Are you thinking of your lecture?" If Uncle Dan said "Yes," that meant this was the end of convoy. And Uncle Dan, concerned with the problems of an ideal community which had ceased to exist even in fancy one hundred years before, turned back to the classrooms of Patapsco and delivered the Republic of Jeffland, an ideal community in being, to the wolves of Today.

The only salvage Jeff ever brought home from various scuffles with Spike McMechan and his gang was a copy of a textbook *History of the United States.* Frenzied by the loss of the tartan lunch box Jeff grabbed whatever he could in retaliation and carried the book home with him. Uncle Dan was mystified when he discovered it, bearing the rubber stamp *City of Chesapeake, Property of the Board of Education.* In idle curiosity he began to read. He soon realized that the young hoodlums of North Avenue were hardly to be blamed for their instinctive suspicion of Geoffrey if by any chance they regarded him as the successor of the British invaders to whom so many crimes were attributed. He understood now what lay behind the boy's remark, "I shall be very relieved when we finish American History."

"Why so?" Uncle Dan asked. "It's extremely interesting."

"Yes, but the redcoats are always brutal, and the boys take it out on me. If the English got licked so many times before it seems too bad it has to be done all over again. Now the kids have invented a game called Hissing the Hessians. They make a noise like snakes."

Uncle Dan supposed that maybe these ancient sneers existed only in the reading allotted to the public schools, but he found the same trend in the history used at Mr. Bolton's. The tale was further enlivened by vigorous woodcuts illustrating the unerring marksmanship of the farmers at Concord, or the invaders' bombs bursting in air at Fort McHenry but always falling clumsily short. The city of Chesapeake, he had noticed in more ways than one, was imbued with ferocious patriotism, perhaps partly due to a certain uneasiness in its own breast for having been on both sides at once in the War Between the States. It was always surprising to his observant spirit to find within a few blocks of each other on the same boulevard (but fortunately looking different ways) imposing monuments in honor of both North and South. These two statues perhaps canceled each other in the all-seeing eye, but Jeff's favorite was left over. This was the white marble edification below which the poet is tossing on concrete billows in a concrete dinghy, and a boatman rests on concrete oars to admire the composition of the anthem. This composition so fascinated Jeff that he once climbed the thwart and wrote with pencil on the empty scroll, "Oh, say can you see. . . ." It was generous of the boy to be so keen about this monument since the legend of Fort McHenry had cost him much pain.

Uncle Dan pondered this matter from time to time. It seemed a pity to foster in a new generation, even a new century, these partisan memories of ancient ill. One evening the rugged Mr. Bolton himself came to pay a call and asked Professor Barton if he were satisfied with his nephew's progress in school. This gave Uncle Dan an opportunity to raise the question in his mind. Mr. Bolton's own subjects were mathematics and science and he confessed himself honestly surprised at the jingo tone of the approved historians. He promised to remember the suggestion in choosing textbooks for the ensuing year but pointed out that much more power was exerted in the public schools where the enrollment was a hundred times larger. This accounted for Uncle Dan's innocent pilgrimage some time later to call on the Board of Education. With Spike McMechan's grimy volume as marked evidence he passed among the impressive graphs and charts with which school superintendents adorn their corridors and found himself courteously received. A young man was sitting with the educator, and seemed so interested in their discussion that he begged permission to stay. Uncle Dan, always disarmed by politeness, assumed that the other visitor was also a teacher and spoke with unguarded candor. Even the most careful professional acquaintance with *Spectator* or *Rambler* or the pamphlets of Dilly and Dodsley does not necessarily prepare one for the humors of modern journalism. The Board of Education, after warily ascertaining that Professor Barton represented only himself and not any large contingent of taxpayers, evaded the issue with noncommittal ease; but the young man happened to be a reporter. The shock was like sickness when unsuspecting Uncle Dan opened the next day's afternoon paper:

REDCOATS NOT ALL BRUTAL SAYS PATAPSCO PROF

ENGLISH TEACHER RESENTS SLURS ON BRITAIN

CALLS NORTH AVENUE BOYS TRIBE OF BOERS

His ten-year-old nephew Jeff (who used to spell it Geoff) has to fight Lexington, Concord, Yorktown and Fort McHenry all over again, to say nothing of Spion Kop, says Associate Prof. Daniel Barton of the English department at Patapsco. The Prof attributes the troubles of young Jeff, bright-faced English laddie, to the crude prejudice with which American schoolbooks are written. As a specialist in the literature of the eighteenth century Prof. Barton believes that American textbooks are unfair to the Tories of 1776, and that sometimes even the embattled farmers did not draw a perfect bead.

"Why throw good blood after bad?" asked the Prof, registering a dignified complaint yesterday at the office of the Board of Education. "It seems to me we are setting the children's teeth on edge even unto the third and fourth generation. The Boers are bad enough in South Africa without setting up a lager on North Avenue."

Prof. Barton was speaking with British humor, and was not alluding to North Avenue's excellent beerstubes. He bids us reread Edwin Burke and says a great deal of unnecessary ill-feeling is caused by the textbook industry perpetuating shallow views. Prof. Barton is a mild-mannered Quaker, but his eyes flashed with indignation as he insisted it ought not to be necessary for a boy to fight his way to school with brass knuckles. He showed a number of marked pages in Wainscott's *History of the United States* alleged to indicate undue severity toward the regi-

195

ments of George III. Mr. P. J. Guldensuppe, local manager of the Middle Atlantic Book Company, says, "We have distributed over a million copies of Wainscott's *History* in the state of Maryland and no one has ever protested before. Chesapeake University is the acknowledged headquarters of American historical scholarship. It seems strange that we have heard no such complaint from the faculty of the larger institution."

Scholars have long memories, it is difficult for them to realize the swift evaporation of newspaper fumes. Even the cheerful young reporter who thought this just one more amusing story in a day's work, an unexpected windfall worth half a column of space, would have been genuinely dismayed to realize how much suffering it caused. But like many unmerited or casual sorrows it brought certain blessings in aftermath. It is true that Dr. Friedeck chuckled when he read it, but there were others, including the Superintendent, who resented the jocularity. The absurd and painful incident roused some lovers of fair play; it helped Dan, later, to recognize the true character of the Town itself, home of music and learning and kind manners.

39. Reading Aloud

"In the city of Chihuahua" (pronounced by the reader in five syllables), "for the most part built of mud . . . overtopped by bald, porphyritic mountains . . . some score of objects . . . tresses of hair . . . *stripped from human skulls.*" Aunt Bee repressed an inward qualm. In fair play, she had to. The understanding was that if Geoff read aloud a chapter from some book chosen by her, he could follow it by a selection of his own.

"Is there very much like that?" she asked.

"Aw, doggone it, that's only the first page."

She resigned herself to the ordeal. Captain Mayne Reid seemed to her much more painful than anything by Thomas Hardy; but the volume bore the bookplate of the Friends' First-

Day School Library and had evidently been thumbed by many young Quakers. The reader was not even dismayed by various ejaculations in Spanish: unconsciously he rose with clenched fist and caballero pride shouting, *"Gringo! Alto el sombrero!"* Imperfect Castilian was covered by the vigor of the performance. Even while trying not to pay attention to the text Aunt Bee could not help glancing at the boy's excited face. Extraordinary, she thought to herself; if he had a tomahawk in his hand he'd scalp me, just to be lifelike.

She allowed the ferocities of Mayne Reid to flow past her, keeping her mind in its own stronghold. The Cozy Corner in the front bedroom upstairs was her fortress. Sitting there she could see the life of Carroll Street reflected in the duplex mirror (outside the window frame) which Dan had thought would be entertainment for her. Actually in that corner by the hot-air register she was more likely to think back to the Thorofare. Over the settee she had hung the old Wilford photographs—a family picnic in the Meadow, a view of the River with Harry Bredfield waving from the cockpit of the *Scandal*, and Geoff's cherished picture of Miss Debbidge with her arm round the neck of a stone deer. The old sewing cabinet was there, rosewood marquetry now crumbling under the hot blast of the register. The ivory darning egg was there and the old ebony muffin-stand—which should have been downstairs but it got cracked in the hold of the *Westernland*. It was useful on those private occasions when Aunt Bee consoled herself with what she called a Wilford tea. There were moments of nostalgia when only a cup of very strong tea in Thorofare china and a slice of buttered bread cut platonically thin would serve as anaesthetic. But Graham bread was no substitute for Hovis, and the hundreds and thousands, if attainable at all, were so much bigger that Uncle Dan called them tens and hundreds.

She came back from reverie to perceive that Geoffrey was breaking the rules. "That's not fair," she said. "You've started another chapter."

"Aw gee, just one paragraph. It's slick. . . . 'The young Kentuckian was half frenzied by the insult, the proud blood of his Republican citizenship was boiling within his veins.'"

Aunt Bee reflected that a few pages of Mayne Reid had quite canceled the benefit of the previous reading, which was *Cranford*. She was always amazed by these sudden transformations. She would overhear a voice in the street which she scarcely recognized as her nephew's. Then came the crash of the front door, the thump of a strapful of books flung down, and up the back stairs came forceful dialogue cozening refreshment from the colored cook in unblemished Uncle Remus. Reading *Cranford* he reverted to what she called the Queen's English; if the book he chose for his turn was his own favorite *Three Men in a Boat* he produced from somewhere a counter-jumper cockney. If *Hiawatha*, he gave her as appetizer a supposedly Indian ululation created by patting a mouthful of wailing vowels. Now Mayne Reid had put him back into the dialect of Bolton's.

"Is the book all about scalps?" asked Aunt Bee. "By the way, when you happen to take a bath, please wash your ears."

"Wait till you get to Chapter 9, that's something fierce, 'a spectacle of fiendish spite.' Those Indians are mighty ornery." He closed the book with a satisfying snap and glanced at the outside mirror. "Cheezit, here comes Do-re-mi Beamish. Aw gee, 23 for her."

"Geoffrey, I don't mind what you say, if you wouldn't always precede it by 'Aw gee.' I'd really prefer it if you'd be honestly blasphemous and say 'Oh God.'"

Jeff was shocked and hastened to continue, "Has she got to take tea with the nobility? She'll be mad because I didn't do my practice. Get the hook, it ain't my turn anyhow, it's Uncle Dan's." He rushed from the room, slid swiftly down the banisters and before Aunt Bee had verified the image in the busybody she heard the simple chords of *Dorothy, Old English Dance* beaten lustily on the piano below.

Miss Beamish, a simple soul from the Music Department at

Patapsco, had been one of Aunt Bee's stratagems. Disturbed by violent renditions of *Bill Bailey, Won't You Please Come Home?* or *Goodbye Dolly Gray,* Aunt Bee considered that piano lessons and a few traditional melodies of the nursery might have softening effect. Geoffrey was dour about this until, to his surprise, Uncle Dan volunteered to take lessons also. He averred that he had always wished to play the piano, and the boy was stimulated by this unexpected rivalry. It had its embarrassments, though, for instance when President and Mrs. Beinbrink, of Patapsco College, arrived unexpectedly while Uncle Dan was conscientiously doing his exercises. The Professor of English felt sheepish at being discovered by his employer pounding with heavy fingers at *The Spider and the Fly* and *The North Wind Doth Blow.* He hastily called Geoffrey to take the piano stool, but when Mrs. Beinbrink said, "I was so glad to hear your little boy practising his tunes," Geoffrey could not control himself. "I can't tell a lie, that was Uncle Dan. You should hear him do *The Happy Farmer,* it's fierce."

Except on the keyboard Miss Beamish's resources were meager and Geoffrey had never forgotten her guileless inquiry when she first came to tea: "Are you related to the nobility?" But though naive, Miss Beamish was persevering. Jeff startled Aunt Bee by exclaiming, "She's like Jim Bludso, she'll hold her nozzle agin the bank till the last galoot's ashore."

40. Uncle Dan Considers the Ideal Community

One problem of scholarship is that the research student rarely finds a table large enough for his needs. Sometimes, late at night, when the little desk upstairs was littered with college work, Uncle Dan brought his special studies down to the dining-room. The secret dream—the work on Susquehanna and other utopian communities in America—involved much allusion and cross-reference. The dining-room table, he pretended, was the best place to spread out, but perhaps its neighborhood to the icebox in the pantry (Aunt Bee still called it the larder) had influence too. In an ancient threadbare dressing-gown, beard kinked sideways where he had leaned chin on fist over piles of sophomore scribble, he laid out his mosaic of learned patchwork with no less happiness than a Rajah of LaGrange mapping new provinces. Consecutively assorted were the heavy tomes toted from libraries, the indexed clippings and scraps of notes, the box of file cards (America's chief contribution to scholarship, he sometimes thought) and the old marmalade pot filled with colored pencils. In his Codex, his master-text, all quotations from Coleridge were marked in red, from Wordsworth in green; De Quincey was purple, Hazlitt yellow, Keats a heavenly blue; Dan had his own logical spectrum in these matters.

He strolled several times round the table, looking askance at Wordsworth or Southey; or maybe shoved Hazlitt to a more commanding position. It was spring, the sudden violent April of Chesapeake when the oyster yields to the soft-shell crab and even frugal Aunt Bee had brought home an armful of daffodils from market. She was shocked when the colored maid Moxie called them "buttercups." Wordsworth himself, Dan mused, would have been shocked by the tragic swiftness of a middle Atlantic spring; even at Greenaway the daffodils were shriveled in a few days by untimely heat and drought. Was that one of the oddities of the American temper, such haste in all transitions? Dan was thinking of a different kind of soft and gradual opening; the Great Spring of 1797, where in a sense his own participation in literature began. It was all clear in his imagination. He saw a queer-looking young fellow run down a lane of honeysuckle in the dusk, vault a gate and hurry across a field to shorten the way. That was at Racedown, in Dorset—Racedown, just what the young pilgrim did—and honeysuckle too: he on honeydew hath fed—for the young man running was Sam Coleridge, on his way to meet William and Dorothy Wordsworth. Even William, the human metronome, was young then. That was the beginning of the Susquehanna dream; and even the beginning of a new kind of poetry. How easy it is to see Beginnings if you're far enough away. Sam and William skipped like minnows in a Turning Tide, he thought; with Dorothy for the perfect audience.

He lit his pipe and sat down to the manuscript. About the second paragraph the tobacco went out and he realized he was hungry. One of his bachelor discoveries had been that great American triumph, condensed milk. Aunt Bee was suspicious of it, but Dan was allowed to keep a can for his midnight snack. Cocoa made with condensed milk, with heels of stale bread cut into strips and dipped were his simple weakness. Scattered brown splashes on papers or dressing-gown testified his peaceful absorption. It was not a scene to please esthetes, but few students have come closer to the cloudland of Kubla than Uncle Dan in those innocent sittings. "At least it's better than laudanum," he said when reproved.

But like laudanum his milk of paradise led to slumber. He was more than half asleep, and at the same time doubting if he was doing justice to Dorothy, when Aunt Bee came downstairs in a mood of concern.

It must be a really disturbing anxiety before Bee broke in upon her brother's meditations. There was probably a little conscious selfishness in the way he had encouraged her to believe his periods of musing were always of delicate import. There were moments of mere idleness when, assisted by his beard, he could assume an air of introspect which Bee took to be the aura of creation. She would say, "Are you thinking?" He was too honorable to lie, but he used a kind of grunt that implied it. This time however he was caught; he woke with a start and spilled some cocoa.

"I thought you were Dorothy Wordsworth," he said.

"I don't believe you were thinking at all." She mopped up the puddle with a sheet of blotting paper. "There was so much noise in the breadbox it woke me up."

"It must have been mice."

201

"Happen it was a two-legged mouse."

"They ought to make breadboxes that don't have so much echo."

"Then I looked for my scissors to do some sewing. I see you've got them down here."

"I borrowed them from Jeff. He had them to cut out soldiers."

"A woman can't sleep until she knows her scissors have come home. Now you're awake too, you might as well listen to me. I'm worried about Jeff."

"You wouldn't believe what trouble Coleridge's father had with his children," said Dan vaguely. "I've got a note about it here somewhere. People in ideal communities always did, I dessay. What about Jeff? I don't see anything wrong?"

"You don't notice, you're not here when he comes home from school. You wouldn't know it's the same boy. Why, he even talks a different language, he and Bert Eutaw come in the back way from the alley and bother Moxie for something to eat, they hang round the yard and sing those terrible songs about Coon, Coon, Coon, and Bill Bailey, I'm afraid she'll give notice. Then there's that gang of Oriole Boys from round the corner, you know they have some sort of feud with Jeff and his friends. They swarmed over the fence to try to steal the piano box for a bonfire. They had it half out of the yard and then Jeff and Bert gave their Cry of Despair and *their* friends came rushing down the alley and the first thing you know there was a pitched battle. If it hadn't been for Moxie running out with a broom and the huckster drove down the alley just about then and took a hand, I don't know what would have happened. I can't understand what's become of the boy, he's a perfect little hoodlum. Is it those funny pictures that he reads in the paper on Sunday, or what? The parents of these other boys seem to be pleasant enough people but their children go rowdying every night. After all, you're a college professor and Jeff goes to that expensive school and I thought he was going to grow up like a gentleman."

Dan was surprised by this unusually long speech from Aunt Bee, but it had given him time to rally. With the timid prudence of the philosopher he would not admit that he had been worried by similar thoughts; he took refuge in a side issue.

"Moxie knows the boys don't mean anything," he said. "She and Jeff get along wonderfully. I was amused the other day when I overheard them in the kitchen. When he discovered she doesn't know how to read he decided to take her in hand and what do you think he was doing, he was reading Uncle Remus aloud to her. I heard him say that I don't read it properly and he was getting her to pronounce things for him the way Uncle Remus would. You know, that's real scholarship."

"But he's such a little tough. There must be some decent boys at Mr. Bolton's school but when he comes home he talks like a bargee. I don't like to bother you about such things but sometimes I wonder if you know what's going on. Because you teach in a college for girls you think everybody is as gentle and sweet as they are. I'm afraid you only see Jeff when he's on his good behavior."

Dan's habitual grunt had a little more groan in it that time. Even a professor at a college of women may be aware of surface tensions. He stifled the obvious retort that Aunt Bee only saw his students at their most demure when they were invited to Sunday tea.

"Listen, Bee," he said, "maybe you don't realize what the boy has been up against the past two years. It's our fault, too. When we got here we tried to keep him a nice little English boy, he went to that dame-school until he was ready for Bolton's, then all of a sudden we threw him into a big American school. You can't run with tigers unless you wear stripes, and the first thing he had to do was to learn to be like everyone else. Otherwise they'd tear him to bits. You remember how that gang down on Joppa Street used to lay for him when he was on his way to school. Remember the time he said it's lucky he only had two eyes because you can't get more than two of them black. When they were both black already, they kicked him in the stomach. Poor kid, it's worse than Mowgli learning to live with the wolves, and I think it's wonderful how he's developed his own hide and horns. Wolves don't have horns but you know what I mean. I think it's fine for a while if he gets completely swamped in America. When the time comes he'll react against it his own way."

"He's swamped all right," said Bee, and the very tread of her feet as she returned upstairs was definite with indignation.

"That's the most American-sounding thing I ever heard Bee say," Dan thought. Looking over his array of notes he realized perhaps clearer than ever that none of the problems of ideal Susquehanna had yet been solved. God help the artist, he thought, who must forever be in his surroundings but never of them. If for an instant he succumbs to acceptance his vision is forfeit; and yet how cunningly he must seem to agree.

On an already crowded slip of paper he wrote and underlined *In but not of*, knowing as he did so that he wouldn't remember later what at this moment he perfectly understood. Let's go to bed, he said, and the " 's" meant both himself and Coleridge.

41. Lexington Market

J. William Sprunt, Choice Quality Meats, would have been surprised to know that his name had been borrowed for an important settlement in the western prairies of Jeffland. Sprunt City was the leading beef market of the pioneer province Westernland, which looked in imagination rather like something from Mayne Reid; it was the center of a Staked Plain, which Jeff interpreted as the place the steak comes from. Mr. Sprunt, who had spent his whole life in old Lexington Market, might well have carried an endorsement on his signboard: "By Special Warrant, Purveyor to the President of Jeffland."

Going downtown to market with Aunt Bee became a joyous tradition. As a dog capers with anticipation when the leash comes out of the closet, so when Jeff saw the string-bag hanging on the newel-post he knew it meant a trip to Sprunt City. After unsuccessful struggles to explain "brawn" or "silverside" for the butcher on North Avenue, and that merchant's distress when she called his chopped hamburger "cat's meat," Aunt Bee learned from Mrs. Warren of the famous old market downtown. The place was as truly in character for Chesapeake as the Peabody Institute or the Pimlico Track. Here an aristocracy of good digestion shopped for its victuals, choosing shad or birds or berries as a bibliophile would scrutinize first editions. Distinguished gourmets, followed by colored men carrying loaded baskets, chaffered from stall to stall; groups gathered in the crowded passages for sociable chat as at a court levee. Conversations overheard might range from crab gumbo to the Kneisel Quartet.

"Please behave yourself on the tram," Aunt Bee said to Geoffrey as they waited for the trolley on Patapsco Street. She said this to divert him from alluding to her first ride on that line, when she had taken the car on the wrong side and went far afield into the country. Jeff quoted at her a rhyme he heard in school:

"Everything comes to him who waits
If he waits in a place that's meet,
But never wait for a downtown car
On the uptown side of the street."

His own form of misbehavior in street-cars was not intentional bad manners, as he tried to explain. When Aunt Bee saw an angry flush rising on the countenance of a stout lady across the aisle she shrewdly traced it back to Jeff, and saw with dismay that he was accurately reproducing on his own features the unconscious frown and pout of the opposite passenger. Aunt Bee nudged him fiercely. "It's bad enough to stare," she reproached him later, "but it's worse to imitate."

"But why did she do that with her face?" he asked. "I can't tell what people feel like unless I do the same thing."

"Don't bother so much what other people feel like. You attend to yourself."

"It's a habit of mine," said Geoffrey. "I feel sad if I don't know the reason for things. There was a nice little colored boy in the car the other day. He looked like the tar-baby but he was crying. Skinny Granger was with me and he started to cry too, he's very sensitive, but we couldn't understand why the colored boy was crying until we saw there was a boy across the car sticking out his tongue at him. So I stuck out my tongue at Skinny to give *him* an excuse. Why did that other boy stick out his tongue?"

"It was very cruel and saucy of him," said Aunt Bee.

"If it was because the boy was black, it must have taught him a lesson, because the colored boy's tears were perfectly white. Everybody's tears are. If we walk up Terrapin Street to market I can save the transfers. Star Lanvale gives me a very good rate of exchange for transfers—he collects them. For five of them I can borrow his *Youth's Companion* overnight."

There were plenty of distractions along Terrapin Street, but Jeff continued to experiment with the facial misfortunes of street-car passengers. Aunt Bee gave him the traditional warning: "You know if you should sneeze while your face is all screwed up, it will stay that way." Jeff produced a loud hopeful snort, but found his features still plastic. Then they reached the windows of the Great Atlantic and Pacific Tea Company, across from the market. Here the scarlet coffee grinders and lithographed calendars were effectual change of attention.

Aunt Bee used to say that the meat stall of J. William Sprunt was her best training school in American life. Though her purchases were small he never minded explaining the different cuts of meat, illustrating them on a large hanging carcase with the steel from his belt as a pointer. Like butchers on the Thorofare Mr. Sprunt had very pink cheeks with a violet threadwork of

206

veins, and wore a straw hat all the year round. "Perhaps it's because his face is so hot," said Geoffrey; "he thinks it's still summer." Jeff usually begged Aunt Bee to buy something that would involve the use of the saw; the thumping chopper was almost too sudden for comfortable watching. But most of the time at that counter he stood in solemn study of Mr. Sprunt's signboard. It was a large painting of a steer's head, hung above the steelyard scales.

"If you stare so long at that ox's head," said Aunt Bee, "you'll get to look like it."

"I can almost see the horns coming out on your forehead," said Mr. Sprunt. Jeff scuffed his feet in the sawdust in pleased embarrassment. But it was not so much the Front de Boeuf mask that charmed him as a suggestion of broad grazing landscape the artist had sketched as background. It had exactly the feeling and color of Henty and Kirk Munroe and Mayne Reid. A green prairie fading into blue highlands was dotted with beeves; small figures of cowboys rode pintos and twirled lariats. One might naturally suppose it was a panorama of Mr. Sprunt's home. The picture brought two wonderful Mayne Reid words to his mind, pampas and champaigns, but there was something bright and quick in Mr. Sprunt's bantam eye which discouraged too much catechism. Geoffrey had a shrewd habit of getting someone else to ask any question which might sound foolish. So when Skinny came along, also marketing under tuition, Jeff persuaded his friend to inquire.

"I think Mr. Sprunt has a picture of his ranch in the West," he explained. "I bet it's the Texas panhandle, what they call pampas and champaigns. But Aunt Bee says I mustn't ask him any more questions, you do it. Here, use my handkerchief first, it's cleaner."

Skinny, among the sharp smells and savors of the market, always wept happily, but so damp a face naturally enlisted Mr. Sprunt's sympathy. He put aside the long knife he was

207

whetting, thinking perhaps this had caused alarm. "Yes, my boy, is anything wrong?"

Skinny prudently attributed his question to still another source. The way the choice quality butcher heard it was "My mother wants to know if you live on champagne?"

Mr. Sprunt was startled into laughter, but wondered afterward. "No, Sonny," he said warily, "meat ain't quite as high as that, in spite of the Beef Trust.—A couple of Peck's bad boys," he said cheerfully to Aunt Bee. "Yes, Ma'am, over here we call it headcheese, but I remember my old gramp called it brawn."

While Mrs. Granger and Aunt Bee did their shopping Skinny and Jeff wandered among the various stocks and smells. Skinny was not above capitalizing the peculiarity of his tear ducts. A stroll among the fish and cheeses gave him a look of pathos which could be useful if they then hung about a candy or bakery stall. But even Skinny grew weary of alms and as they waited outside the A & P he confessed his impatience. "I'm too proud to go on getting things by crying. It's undignified. I think we better earn some money. Twenty cents a week pocket money isn't enough for a Rajah. LaGrange has got to have a sinking fund."

"I get twenty-four," said the President. "That's because it's a shilling, equals twenty-four cents."

"I've got an idea," said the Rajah. "If you'll split your four extra cents with me every week, I'll tell it to you."

"Maybe *I've* got an idea," said the President. "I'll be genteel. I'll mention it without charging you anything. I heard Major Warren say he would have to let people paint Mandrake Pills on his barn if he got any worse hard-up."

"But we haven't got a barn to paint it on."

"We could paint it on boards like those sandwich men and carry them around the street every Saturday. Then we send a bill to Mr. Mandrake."

"It isn't Mr. Mandrake. It's Mr. Schenk. You haven't been

in America long enough to know the institutions. Besides it's for impurities of the blood and that's only in the country. People in cities have doctors to go to and besides if they're impure they're too stuck up to admit it."

"We could sell some of the pills to J. William Sprunt. His blood is just raging in his cheeks."

"My idea is better," Skinny insisted, "besides I've given you half of all my tear-duct dividends."

"I know how I can get a dividend. Aunt Bee said she'd give me a nickel extra if I'd stop reading *Hiawatha* to her. She says it puts her to sleep because it tells everything twice. It's fun to read, though."

"Shucks, that would be only chicken feed. What I'm thinking of would be real money."

"Cross your heart?"

"I'll bet you a chocolate mouse. We'll each buy one, if there's a penny in them you can have it."

The chocolate mice were a specialty of a small candy store which had never heard of hygiene. They were disapproved by Aunt Bee not only for themselves but for the display of Nick Carter booklets which adjoined them. The chocolate was only a thin wash of syrup and the inwards could not compare, Aunt Bee said, with Bessie Barritt's cocoanut ice. But two or three in every layer had copper cents imbedded. Accordingly Jeff and Skinny regarded these confections as a form of investment. They couldn't do that in England, Geoffrey remarked, because their pennies are too big. But Aunt Bee and Mrs. Granger took charge of the boys before the mice could be bought.

"Meet me at the clubhouse tomorrow morning," said Skinny as he was commandeered. "I'll tell you my idea then. We'll have to let Bert and Star in on it."

"There'd be more profits if it's just us," Jeff suggested.

Skinny made a final twist under his mother's grasp, sniveling with his great idea. "They've got to be in it," he said mysteriously. "They've got the equipment.—Hell's bells, Mother! Do

I have to have a new overcoat? If it has a velvet collar it makes my neck feel like camphor ice and I can't stop crying."

Customers on the crowded pavement outside the A & P probably thought Skinny's mother was very cruel to him.

"The tiger's roar filled the cave with thunder—*Hurrp!*" Uncle Dan's bearded face really did look almost tigerish as he opened the door and growled this morning cry. *Hurrp* was a word of their own which compacted the sense of "Hurry up" into more urgent sound. The tiger's roar of course was quoted from the picture in *The Jungle Book*.

And as Geoffrey liked to think, his sleeping place really was a kind of cave: the small cubicle between Aunt Bee's bedroom and Uncle Dan's. Its real name was the box-room; Jeff's cot was surrounded by trunks and bags still plastered with their ocean labels. This interior space had no windows but the great luxury of a skylight; to be properly realistic in the morning summons Uncle Dan should have crawled on the roof. Jeff was usually awake sooner, the hurrp meant that the bathroom was now free. He could tell by the sounds of plumbing and footsteps when the moment drew near for the tiger's roar. It was perfected plotting to go deep below blankets and wait. "You were so still under there I thought you had smothered," said Uncle Dan. "I was expecting," Jeff said.

Expecting was best under a tattoo of rain, though bright mornings had their pleasure too when a swath of light lay over the roof without damaging the soft dimness of the cave. From downstairs came the mixed voices (one shrill, one mumble) of Aunt Bee and Moxie discussing the rations of the day. This was usually followed by the squeak of Aunt Bee's slate pencil as she made notes for her orders. She was careful not to rub out the cat (supposed to be Jue) drawn by Jeff in one corner of the slate. This, he said, would frighten away the slate-mouse which made such painful screaking.

"Hurrp!" Uncle Dan repeated. "I envy you a room with a

skylight. It's like having your mind open at the top. Did you ever think of that?"

"I think of all sorts of things. I like your window too. You can see people's bath-water going down the gutter."

"That isn't very interesting, is it?"

"You can tell whether they've used soap."

"If you're going to have that club meeting you'll have to hurry, because Aunt Bee says you mustn't miss First Day School."

This meeting of the club was unusually orderly, probably because the members were geared for religious duty and partly throttled by starched linen. Bert even had a standing collar whose points gored the underside of his chin. Mrs. Eutaw thought this the only way to encourage a cherub look of upward attention in church, but Bert had found a way of retiring the whole front of his face inside the stricture. Rallied on his gruesome looks he explained, "It's my Sunday collar."

"My family don't believe in Sunday," said Jeff unguardedly. "We call it First Day."

"First Day isn't as religious as Sunday," said Star with contempt. "You'll go to hell, you poor little squirt."

"Yay, yay, yay—old First Day," said Bert, hoping to start a rhythmical blasphemy, but it got lost around his Adam's apple.

Skinny, who had summoned the meeting, was very business-like. "Listen, we've got important business. Jeff and I decided we've simply got to earn an income, it's shameful to be so impenurious, and we'll let you fellows in on it because you've got the rolling stock. What do you suppose is the greatest monopoly people want?" He sneezed with hay fever and excitement; the earnestness of his streaming features compelled the other members to discussion. Ice cream, street-car transfers, free-wheel bicycles and other suggestions were offered, but he swept them all aside.

"It's a drink of water. You know how it is in this old pest-ridden town. Everybody has to boil their water because it's full of malaria. You ought to know, Bert, your father is a physician and surgeon, and what's the result? You have to keep old kettles of water boiling on the stove all day long and when you do get a drink, it's most likely tepid because you can't put ice in it, the ice is an epidemic too, and over on the other side of town the kids live in luxury because they're out every evening to that spring in the park and sell bottles of water."

"Geez, baby, that's a smart idea," exclaimed Star. "We could get up early and go across the bridge to Druid Hill spring and bring back a load of bottles. I bet people round here would rather buy water from their own children instead of that old Dulaney Valley Artisan Company that carries it round."

"You've got a big express wagon," said Skinny, "and here in Bert's barn is a lot of old glass jars I saw lying around. That's what made me think of it."

"I don't know about those jugs," said Bert. "They had all kinds of coal oil and carbolical acid in them. My father is crazy about emetics, but we could give them a scrub."

"The smell would soon wash out," said Jeff. "Nobody would be expecting to taste it, so they wouldn't notice, only maybe the first few pioneers? We'd keep it in our own personal families until the bottles got good and clean."

In this way the T.S.O. 4 Artisan Water Company was founded.

42. *The Artisan Water Company*

Star Lanvale hadn't used the express wagon much, partly because his sisters had pre-empted it for giving their dolls an airing, also because he felt obscurely that the inscription *Dandy Racer* was too juvenile. But now repainted with the fresh blazon of the T.S.O. 4 Artisan Water Company there was even a rivalry (at first) who should pull. No commercial enterprise was ever founded without quickly meeting the unexpected. By Euclid the shortest route to Cotton Duck Bridge and the spring was the obvious diagonal across the Vacant Lot, but until they tried it with a freight of glass bottles they hadn't realized how rough was the terrain. There was frequent discussion among the promoters whether it was better to take the longer way up Carroll Street and then along Division Road than the Oregon Trail across wilderness. Scholarly Skinny nicknamed the bumpy diagonal the Hypotenuse and said it was a useful lesson in plane geometry. To which Jeff, captious as usual, replied, "Yebbut it's not a plane."

Paradise for boys is any region on the outskirts of town where civilization has not yet reached full control. That big spread of undeveloped ground had all the prime factors of charm. It was bounded on the west by steep slides of tawny gravel under which ran the line of the Ma and Pa and then the stream of Jones's Falls. The usual flavors of the creek were frequently invigorated by dead kittens or squirrels. Ma and Pa had defended themselves by a strong barrier, to buttress off a constantly slipping talus of rocks, tin cans and various jetsam, but there were ways of getting through the fence for exploration. Sometimes, if the chocolate mice had been fertile, pennies were laid on the rails but Bert Eutaw advised Jeff against trying it with an English coin. He said it would throw Ma off the track. The central expanse of this small prairie had been successfully parceled out in tenure by various gangs who occasionally met in a level patch in the middle for any sport then seasonable; the outward fringes, well thicketed with brambles and sassafras and hay-fever carriers, were accepted as open to squatters' claim by rival clubs. The T.S.O. 4 were not numerous or warlike enough to acquire one of the more desirable gullies, or even the bubbling marshy sump called Pogeypond. This was thrillingly rumored to be a quicksand, filled with bones of orphans from a near-by asylum. But their own small eyrie at the brow of the western scarp had great advantage for the heaving of missiles. These were thrown more as experiments in ballistics than as volleys of malice. It was probably accidental when Star Lanvale

213

hurled a rotten apple clear across the stream and smote a brake-man on a box-car of the Northern Central. (No one ever threw things at the Ma and Pa, that was too much like picking on a weakling.) The impact was superb, the apple burst on the train-man's jowl, and a scouting vedette of the powerful Oriole Boys was impressed. A formal invitation was issued to the T.S.O. 4 to join forces with the Orioles, who coveted such a marksman. The T.S.O. 4 declined, which caused them much harrying by the other tribe.

The vacant lot, as Jeff afterward meditated, had considerable sociological value. It served as a general Gehenna for that whole neighborhood, and as the city of Chesapeake was in those days not meticulous in the disposal of rubbish, householders along Carroll and its rear neighbor Schier Street dumped into the open space all kinds of outcast. It was certainly an education in life's rich complex to find such miscellaneous trove—anything from broken baby carriages to bed-pans. Skinny was particularly pleased when he found an old eye-cup, sooted by fire; Jeff suggested that it was intended for black eyes but Skinny put it to good use as a drinking cup for humming birds. Jeff, still innocent of the extraordinary American passion for throwing things away, remarked, "Everybody round here must be very rich if they can waste things like that." He mentioned this theory to Aunt Bee who had also been astounded at the relics of previous tenants found in their backyard. It was very different from Wilford's frugal habit. She quoted a remark made by one of their neighbors when they first moved in. Mrs. Magothy, the attentive housewife at 1908, had been assessing the new-come Bartons in the usual way by study of their backdoor doings. Mrs. Magothy was overheard (and quoted): "I don't think they're really consequential, they have such skinny garbage."

"Best compliment I ever had," said Aunt Bee tersely. Jeff nicknamed the watchful neighbor Mrs. Maggots.

He was distressed when they found the ripely defunct corpse of a cat in Sassafras House, the Club's wildwood sanctum. It couldn't have happened if Aunt Emma were here, he thought. Even Uncle Dan occasionally took an observant stroll round these playgrounds and was astonished by the profusion of waste. "If this country ever really gets hard up," he said to Major Warren, "it will certainly hurt."

Such reflections were not more than subconscious in the hopeful merchants of the T.S.O. 4 Artisan Water Company as they plotted their sales campaign. They had not realized that the spring of fair water across the bridge was considered private property by the boys of that other region. The first time the T.S.O. 4 made the journey with fresh-painted wagon and diligently purified containers, they were startled to find the well-head surrounded by a whole company of toughs (so they promptly classified them) with wagons and bottles of their own. These experienced water carriers looked formidable and lusty, as boys from other neighborhoods so dangerously do.

Nursing the bright wagon down a steep grade the quartet came to the hollow where the drinking fountain was niched in the hillside. All four were intent on their task: one to guide, one to hold back from behind, one on each side to keep the precious bottles from joggling. In their pride and concentration they did not notice the threatening silence of the boys already gathered round the iron water-pipe. Skinny, always alert for psychic vibrations, was first to look up. "Aw gee," he muttered, "there's the Shawbuck boys." I'm glad there's four of us, he added to himself.

"Well, for Deity's sake," remarked Bill Shawbuck, the noisier but perhaps less dangerous of the two Shawbucks. "Who do you-all think you are with your nice new cart?"

The T.S.O. 4 artisans now realized how deplorably shiny and young their delivery wagon looked by comparison with the battered vehicles and home-made scooters of the others. It was queer because all the way along Division Road and across the bridge they had been thinking how splendid and big it was.

Bill and Jack Shawbuck took lounging attitudes on each side

215

of the rusty iron standpipe, leaning elbows on its rounded top. They were so evidently in command of the situation that the rest of the crowd, respectfully waiting until the Shawbucks finished their bottle-filling, began to express what was evidently power politics.

"Ain't you kids got any hydrants your own side of town?" sneered one objectionable dwarf with crossed green eyes.

"We'll take our turn," said Jeff politely.

"Gee, I guess this spring belongs to Druid Hill Park, don't it?" said Star. "I guess everybody has their rights in a public park."

"Old Francis Scott Lanvale, the Star-Spangled Banana!" cried the offensive Bill, as though addressing the sky at large. There was a threatening jostle around the basin as the forces in occupation shifted to positions of vantage. The half-dozen express wagons and home-made scooters already gathered at the spring were being reinforced by others coming down the hillside. It was the after-school time about 4 o'clock when family supplies of drinking water were replenished. On some of these new arrivals Jeff noticed scrawled in chalk—how different from their own careful paintwork—the menacing legend MOUNT ROYALS. Excursions of this dangerous tribe, which dominated the heights of Park Avenue and Mount Royal Terrace, had spread even across the valley of Jones's Falls; Spike McMechan was their satrap at P.S. 16. Jeff nudged Star who was at the handle of the wagon. "I guess it's not urgent," he said to Bill, who still seemed to be gazing anywhere but at them.

"Oh, it's not urgent?" declaimed Master Shawbuck. "You hear that, Jelly? It's not urgent!"

How unfortunate, Star (a bit of a diplomat) was thinking, that in moments of stress Jeff unconsciously adopted such formal jargon. "Come on, kids," he whispered, "we'll back up till they get through."

"You're damn tootin' you'll take your turn," announced another sycophant, moving outward as if to flank a retreat.

216

Geoffrey still could not believe that even such uncongenial schoolmates as the Shawbucks would be so intentionally disagreeable on this distant ground. It was a shock to find that their hostile manners, constantly exhibited in the hallways and playground at Bolton's, were carried even into the outside world. He met the penetrating gaze of Jack Shawbuck and unconsciously adopted the stuck-up tone for which he was infamous. "I think you're extremely unreasonable," he piped.

"We'll wait till you and Jellybean get through," squeaked Skinny.

One hopes and believes that in after years Master J. J. Shawbuck encountered his due share of humanity's woe; but in that epoch he had his own secret annoyance, the family and respected middle name Jellaby. Its conversion to Jellybean was obvious, but reserved for intimates. Trebled out in poor Skinny's liquid snivel it was peculiarly humiliating. He conned the field steadily, with a special eye for Star Lanvale, the only visitor who looked dangerous. Brother Bill usually did the preliminary parley, shrewdly toning up J. Jellaby Shawbuck for the kill.

"Guess this T.S.O. 4 Water Company must be ole friends," said Bill. "Must be some mistake. I didn't know what Star-Spangled Banana and Baby Granger and kids would be doing over this side of the tracks."

Jellybean made a sudden rush. The T.S.O. 4 Company were already backing away so their pride was somewhat salvaged, but the gesture of ferocity was emphatic enough. He seized Jeff's arm, twisted it violently backward and scoured his nape with a stone which no one had seen him pick up. The nimble Star sprang to reprisal and the ecstatic yell "Fight! Fight!" rose in many voices. But the Park policeman who always prudently strolled through the hollow just about that hour quieted the fracas. He was surrounded by a clamor of repartee, and the T.S.O. 4 Company, rather sadly considering these unexpected problems of industry, waited patiently on the outskirts until all

217

squadrons of the Mount Royals had taken their fill and rumbled away.

At last they found it possible to approach the fountain. They had supposed that one or at most two members would be enough to take the job in turns. But surrounded by unfriendly watchers all four were needed: one to hold the water handle open, one to fill the bottles, and a guard on either side to watch for any movement of malice. It was already growing dusk when they completed their load. They realized now how desirable would be an arrangement of pigeon-holes to keep the jugs from dangerous vibration, and also how much heavier was the return. As they heaved uphill toward the bridge Bert called attention to sounds of argument and distress on the other side of the glen. There was the crash of breaking bottles accompanied by profane yells and retorts.

"Gosh," remarked Skinny, "those Mount Royals are terrible muckers. They're fighting among themselves now."

"Unh-unh," grunted Star, tugging at the load. "I know what's wrong. While they were all yapping at that cop I pulled out their axle-pin."

Jeff and Skinny found that by making the trip to the spring before breakfast the problem of meeting enemies was avoided. The delivery wagon of the water company rumbled cheerfully up the pavement by the vacant lot, past the Chestnut Woods on Division Road, and over the echoing planks of Cotton Duck Bridge. In bright morning air the two rulers found much to discuss. Jeff explained that because he slept in the box-room he could not get out without passing through either Aunt Bee's room or Uncle Dan's. "It's like an uncle and aunt sandwich," he said, "but if I have to wake up one of them it's better to be Uncle Dan because Aunt Bee is most likely saying her prayers. She must know a lot of prayers, she gets up so early."

The topic of religion was appealing to Skinny. Jeff's allusions to First Day School and Friends' Meeting had roused his curiosity. "My father's very liberal, he's a Unitarian. He says it would be all right for me to go with you to Meeting some Sunday. He says the Friends have the root of the idea in them."

"Maybe that's why Aunt Bee is so crazy about root beer," said Jeff. "She got a lot of ole extracts and condiments and made a whole vintage but it exploded. There's a piece of bottle sticking in one of the beams. I'm going to start a museum in the cellar, Relics of the Great Carroll Street Explosion. Do you think people would pay?"

"Nothing ever happens in my house that would be worth making a museum about," said Skinny sadly. "That's because it's full of girls. I don't know why, but my Dad says Unitarian ministers always beget girls."

"I thought Unitarians were pastors," said Jeff. "I always read the notice boards on the churches. I don't think it's really Holy Ghost unless they have a sexton."

"Pastors is Baptists and Lutherans, I think. It's like what they call evangelical. They herd the congregation around like sheep."

"At Friends' Meeting we have caretakers, they don't go in for sextons. They have one on board ship, though," he remembered. "Captain Bompjes had one to tell him where he was."

"You've got to have sextons or people won't know what to do when you die. Sextons have to see there's smelling salts ready in case people feel sick at the funeral."

"Shucks, people don't carry on like that when Quakers die," said Jeff.

"My father preached at a funeral where three ladies fainted, but he said he didn't really take the credit for it. It was very oppressive weather."

"Did you know colored people have churches too? Moxie told me, she goes to African Methodist, they have a black bishop."

Skinny looked about to make sure he was not overheard. "I

bet you something, if you don't tell on me. I bet you God don't give a damn *what* color you are. So there."

Since they were being so frank, Jeff felt he could even venture a question suggested by dreadful rumors in school.

"Do Jewish people believe in God?"

"Aw gee, sure they do. My father says everybody believes in God, but he says Jehovah ran them so ragged in the Kingdom of Israel they got sort of panicky about the whole thing. My father's terribly outspoken, he even had a priest and a rabbi at the house to dinner one night. I was scared to say anything. I guess it wasn't real dinner, just a kind of bouffé. We had fishcakes.—You know they used to burn Unitarians for being so outspoken," he added with pride.

"They put lots of ole Quakers in prison," Jeff countered. "That was because they wouldn't go to church, but you don't have to have churches. Aunt Bee says ole George Fox found God in a hollow tree. It sounds like Brer Buzzard. I think it's all very peculiar."

"I haven't decided what sort of religion they have in LaGrange," admitted the Rajah. "Of course they have Christmas, it's good for piety. Candy canes could be a gov'ment monopoly. They have a bang-up Sociable on Christmas, and nobody has to sing *We Three Kings of Orient Are*." Skinny and two other young victims had once been swathed in robes and turbans and made to pull a cardboard camel which collapsed on them. The experience still rankled.

"Star of wonder, star of night," hummed Jeff. "Star with royal beauty bright. Westward leading, still proceeding. I rather like that song, I like those little short lines, they sound good some way."

"Field and fountain, moor and mountain," mimicked Skinny in falsetto. "We better get on, those toughs will be ahead of us."

The wagon clinked faster, each artisan pursued his private thought for a space. Morning sunlight on the load of glass bottles faintly reminded Jeff of the warehouse on the Thoro-

fare; spangled brightness from a window overhead; Miss Debbidge among the breakables. Are human errands always among
such fragile things? Skinny presently remarked, "You don't
know how lucky you are on Sundays. You haven't got a crowd
of grabbing sisters. You can read the funny paper all to yourself."

"Do Unitarians have a Spring Sociable?"

"You bet. Gee whiz, we have Interdenomination Picnic, every
sex invited. My father hires the old steamer *Louise* and we
go down to Tolchester Beach. Listen, if you let me go to meeting at your church I'll get you a bid to the picnic at Tolchester.
They have a toy steam train down there runs on a track round
the field. It's an engine about the size of this wagon and each
car just big enough for one person to sit. The kids all raise
Cain on the steamer. They play Monkey, monkey, bottle o'
beer; honest, you'd never know they're a Sunday School."

This was a tempting offer. "It's a bet. But Aunt Bee says she
hopes you don't want to go to Friends' Meeting just for curiosity. You have to sit awful still and there's no music and hullaba-
loo to take the load off your mind. Uncle Dan doesn't go very
much any more because he got to thinking out his lectures in the
Silence and he forgot where he was and said some ideas out
loud. I guess it's pretty hard for a lecturing teacher ever to
keep quiet. The elders spoke to him about it and he was sore."

"Gosh, you got elders? It's like the Bible. That must be real
religion." Warily they looked down into the hollow to see that
no Mount Royals were at the spring.

"Going to the well, that's kind of biblical too," said Jeff.
"Nobody there. All quiet along the Potomac."

43. *Aunt Bee Writes Home*

"I'm sorry about that stain," said Aunt Bee, "but if you *will*
leave the map and the paints on the floor somebody is likely

to trip over them. I mopped it up as fast as I could but I'm afraid it made a smear on the map."

"There's no harm done," said Jeff, using one of Uncle Dan's favorite phrases. "It made a very interesting shape so I drew round it and founded a sort of Reservation specially for you. It's called 'Privacy.'"

Aunt Bee did not exactly smile but her mouth loosened slightly. She had her knees on a doormat in the backyard, turning the earth around her tulip bulbs with the big carving fork. Uncle Dan and Jeff had long intended to get her some garden tools for her birthday but she said the digging was an excellent way to polish the fork. Moxie had no gift for keeping things clean according to Bee's standards and did not even understand what knife-powder was, as they learned when she sprinkled it in a salad.

"Presents have a way of going wrong in this family," Jeff remarked. "I don't suppose Uncle Dan really wanted that nose-guard I bought him. It was unlucky for him his birthday came just at the beginning of the football season."

Conversation between Jeff and Aunt Bee was syncopated in a way that made it mostly unintelligible to others. Even Mrs. Magothy, who cocked a dirigible ear at the window sill next door, would not have guessed that the new parish of Privacy was named on her account and that just outside its boundary was the eavesdropping village of Old Maggots. Aunt Bee disliked Chesapeake's cheerful habit of sociability at front stoop and back fence. She hankered for a small patch of open air to herself, and in her first attempts to start a few flowers in the yard she was constantly irritated by the critical gaze of Mrs. Magothy. One could almost feel the tremor of the neighbor's loosely hinged lips shaping for comment. "You can imagine a balloon coming out of her mouth like the funny pictures," said Jeff. But it was better now since Aunt Bee had tacked a roof of chicken wire over the brick walk and started some rapid and brilliant creepers she found in Carroll Woods. Her first experiment in planting had to be quickly removed.

"That was a good joke on you," said Jeff, "planting that poison ivy. I guess there's a lot of stuff grows at Wilford that doesn't flourish here." He was thinking of the clumps of primrose roots the aunts had sent over by post. They soon expired in the hot and shallow earth of Carroll Street, which seemed underlaid a few inches down by a subsoil of rusty cans. Uncle Dan thought the previous tenants must have had a Tin Wedding.

"I must write to Wilford," said Aunt Bee. "I've been putting it off too long. You ought to do it too."

"I've been putting it off because things need so much explaining. Doggone it, they just wouldn't understand."

"It's very difficult," said Aunt Bee. "When you try to think of two countries at the same time, you can't be fair to either of them."

"That's why I like to take a little jaunt round Jeffland when I feel depressed. It's very jolly. You can put things down on the map the way they like to be."

No, it was not easy, Bee reflected, as she got out thin notepaper to write to the Thorofare. From the beginning she had transmitted so simplified a picture that she could hardly begin now to suggest its more grotesque phases. For instance the aroma of what Geoffrey called "Lion Steak" which just then dominated even the vapors of Jones's Falls. Jeff said it gave him an appetite, but Bee felt otherwise. It would be too gruesome to describe how the old tinder-box skating rink on North Avenue, converted into a menagerie, had burned down one stormy night. All sorts of beasts from elephants to midget ponies had perished in flame and panic, and the T.S.O. 4 were morbidly interested by the sight and whiff of charred lions in the tragic embers. Jeff had rather too vividly described how the iron bars of the cages had even made a gridiron pattern on the cindered haunches. At this very moment Mrs. Magothy and many other pairs of roving eyes were alert for escaped monkeys supposed to be at large, and scouting parties of Orioles and Mount Royals were shrill in vacant lots. So horrifying a story would only agitate the aunts. It was perplexing enough to explain such simple phenomena as Breakfast Food and creamed chipped beef, or the tocsin of the rag-bone-and-bottle-man's cowbells. The first time Bee heard these she hurried out to the alley. "I thought it was an American muffin-man."—Or how would you describe the boys playing lacrosse along the cobbled street? When she tried to draw a picture of those queer netted implements, Grandma thought it was battledore and shuttlecock.

She looked younger as she began to write:

MY DEAR MOTHER,

I am very ashamed not to have written lately. I wish I could console myself as Dan does, he says he doesn't fare to write letters this spring because it's such a shock to write 1900 instead of 1899. You can see that even being an American hasn't changed him. It's really too bad the new century should begin with all this trouble in South Africa, and now we read threatening news about China; but Geoff says people called Boxers can't be so bad. That was the barber on board the *Westernland* that took such a fancy to him. Dan thinks that surely now Lord Roberts is in charge things will be better? I was glad Wilford Meeting drew up a minute questioning the war. I have begun this letter in a confused way but Moxie interrupted me to ask what to do with the crumbs left over from the baked oysters. How I wish we could use the crumbs for treacle tart, but the real treacle simply doesn't exist here. We gave a little supper last night for some of the faculty who have been very kind. I served the oysters in those silver-mounted scallop shells you let me bring from home. People are very careful here about only eating oysters in months with an "r" so we won't have many more this season. I was amused last night by President Beinbrink of Patapsco, so very Southern and talks in that drawl as if their teeth didn't meet, and never pronounce the "r," he was joking about the months for oysters and Dan said, "Of course, Mr. President, in Chesapeake there are *no* months with an 'r.'" I don't think Dr. Beinbrink really understood poor Dan's little joke, but Dan is accustomed to that. In our college circle there's a strong Wesleyan influence, and they do like their jokes to come head-on, not a little bit sideways. We always enjoy overhearing remarks about ourselves. If you think Wilford is a place for gossip you should try a college like Patapsco. Anything said by a faculty wife is all over the "campus" (three city squares of *hideous* buildings like the Anker Blocks Geoff had). We soon learned that one of our most stolid professors said of Dan, "he's a fine fellow but I don't think he has any sense of humor!" But we have to be careful about Dr. Beinbrink because Dan's promotion naturally depends on him. It would be fatal if they ever got wind of Dan's great ambition to have a post at the University. Of course Patapsco is small beer in the world of scholarship compared to Chesapeake University.

Really you would be amused to see Dan as a "family man" as he calls it. He says that as a solitary student living in lodgings he had no idea life could be so complicated. He asks me, "Did these weird things always happen or is it just some fatality of my own?" I tell him that probably everything always happens everywhere but he never began to notice until Geoff and I made things interesting for him.

As for Geoff, you wouldn't know him, he's so big and stout, always bursting his trousers. I dare say he has had more troubles than he tells about in acclimating himself to other boys. Because his natural way of expressing himself is rather precise and old-fashioned, he adopts an exaggerated toughness and slanginess as a kind of protection. Dan is always at him about his language but after he has been in the house a little while it wears off and I get him to read aloud to me as much as possible. He always surprises me because he acts out whatever he reads and sometimes it's quite thrilling. Dan left *The Ancient Mariner* lying around and Geoff said he would read me some of it. He said he was interested because it had things written at the side of the page like the Bible! He asked amusing questions such as "Why were the mariners hollow, they were hungry?" and then he got excited and really, I had quite a chilblain on my spine when he said in a dramatic guilty whisper: "With my crossbow, I *shot* the albatross!" For an instant he looked like old Ben at Sutton ferry, or one of the old Seckford almsmen! Then he burst into tears and I think I would have done so too except for my Wilford training. Perhaps it's the climate, everything is more emotional over here. You remember how upset he used to be by the rabbits hanging on hooks. That reminds me, our kind friend Major Warren gave Geoff a book of stories *Wild Animals I Have Known*. He read me one about "Molly Cottontail" which left us sadly depressed. Geoff said, "I think literature is very cruel to rabbits."

Our little feast last night was really a success, I think. I've told you about my struggles with Moxie which were partly because it took me so long to realize not only she can't read, but she doesn't know right from left. You can't believe how difficult it is to explain that to someone who has no idea of it. Mrs. Warren suggested I try her with *near* and *off*, being terms of horses, but we finally got it straight because she has some wonderful gold stoppings on the left side of her mouth, so now we call the left the "gold-tooth side" and she understands. The ladies last night were all excited about the new movement in women's clubs which are so powerful here. They say that all over the country New Century Clubs are being started for the betterment of social conditions, &c., and they are agog to change their Browning Society into a New Century Club. They say they have "gotten" everything possible out of Browning and he has been dead quite a while.

They were disputing, when does the twentieth century really begin? Dan insists not until 1st January 1901, but that seems to me absurd. I think it's a mathematical quibble he got from Blanche Bristol! By the way, one of Dan's advanced students (Miss Towson, the one who's always talking about "poitry") let out a secret: this year's graduating class is going to dedicate its *Yearbook* to Dan, a great compliment because they only do that to their favorite professor. I'm trying to write fast. It'll soon be lunch time. We're going to have minced kromeskies (leftovers from last night) on the old blue Thorofare platter— I always wash it myself for fear of accident. Dan calls Moxie the Girl with a Thousand Thumbs. This afternoon if it stays fine Geoff wants us to walk to the tadpole pond in the Park. We will probably have to bring home a jar full of the unfortunate creatures. Then they turn into frogs and hop round the floor. They have a kind of frogs here in the swamps that make a wonderful whistling music at night. Geoff took me for a walk in the vacant lot to hear them. The stars were very bright and he said such a pretty thing. "They sound so silver and sad and far-away, you'd think it was the stars and not just frogs."

How is Lizzie Batts? When Geoff has to go to the dentist he always thinks of her. Our dear love to all, G. will add a P.S.

BEE

P.S. My dear Grandmother & Aunts: She did not leave much room but I don't believe in "crossing" letters as people used to. There is plenty of paper in the U.S., and everything else too. We are doing splendidly and I enjoy taking Aunt Bee for adventures which give her an idea of American history. Next week we shall go to an old museum that has a famous painting, Exhuming the First American Mastodon. She is a little aprehensive. It sounds like a terrible fire we had where elephants & lions were burned, but this is only a historical painting. Aunt Bee said a witty thing about the First American

Mastodon: "Who was that, George Washington?" Love to all and Miss Debbidge,

your loving JEFF (Geoffrey)

P.S. 2. Aunt Bee didn't really say it, I thought of it myself.

44. Pleasures of the Scholar

In his study at the back of the house Uncle Dan was intent upon the mild pleasures of the scholar. His teaching schedule began early in the mornings—he used to say he had grown a beard on account of the 8:30 class—but allowed him an hour at home before lunch. He often found it the most fruitful concentration of the day. Time at the meridian seems packed more tight, pressed solid under the hammer strokes of activity outside. At that hour the noises of the alley softened into distance, housewives and colored maids after long forenoon vociferation settled down to duty. A carpenter had put double sash in the window that overlooked the yard. A storm-window was the American name for it; it kept out the storms of Moxie's conversations with hucksters. Moxie's full name was Monocacy; Jeff reported, "She says she was named for a battle, and she makes as much noise. There's interesting names in her family, she has a sister called Zouave. She says her ole mammy got run over by a Federal supply train, they got no more morals than a sutler mule."

"Sumpter mule," Uncle Dan corrected. He reflected how rich language is in these falsifying doubles; what the Oxford philologers later called pairs and snares. He himself, like all teachers, had some favorite confusables for his students, asking them to distinguish Thomas Lovell Beddoes and Thomas Love Peacock; or Vivian Grey and Dorian Gray.

Zouave was to Jeff a name of pageantry, an earfiller like Ringling Brothers or Forepaugh and Sells. The Zouaves were the most vivid of all the cardboard troops, they were dressed in a Turkish fashion and were called upon to make Last Stands.

"They wave their glittering chibouks," said Skinny, who thought these were cutlasses. Like Chesapeake itself they seemed to have fought on both sides.

Uncle Dan kept the double window tight shut, even in warm weather. He liked to contemplate the dusty space between the two panes, imagining invisible sound-waves trapped there, only half strangled and still trying to get at him. His shabby flat desk stood under the window. It was not nearly large enough: he had to be careful not to elbow the kerosene student's lamp which had a green china shade and a gurgling nickel cylinder. He might have used a gas fixture (with a Welsbach mantle) but the kerosene lamp, a relic of his boarding-house era, was the memento of many quiet hours. He believed it helped him to concentrate. Aunt Bee always trimmed and filled it with her own faithful puckered hands. In the silence of evening study the lamp made small inward gulps and swallowing sounds, rather like Bee herself. Half a century of Wilford suet, pork and pastry, Dan realized, caused strange convulsion inside.

Aunt Bee had brought over a few old family pieces from Wilford, but most of the furniture Dan bought secondhand when he set up his own home on Carroll Street. There is a psychic value in furniture of alien origin; the old slippery couch against the left wall came from a doctor's office, and when he lay there after lunch with *The Prisoner of Zenda* or *The First Men in the Moon* or *Captain Kettle* it added to the peace of his nap to think vaguely of painful or embarrassing examinations that had probably been conducted on its rigorous horsehair. To the left of the desk was a quavering bamboo stand which had never expected such burdens as his broken volumes of the *Edinburgh Review* or the half set of De Quincey. The latter he had bought cheap at Cambridge in partnership with a friend: they split the set between them, one taking the odd numbers and the other the even; it grieved him that his research in De Quincey was based mostly on Volumes 2, 4, 6, 8, 10, 12, and 14. Only the faded brown Morris chair at the right of the desk was strong enough to carry one volume of the 1755 Dr. Johnson's Dictionary, borrowed for study from Major Warren. In the right-hand corner and also behind him were unpainted shelves put up by the carpenter. At the foot of the couch was another window which could be opened for ventilation but was less pleasing for view: it opened directly opposite the corresponding window next door, at some six feet distance across the dividing fence. This was the boudoir of plump Mrs. Magothy who had less than the Barton instinct for concealment. Through this open window came the sounds of bath and dishwaters as they seethed along a brick gutter toward the alley; and the tinkle of a Japanese windbell, thin strips of flowered glass hung to catch the draught. This was a discovery of Aunt Bee's and relished by Dan to remind him of S. T. C.'s aeolian harp in the window at Keswick. Another sound that came occasionally across the yards to westward was the whistle of Pa or Ma, winding their way up the valleys toward Susquehanna.

He could dimly hear Aunt Bee and Jeff talking together in the yard, but returned his mind to his notes. He was in good form, he had just given his lecture on Hazlitt in English VIII (History of Criticism) and the timing had come just right for Hazlitt's April birthday. He had freshened up the lecture in spots that had grown too familiar, particularly by his happy discovery that Hazlitt applied the phrase "The Fourth Estate" to journalism some years earlier than Carlyle or Macaulay to whom it was usually credited. A note for the Modern Language Association: he visualized it in the dense type of academic journals, modestly signed *D. Barton, Patapsco College*. Vicissitudes of weather had made pleasantly apropos his reference to Hazlitt's April temperament. Something too of an April look in the large brown eyes of Rozanne Towson, his only graduate student, his ewe lamb in the pastures of The Romantic Movement, had given special felicity to his account of the Silver Buckle episode. He reminded the girls that Hazlitt as a child had lost a cherished silver shoe-buckle in the sand beaches of Cape Cod. Of all possible souvenirs, he suggested, that forgotten ornament would be the happiest find for the amorist of English prose.

"But, Professor," bleated the adenoidal fatwit in the front row, "it would be all rusty."

The class's cackle, and the look of admiring sympathy from the ewe lamb, warmed him to peroration. "The rust would be like some students," he said amiably, "merely superficial. Rust is only a peripheral oxidization caused by exposure to unpropitious elements." (It was for such impromptus that his classes adored him.) "As in Hazlitt himself, the fine metal is there, under whatever temporary crust caused by change of manners. I like to think of that perished silver buckle as a conjunction between English and American letters; if you like, as a symbol of the great critic's argentine precision; he was himself a connecting link, a clasp, a conjunction, between journalism and literature. Even a buckle has a tongue," he added, pleased with himself.

"You took a terrible chance," said Miss Towson afterward. "When you used the word *argentine* I'm sure that girl will believe Hazlitt lost the buckle in South America."

"What I wanted to say, and checked myself just in time, was what Hazlitt said to Gifford of the *Quarterly:* 'You are a nuisance, and should be abated.'"

They proceeded to discuss the matter of Miss Towson's thesis for a Master's degree on Wordsworth as a Writer of Prose. This was giving them both much satisfaction, particularly the ingenious idea of condensing *The Prelude* from verse into the more stringent form. With the vapors squeezed out of it the poet's monologue was becoming a strong essay in luminous prose. They even believed that Miss Towson might find a publisher for it, and secretly Dan suspected a modest dedication: *To D. B., Inspiring Teacher.*

Such compost germinated his mind as he recapitulated the

morning's work, and unclipped the loose-leaf notebooks to insert any new notions that had occurred to him. Such are the hours that Hazlitt called Living to One's Self; they are not easy to find, and worth strong sacrifice. Almost unconsciously he blew a perfect smoke ring—which he could not always do by intention—and watched it dash itself against the barrier of double glass. Jeff, palavering with Aunt Bee in the yard below, waved to him and made the raised eyes and lip-motions that meant "Are you working?" Uncle Dan nodded happily. "He says he's working," Jeff reported. "That means we mustn't catch his eye."

It was the pleasantest kind of work, when Dan felt himself getting ready to think about something but didn't quite know what. He looked across the disorderly view of wood-fenced yards, cobbled alley, the balconied backsides of the houses on Schier Street with their clotheslines of lively garments. He had nicknamed this region The Backs, with ironical allusion to the velvet lawns on the Cam, behind the colleges at Cambridge. It should be Sheer Street, Jeff said, because it runs along the top of the canyon. "The clotheslines get older on different streets," Jeff noticed. It was true. Schier Street, Uncle Dan once remarked, was a regular begettery: the garments exposed there ranged from infants' gear to age about seven. In the yards of Carroll the average would run from ten to twelve; as one moved to more stately Key Street the wooden pins nipped more elaborate female ruffle and full-length merinos. Eastward of Key the rigging of Patapsco Street showed younger again, the undervests of the college. All these humilities rippled and struggled in the flow of early spring. Ten thousand saw I at a glance, Dan thought, tossing their tails in sprightly dance. He had never truly perceived the humane quality of the city until he became himself a householder. Now he saw it with eyes of membership. Why, it's perfectly hideous, he said to himself: hideous, and homely, and dear. I love it! Oh, the wondersheen of spring. The word was from a mint of his own. Nothing is so comfortable as to take a foreigner's word and capture it for one's self. That is an invasion I enjoy. Wondersheen!

It wasn't only The Backs that he had learned to love. Sometimes, in those parenthesis moments before lunch (when his mind was just feinting for position) he went out to love the sidewalk in front of the house. He would have been too shy to tell anyone but he thought of the sidewalk as Reality. He didn't dare wash the marble steps; that had to be done by Moxie; to do it himself would have declassed him forever on Carroll Street; but it was all right to get out the hose (which had no nozzle) and wash the brick pavement, specially after the coal man had blackened it with dust; or sweep a late surprising snow; or astound the dealer in firewood by paying him to dump the logs outside and let Uncle Dan put on gloves and heave it through the little window into the cellar. The patient log-man (as Dan collaborated with Shakespeare in calling him) simply thought that Professor Barton was queer, because he himself would have stacked the wood in the bin for the same money; but to Uncle Dan it was important. It was one of his few contacts with physical decency. It was a sardonic parable of college education: the teacher (he mused) goes out into the forests of literature and cuts down the tall trees, delivers the chopped billets of doctrine for his customers; all they have to do is pile them orderly in a breathless basement. What do they know, or guess, or care, of the music of wind in the boughs; the ruinous crash of the great diseased chestnut; the twangling drone of the saw (cutting steadily into tough fiber, as language bites its way into meaning); the sweat of the workman, tickling the ears and wiped cool from the brow? What do the young know of anything? he thought sourly. They just want it delivered in convenience so they can pile it up and pretend they've "passed" it.

The backyard, maybe, was Hazlitt for Uncle Dan, but the sidewalk was Coleridge. To sweep or sprinkle was allowed a

233

legitimate chore of citizenship, and involved more casual conversation with neighbors than he really enjoyed; but a man with a beard always looks more thoughtful than others and by putting on a look of absence he was able to avert too much salutation. The Carroll Street brick pavement, laid in cunning sideways pattern, often took him to thought of the old wall at the top of the Wilford garden. It was rather like that wall laid flat on the ground; the walls of Jericho prostrated by divine bugle. A wall that kept no one out. Cooked by Chesapeake sun, scoured by the furious rainstorms, it was never so lovely pink as when the last snow of winter had to be swept. The Oriole Boys, who had a monopoly of snow-cleaning in that neighborhood, thought Uncle Dan a tightwad because he liked to do it himself. They couldn't possibly know that it was his luxury, his parable of walls fallen flat so he could think about what interested him. As he shoveled and scraped he mumbled to himself, "Twice five miles of fertile ground With walls and towers were girdled round." Then came spring, scurfy sycamores swelled in bud, and in the cracks of the pigeontoed bricks sprouted random seeds of the buttonballs, picked open during the winter by civic sparrows. Yes, the brick pavement was Coleridge himself, who had blown all fortresses flat in two terrific trumpet calls, and then had fallen palsied among what Wilford called rubbidge. Why couldn't S. T. C. have known, Uncle Dan asked himself as he swept the bricks in ecstasy, why couldn't that tormented god have known how his own buttonball skein ("many an incense-bearing tree") would fall, so far and long away, among the careful bricks of men's footing? He thought his most frequent vision: the wonderful boy who leaped over the fence and careered across the meadow to meet William and Dorothy— No, Dorothy and William—he thought of that magical-tragical head: a pleasure dome with caves of ice— The first Englishman who ever loved America as she needs to be loved,—"In Xanadu did Uncle Sam"—I must tell that to Major Warren—I never saw brick look so rosy—a professor of literature can't afford to be too fanciful—and he was summoned for lunch.

45. Big Fiends

It was not always necessary for the T.S.O. 4 Water Company to visit the spring so early in the morning. Unexpected auxiliary presently reinforced the young merchants. Aunt Bee had been curious about a much larger boy whom she had seen accompanying the expeditions. Her first impression of this odd-looking lad was memorable. The doorbell rang, she went to open, and a tall spotted youth in a very long overcoat removed his cap from a shock of bristly black cowlick, made a low bow and said, "Good morning, Madam. Is this the eminent Miss Barton?"

There was something so grave and intense in his demeanor that Aunt Bee's first thought was, it must be some instructor from the college.

"I'm very amenable to your kind acquaintance, Madam," continued the visitor with portentous solemnity. "The despot's foot is at your door. I've been instructed by the supreme council of unction to deliver this small package as a token of their assiduity." He again bowed almost to a rectangle and held out a bumpy-looking parcel untidily wrapped in brown paper.

"I'm afraid there must be some mistake," Aunt Bee began, astonished. "I'm not expecting—." The package wavering uncertainly between them fell to the marble step and burst open, showering the stoop with small pebbles, oyster shells and chestnut burrs. The face of the messenger, bent over toward her in exaggerated humility, suddenly flushed a deep red. His large opaque brown eyes rolled rapidly from side to side. Without a word he turned and fled down the street. He ran with amazing swiftness, leaning over with long arms swinging like a gorilla and throwing his knees very high under the flapping skirts of

235

his coat. From concealment behind a neighboring stoop appeared Jeff and Bert Eutaw screaming with laughter. "There's no harm done!" cried Jeff.

Bert Eutaw tried to explain while Jeff picked up the fallen rubbish.

"It's Ingram Sylvester Duffle. He's not quite all there, but his father sent him to live at my house so he could be around with kids and lead a normal life."

"It doesn't look exactly normal," said Aunt Bee; she could see an agitated face looking nervously round the corner of the block a hundred feet away.

"Just ole nervous spasms, he'll outgrow it," said Bert. "And he has such beautiful manners, my mother says he's really a good example. He's going to be mighty valuable. He'll do anything you suggest if you're quite serious about it. And he's terribly strong. My father says he has delayed reflexes or something. He's much older than we are and he's only in the fourth grade, but you should see him clean up those Orioles and Mount Royals. He's got them scared to death and he's going around with us as a bodyguard."

"He's like Centurions in the Bible," said Jeff. "He can throw the biggest kind of rocks and skin right up a tree. When he gets really excited he champs."

"I've seen him foam if you tease him too far," said Bert. He whistled and Ingram, like an obedient mastiff, came loping up the sidewalk. Again he made a sweeping bow and gesture to the horrified Miss Barton.

"They're big fiends, they're big fiends," he muttered apologetically. "Did I do something wrong? They told me exactly what to say."

"He has a wonderful retentive memory," said Jeff. "If you tell him the words, he never forgets. We're going to get up a parcel delivery service so he can ring doorbells and make speeches. He holds the maid with his glittering eye."

"Sometimes they slam the door on me before I can make it

236

glitter," said Ingram sadly. "It takes practice to make it glitter, you big fiends." This was evidently his usual description of his companions.

"They don't tell me what they put in the packages," said Ingram Sylvester Duffle. "They say it's better to keep my mind on the speech. I can say it again: 'Is this the eminent Miss Barton? I'm certainly amenable to make your kind acquaintance.' They said that would sound like the age of chivalry." He fixed her with a gaze of humble imbecility and again mumbled, "The big fiends, the big fiends!"

"We're digging a trench out in the lot," said Bert. "If the O.E.A. wagon comes round it will find it full of the bones of the Oriole Boys. Come on, Stinkin' Jim, it's your turn to dig."

"That's not my name," said Ingram anxiously. "You call me that it's not chivalry, it makes me sick to my gorge."

"I hope Dr. Eutaw approves of your treatment," said Aunt Bee doubtfully to Bert.

"He says they're such normal wholesome boys," insisted Ingram. "The big fiends. Good morning, Madam. I hope we will meet often." His small companions took him one by each elbow and escorted him up Carroll Street. Aunt Bee could see him tilting a large red ear downward to attend instruction.

It did not take long to exhaust the possibilities of parcel delivery. The ingenuity of carefully wrapped packages of old banana skins or vacant lot antiques was worth admiration; so also the labels "To the Lady of the House, Special Delivery from Strauss's" (a distinguished department store), and Ingram was never deficient in his instructed recitation. It always worked the first time. At a dignified front door on Key Street the earnest messenger would appear, startle the Negro maid with his extreme obeisance, and gabble, "Now is the time for all good men to come to the aid of the Madam. This little trophy is brought you by hand from Strauss's delicatessen, Forepaugh and Sells, Ringling Brothers and Twenty Mule Team Borax. Please de-

237

liver at once or place in your refrigerator, keep away from light and dark, heat and cold, whether this parcel so conceived and so dedicated can survive." There might be plenty more memorized text (tutored to the messenger with difficult gravity in Sassafras House) but that was about as much as any door-opener would accept without either terror or suspicion. It was not long before various householders kept a broom or an umbrella handy in the front hall; one Amazon Irish maid, too often pestered, first heaved a pail of water and then pursued Ingram Sylvester Duffle dangerously near the local police station. The itinerary of the parcel delivery could of course be extended to more distant streets, but like all good mischiefs the idea soon palled and the prudent Star Lanvale thought it wise to plan a change of tactics. This much explanation is needed to account for what happened when Skinny Granger made his first visit to Friends' Meeting.

Perhaps a sexton with his sharper sense of mortality would have been better prepared (than a mere caretaker) to anticipate trouble. But on so fair a sabbath no one was looking for trouble. Skinny, who already esteemed himself a connoisseur of church rituals, had probably boasted too much of his privilege in being invited to attend a Friends' Meeting for Worship. When Ingram Sylvester Duffle so very politely called on Miss Barton, expressed his amenity as usual by louting low and asked if he could go too, Aunt Bee was innocently touched. What, she thought, could be more wholesome for the poor fellow than the peaceful silent meeting? She may have had twinges of doubt but when she consulted Uncle Dan the latter believed Ingram's request a moving tribute to the kindly influence of Quaker doctrine. There may have been a little selfishness also in Dan's encouragement. Every additional boy moved away from Carroll Street on Sunday morning he considered an achievement. That period, when as many as possible of the world's noisier tenants are briefly and blessedly segregated for devotion, is an intimation of paradise for the student. "Never say I don't believe in religion," said Uncle Dan; "I get my best work done while other people are in church." So he watched with affectionate cheer as Aunt Bee went off toward the Key Street car with Jeff and Skinny at each elbow, while Ingram Sylvester Duffle rearing his long neck out of a very tight collar skipped ridiculously from side to side of the party in his efforts at seemly escort. It was ominous, perhaps, that Bert and Star leered at them unseen round the corner of Twentieth Street. Ingram was wearing the outsize overcoat and his first suit of long trousers, a light sandy color, rigidly creased. "Be careful of those store pants," yelled Star. "Shut up, you big dudes," Ingram muttered, almost tripping over a sycamore root. "If I can take your arm, Miss Madam, it will be more lady-like for you, and I can keep my mind on my instructions."

Meeting was preceded by Bible School, in which Ingram scored an unexpected success. Good-natured Miss Broker who supervised Jeff's class recognized the obvious frailties of Ingram Sylvester Duffle and wanted to give him a chance to show. It appeared he had been solidly tutored in the more dramatic fables of Israel. The episode was mentioned of the ill-mannered children who teased the bald-headed prophet. "And does anyone remember what happened to them?" the teacher asked.

"They were eaten by she-bears," said Ingram, rocking to and fro and grinning with satisfaction.

"Yes, and there are still bears in the mountains of Lebanon," said Miss Broker, who had duly studied her International Lesson. She could not have guessed that the T.S.O. 4 had made an expedition to the zoo only a few days before, where Ingram had been specially pleased by the grizzly which they always called Mr. Bolton; the animal's bandy legs and meaningful eyes gave a ribald suggestion of the schoolmaster. Ingram was already tensed by subtle pokes and proddings from Skinny and Jeff who had rather hoped for an outburst. He felt his mind lighten and leap with that uncontrollable inward flame.

"Bears!" he exclaimed. (He saw them emerging from the

underbrush of a cedared mountainside.) "Great ole sinful cinnamon bears! Those children tormented the prophet until he was sick to his gorge. He was compelled to abolish them. He whistled up his marauding she-bears and they just onslaughtered those kids. It hurt them more than it did him, it was a lesson to them, the big fiends, the big fiends. Their fathers and mothers and Dr. Eutaw came rushing out from their ole synagogue and the bears had them all worried to bits. Grrrr!" With gleaming eyes and shock black hair Ingram was on all fours in the orderly little circle, growling and pawing and pretending to attack his astounded neighbors. "You big fiends, I mean you big dudes, you better go way back and sit down, those bears forgot their instructions."

The other members of the class hoped that Ingram Sylvester Duffle was going to be a regular visitor. They speculated in Quaker decorum, what fascinating sect might Ingram belong to? and made innocent suggestions among themselves. But though Ingram quieted down without further disorder, the class was dismissed a little early.

Geoffrey tried to apologize to Miss Broker for the outbreak. The teacher's chief alarm had been that the superintendent of the First Day School would appear, as she was sometimes supposed to be too lenient in correction. "At any rate," she said, "I'm glad to find a boy who takes his religion so seriously. What is he, a Methodist?"

There was always a few minutes' recess between Bible School and the Meeting for Worship. During this time small girls swarmed into the library to borrow copies of the Prudy Books, the Little Colonel, Chatterbox, or Little Miss Weesie. The boys had their chance for an airing in the courtyard between the Bible School and the Meeting House. This was the time for Ingram Sylvester Duffle to obey the instructions that occupied his frail tenacious wits. Star and Bert had explained it all with care, though even they could not have foreseen the accident

240

that the Meeting House caretaker had gone off to find drugs for a grinding toothache. Ingram's kind heart, always friendly to the unfortunate, had been wrung by Star and Bert, who had explained to him the poverty of Quaker ritual. What the Friends subconsciously desire (these big fiends had explained) is incense. They sit in a bare room, Ingram was told, with nothing to do but twirl their thumbs and listen to homilies. It was now understandable why Ingram Sylvester Duffle had worn his long flapping overcoat on this bright spring day. For he had been given a parcel of incense to carry in his pocket and told how to find the Meeting House basement and put the perfume in the furnace. "Is it frankincense and myrrh?" he asked hopefully. They assured him it was. So when Ingram Sylvester Duffle remarked to Jeff and Skinny that he would just go and hang up his overcoat, and skipped with an extraordinary air of stealth across the courtyard and into the cellar, they only thought it was amusing he should suppose the basement was the cloakroom. He reappeared promptly with an air of conscious piety, and grasped Miss Barton's arm with solicitous dignity as they approached the Meeting House. "Now, Ingram, you behave yourself and no she-bears," whispered his tormentors.

"Shut up, you big dudes. I guess I know how to behave in church," he growled. His voice came out unexpectedly loud, startling some placid Friends entering with them.

Skinny of course was keenly interested in the routine of Quaker devotion. Since he knew he was in for a long sit he was relieved to find the cushions softer than anything Unitarian—probably because a Friends' congregation has less opportunity to take the weight off its hams.

"Who are those?" he whispered, observing several men of grave demeanor sitting on raised benches facing the meeting.

"Those are the elders," whispered Jeff.

Just then a solitary old lady in a dove-colored bonnet took her place on the female side of the dais. It was natural for

Skinny to ask was this Susannah, but Aunt Bee decided to divide the boys and sit between Ingram and the other two.

Natural human rustlings subsided and Skinny, all eyes and ears, found himself in a silence more intense than he had ever known. He could even hear the small rhythm of Aunt Bee's breathing. The air was warm to the edge of drowsiness; the conscientious caretaker, in spite of his tooth, had built a strong fire to dispel the Puritan frigor which accumulates in an unused building in a cold April week. Aunt Bee, before passing into an innocent nescience, reflected how well the boys were behaving, and Ingram especially. He had shown a spark of excitement when he saw a bunch of artificial Quaker ladies on a spring hat. This seemed to him so appropriate that it required admiring comment. But he was safely separated from the other two and except that he frequently spread his large nostrils and sniffed oddly, he seemed docile enough. Perhaps he has caught cold, thought Aunt Bee, and made Geoffrey pass over his handkerchief.

Skinny, by sloping this way and that, could get a good view of the elders; one of them had a very pale face and a large pink beard which particularly fascinated him. He could just see the head, truncated by someone's shoulder. Somehow it made him think of John the Baptist beheaded. He was shocked that some of the elders still had their hats on. This seemed to him to nullify the whole idea of a religious service. Why should this dreadful accident happen just the day he was there? Would they have to cancel the meeting and hold it over again? He whispered to Jeff, "They've gone to sleep and forgotten to take their hats off."

Jeff started to laugh but managed to turn it into a sneeze. Then the queer thing was he couldn't seem to stop sneezing. He leaned across Skinny and prodded Aunt Bee. "I want my handkerchief back," he whispered. But at that moment Ingram sneezed also, a beauty. Even the filaments on Aunt Bee's hat quivered, and a man with a large naked nape just in front of

242

Ingram shivered slightly. He wiped the back of his neck, which looked as if it would turn round, but the Quaker discipline is firm.

They were sitting alongside the center aisle and close to a large hot-air register. It was perhaps right that Ingram Sylvester Duffle was among the first to feel the effects of his incense, which was a couple of pounds of prime red pepper. Skinny was later than the others in feeling the irresistible tingle. He had been watching the face of John the Baptist. Experienced Friends would have known that this chandelier of the inner light was by no means asleep. A rapid pulsation of his eyelids and several unconscious tremors of the well-broad-clothed diaphragm were recognizable symptoms. The benches of the hierarchy were further removed from furnace outlets and although it seemed to Friend Eli Caton that the meeting was a little restless, he was too happily introvert to be disturbed. It was several weeks since he had given testimony and he had a Concern. The scriptural injunction to give no heed to one's message, it will be forthcoming when necessary, was one that he strictly obeyed. Indeed this was one reason why Uncle Dan came to meeting so seldom. But Skinny, inexperienced to the symptoms of ecstasy, watched absorbed. He saw John the Baptist rise abruptly, knit his fingers together and turn the palms briskly outward, and announce, "Did not our hearts burn within us by the way?" The bright eyes of the speaker seemed to fix Skinny with an unseeing stare and he waited for an answer to the question. At that moment the face of the heart-burner underwent strange transformation. Again the eyelids flapped repeatedly, all the massive features seemed to ripple together and then fly apart. Friend Caton horrified himself and the Meeting with a roaring sneeze which blew his beard sideways. It was like a signal of release. Those who had writhed and strangled in secret unconsciously let go. Tears rolled, handkerchiefs flashed, and Ingram Sylvester Duffle, now realizing that something was wrong, gargled and wept and turned tragically to Aunt Bee. "The big fiends, the big fiends!" he exclaimed. Jeff with streaming features snatched back his handkerchief.

But it takes more than hysteria to dominate a Friend just embarked upon a Concern. With a very large handkerchief to his face Friend Caton reached down and shook hands with the elder at his side. This formally dissolved the gathering. "I am sorry, Friends," he said. "There seems to be something wrong. The meeting will migrate to the Assembly Room in the Bible School." And when some fifteen minutes later all were transferred and the silence resumed (punctured with a few snuffles) Skinny was astounded to see John the Baptist exhibit the same preliminary gestures, and continue his discourse without even repeating the text.

"It wasn't our hearts that burned, it was our noses," Jeff explained later to Uncle Dan.

The caretaker returning to duty with a mouthful of oil of cloves was horrified to see his clients streaming across the courtyard with wet eyes and pink noses. "It looked like a rum demons' convention," he reported at home, "but anyway, the excitement cured my tooth."

Subsequent question caused pain to Bert and Star, who wailed and confessed their ingenious plot. But Mr. Lanvale, a lawyer, admitted to Uncle Dan that under cross-question his son had shown unmistakable talent for the bar. "What do you suppose he put up as a defense?" said Mr. Lanvale. "He said I'd been all the time telling him to read Huck Finn and Tom Sawyer, so he did, and the tricks Huck and Tom played in church put this idea into his head. I wouldn't be surprised there's been a whole generation of kids cutting up in church on account of Mark Twain. I guess maybe literature has more effect on actual life than I supposed."

Mark Twain might well have considered the aftermath a tribute to his art. Star and Bert were ordered to write letters of contrition to the Clerk of the Friends' Meeting, also to apologize to Miss Barton.

"Maybe she wouldn't mind waiting till tomorrow, my eyes are still red," said Bert.

"So are hers," said Jeff. "You can apologize to me instead."

"It's not just my eyes that's red," said Star, who had been contemplating Mr. Lanvale's efficiency by examining himself backward in a mirror.

"I'm embarrassed," Jeff said to Uncle Dan, "because both Star and Bert got a terrible thrashing. In the T.S.O. 4 we're supposed to go dibbies, share and share alike. It's Article Six in the Constitution. You better give *me* a licking too."

Uncle Dan said he couldn't do it in cold blood.

"If you don't, the boys will. I'd rather have it in privacy."

"Try Aunt Bee," said Uncle Dan. "She's got a stronger character than I have."

Aunt Bee was not loth to oblige. She said it was overdue on many counts. "Bend over that chair," she ordered tartly. "I'll get Uncle Dan's old razor-strop. I always wondered why we saved it. Now I know."

Dan left the house hastily, not to hear the sound of leather. He knew that Bee would lay on with vigor, and probably weep in secret afterward. It wouldn't do Jeff any harm, and would be a catharsis for her.

"Say, you're strong," said Jeff. "I couldn't help yowling. I guess I feel better now. I mean, I feel more democratic."

Even Skinny did not escape; the other three overpowered him and handed on their own concussion. Ingram Sylvester Duffle felt almost slighted that he himself had escaped punishment, but the boys agreed that he was really blameless. "The Constitution don't apply," they said. "You're only an honorary member. You're not really all there."

"I am so, you big fiends. I'm the most there of anybody in this crowd. I'm sick and tired of such nonsense. You're stuck up." He threatened them with his large fists.

"Well, you're too big and powerful," said Star tactfully. "You might get excited."

"Let's go up in the barn," suggested Bert. "There's straw to sit on."

They retired to the hayloft to talk things over. There were a few mouldy jujubes, gumdrops and crackers left in their cache in an old cupboard. Gumdrop sandwiches were an invention of their own. Skinny's tasted saltier than the others.

After a good deal of face-mopping Skinny said he was surprised that things didn't happen in Friends' Meeting more often, because there was nothing to read, no distractions against mischief. "You sit like that, all alone in your mind," he said, "and maybe it's not good for you. Even the ladies' hats are not very amusing at that Meeting. I'd think there ought to be a hymnal."

"Sure there ought," said Bert. *"Hymns Ancient and Modern.* I think they're all ancient. I never could find any modern ones."

"It's bad to read hymns without singing them," said Star. "They sound awful exaggerated."

Jeff naturally stood up for the Quaker doctrine. "You-all are just bigoted. You gotta have enough Holy Spirit in you to understand that kind of thing; yes sir, you're bigoted."

"Yay, yay, old bigoty-bigot," cried Star, turning a handspring. "Let's play leap-frog."

"Shut up, you big fiends, you're punko. Go way back and sit down. Twenty-three for you, now we're having a nice talk," mumbled Ingram Sylvester Duffle. He enjoyed serious conversation and resented its turning into horseplay as it so often did. Poor soul, he knew intuitively that if excitement got the better of him anything might happen. He dragged Star back to a sitting posture.

"Now look what you did, you dumb ox," Star squawked, "you sat me down hard on a broken bottle. I've got Bromo-Seltzer in my tail and it was sore already."

"You shut up yourself, you're just vulgar. If Dr. Eutaw knew how I have to associate with you he'd send me to a sanitarium, he said so."

"There's worse things than red pepper happens in churches," said Bert.

"You bet," said Jeff. "I went to your kind of religion in England one time but it's got more class to it, I guess, it's Established Church. Gee, they've got some terrible bad words. They're pretty near ashamed of them themselves because they turn sideways and duck their heads. There's one word they use I wouldn't even think of."

"What is it?" exclaimed Star and Bert.

"No *sir*," said Jeff firmly. "Besides maybe I don't know how to pronounce it. They mumble it so you can't be sure."

"Spell it backward," suggested Star, "and we'll pronounce it for you."

"No, I guess it's just an English word," said Jeff.

"I bet they don't have any dirty words in England as dirty as we have," said Star.

"You're crazy, all the smutty words came from England to begin with. They were busy thinking them up while this country was nothing but Indians."

"You could write some down in the minutes," said Bert, "and then go away while we read them. We could tell you if they're really so bad."

"Now you big fiends," interrupted Ingram, "let's keep this meeting on a high plane. I'm going to be a good influence in this club."

"I didn't know how rotten things are until my Pop left his bookcase unlocked," said Bert. "It was worse afterward because I dropped licorice on the pages."

"Aw shucks, that's nothing," said Star, "we got the Century Dictionary right out in the sitting-room."

"Dictionaries ain't any good," said Bert. "You gotta know how to spell anything before you can look it up."

"You sound awful dumb to me," said Ingram. "What was it happened in your church, Bert?"

"I had a slick way to get even with my sister. She had some kind of a tizzic."

"How do you spell it?" asked Jeff.

"I don't know, I guess it's not in the dictionary. Kind of hay fever, she was sneezing all the time. She kept on scolding me about bad manners, you know what girls are, so one Sunday when we went to church I took along her atomizer. I had it hid under my coat and every time she sneezed I sprayed it all over the lady in front. She was like to go crazy because she thought Judy was snotting all over her. She turned round and made an awful fuss. They got the ushers into it, too, as a matter and fact it was really kind of antiseptic but my Pop took it out of me in the long run, like they always do. Gee, I'm so tanned behind I could sit on broken glass and never feel it."

"We better vote," said Star, "or we'll be late at the spring."

The subject of the ballot was which form of religion the club considered most promising for Salvation. The result was as might have been expected: Presbyterian 1, Unitarian 1, Episcopalian 1, Society of Friends (thanks to the novitiate of Ingram Sylvester Duffle) 2.

"Fen crowning King Edward," shouted Jeff.

"Dibbies on Master of the Horse," cried Ingram. He was so proud of this nomination that he always forgot it involved pulling the wagon up the hill.

The crowning of King Edward VII, then much mooted in the press, was a new ritual of the Water Company. It was supposed to give their cargo a royal sparkle. Jeff had noticed that the rounded iron standpipe resembled the pate of the elderly monarch. To fill the drinking bowl which hung on a chain, hold it solemnly aloft, then clank it deftly on the metal skull so that the water flowed evenly over the scalp, was the procedure they called coronation. It was very satisfying when well done, while the other members stood at courtly attention. The

248

guerillas of Mount Royal looked on with sneers but one growl, "Skiddoo, you big fiends," from Ingram was enough to keep them at a distance. Perhaps inspired by the ecclesiastical discussion Jeff accomplished the rite with unusual skill. "Oyez, oyez! The Archbishop of Canterbury approaches the historic throne," he announced. "Is the Stone of Scoon under the chair? It is. Are the Master of Horse and his Equerries ready for the Unction?"

It was desirable to make haste; Ingram was already tremulous with hysteria.

"I crown thee Edward, in the name of the T.S.O. 4." A word came into his mind, he didn't know why. "A chrism!" he shouted.

46. *The Dressing-gown*

Please act as arbiter in a linguistic dispute (wrote Uncle Dan to Blanche Bristol). Bee and Geoff submitted it to me but now they've got me confused. I had no idea I was raising such a young stickler. Bee and Geoff were out in the yard planting some lilac stubs we brought from Greenaway. It's wonderful what Bee has done in the way of beautifying our wretched little space. She's perfectly happy if she can grub around in a patch of dirt, no matter how small. She remarked to Geoff that she was "happy as a grig" and he demurred. He said that grigs aren't "happy," they're *merry*. They argued about it until now I'm uncertain myself. If it has to be merry, then Bee isn't exactly a grig. She has her own stoical mode of showing satisfaction, but *merry* is not quite in character.—Character is Geoff's specialty: if people aren't in it he'll put them there. You remember Mrs. Maggots next door, from whose basilisk eye we will soon be mercifully shielded by masses of Virginia creeper. She fascinated Geoff from the beginning, he used to sit on a box in the yard and fix her with a retaliating gaze. One day he came indoors in triumph announcing, "I made her flinch." Bee took him down, however, by saying, "You haven't made her cower." But the boy had to account to himself somehow for the poor lady's persistent stare. He invented all sorts of fantastic motives and explanations, including even a romance in which she was the relict of a frustrated jerrybuilder who had buried a hoard of treasure exactly in our backyard; so that every time Aunt Bee goes digging Mrs. Maggots fears we'll find her doubloons and pieces-of-eight. But this was only the beginning: it developed into a series of comic drawings, "The Melodramas of Mrs. Maggots," in which she passes through successions of adventure and outrage, undergoing every kind of calamity and triumphing over disaster by the steadfast fixity of her gaze. Killer whales, jungle tigers, Indians, cyclones, volcanoes, on-rushing trains, are all shown in these pictures as quelled and sidetracked by Mrs. Maggots' superhuman orb. Her only human weakness is the exclamation which concludes every series: with a memorial sigh she relaxes and says *Phew!* This perhaps is out of character. Geoff got it from my earnest graduate student Miss Towson. It is Miss T's only sign of emotion.

Eventually, of course, The Eye proves to be glass. One of the best of the cartoon serials is where Mrs. Maggots thinks she has discovered the treasure but Geoff refutes her by showing they are not doubloons but only singloons. I never saw a child have so much fun with words: the fiscal system of Jeffland has been revised lately, due, I daresay, to some school allusion to "resumption of specie payments," a phrase that tickles Geoff for some reason. The monetary unit of Jeffland is the *specie*, but all its petite monnaie is now reckoned in coins called *reps* and *demi-reps*. As a result of recent unsuccessful wars with LaGrange, Jeffland is paying an indemnity and you may imagine me smiling as I overhear Skinny Granger remark, "You owe me another shipment of ten thousand demi-reps." The North Avenue Unitarian Church would be surprised to know that its neat little envelopes for Free-Will Offerings are used to hold these shipments.

Bee reproaches Geoff for all the irresponsible fables he invents about Mrs. Maggots or other neighbors. In the good old Wilford tradition Bee draws a rather definite line between truth and falsehood but I urge that every artist has to account to himself for phenomena he observes—and as a child cannot possibly know enough facts to account for the world's grotesque behavior he must naturally invent plots of his own to explain it.

I didn't mean to write all this irrelevance, it's just a way of postponing what was most uncomfortably on my mind. I didn't get the appointment to the University. Naturally it's a blow, the professorship would have been a step up in so many ways. I know it seems absurd, but I rather believe it was still an aftermath of the old Friedeck trouble. I don't remember any too well just what it may have been that rubbed our Prussian friend the wrong way. You'd think he also might have forgotten about it by now, but I have it from trustworthy report that when my name came up at the academic council Friedeck insisted that I am not a genuine scholar, have no doctor's degree, in short, no philologist. Which I fear is true. I felt pretty badly about this for a while and for some quite special reasons which I need not enlarge. One piece of good news, though, they have just appointed me official delegate from Patapsco for the inauguration of Woodrow Wilson at Princeton next fall. I take that to mean that Beinbrink has it in mind to promote me: they would hardly send anyone below a full professor to such an academic gala? There will surely be a notable attendance of people from all the colleges and some of them will be useful to meet. Do you know who will be going from Radnor? Tell Kilda I wish I had a Dublin gown, those wonderful sleeves in McGillicuddy green.

I've been a bit tired and jaded. If you knew what my students can do to the eighteenth century you'd forgive anything. I'm going off for a few days' jaunt with my friend Huffy (Dr. Huffenbutz), or as the students call him, Hoof-in-boots. He's a good companion for a vacation; as he's a physicist we don't either of us talk shop. He endeared himself specially to me when we were cycling together—whenever I got a puncture he insisted on repairing it because he said it was a pretty little problem in pneumatics and he likes above all things to work with his hands. That suited me perfectly. As reciprocity he always lets me do the bargaining for a night's lodging. He says my air of false naïveté blandishes the rustic housewife. He's really wonderful in any practical dilemma and very kindly fixed Geoff's steam engine for us when I was baffled. Did it ever strike you, if you scratch an American you find a mechanic—

Dan interrupted himself. And if you scratch *me*, he thought somberly, what would be found? An uncle . . . but this kind of self-question is too destructive. "If the sun and moon should doubt, they'd immediately go out." For consolation he approached a sentimental hiding-place on one of the bookshelves. Discreetly slipped between Coleridge and Keats (the exact neighborhood had been given much thought) were three thin pamphlets: *Transformations of a Quartic, Bimagic Squares,* and *A Note on Determinants.* Two of these were primly inscribed "D. B. with the author's compliments," but *Bimagic Squares* seemed more intimate. On it was written "D. B. from B. B." Though the pages consisted mostly of inscrutable blocks of numbers completely mysterious to Dan, this was his favorite. In the world of scholars there is no gesture of regard so tender as the exchange of reprints. The pamphlet extras of contributions to professional journals are the bonbons and nosegays of the higher faculty. It may be thought that in these austere exchanges Miss Bristol had something the better of it. Professor Barton's most esteemed research—*On the Decline of Visualizing Power in Wordsworth After 1820*—was at least legible to its recipient. Indeed he had even embarrassed her by introducing her in a very small footnote. "For climatological graphs bearing upon the topic I am indebted to Miss B. Bristol, Radnor College." To casual readers (if there are such) of the *Modern Language Quarterly* this footnote would seem just the fine conscience of learning, but it could also be estimated as a form of academic showing-off.

He sighed gently as he glanced again at the leaflets, printed mostly in the runic symbols of that printing house in Lancaster, Pa., which is the Mount Sinai of the polymath. Perhaps even Blanche herself had realized that these essays were meager nourishment. What a stride it had been when after her visit at Christmas she sent him the dressing-gown. She must have noticed that he had given up his room for her and slept in the study. Or worse, Geoffrey might have told her. . . .

He returned to the letter:

Bee and I were disturbed when you wrote you had been plagued all spring by "an obstinate quartic." We thought at first it was some kind of fever or migraine. Bee was going to advise rhubarb and soda. I went so far as to look up those price-less passages in Dr. Johnson's *Letters* where he recommends his orange-peel specific to an accomplished female friend. But I have just looked again at your Works and realize that the Quartic is some kind of recalcitrant equation? So we feel re-lieved. If it has yielded to analysis, why don't you come down after the end of term and pay us a visit? Bee has been brewing a new vintage of root beer which she annunciates as tête de cuvée, and I know Geoff would welcome some help with his algebra now just beginning. I'm not much use at that, like S. T. C. I find the trunk of the Tall Tree of Mathematics very slippery to climb. I see you up there in the branches as inde-pendent as the Cheshire Cat—or the Shropshire Possum.

It is very sweet of the good Possum to let me unload like this. I began this letter in a fit of the dumps, but I got into my dressing-gown here in the study, even the alley is relatively quiet, and I feel better. After all a dressing-gown is the most spiritual present anyone can give. It wraps the mind in and the world out in the hours when one most needs to make friends with one's self. Perhaps that was why your hero Sherlock

Holmes solved his problems with one.—But myself, I carry the fancy farther still and think that the thaumaturgic mantle Prospero used to put on for his doings with Ariel was really the dressing-gown he wore at his studies.

I better not let Geoff get hold of that word thaumaturgic—he'll run it into the ground.

47. *The Shawbucks Look Daggers*

It had been a bad day from the beginning. Mr. Bolton, looking even more like the grizzly than usual, gave a talk to the whole school in morning assembly. Even though this reduced the first classroom period by several minutes its purport was devastating. Nobody had confessed about setting the lumber pile on fire. There wasn't a boy above the kindergarten who didn't know that Bill Shawbuck, in a pang of nausea, had dropped a lighted Little Recruit between the scantlings (they were building an addition to the gym) but it was no one's business to tell if Bill didn't. Now Mr. Bolton said that unless the guilt was honorably admitted there would be no leave that noon to watch the circus parade go down Cardinal Street. A low moan of despair sounded among two hundred boys. If Mr. Bolton was as shrewd as one believed, he could guess the culprit pretty well by seeing the instinctive lining up of glances toward the callous Bill.

Yet perhaps Bill was not so hardened after all. In the damnably complicated psychology of fourteen his feeling probably was that he had fessed up once already and surely that was enough. He still bore on his forehead the mark of the ashes of penance from the Lenten Mass that morning. He had confessed his guilt to the priest and that practical theologian had of course commanded him to tell the truth at school. And Bill had done so: he took his brother into the furnace room and told *him.* "Maybe you better tell Mr. Bolton," said Bill to Jellybean. But even for one of Jellybean's tough fiber this was too painful a dilemma. He suspected that Bill wanted to come clean, but for Jelly to serve as informer would put him on record forever not only as a tattle and sneak, but a traitor to his own blood.

It was strange to see the usually carefree and domineering Shawbucks oppressed by the power of mass opinion. Indignant looks seemed actually palpable as the crowd clattered up and down the iron stairs—and how iron the treads can feel to the heavy feet of shame. In moving masses of boys that shuffled through the halls the Shawbucks encountered knees and elbows and sharp anonymous pinches which they well guessed were administered by companions usually timid and respectful. Jeff and Skinny, who had suffered many indignities from Shawbuck hands and feet, were elated to join the general disgust. "Why don't you wash your face?" said Jeff, addressing Bill with a look of such frank hatred that even Bill was startled. This was the extreme of insult. Jeff, quakerishly ignorant of the religious symbolism, quite honestly supposed the Ash Wednesday smear was just Shawbuck sloven. The attendant Jellybean, with every muscle cocked to glean whatever small salvage might come his way, projected a hardy shin and Jeff went sprawling. But Bill for the moment seemed cowed.

He may even have lain awake the night before anticipating disaster, though indeed that would be rare in the confident house of Shawbuck. At any rate Bill had not studied his lessons.

They were in English III when Ringling Brothers went down Cardinal Street with chariots and white horses. The classroom is often very apropos in satirizing the current event: there was a painful timeliness in the early stanzas of *The Ancient Mariner*, their assignment that morning. They heard the loud bassoon (the screaming warble of the steam calliope), but the parade itself was hidden behind the gym. Looking desolately across the pebbled playground they could see for an instant the lofty head of the giraffe riding in its wheeled and gilded crib. The first giraffe ever to Participate in a Public Pageant, the

255

Sun-Paper had assured them; and just then the gangling quadruped gazed across with bulging eyes as if to reproach them for not being out on the street to welcome it. What was worse still, the scaffolding of their own gym was swarmed over by small colored boys enjoying a perfect view.

The teachers themselves were a trifle acrid that morning. They wouldn't have admitted it but they enjoyed parades as much as anyone. "This is just as exciting as any circus," said Mr. Lidgate sharply. "Granger, close the windows."

Skinny tarried at the task as long as he dared but the big sashes were finally pulled down; the chords of the steam organ and all the brazen ta-ra-ra (which seemed to be saying Ringling Brothers in a thousand voices) faded away.

"Instead of Ringling Brothers, let's try Shawbuck Brothers," said Mr. Lidgate. "Bill, read from there."

"The ice was here, the ice was there," mumbled Bill. His enunciation was never very clear but today his private sorrows made him specially gruff.

"Please hold your head up and read as if you thought it made sense."

Bill straightened his long neck and a deeper flush seemed to blend into one color his rich dapple of orange freckles. A rub of his arm across a damp forehead transferred the symbolical ashes to his shirtsleeve. Jeff and Skinny, who flanked him from behind, rejoiced with malice in these signals of distress. *He looks like a giraffe*, Skinny wrote hastily on the margin of Jeff's book. This drew Jeff's attention to one particular word on the page. It was a new textbook just handed out to them the day before. Jeff of course had not prepared the lesson. He had spent his time on Caesar for he knew most of *The Ancient Mariner* by heart anyhow. But now he saw in an ecstasy something on the page which might cause the downfall of the unsuspecting Bill. He pointed it out to Skinny and they nudged each other with joyous expectancy.

"The ice was here, the ice was there," gabbled Bill, "the ice

256

was all around: it cracked and growled and roared and howled like noises in a sound."

"Like a circus parade," said Mr. Lidgate, getting an insincere titter from several bootlickers. "What does he mean by the last line?"

"Just noises," said Bill sulkily. "Noises in a sound, a sound made up of a lot of noises." Jeff's and Skinny's arms were waving furiously on Bill's left. He looked round at them with a curious mixture of threat and appeal. Mr. Lidgate paid no attention to these gestures which were sometimes too frequent.

"Noises in a *sound?*" he said. "Can't you read?"

"Sure he can read," growled the loyal Jellybean. He and Bill sat together and shared the same book. "It's just common sense."

The rest of the class sat in prudent dumbness enjoying this unexpected episode, but Skinny and Jeff were almost on their feet with eagerness.

"Granger and Barton, the Heavenly Twins," said Mr. Lidgate. "What seems to be the agitation? Granger, borrow a handkerchief if you haven't got one and wipe your face."

"It's a misprint in the book," screamed Geoffrey. "It says sound. It ought to be *swound.*"

It took some time to clear up the misunderstanding, because Mr. Lidgate was using a different book. Until he had come down from his desk and examined the new texts he thought perhaps some sort of joke was being played. To the delight of the class he then took time out for a sermon on the relativity of error. This gave opportunity for some ingenious drawings of circus parades at the back of the room.

"Nobody should be blamed," he said, "for an error of judgment where the data were not available for making a correct choice. To get a thing wrong is not discreditable if you were given erroneous premises to start from. I cannot help thinking, however, that you might have been familiar with one of the most famous passages in literature." They proceeded to a dis-

257

cussion of swoon and swound. "The latter," said Mr. Lidgate, "was an old-fashioned or rustic pronunciation." But Bert Eutaw insisted that his father always said it that way. "My mother fell downstairs in a swound," he said, "it was just her time of life."

"Never mind the family details," said Mr. Lidgate. "You can read from there." Again there was trouble, for in his agitation Bert read "through the fog" instead of "thorough the fog." "Why do you suppose he said 'thorough the fog'?" asked Mr. Lidgate, thinking sadly to himself what a way to treat a poem.

"It's meter, it sounds better," piped Geoffrey.

"It sounds more difficult," added Skinny, "like the bird finding its way in the fog."

Bill Shawbuck breathed more freely to find attention diverted. He parted his lips very slightly in a syllable audible only to his brother. Skinny and Jeff had saved him but he knew that was not their intention.

After the excitements of *The Ancient Mariner*, orchestrated by the bassoons of Ringling, Jeff looked forward to the usual tranquility of Caesar's campaign in Gaul. That general would have been surprised to know that his diary of campaign could become a noontime sedative for small boys. But Mr. Rhodes's class was conducted on principles of order and method. The pupils were called upon regularly in turn so that one always knew one's safety margin against question. Rather like G. J. Caesar himself, Mr. Rhodes (naturally known to the class as "Dusty") would almost prefer not to conquer the enemy than to succeed by unconventional maneuver. Action was proceeding on the left wing of the front row. Jeff and Skinny were still protected by several intervening auxiliaries. The invaders were not yet very deep in Gaul; indeed they had only just become familiar with the awkward preference for the subjunctive mood shown by Diviciacus the Haeduan. Little did they realize that this peculiar form of syntax would spread all the way from

Mediterranean to English Channel and even embarrass tourists two thousand years to come. As Skinny once remarked in a moment of bitterness, "I wouldn't have minded the Romans walloping the Gauls if they hadn't taught them to talk in subjunctives." Well did Allen and Greenough in their Preface speak of Indirect Discourse as "the bugbear of Latin education." Skinny had adorned the margin with a picture of a bugbear, a cross between Mr. Bolton and the grizzly.

"Chapter 29. W. Shawbuck, take it from there," said Mr. Rhodes. Skinny nudged Jeff; he knew this was going to be good.

"*In castris Helvetiorum,* in the camp of the Helvetians, *tabulae repertae sunt,* tables are found, *litteris Graecis confectae,* littered with Greek confectionery."

A blissful and suspended silence concealed all small sounds or distractions. The class held its breath. Was Bill so besotted that he would try to bluff it through? Did not even Jellybean have sense enough to say "We are not prepared"—since everyone knew that the Shawbucks performed mutually. Even Mr. Rhodes's young and austere face showed the innocent pleasure of one finding some shining gem among rubbish.

"How do you suppose the Greek confectionery got there?" he asked. His deceptive serenity lured Bill deeper into the mire.

"I suppose it was those merchants who sold stuff to the troops. It says so in the next clause: *quibus in tabulis nominatim ratio confecta erat,* on which tables was the aforesaid candy ration."

"What kind of tables do you think these were?"

Bill was beyond succor. "Sort of lunch tables."

"Since you all seem to be translating at sight this morning," said Mr. Rhodes, "let's go on to Chapter 39 and try a bit of unseen. This will tell us more about those candy merchants. It's a very interesting passage because it shows the effect the Germans had on all those little Mediterranean peddlers. In case it hadn't occurred to you that Caesar had a sense of humor, you'll find it in his description of the panic that runs through the camp, and Caesar's civilian friends, sort of members of Congress who'd been looking over the campaign, suddenly discover that urgent personal business needs their attention at home; others send out for a lawyer to make their wills. It's a difficult little chapter, look it over for a couple of minutes and then we'll see who wants to try it."

Skinny's hand went up first. "By the talk of our men," he said, slowly exploring the layers of indirect discourse, "and the reports of the Gauls and traders, who kept saying that the Germans were of such huge bodily size, of incredible valor and skill with their weapons—often when they met them they couldn't bear to look them in the face and the—*aciem oculorum* —gosh, I can see what that means, but I can't think how to say it."

"We might say 'penetrating gaze,' " said Mr. Rhodes, "but perhaps we can do better. *Aciem:* that means first something sharp, a point or a keen edge, and then a line of battle—"

"The flash of their eyes," suggested Skinny.

"Their steely gaze," offered Bert.

"They looked daggers!" exclaimed Jeff.

"Good! *Very* good!" said Mr. Rhodes. "Now that's the way to translate."

The Shawbucks were of the superior clique who ate lunch in the school's dining-room on the top floor. Boys who brought their own sandwiches usually took them out to the playground where they clustered in small groups of mysterious congeniality. This day Jeff and Skinny had so much to talk over they repaired to a window-sill in the locker room in the basement. Bill Shawbuck, at recess, embittered by his various woes, did not feel like encountering the inevitable chaff of the dining-room. Jellaby had been detained for ominous questioning by the headmaster. Bill, without his ally and feeling every hand raised against him, decided to sneak out through the basement and get a hokey-pokey from Santa Claus, as the neighboring vender Pappanicholas was nicknamed. In the rigor of the law this was taboo, since the *Sun-Paper* had alarmed parents by a headline BUGS IN HOKEY-POKEY; but to Bill it seemed that nothing mattered now. Getting ball and glove from his locker to do a little bouncing on the outdoor pavements, he did not at first notice Jeff and Skinny colloguing in a remote corner. Except for them the gloomy basement was empty. "I guess he's going out for some of that Greek candy," Jeff chirped.

Bill looked furiously in their direction. At first he did not recognize them, darkened against the wired window.

"Oh, it's you, hey? Greasy grinds. Crybaby and Gee-offrey. Guffrey, Fatguts Guffrey. Eating your nice little sandwiches, hey? Just too cheap-skate to spend a few cents upstairs. I guess you're afraid they'll give you chicken soup."

This alluded to Jeff's very first day at school, when he had eaten in the lunchroom and was hailed simultaneously by two boys. One said, "Hey, new kid, what's your name?" and the other: "What's that you're eating?" Confused, Geoffrey had replied to the one who asked his name, "It's supposed to be chicken soup." A shout of pleasure rose along the table. "Here's a new kid says his name's Chicken Soup." This humiliating label still irked him.

"Why aren't you up there yourself?" was their natural retort, which seemed to enrage Bill. He snatched Jeff's package of lunch and scattered the sandwiches on the floor.

Jeff had a horrible feeling that he was going to cry, his mouth shook so with nervousness. It was a kind of sickening disgust at seeing Aunt Bee's patient handiwork, the carefully trimmed sandwiches of crab-apple jelly which she cut so carefully, strewn on the dusty cement. He tried to control the quivering of his jaw and slid from the window. Tears of excitement were already streaming on Skinny's face, which probably encouraged Bill further.

261

"Going to do something, hey? That's fine. Fatguts Guffrey. Want to fight?"

"Come in the furnace room, I'll have it out with you," said Jeff with something of a shake in his voice but with such evident resolve that even Bill was surprised. He pushed Jeff roughly, playing for time since he expected Jellaby to join him at any moment. "Aw, you're ensi-ent," he jeered; a word he had heard his grandmother use mysteriously and which he must have misunderstood; at any rate he had reserved it as an ultimate reproach. "What you going to fight about?"

"About you," blurted Jeff; or that was what he meant to say. He thought afterward, in humiliation, that it must have sounded ridiculously like a sneeze: About-*choo*. But at the moment long-suffered anger and alarm blotted all other awareness. He led the way to the furnace room, which was far from ideal for such encounters, but it was the first place he thought of.

"I'll *attend* to you," he muttered.

"Kill him, Jeff," wept Skinny, following, "and I'll see fair play. You can have half my sandwiches."

"Stung!" shouted Bill, seizing Skinny's lunch also and throwing it into the open door of the firebox.

The beautifully scientific and maneuvered combat that Jeff had often imagined did not take place. Outraged Skinny, whose tear ducts belied his valiant heart, threw himself bodily on Bill with a howl of rage. With teeth and knees and nails and feet all working he staggered the larger boy, while Jeff must also have exercised a useful fist since his knuckles ached for days. There was something so berserk about the attack that Bill was appalled. He dodged backward and was about to seize a lump of coal from the bin.

But the janitor, before going off for his own lunch, had shaken down the fire and raked ashes into the pit where the furnace stood. Bill, stepping too far, went over into the depression. It was quite a fall in itself, but also he landed full sprawl in the pile of cinders. They looked like gray clinkers, but there were red coals underneath and the mass was fiery hot. With a yell of anguish and a smell of burning cloth Bill sprang up and fled wildly to the washroom. Even his enemies were horrified and helped him anoint his blisters with soap. He mumbled unintelligible grievance, said he felt sick, and departed for home without waiting for further disaster.

Grimly LaGrange and Jeffland watched Bill hobble up the bicycle ramp from the basement, with two smoldered gaps in the rear of his pantaloons. "I bet he won't forget Ash Wednesday," said Skinny. "Lend me your snot-rag."

Jeff suddenly realized his nose was bleeding, so Bill must have landed at least one good blow. At any rate, he reflected later, one fine thing about that fight was, it didn't start a lifelong friendship. He never had any use for the Shawbucks and that was undoubtedly mutual. But he still blushed in secret for his agonized outcry: About-*choo!* That was a crude thing to say, he thought sadly.

48. Mythology in 1903

Perhaps it was the Album at Greenaway that stimulated Aunt Bee to compile a new series of scrapbooks. In the evening, when Uncle Dan had retired to his study and Jeff spread out homework on the dining table, Aunt Bee had a chance to settle down in her cozy corner and take the evening paper seriously. She was delighted by the miscellany of reprinted poems and household hints that lurked in its pages. Her private scissors and paste, if Jeff hadn't made off with them, were busy fastening these into exercise books that fattened rapidly. Her secret fantasy, as she sat in winter in the gust of the hot-air register, or in summer by the open window and the busybody mirror, was to imagine going through these scrapbooks with the old family circle at Wilford. How much Grandma would find to interest her, and what a range of sentiment: from Joaquin Miller, Behind him lay the gray Azores, to Removing inkstains with skim-milk.

Reared on the *Wilford Reporter and Wickham Market Gazette*, it was natural that Aunt Bee took her journalism with patient gravity. After a while, however, she began to perceive that here and there were items deliberately in fun. One evening Dan heard her chuckle over something in the *Sun-Paper*.

"What is it?" he asked.

"It's a letter to the Editor," she said. "It says: 'Dear Sir, to settle a dispute, will you inform me, am I right or is she?'—And it's signed HUSBAND."

"How perfectly idiotic," said Dan. "The printer must have dropped something out. How can you answer without knowing more details?"

"That's just the point," cackled Aunt Bee. "The Editor prints the answer. He says 'She is.—Ed.'"

Dan was startled to realize that Bee was actually aware of the American relish for the absurd.

Jeff had no interest in the newspaper except on Sunday, when a much put-upon character called Mr. Bowser made his weekly appearance. A short story, with a lively illustration, described Mr. Bowser's Trials and Tribulations: his wife, or the cook, or the child, the neighbors, the steam laundry, or the cat, got the better of Mr. Bowser in some domestic problem. These fables, mysteriously signed "By M. Quad," were Jeff's introduction to the American defensive humor of self-mockery. He rose early on Sundays to read them before breakfast, pasted them carefully in his own scrapbook, and then went through them again, aloud, for Aunt Bee. "Poor Mr. Bowser," she would say, "no wonder he feels sadly."

Sometimes the ghost of Mr. Bowser even accompanied the Bartons on their Sunday afternoon walk. This expedition became as traditional, on pleasant afternoons, as the stroll on the river wall or to the Valley of Fern would have been in Wilford. It was taken gently, as Aunt Bee was not valid for large distance. Rheumatism gave her a slight sideways veer which needed frequent correction by her escort. They used to point out a distant landmark and tell her to steer for it, but as soon as she forgot she made leeway, and her struggle to keep straight gave a nodding tremble to what Jeff called her whisk, a little brush of sensitive antennae on the Ipswich bonnet. This, and Uncle Dan's knotted stick, were the signs of an Occasion. The favorite route was across Cotton Duck Bridge and as far as the old Pavilion Latrobe in the park. This was a pagoda or summerhouse of Moorish form; it had a polygon ledge a few feet above ground, much favored by children for groping round and weaving through the window spaces. Pavilion Latrobe stood on a wide slope overlooking the lake; while Jeff clambered Uncle Dan and Aunt Bee could rest on a bench watching the sparkle of carriages round the lakeside drive, and perhaps the stampede caused by the staccato of a primitive buzzwagon. Or the goal might be the tadpole pond, more remote in the park; or sometimes a walk through Carroll Woods to hunt chestnuts and chinquapins. On autumn Sundays these groves were thick with flying billets where the Oriole Boys were trying to bring down high-hanging burrs. Once Uncle Dan rashly flung his walking stick high into a tree, aiming at a lofty clump of nuts; it hooked on a branch and they had to leave it there until a gale brought it down weeks later. Just the kind of thing, Uncle Dan said, that would have happened to Mr. Bowser.

Rozanne Towson, the favored graduate student, sometimes joined these expeditions and came back for a real Wilford high tea. It was she who introduced Aunt Bee to waffles, which Miss Barton described as crumpets with patterns on them. But as is often the case with professional students, Miss Towson was well schooled in all forms of imagination displayed in the approved classics but rather baffled by it when encountered in daily life. She was surprised to find that the homeward way was usually devoted to an impromptu story about Mr. Bowser; she thought this very unliterary. But Jeff had taken Mr. Bowser's troubles to heart and wished to compensate. An idyllic region of Jeffland had been allotted; it was called Bowser, and here that harried citizen ruled as Prefect and everything happened to his satisfaction. Here, as Uncle Dan suggested, Mr. Bowser was ert and ept; he was gruntled and comfitured. Often on the homeward path Uncle Dan was urged to tell a story in which Mr. Bowser would be heroic and triumphant. From much study of *Puck* Uncle Dan was now familiar with the comedy stereotypes of God's country. But to Jeff, perhaps even to Aunt Bee, it was all a new and vivid mythology. The boy listened with delight to these simple inventions; across the vistas of his ever-changing republic (which looked just then rather like Druid Hill Park) he saw a deified Bowser outwitting Chinese laundrymen and German bands, Irish cops and bowing Frenchmen and monocled Britons, Dusty Rhodeses and Weary Willies, dudes and chollies, fresh drummers and summer boarders, actors on railroad ties and hats concealing bricks. At the peak of these narratives, when Mr. Bowser stood on the brink of some crisis, Miss Towson would ejaculate her innocently sympathetic "Phew!" Aunt Bee, less impressionable, carried on her own meditations; perhaps reflecting that the wilderness of America was quite different from her anticipation. It was not a wildness of the frontier but a wildness in the mind.

Uncle Dan occasionally apologized to Miss Towson for the crudeness of his effects. "It's astonishing that no one since Aristophanes seems to have invented any new jokes. Not even Molière."

"Who was Mulyare?" Jeff asked.

"He was a Frenchman."

"Is M. Quad a Frenchman?"

If the walk took them up Key Street Avenue Extended, where new suburbs were beginning to build, they played Uncle Dan's game instead. This was Dan's own version of the Imaginary Country; it was an Imaginary College. In those days a group of generous citizens had recently given Chesapeake University a beautiful tract of land (including Carroll Woods) on

266

which it would eventually build its new home. Uncle Dan, jealous for the future of little Patapsco, enjoyed choosing a building here or a landscape there and imagining it part of an ideal campus for his own college. Many a flourishing merchant, just settled in his dwelling of New Century Colonial, was unaware that it was lifted over his head and requisitioned in fancy as "That's the Dean's house," or "That might be the Faculty Club," or "That would be nice for the professor of English." It was part of the game to settle these migrants in quarters appropriate to their duties. For a teacher of literature or pure science a home would be chosen that had some chance of solitude. They passed a very modest cottage on a byway, which Jeff nominated for the Professor of Bible Studies; "it would remind him to be humble." The game was at its pleasantest when they discovered houses in the process of building, fresh in the excellent smell of damp mortar, new-cut wood and paint. Here, on Sunday afternoons, they could wander and plan their adaptations.

The problem of dormitories for the students, an old anxiety at Patapsco, offered spirited discussion. The girls either hustled to and from college in street-cars or lived in boarding houses adjoining. "I think it's better if the girls don't live at the college," Jeff remarked, from his observation of the lodging houses on Patapsco Street. "They'll only fill the place with mandolins and sofa pillows." His acute ear had already been distressed by the stridulous and wiry tinkle of that abominable instrument. "I don't mind it," said Uncle Dan, "it's damsels with dulcimers."

"If we put the dormitories out here," said Jeff, surveying a region of woods and meadow, "it'll be too far from Spontoon's. The girls won't be able to get their molasses candy. I think it's better if they live at home and just come to college to study. Girls are a terrible nuisance around a place. I know what the other boys tell me about their sisters. I guess I'm spared some awful sights."

267

"You mustn't be too hard on them," Uncle Dan suggested. "I had sisters, you know, and they grew up quite nice."

"That's true. You never think of your aunt as being a lady."

"Maybe we should sometimes," said Uncle Dan.

"Well, anyway in Jeffland they're not allowed to wear bloomers. It's such a shock when you see those fat legs."

Uncle Dan inferred that some of the club discussions in Sassafras House were beginning to deal with the ignominies of the other sex. The T.S.O. 4 were probably fortifying themselves in that instinctive suspicion of the female which is the Custer's Last Stand of boyhood.

"You must always be respectful to women," said Uncle Dan, almost automatically; it was the accepted doctrine. Then he realized sadly that this could not be more than half-truth; natural enough in any statement dealing with only half of humanity. Perhaps people being respectful to them was what infuriated them so?

Very likely it was a reaction from this theme that led to the incident of the new bonnet. The Ipswich confection with the whisk had grown a bit familiar. Perhaps Bee clung to it as a sort of last loyalty to East Anglia and Wilford Meeting; it was a sort of Martello Tower in her mind. Yet there were times, perhaps meeting Mrs. Beinbrink and Mrs. Huffenbutz at a college festival, when Uncle Dan and Jeff dimly realized Aunt Bee's hat was a museum piece.

It was a windy day in spring. Jeff and Skinny were on one of their excursions downtown. They had stopped at the dentist long enough for Skinny to have his tooth-braces tightened. When this happened Skinny was allowed to have money for an ice cream soda, to test his theory that the cold drink would shrink his protesting gums and numb the pain. But even their favorite flavor (nectar: a mixture of vanilla, pineapple and strawberry syrups) did not seem sufficiently astringent and Skinny was weeping copiously as they proceeded to look for adventure. Jeff was eager to console, for walking with a tear-stained companion is always humiliating. He made various suggestions. "Let's go to the Pratt and get something by Jules Verne. You haven't read *The Steam Elephant*, and there's *Tigers and Traitors or The Demon of Cawnpore*."

"Damn the Liberry," moaned Skinny ungratefully.

They were moving in the general direction of Chocolate Mice when Jeff noticed for the first time an alley that led to the stage door of a famous old theater. It was a palace of miracle: there they had seen Shakespeare, and the chariots of Ben-Hur, and (best of all) Jeff had seen what he called Sherlock Holmes in *William Gillette*. "Let's go and look at the stage," said Jeff, and Skinny dried his eyes.

By happy chance the rearward door stood open, the house was empty, the guardian probably off dipping a scuttle of beer. The vast gloomy stage was dimly lit by a hanging bulb, tall canvas wings (trees, scarlet curtains with tassels, marble pillars) were stacked against the back wall. They tiptoed cautiously toward the front of the stage, gaped into the silent cavern which seemed heavy with utterance just below hearing. Shadowy rows of seats were overhung with cliff-like balconies, curves of gilding caught faint light like reefs and veins of mica. "It's like Aeolus's cave of wind," whispered the classical-minded Skinny. To Jeff the whole twilight hollow begged for words.

"Aye, tear her tattered ensign down!" he ventured. He was astonished how the empty space gathered, amplified, resonated his voice. He spoke more strongly:

> "Long has it waved on high,
> And many an eye has danced to see
> That banner in the sky."

The clear young tones rang thrillingly in receptive space, he forgot himself with pleasure:

> "Nail to the mast her holy flag,
> Set every threadbare sail,

And give her to the god of storms,
The lightning and the gale!"

"Gee whiz, that's slick," exclaimed Skinny. "Let me try.
Don't tread on me!" he proclaimed rather huskily to the empty
house. Perhaps the lingering sniffle in his head made his elocution all the more appealing as he recited:

"The despot's heel is on thy shore, Maryland!
His torch is at thy temple door, Maryland!"

Jeff chimed in with his favorite lines, which they shouted
together:

"For life or death, for woe or weal,
Thy peerless chivalry reveal,
And gird thy beauteous limbs with steel,
Maryland, my Maryland!"

"When I say that, I feel quite sore at the British myself,"
said Jeff, who had always thought the song was another sneer
at the luckless redcoats.

"Aw gee, that's got nothing to do with the ole British," said
Skinny. "That's talking about damyankees."

"What the hell you kids doing?" shouted a voice. "Clear
out of here." They fled.

"You've got a nice voice," Skinny complimented his friend
as they continued their walk. "It's a pity they don't have any
singing in Quaker Meeting."

Jeff shuddered at this pagan idea.

"I been reading a wonderful story," continued Skinny,
"called *Master Skylark,* about a kid that could sing and made
friends with Shakespeare. That's the only good thing about
having big sisters, you get their old *St. Nicholases* to read."

"Shucks, the best story ever was in *St. Nicholas,*" said Jeff,
"was *A Boy of the First Empire,* about a kid that worked for
Napoleon. He was a courier and wore a cocked hat. 'Ride like
the wind to Paris; tell them the battle is won!'"

"I bet Shakespeare and Napoleon were the two most important people ever lived," mused Skinny. "Gee, I bet they never had their teeth straightened either."

"I bet Shakespeare would cry even more'n you do," said Jeff generously. "He was terribly emotional. I think I can understand Napoleon better, he's more my type."

"Maybe we might go to the Liberry," said Skinny. "I been trying for six months to get *The Hound of the Baskervilles*."

"In the National Library of Jeffland there's fifty copies of every book by A. Conan Doyle. Nobody has to wait."

They turned eastward toward the Library; their way led them through one of the dipping valleys that carve the city. It was spring's breeziest weather, the crosstown street was a funnel for the western gust. As they came down the slope they saw a colored man with a dray backing his horse into the gap of an alleyway. The big wagon was filled with little round bonnet-boxes of lilac pasteboard. Evidently they were to be delivered at the back door of a Key Street milliner, one of those famous caterers of finery for Chesapeake belles. Probably the colored citizen was impatient with his fragile freight after a long haul from the box-factory. Without pausing to consider meteorology he cut the cord that bound his bulky and toppling cargo. Aeolus was on cue. As the driver let down the gate at the tail of the wagon the entire mass of paper cylinders flew like confetti or toy balloons.

The boys gazed in astonishment. In an instant the whole block was a sprinkle of rolling and soaring cartons, some flying in air and dodged by astonished pedestrians, others wheeling on one rim and scuttling like rabbits into byways and corners. The bewildered Negro sprang this way and that, grabbing at his dispersing cargo; he managed to seize a couple and then stood clutching them, helpless to collect more. The whole covey of flying cardboards now burst suddenly across the intersection of Key Street's afternoon traffic. Horses reared, a primitive taxi stalled, blocking the trolley track; ladies screamed, an elderly gentleman from the Chesapeake Club capered along the gutter pursuing his own silk topper which must have been lifted by a fellow-feeling. An alert motorman leaned out from the front platform of his street-car and fielded a cylinder in midair. So many geometrical forms in motion at once were like an explosion from the pages of Euclid, but Madame Hyacinthe (Chapeaux of the Mode) was not amused. Easter was late that year and so were the boxes.

Jeff and Skinny in ecstasy pursued one agile container down the alley. It was unblemished by its flight and they decided to take it home. The Zouaves of Jeffland had long needed a new barracks; or it would make a perfect roundhouse for the Great Eastern and Western Railway shops in Sprunt City. Jeff had laid first hand on the box so Skinny feared he would not get one, but a passer-by who saw his face had pity. "You poor boy," she said, "did you lose your boxes? Don't cry. Here's one. It almost knocked me over." They fetched a careful detour to save their trove. Two or three blocks away they thought it safe to come out on Key Street and at this corner they ran into Uncle Dan. Hat-boxes are impossible to conceal and explanations followed. It would be honorable, Uncle Dan suggested, if they returned the boxes to Madame Hyacinthe, whose name was printed on them in very French script.

The statesmen made ingenious argument. "If she only gets back two," said Skinny, "it will make her feel worse than ever. It will remind her of the others flying down the street."

"I saw a horse put his foot right through one," said Jeff. "It was cheval de freeze round his ankle like the White Knight's horse."

"By Sir John Tenniel," said Skinny, still hoping to distract Uncle Dan.

But they returned to Madame Hyacinthe's, where other good-natured people were also delivering the escapading cartons. No street in the world is more good-humored than Key Street. But the unfortunate colored man had completely disappeared. Seeing the miraculous and irretrievable dispersion he whipped up his horse and fled.

"This season's bonnets must be rather frolicsome," said Uncle Dan politely to the Hyacinthe. "It seems to me I read something in the paper about flyaway hats?"

"Such lovely little creations," said the lady. "I think people are getting tired of great big hats. Now I'll have to sell them in paper bags. I can't get any more boxes printed before Easter."

Jeff had his inspiration. Certainly there was a way they could honestly acquire one.

"Aunt Bee needs a new hat," he said. "And I bet Skinny's mother would like a new hat too."

"She's got one," said Skinny sadly. "I heard them talking about it. Father said Unitarians ought to stick to one color. It's got botany and cherries. It's conspicuous," he added proudly.

Choice was difficult. It was the first time Uncle Dan had ever bought a female hat and before decision was reached Jeff and Skinny were told to stop advising and wait outside. They argued happily about it on the way home.

"I'm glad you got the one with wings," said Jeff, "because that's the way the boxes acted."

"What kind of a bird is it," wondered Skinny. "Maybe it's a bird of paradise?"

"If it's real," Jeff meditated, "Aunt Bee won't like it. I shall tell her it's a bird of prey."

The bird was probably not in Audubon, but that was how Aunt Bee got the new hat—and the Zouaves their new barracks.

49. The Major Drives Tandem

Everyone needs reassurance sometimes. When the Major felt like trash—"I feel right shabby, honey. Sort of a mizzry in my wits"—if the weather was right he abandoned Ma and Pa and ordered out the oriole-colored dogcart. Then there was reassurance in the stable too. Lightfoot would pass along the word, there was skirmishing and flourish in the tack-room, neat's-foot oil and saddle-soap, bath brick and chamois. Cinders, the old groom, was busy with currycomb and hoof-blacking and toothpaste for Dido and Aeneas. Dido was his favorite, but he was tactful to do Aeneas first. The groom's hissing (to prevent swallowing dust and horsehair) acted on Aeneas like a cocktail; if he heard it first in Dido's stall he got rambunctious. Then Cinders had chance for special endearment with Dido. "Now, lady, jes' hol' still while I wash yo' mouf. Don' you curl up no nozzles at me, no'm. You's a handsome lady-hoss ef you don' stargaze, dat hoss hold her haid so high she nevah need no check-rein. Mutual, tie up dem dawgs befo' dey go crazy, see ef de good whip is coil up pretty, an' get me out my good cap, dis' one too whiff to ride with white folks. Jesus Gawd, de whole yahd in a flux, Major take tandem to town."

The Major was the last of Chesapeake's cavaliers who drove his animals to the office—and tandem at that. It was only done when the horses really needed exercise, and the Major admitted to himself that they were getting a little beyond him. It was a secret between him and Cinders that after they left Greenaway in a flying sprinkle of gravel, when they reached the valley road, out of sight, the Major turned over the reins to the groom. But he always took them again (Dido and Aeneas a little chastened by now) when they came to the broad slope of Key Street Avenue Extended and went spanking down that highway into town. Not even the twin steeds imagined by Plato as rival couriers of the soul were more accoutered in beauty than the gleaming mare and gelding as they swung (Dido in the lead) round the wide sloping driveway where Cathedral Station lies in its great bowl of turf. The Major kept his desk at the leisurely uptown depot, not among traffic managers and freight accountants in the company's office building. He said a railroad man ought to keep company with trains. Clerks, ushers, a dispatcher and an old brassbound conductor off duty looked

274

out from station windows as the Major tightened rein on the downward slope. Leader and wheeler slackened to that prettiest pattern of feet, each hoof with its separate strike of sound. "By God, he slows 'em down as sweet as the Royal Blue Limited," said the conductor, and an artist in the tower, working on a Summer Tours booklet, tried hastily to do a sketch.

Not until the equipage came to a softly chiming halt, and the Major twirled his whip into its lapping spiral, did Cinders relax African gravity. His soot-colored jowl opened white and pink. "Yassuh, Major, mighty pretty singlefoot. Ole Dido sure a pretty hoss. She kin still trot wid de front laigs while de rear-quarters slowin' down."

"I feel that way myself," said the Major, putting the whip in its socket. The groom gave him a firm elbow to descend from the high seat, then stood at Dido's head with some confidential compliment. Maybe the mare enjoyed a reassurance too. The traditional one, as between groom and thoroughbred, goes something like this: "Honey, yo' haid's as high as de lady's maid and yo' rump's as broad as de cook's."—Aeneas got his kind word too, but Cinders needed none. The faces of the admiring colored porters were his elixir.

And the Major, a little lame, moving stiffly up to his office in the tower, reflected that perhaps this was the last great railroad station that had a right to call its castellated vestibule a porte-cochère. To his good heart the locomotive still really was the iron horse, and the ornate old station was his fortress of romance. If one of the ancient varnished rocking chairs in the waiting-room was empty he often sat there to take the travel off his feet, but also in a godfatherly pleasure of treating the public as his personal guests. Many a lady baffled with children or parcels was surprised by an elaborate greeting from this unidentified hidalgo. "You-all won't have long to wait, the train's right seasonable this morning. Ah'm glad you toted yo' luncheon-basket, won't have to be movin' the youngsters into the dinin'-car.—Deer Pahk? Yes, ma'am, that's a right scenery ride."

By the time he looked out from his lofty belvedere above the station Cinders and the tandem had jingled away to take their ease at near-by Ellicott's Livery. His wrists were shaking a little; each of these drives he felt should be the last. The bravura turnout twinkles away into distance, up the smooth pull by Patapsco College and the chinquapin forest, juggling sunlight on silver trappings, last glamour of a jovial age. Sunlight was part of that picture. It flew in sparks from mirrored hooves and lacquered spokes. When it was time to turn homeward in afternoon the Major could even tell the hour by the shadows of his pair. He had taught Cinders, waiting in the circular paved plaza, to head them due north so they served as a sun-dial. Dido, who had also had her afternoon snooze, danced a little when the 4:10 train rumbled out of the tunnel, jetting crullers of steam. That was always Cinders' moment. Sitting at high alert, he could bring her to order with the long whiplash, exact as a trained conscience to sting the ticklish spot. This was the company whip, with the Major's stable colors (blue and yellow) braided into the lash. The Major admired to see it perfectly handled, a reminder to Dido while bypassing and pleasing Aeneas. As old horsemen knew, the whip isn't just punishment: it's reassurance too, like a telephone call between friends.

That afternoon the Major didn't wait for those well-trained shadows to stretch very far. He had seen the Mayor in the Chesapeake Club at lunch time, and His Honor had twitted him a little too brightly about disrupting homebound traffic on Key Street. The Mayor came of a later generation which did not understand that even intended as endearment the term Unreconstructed Rebel sounds better after juleps than before. "I'll take it as a civic suggestion, suh," replied Major Warren; and checked himself from saying, "I prefer my jokes either brand-new or else better seasoned." Now it occurred to him, since he would be driving so near, why not stop on Carroll Street and have a cup of tea with Dan Barton?

He did not realize that the clatter and novelty of his tandem would almost cause riot in that modest byway. "Yay circus parade! Whoa, Emma!" yelled Spike McMechan and his crew, following up the street. Even the girls at Patapsco College, exercising in full bloomers inside a modestly screened enclosure, came out to squeak and coo. Aunt Bee had just put the kettle on for a solitary cup when she heard clatter and shouting, followed by a ring at the door. At first she thought it must be some climactic exploit of the T.S.O. 4 Parcel Delivery Service. It was Moxie's afternoon off so she answered the bell and was astounded to find the Major himself on the steps. Cinders was arguing with Dido and Aeneas, who were doing a tap dance on the cobbles; boys were swarming round the cart. The excitement was such that the Major saw conversation would be impossible. He had one of his inspirations. Spike's look of homage, carefully twisted into a sneer, reminded him of his own boyhood. He could see that Spike was the leader among these bandits. "Hey, you boy, if you clear away this gang so Miz Barton can have some peace you can climb up with the groom and take these hosses for a run." They rattled away and probably this more than anything else convinced Master McMechan that the T.S.O. 4 might be useful friends.

It was the first time the Major and Aunt Bee had enjoyed a tête-à-tête. "I'm sorry to miss your gentleman folks," said the Major politely, "but a cup of tea with yourself is a privilege." What good fortune, Aunt Bee was thinking, she had been amusing herself by cutting some of her lace-fine bread and butter, and had even got out the old tortoise-shell tea-caddy. These were *her* reassurance. She settled the Major under the water color of Wilford church, and was pleased that the potpourri bowl had its crack (or rather Moxie's) turned to the

277

wall. She hoped his eye didn't notice her Album on the bottom shelf of the whatnot.

"Dan's away for a jaunt with his friend Dr. Huffenbutz," she explained. "He's been working too hard and I urged him to go. He said he simply must see some hills. They went on a walking trip to Susquehanna."

This region was only a mystical name to Aunt Bee but she had learned to pronounce it with an air of reverence.

"Shucks, Ma'am, that ain't much in the way of hills," said the Major. "We-all can do better fo' him than that. I been teasin' for years to get him up to Blue Ridge. What part of the Susquehanna is he at?"

"I don't know very well. He sent a postcard from Safe Harbor. Is that really a place, or does he mean a figure of speech? It's hard to tell with Dan, he gets quite fanciful when he's off on a trip. Here's his card: he says they walked from Peach Bottom, through Castle Fin, Slab, and Shanks Ferry. American names are always so vigorous."

"They tell me that country's very pictorial. I never got called up that way myself. I recollect Mr. Bayard Taylor said the Susquehanna was prettier than the Rhine, but I think I'd miss the wine and the castles. The Yankees say that about a whole parcel of rivers; would you believe it, Ma'am, they said the same thing about the Hudson."

"I'm afraid Dan's a little disappointed," admitted Aunt Bee. "He says they went to Red Lion, P.A., but it wasn't like Martlesham. They wanted to camp out but they were tortured by mosquitoes and something he calls flying roaches. I'm always confused about P.A., is that short for Pennsylvania?"

"Either that or Penny Ante," said the Major gravely. "He ought to know better than to go trapesin' across the frontier. We can show him more-account mountains than that.—And my young friend Jeff, is he with him?"

"He's off with his club on a picnic. It's their spring holiday, they've gone to spend the day in Washington—D.C.," she

278

added a little uncertainly. "I trust they're behaving themselves. It would be just like them to send Ingram to the front door of the White House with a parcel of shad roe and banana skins. I shan't be easy in my mind until they're back. You can't imagine how saucy they are when they're all together. They were told at school they must go to Washington to see what the government looks like. I told Jeff I thought Congress ought to be warned they were coming."

"Don't you worry, Miz Bee, government has been through plenty of rumpus. It'll take care of the situation. I declare, the most likely trouble they'd meet in Washington is if they run up with Teddy Roosevelt. He might lead 'em into some sort of fandangos. What was the very first thing that man did when he got in the White House? He invited colored folks to sit down to lunch with him. Lightfoot and I were certainly put out about that."

"What worries me is that Washington Monument. I hear it's terribly tall. I hope there's a good high railing round the top?"

"Well, it's right prominent for an obelisk, but so far as I recollect there's no way to fall off of it. Don't you fret yourself about their cutting capers. I wouldn't give co'nshucks for a boy that didn't."

"They have a bad reputation in monuments," said Aunt Bee. "They went up the one in Mount Vernon Place. There were other people up there on the balcony. The boys came down first, and by climbing on Ingram's shoulders they could reach up and turn out all the gas jets on the winding stairs. So when the others wanted to come down it was pitch black. The ladies were dreadfully frightened and had to scream from the top of the tower until the guards noticed them."

"That was a cute idea," said the Major. "I'm humiliated Randy and I never thought of it. We thought up some right flibberty monkeyshines, though. First time we went to Washnton, that was befo' the War, they were building Cabin John Bridge and we walked on the parapet all the way across. I reckon it was that crazy Blondin at Niag'ra Falls put it in our heads. I declare it makes me shudder when I think of it.—As a matter and fact the whole country was sort of walkin' on a parapet about then."

"Well, please don't mention it to Geoffrey."

"He takes suggestion as a cat laps milk, like the Bard says. Well, Ma'am, they have to work off their energy. I declare it's a pity, by the time a fellow finds out what he wants to do with it there ain't much of it left."

Aunt Bee was always fascinated by Chesapeake's habit of "I declare." No wonder, she thought, these people had issued a Declaration of Independence.

"I had a struggle with my conscience," she said, "about the boys spending so much time fighting wars with paper soldiers. It seems very unFriendly, but I dessay it's better than ringing doorbells and playing practical jokes. Of course poor Dan does his work at home and I have to get the boys out of the house as much as possible."

"I wouldn't worry about paper soldiers being unChristian. It's a lot better than the real thing. Best Christian I ever knew had four legs, my old war-hoss O'Malley. He was blue roan, a great big feller and full of good humor. He was a bit absent-minded sometimes but a real pious hoss. Come to think of it, for a hoss he was what Dan is for people, sure enough quality-disposed. When we was in winter campaign along Shenandoah Valley the only way we could keep warm at night was get O'Malley to lay down somewheres and we all snug up to him. That old belly of his was as good as a stove. I declare, Ma'am, you'da laughed to see me an' Lightfoot and half a dozen other boys all packed round O'Malley like Brer Rabbit on the tar baby. We sure clove to that hoss, an' do you know he enjoyed it too? It kept the draught off of him and he was so considerate he wouldn't even sneeze if he could hold it in. If he felt ticklish he wouldn't lift his hoof to scratch until he'd kind of give warning. He didn't even rare up in the morning until he knew

280

we were all clear. I always figured that's how O'Malley got rheumatism, he squandered so much natural heat laying out with us in the co'nfields, likely that's why Lew Wallace caught up with us later on. It was kind of a humiliation to be captured by an officer who was more of a writing man than a tactician. Just as well maybe, I'd have been in a social quandary if I'd been with Jubal Early when he scared the gizzard out of homefolks here in Chezpeake."

Aunt Bee did not always understand the Major's allusions, but she was amused at the picture of himself and Lightfoot sleeping together cheek by belly with the recumbent steed—and yet the Major was so shocked at a Negro taking lunch in the White House. She didn't know, of course, that even in bunking with O'Malley there was a Jim Crow etiquette: Lightfoot took the weather side. The Major was so easy to talk to, she found herself telling him more than she realized. Dan was to make a quick journey back to Wilford that summer; the foundering china business had to be closed out, the old house sold, and arrangements made for Grandma and the aunts. He couldn't afford to take Bee and Jeff with him, and she had been worried how they would spend the interval. Carroll Street was unbearable in midsummer, but they could not afford to go far. Without quite knowing it she suggested these problems more fully than she would have done by intention.

"You give me great pleasure, Ma'am," said the Major, "because there's a notion I've had for some time. Your perplexities about young Jeff is mighty slim compared to Teackle. At least yo' young scalawag is good at his studies. I been figuring out, could I suggest to Dan to give Teackle some tutoring? He'll get left back in school if he don't mend his paces. I recall how my old Tullius Teackle talked about hirin' a scholar to give me a little doctrinairin' about that age. Tullius Teackle always said the best kind of an American is one that's been tutored by an Englishman and vicey versa. He even had a young Englishman picked out for me but the feller had to go back home and

I missed all that good learnin'. Matter an' fact it was a feller named c-l-o-u-g-h. Randy and I called it Clow but Tullius Teackle put us right. He said, 'Boys will not bluff, When tutored by Clough.' This Arthur Clough had a feelin' for the States; he was raised with gentry down in Cha'lston. He was teachin' boys up in Mass'chusetts but Tullius Teackle figured he'd likely be relieved to come South. Of co'se he's forgotten now, but they tell me he got to be considerable of a poet. I always been too busy to read after him."

Aunt Bee was a little bewildered. She covered it by refilling the Major's cup.

"I'm certainly beholden to you for this good tea," said the Major. "And I ain't seen bread cut so flimsy since Lightfoot lost the knife-sharper. What I'm thinkin', Miz Bee, since you say Dan hones for some real hills, why don't you and him spend the summer up at Sandy Hole? You can take Teackle with you. You know how it is with a boy of sixteen. He's just a mass of corruption but he has right genteel instincts. Dan can fill him full of scholar's instruction till he has to make his trip across. Then the boys can squire you while Dan's away."

"It sounds lovely," said Aunt Bee, though wondering inwardly what a sandy hole was like. Her imagination suggested a sort of oasis in a desert.

"It's up in Blowin' Gap," continued the Major. "That's in the Blue Ridge, just a nice little scenery ride in the cars. There's an old farmhouse, Wicker's. I've known the place since I was Teackle's age. Maybe it's a mite slatternly but it'd be like yo' own house-at-home.—You know what I mean.—They can make you and Dan real easy. It's plentiful table, and what tickles me, down by the falls is an old cabin where Jeff and Teackle can camp out. There's no doorbells to be rung and they can work off their steam swimmin' and fishin'. I know what's frettin' on Dan's mind. He's been studyin' too much Wordsworth and Coleridge, an' there's too much literature he just can't talk about to his young ladies. We got real hills in the Blue Ridge will be physic for his symptoms. And you wouldn't be bit up by mosquitoes like Susquehanna. I have a notion he's trying to live up to someone else's Susquehanna and it just can't be done. You got to find one of your own."

"It would be marvelous for Jeff," said Aunt Bee, who was perhaps a little frightened.

"It's a mighty sweet landscape," said the Major. "You look down on that valley full of co'nfields and apple o'chards, and you come smack up against the mounting, a thousand feet up. The crick makes a circumbendibus right under Wicker's farm, falls over a ledge into Sandy Hole—like what Uncle Hartley used to call whisky and potass. I ought to know, when I was a young engineer I helped build the bridge through the Gap. We had a flood washed us away, but we got it finished eventual. There's my initials onto one of the piers, and the cabin I spoke of we put up for the surveyors down by the falls. If Dan don't have to sail till late July there'll be a passel of time for you-all to get settled."

"I always wanted to see the Far West," said Aunt Bee bravely.

"It ain't awful far, but anyways it's got different feelins," said the gentlemanly old Major. "It'll give Jeff a kind of a skyline on the back of his mind. I wouldn't want him to figure that the sun sets in Druid Hill Park."

There was a clatter in the street outside. Dido and Aeneas drew up in front of the house—as a matter of fact, in front of two houses. It was an event for Mrs. Maggots.

"Reckon I better move my cavalcade away from yo' stoop," said the Major. "I didn't figure they'd make themselves a nuisance."

Cinders was actually smiling; evidently he and Spike Mc-Mechan had got on well. Spike held a pose long enough to savor what envy was available among his followers. "Beat it, trash," he exclaimed, with his hand nonchalantly on the whip, as if he had just furled it after expert use. Then he jumped down and rang the bell at 1910. "Here's your team, Sir," he said, taking off his cap to the Major. "Gee, those are certainly wonderful stallions."

They weren't, either of them, but the Major realized this was the most impressive word Spike could think of.

"Make my compliment to your brother, Ma'am. I hope his little trip don't spoil Susquehanna in his mind. I declare, it's right tragical, an idea is always lovely if you don't have to put it in touch with reality. It's like that bridge I was telling you of up at Blowin' Gap. In the drawings those tension members were pretty as a morning cobweb and when we got it built it was just a picayune old trestle."

"Sure enough," said Aunt Bee, startled to find herself imitating the Major's talk. "Like a rosebud if there weren't any caterpillars."

"A right pretty simile, Ma'am. Tell Dan to get you some nicotine, that'll fix the bugs."

She blanched slightly—on the Thorofare bugs meant only one thing, and unmentionable: the infestation of beds. But he continued gaily:

"Nicotine and mint, best two medicines I know. You-all must come pass an evenin' at Greenaway right soon, we can talk Dan into the notion of Sandy Hole. It'll be warm weather, we'll set out in the garden and watch the fireflies. They sparkle mighty biggity when they smell juleps."

He drove speedily away and Aunt Bee reflected guiltily that she had forgotten to ask him to smoke. Dido and Aeneas freshened with homeward zeal, sparks hovered like fireflies round their timing hooves. They were pursued as far as Key Street by a posse of enthusiastic Orioles, but on that smooth highway the boys were soon outpaced. The Major handed the reins to the groom and got out a cigar.

"Appears like we make too much commotion in this rig," he remarked presently. "Reminds me of a song folks used to sing:

An old-fashioned house in an old-fashioned street, Where the old-fashioned cobblestones trouble the feet."

"Yassuh. I take notice of Dido, she's kinda tender in the off-hind. Think she's a mite elderly fo' this rampagin'."

Probably the Major's cigar was sufficient excuse for his not making any comment.

He took the reins again as they thudded up the gravel drive. Trundle was playing with a puppy on the lumpy meadow. She hurried floundering through the thick grass, and tripped over the dog. Her mouth and the puppy's were both so wide-open it would be hard to say which one was calling. The Major drew in the impatient horses with difficulty.

"Let me ride to the stable," Trundle demanded.

"Ride with Cinders, honey." He felt his way down from the high cart, lifted her with an effort, and restrained the wriggling pup from danger. He felt shaky as he walked into the portico, picking up a doll cast aside on the brick terrace. Lightfoot met him at the door.

"Howdy, Lightfoot. Glass of Madeira."

"Nosuh, Marse Ha'tley," replied that black Achates. "You'll take a dram o' Bou'bon."

"Reckon you were right," said the Major a little later. "I declare, it's queer to see the old house sort of stretchin' its thews, ready to begin all over again."

Meanwhile the T.S.O. 4, returning that evening from the all-day excursion, had spent all their cash (to the last demi-rep). They trudged wearily from the Short-Line station. The nearest way led them through a known ambush of the Orioles. They tightened what muscle-fiber was left, in case of assault; great was their astonishment when Spike McMechan joined them politely and offered to walk with them as far as North Avenue. He even repeated the earlier suggestion of amalgamating the two clubs. Star explained that they were too fatigued to discuss matters of state, but this advance put them in excellent humor.

So much so that when they found Aunt Bee had cocoa and sandwiches waiting they were eloquent to describe their adventures. Aunt Bee, who had never visited Washington, must have received confused impressions.

"We saw the President."

"They've got double-header trolleys."

"Streets as wide as a football field."

"It's like alphabets. All named for letters and compasses."

"Every old address looks like algebra. We met a kid lives at 3416 13th Street N.W."

"T. R. was coming right out of the White House, on a dandy horse."

"He smiled at us."

"That wasn't a smile, that was a grin."

"That wasn't a grin, it was a grimmus."

"Not grimmus, grim*ace*."

"Aw, go chase yourself."

"They've got an echo in the Capitol. You just whisper and it comes back like a windstorm."

They hadn't intended to confess their special triumph but excitement carried them on.

"We got run out of town by the cops!" shouted Skinny.

"Cheezit," warned Star. "We said we better keep quiet about that."

"Aw gee, you're an old fraid-cat," Jeff proclaimed.

"Suppose the Secret Service hears about it?" said Bert. "Anything that happens in the District of Columbia is national dishonor."

"We could appeal to Teddy," moaned Skinny, moistening with excitement. "He looked right at us. He'd recognize us any time."

"I dessay anyone would," murmured Aunt Bee amid the clamor.

"I bet he said 'Bully.' I could see his teeth saying it."

"Aunt Bee won't tell, she's a faithful friend. It was really Ingram because his feet are so big."

Ingram had been silent, perhaps because impeded by sandwich, but this allusion lit all his fuses. He swallowed with a rapid convulsion and burst into narrative:

"The big fiends, it was not, Miss Barton, it was all unanimous. That old Secret Service only jumped on me because I'm bigger and it was Jeff's idea, the big squirt. We went high up on that Washington Monument. You look down from those slanty windows and every time I was admiring, somebody always pinched me behind and then said it was Secret Service. I knew who it was allright allright. Secret Service would pinch higher up and I'm sickantired of such nonsense. I was going to appeal to the government. Nice normal boys got no doings to behave that way on top of sacred buildings. It don't make any difference if people are all there or not."

The other members were now in such a state of hilarity that they all tried to tell the story at once.

"The elevator was absolutely packed."

"All those old sightseers, just a lot of yokels."

"So we played a practical yokel," screamed Jeff, beside himself.

"Ingram acted like a big fiend, he said he wouldn't go down in the elevator, he'd run down the stairs for relief."

"Five hundred fifty-five feet," wept Skinny.

"They were pinching me, they said I'd get numb, and I didn't."

"It was sort of an experiment."

"Mr. Bolton will give us an A in science."

"For goodness' sake," begged Aunt Bee, "quiet down and explain what happened."

They all mopped up and Ingram subsided to an occasional mutter but his face showed that he was enjoying this as much as any.

"Now, Geoffrey," said Aunt Bee, "control yourself. Try to behave like a gentleman and tell me."

"It was very instructive," said Jeff. "Ingram started to run down the stairs. I guess they're just for emergency panics but anyway the janitor wasn't looking. I guess there's about a thousand of them, stairs, I mean, and a big iron landing on each flight. So we followed Ingram, it's club rules, anybody does anything different we all have to do it, like espree de corpse. Ingram has such powerful legs he can go four steps at a time. He runs like fury so he went down each flight jump-jump-jump, Bang."

"Surest thing you know," said Ingram happily. "It was like drum majors. I could time my jumps all the same and then land on the floor with both feet, BOOM!"

"Feet like that, it means something," said Bert. "Like a tidal wave."

"Shut up, you horse's horse," muttered poor Ingram.

"We all followed him," Jeff continued, "we ran down keeping in step, just an idea that came naturally, jump, jump, jump, BOOM. Gee, it was like a poem, like *Hiawatha*—"

"No, it was different from Hiawatha," Skinny interrupted. "Heavier, more like that ole Mariner. Noises in a swound! That's what I was thinking when we could see Ingram fleeing down those terrible stairs. I was saying it to myself in time with jumps: Be*cause*—he *knows*—a *fright*ful—*fiend* doth *close*—be*hind*—him *tread!*"

"I know!" Jeff exclaimed. "It was like *Breathes* there the *man* with *soul* so *dead*, Who *never* to him*self* hath *said*—see, it was Bumpety, bumpety, bump, *boom*."

"It was like the school yell," Star insisted. "Ripity, bipity, bim-bam-BOO; Bolton's, Bolton's, hoo-rah-ROO."

"It was pretty darn slick, Aunt Bee. You see that monument is like an awful long tunnel up on end and all of us doing everything together the noise got louder and louder."

"Bumpety, bumpety, bump, BOOM; bumpety, bumpety, bump, BOOM!" exclaimed the others in unison.

"Cheese, it was out of sight."

"But not out of hearing, I suppose?" said Aunt Bee. "You might remember Mrs. Maggots. We've had a good deal of racket here this afternoon."

"I was almost sorry I didn't have my K-boots any more. They'd have been like sledgehammers. We kept on running and jumping and booming all together on the platforms until, my gosh, it was like a thunderstorm. Time we were half way down, honest you could feel the whole shebang tremble."

"I got there first," said Ingram, "and I could hear yells from the cops downstairs, the big fiends."

"We got two-thirds of the way down," said Star, "and there was a whole squad of cops and Secret Services running up like crazy men, and folks hollering up and down the shaft. It was bughouse. I bet they thought it was that old Mount Pellay bust loose again in Martinique. Nobody ever thought of doing that before, not even Coxey's Army. They took us by the neck and run us out of there pronto. Specially Ingram, we had to pretend he was anarchist and we didn't know him."

"They were sore because Jeff called them janissaries," Skinny remarked. "That's just janitors in uniform."

"We tried to tell them it was an exercise in sound-waves. Mr. Bolton sent us all the way over to make a test. It's what they call propagation of sound."

"Resonance," sniveled Skinny. "You do a thing like that in a closed pipe and the waves just multiply. You can break down a bridge that way."

"One of the cops watched us clear to the train," said Bert proudly.

"Happen the Major was wrong," Aunt Bee concluded the discussion. "He told me Washington D.C. Monument was one place you couldn't get into trouble. I'm glad school starts next week."

"This club's good about monuments," Star said. "I bet it's because my family wrote a national anthem."

They disbanded in good spirits. "We're certainly beholden to you, Ma'am, for that good cocoa and cake. Let's give our new yell for Miz Barton. We made it up coming home in the cars."

They were urged to render it in a whisper; but if Mrs. Maggots was listening she might still have heard:

"Siss on Harvard, siss on Yale:
Ingram Duffle's gone to jail.
Don't get sore,
T.S.O. 4,
Fiends, fiends, fiends!"

They gave it again, considerably louder, from the corner of the street. "Dessay Sandy Hole will be a good idea," thought Miss Barton. "The city's no place for young animals."

50. Uncle Dan Prepares a Lecture

To Jeff's surprise the call was for Uncle Dan. Professor Barton hadn't guessed—few people had in 1903, when he subscribed—what the telephone was going to be like. Their number was Patapsco 1001-K; Dan soon interpreted it as a thousand calls and a call. In the hour after supper, when Uncle Dan and Aunt Bee enjoyed a little talk about the events of the day, the number might almost have been Patapsco T.S.O. 4, as the instrument rapidly became the medium of all club business, or exchange of advices on the next day's lessons. They would overhear Jeff talking at Bee's desk in the dining-room:

"Say, isn't that the limit? How did *you* do it?—I thought it was one of those crazy *as to* accusatives, 'having been collected as to her flowing bosoms in a knot.'—That's what it says, I got the book right here: *nodoque sinus collecta fluentis.*—Gee, *sinus* is a stinker, the vocabulary gives ten meanings for it: a fold, a bend. a coil, a curve, a bay, a gulf, a cove, a bosom, a lap, an embrace.—Well, *which* is in a knot, she or her dress or her bosoms?—Yeh, somehow it sounds rude in the plural.—Accusative of specification?—Let's tell him we're puzzled by that word, ole Dusty'll spend ten minutes explaining.—See you in the morning, stop by for me?"

It was soon necessary to limit Jeff to three calls per evening, whether inward or outward. He protested that by the principles of Algebra III it required $4 \times 3 \times 2 = 24$ calls to accomplish complete circulation of dialogue among a club of four members; and even this left out Ingram Sylvester Duffle.

"That's all right," said Uncle Dan, who was trying to concentrate on his pipe and the newspaper. "If you ring through to Ingram and say 'Are you there?' he would have to reply 'I am not all there,' and the Chesapeake and Potomac Telephone Company would be embarrassed."

"Aw go on, you're kidding. 'Are you there?' is what they say on the phone in England. Of course they're there or it wouldn't be answered at all. Americans say hello. It's more mannerly. That's what the mariners said to the albatross," he added.

Uncle Dan was thinking this out when the bell rang. Jeff yelled "I've only had two," and ran. He had to hurry to reach it before Moxie got there. She was as much thrilled as anyone by this new installation. "When that bell chime fo' you, it make you feel celebrated. It pleasures me good to say Thiz Professor Bahton rezzident. Jeff tell me that rectory all full of folkses names in print. Mighty God, ef they all feel conversable, what a shivaree."

Since it was a party-line various other subscribers had opportunity to hear Moxie's heavy breathing as she listened in. When other people were called the phone made small ticking sounds; Moxie said it was scratchin' to be heard, and usually obliged it. She always reported these eavesdroppings to Aunt Bee; there was one unknown and frequent voice she had nicknamed Miz Shrill. "I heah Miz Shrill fixin' to have a dress-up dinner. She ohder frizzlin' beef, all I could do to refrain my tongue. Dat's too puny fo' company. When *we*-all economies it always come out fancy, like dem currycomb oysters or Miz Bee's kromeskies or Marse Jeff's long-sweetenin' pie.—But I heah Miz Shrill tell out the documents fo' a fool-proof Boiled Dressin'. I'm thinkin' we might try it."

This time it was neither Skinny nor Star nor Bert, nor even Mrs. Shrill, but the solemn tones of Dr. Beinbrink asking for Uncle Dan. "I'm certainly distressed to bother you, Professor, but Dr. Outward is sick. By what Mrs. Outward says, I'm afraid he's real poorly and I'll have to ask you to take his Shakespeare class tomorrow afternoon."

"Of course, Mr. President," said Dan politely. "I hope it's nothing serious?"

Dan had not accustomed himself to holding the ear-piece; he had an odd way of tilting it at right angles. Don't hold it like that, Jeff kept on saying, the sound gets lost in your whiskers. Dan held it in such a way that anyone else in the room could hear the voice, and Jeff was much amused by President Beinbrink's reply.

"He has a misery in his guts. We hope it ain't appendicitis. That's so popular nowadays."

"That's a careless way of talking. He doesn't mean popular, he means frequent."

"What was the assignment for tomorrow?" Professor Barton asked.

"There seems to be some dispute among the girls," said the President, "but Rozanne Towson is more trustworthy than most, she says Dr. Outward was going to talk about *The Tempest*. But don't let that trouble you none, Professor. You just skirmish up anything you have in mind about the Bard. What is it you literary scholars always call him, the Sweet Swan of Avon? I declare, when Mrs. Beinbrink and I visited Stratford that river was a disappointment. On a hot day it's positively septic."

"Like Jones's Falls," said Professor Barton.

"Ha, ha! You're always the wag, always quick on the up-take. I'm glad you're on the telephone now. It'll give me the pleasure of ringin' yo' bell from time to time, a little friendly tintinnabulation. I really do enjoy our chats. Well, Sir, I'll have a notice put up so the young ladies won't cut the class. I take it very kindly that you'll come to my rescue. Don't let it prey on your mind, Sir; just any little notions you feel for about the Bard. You can be extempore rather than, hum, ex cathedra."

That was easy for President Beinbrink to say, but Dan worked late that night. A glance at the calendar showed him the coincidence that the next day was Thursday, April 23, Shakespeare's birthday. It was also a coincidence that on his desk were some of Bartholomew's cycling maps. Secretly he had been visualizing favorite roads between Wilford and Cambridge. He didn't wish to rouse nostalgia in Aunt Bee, but in his mind he was planning a jaunt on wheels when he would go back to Suffolk that summer. Sitting in a drift of tobacco smoke (which eddied gently toward the gulping lamp-cistern, then suddenly funneled up inside the green shade) he brooded what he might tell the Shakespeare class. It would be rash to offer his own ideas about any particular play; they might conflict with what Dr. Outward had said or planned to say, and disagreement among magistrates is marshmallows for the pupils. And also he must refrain because he specially hankered to cross foils with Erasmus Outward, Ph.D., who had so capably and profitably reduced Our Fellow Shakespeare into soluble bouillon cubes. This active dominie was reputed by envious colleagues to double his salary by a summer Chautauqua circuit: *The Forest of Arden, with Slides. . . .*

Perhaps I could try, Dan thought, to suggest to them what lies behind Shakespeare or any other desperado of the island tongue: the feeling of England itself. How suggest it to these flippant or incapacious children, naturally suspicious of any kind of beauty they had never seen or guessed? He conned the col-

293

ored maps spread under the lamp: the great green buttress of East Anglia rumped into the blue; and all the westward-reaching shapes sloped toward the open Atlantic like a venturesome child dipping its foot in surf. He knew already, months ahead, how Cornwall's opal air would feel and taste as the ship came up the bend of narrowing seas. The white three-pointed trident of The Needles; Alum Bay with tinted cliffs; Harry the Eighth's Hurst Castle. Or, if they were going round the Foreland there'd be Lear's chalky bourn (ten masts make not the altitude), the samphire gatherer of dreadful trade, the blink of the Gull and the Mouse. What was it young Kipling had said: "The Mouse swings green on the Old Trail, the Gull Light lifts on the Long Trail, the trail that is always new"— Did they think these things were only scenery, or "literature"? They were the blood of men's hearts. . . . The Gull, the Goodwins, the Girdler, and beyond these lights and shoals the working Thames. Mind's eye moving inward over naked hill and such gnarled forestry sees Shakespeare's frightened hare in Warwickshire, pricked up to listen and sunlight veins his ears. Not even Uncle Remus knew more about rabbits. . . . The samphire on which the sun never sets. . . . Now stop fooling, Barton, and think it out. He put away the maps and set to his notes.

Not scenery indeed: beyond these lights and shoals were the bonfire of Shakespeare, the glow of Milton, the frosty sparkle of Pope, the foxfires of Swift. If *The Tempest* really was the lesson for the day he could begin with that—as a fable of ideal education for girls? Here he better step lightly. Shakespeare as an American citizen, or Miranda as America's First Lady? No, they would think he was being fanciful and that must be left for Shakespeare himself. But whom should he try to please: the girls, or The Bard, or the ailing Ph.D.? It was even possible President Beinbrink might drop in at that lecture, to examine whatever little notions would mature in the drooping tempo of three o'clock in the afternoon.

Thursday the 23rd was almost able to stand up and walk when Uncle Dan went to his couch, mumbling to himself, "A ship at sea and afterwards an island."

But *The Tempest* is a fable not so easy to dismiss. It lives in the subconscious mind, and when that element took charge of Uncle Dan asleep, he found himself in a world more tropical. The Island was not the precious stone set in the silver sea but some circling atoll of the West. Perhaps the island was himself. It began as a pale smoke ring inside which he sat with dressing-gown and green lamp and strong notebooks checked with colored pencil; the light sparkled on their shiny fasteners, like Hazlitt's shoe-buckle. The green lamp grew and domed with foliage; the ring of smoke widened to a barrier reef, cliffs and perimeters of yellow sand; on those dazzling shallows pounded the monotone sea. The beaches were not our coarse northern gravel but burning powder-sand, as though some world-huge hour glass, the crystal bulb of sky, had cracked and poured it down. Time was spilled and sifted flat. There were cries of shipwreck under the bluff and a purple distance tigered with lightning but twice five miles were girdled round with magic, no harm was done. In that central glade of thinking the sun was burdensomely bright, crayon-colored birds screamed in gangs, flies and mosquitoes stung like telephone bells. A woodcutters' stump, a cloven pine, sweated resin; it had a sun-dial on it. Miranda played about, crawling in a loincloth. I should warn her about poison ivy; damn it, you have to think of everything. It was a queer smell; hot, oily, metallic (Jeff's old magic lantern); flowers like pictures in children's linen books but they breathed of Jones's Falls. "It's laudanum and garlic," said Coleridge, who also wore a dressing-gown (Dorothy made it for him). "In Malta they call garlic Italian vanilla." The shipwrecked mariners crackled through the marshy underwood and revealed themselves as the T.S.O. 4 led by their own Caliban, Ingram Sylvester Duffle. "Phew!" said Baby Miranda, pivoting on her rump, and closed her long-lashed eyes in disgust. Jeff apologized: "It's baked onion. I had a rotten ear-ache and they put a baked onion in my ear and gave me *Treasure Island* to read. The inside of my ear crackled like a telephone. Where's the spade? This is the place to hunt."

"You big fiends," said Caliban. "I've got to go and haul some wood. You're as bad as Egyptians. You brought a plague of flies."

It's like Susquehanna, Dan was trying to say, but it's a difficult word in a dream. I must say only the simplest things or I'll wake up. I might have known, as soon as I found an island to myself someone would be shipwrecked on it. But when he looked round to tell this, Coleridge was already dodging behind the woodpile. A bell was ringing—Ariel?—or probably Porlock 1001-K. . . .

By lunch time Dan had rationalized all this; it was under nickel handcuffs in a loose-leaf notebook. Inquiry reported Dr. Outward improved but still off duty. Uncle Dan had his lecture comfortably stowed in five mental pictures. "You're making something out of it that the author couldn't possibly have Had in Mind," Miss Towson would say. "Why not? Isn't that the glory of literature?" he might retort. His symbol-sketches were clear as lantern slides: he wouldn't even need to draw them on his fingernails with ink—as they said Mark Twain did, so he could glance at them and then lick them off one by one as he pretended to stroke his mustache. This is really better than a lecture, Uncle Dan brooded; this is testimony. He was in that happy fullness of conception known to one who has really grieved upon his topic and is sure what he wants to say. It was further bedded down by Aunt Bee's steak and kidney pudding, since it was Moxie's day out. His sister, fatigued, retired to her room; Dan sat pensive at the ravaged dining table, half Prospero, half suet and gravy.

He set off at the proper time, recapitulating the sparse precision-points of Shakespearean biography. At least the death date, 1616, is easy to remember, he thought; perfect prosody, a quatrain rhyming in pairs. He left the house without disturbing Bee; he saw tucked in his hat the usual list of Thursday afternoon errands including "cat's meat" from J. William Sprunt. He was buried seventeen feet deep (Shakespeare, not Sprunt), but most of the commentators have buried him deeper still. Going down Carroll Street Dan passed 1850 (Wordsworth died)—1800 (Macaulay born)—alas, there was no 1797. That magical date hovered a rainbow twirl in air between two blocks. The eighteenth century began (on the other side of the street) at 1745, so he was torn between crossing over to homage the death of Swift, or stay hither for Pope's obit at 1744. This block ended with the side door of Spontoon's, fragrant with paper soldiers, at 1702, the Age of Anne. Before he knew it he was across North Avenue and in the miraculous 1600's. 1648, Herrick's *Hesperides* was a good beginning, but his mind was hurrying on. His goal now was the humane and considerate Chaucer who chose his dates so easily memorable for even the frailest student. The greatest of all Geoffreys was exactly spanned in the crossing of 14th Street, below P.S. 16. Not impossibly Spike McMechan and his gang had picked up some brisk language from their proximity to Chaucer's dates. . . . If you have always gone downtown to do errands on Thursday afternoon, and if you are comfortably drowsed with lamb kidneys and warm April, you will probably pursue the accustomed track. Uncle Dan did so and about half-past three was enjoying a little conversation with Mr. Sprunt. "She writes it down 'cat's meat,'" he said, realizing too late he had handed Mr. Sprunt the list, "but we don't really call it that. It's a family joke."

"Oh, yes, we've had some good laughs about that," said Mr. Sprunt. "That's the kind of family I like, that has its own jokes even if they aren't amusing to outsiders. You should have known my old grampa, he was a one. You said anything comical to him, he came right back at you like a bufferang."

"Miss Barton always visits with me when she's puzzled about her marketing," continued Mr. Sprunt. "She's told me about some of your high-class English dishes, like bubble-and-squeak and toad-in-the-hole. She had me up a stump, though, time she was hunting for an Italian warehouseman. It took quite a while before I made out she wanted a delicatessen. This here bottom round, ground for hamburger, in the carriage trade we call it Salisbury steak. When you want real cat's meat I keep scraps here in the bucket. I like to give them a treat when they look real anxious. 'Care killed a cat,' like Shakespeare said—"

"Shakespeare— Oh, my God! Excuse me, Mr. Sprunt, I'm lecturing on Shakespeare this minute."

Uncle Dan fled along the crowded passageway, not even waiting for his parcel.

BLUE RIDGE

51. *The Greased Pole*

It's only seventy miles to Blowing Gap, but what a different earth and sky. Uncle Dan was a little disappointed that on the train Jeff didn't seem to pay much attention to the gently rising landscape. Dan had expected that apple farms and cornfields, hogs and mules and little slattern towns where the locomotive belled along the street, would be claimed for Jeffland. But without the rivalry of LaGrange the game of Countries was in abeyance; also the young traveler was reading *King Solomon's Mines* for the first time. He did not rouse from absorption until Teackle, to whom this journey was familiar, appeared from the baggage car wearing the news-butcher's coat and hat and shouted, "Here you are, folks; get 'em while they're hot: *Life, Puck, Judge,* pepsin gum, Velvets and chocolate cherries." But Jeff's ear had been recording subconsciously. "Didn't fool me," he said. "You don't say it right, it isn't chocolate, it's *chocklut.*"

"Up from the meadows green with corn," remarked Uncle Dan as they traversed broad fields and saw the blue profile of the hills rising beyond. "Shucks, that ole Barbara Fritchie," protested Teackle. "Major says that's just Yankee telltale they rumored into the schoolbooks. He knew the ole lady. She couldn't sing out like that. She was mo'n ninety years old and bedridden to boot."

Evidently Jeff took his literature more credibly, for his first comment when they descended at Piedmont was a quotation from the geography of Rider Haggard's romance. As they stood on the station platform looking toward the Appalachian bulwark, the twin contours of Carrick Knob and Roundtop were outlined clear in afternoon light. He surprised Aunt Bee by exclaiming "Sheba's Breasts!"

Since the trip was first planned Uncle Dan had been repeating the Major's phrase "a thousand feet up." It was as conventional and as inaccurate as the label "Ten-Day Boat" for the *Westernland* and her sisters. After Uncle Dan wrote to Washington for the survey map of that quadrangle he saw that even at Wicker's Farm the elevation was only 910; but Jeff, an alert sophist, said he was satisfied because the difference between 910 feet and 1910 Carroll Street was an even thousand.

"That don't make sense," said Teackle.

"Oh, yes, it does, the way Jeff and I argue," said Uncle Dan. "It's a perfect quibble. Thirteen is the Age of Quibble."

"How old is Quibble?" said Aunt Bee. "*You* haven't outgrown it yet." No one else was amused by an apparently endless game of argument which Dan and Jeff enjoyed. Each would try to lead up to a dilemma which the other could only pass by evasion. This was known as a Caudine Fork or a Quibblespringe. Jeff learned to see one of these logical ambushes before him, cry "Quibble-springe!" and yell with laughter. But this esoteric sport was avoided for a while since it baffled Teackle. There were plenty of other games that Jeff could learn from the older boy, who was now sixteen.

The farmhouse, mottled stone with broad wooden verandas, stood on a hump of meadow above the creek. The smooth dome of Roundtop rose another 900 feet behind it; across the ravine was the long ridge of Catoctin Mountain. There were only a few weeks before Uncle Dan would leave, and as Teackle said sadly, "I guess I've got practically the whole of literature to make up." Every morning there was brisk tutoring on the balcony upstairs. This was more grievous for Teackle than for Jeff. The young Warren was adept in anything of horses, guns, or fishing tackle but he had not inherited the Major's taste for Virgil. In a year's time he must face ordeal by Princeton, and even those modest requirements gave him palsy. He was at his best when lessons were over and the boys retired to the abandoned cabin down by Sandy Hole. They put mattresses and blankets in the musty old bunks and were allowed to sleep there and cook their own breakfast.

Jeff sometimes wondered, long afterward, if he would dare revisit the lost paradise of Blowing Gap. The hot winding road, whether mire or powder, climbed the steepening gully and over the star and daisy field; iron wagon-tires jarred and slid on rocky outcrop. It may now be a swath of concrete with a lubritorium and a Log Cabin Rest; instead of the bassoon of frogs by the millpond the suck and crackle of hot rubber. Perhaps, afterward, as much education could be traced from old Doc Wicker as from Virgil. The shrewd old Doc, so-called because he began as a veterinary—he was a German-American horsecoper when the Major first knew him—was the leading character of the Lutheran settlement of Slabtown. He lived on a triangle; his three enterprises were the farm, the excelsior mill by the pond, and the general store at Slabtown Corners. Uncle Dan and the boys thought they had never seen so busy a person. It was Aunt Bee, more shrewd, who analyzed their landlord. "He's always on the way somewhere to see if somebody else is doing the job." As soon as this was pointed out they recognized its truth. His amiable frau ran the house; she had no eyebrows and Teackle said she had toasted them off leaning over the stove. The son Joel, graduate of the State agricultural college, managed the farm; the foreman at the mill sliced up the excelsior; the old Doc chewed tobacco, uncomfortably close to the sugar barrel, at the Slabtown store. Even there business was not oppressive until Saturday nights, when the boys were more than happy to lend a hand. In the fly-speckled candy-case were cardboard boxes of chocolate mice so Jeff accepted payment in that tender, or in fishhooks. There were shelves of queer smelling calico and dress goods which it was fascinating to measure off on the counter with the yardstick; Jeff regretted that he couldn't "smell a yard" as the Doc called his own way of measurement, stretching the cloth from the tip of his pocked nose to the end of his reach of arm. If there was a packing case to be opened or a freezer of cream to be dished out it was Teackle and Jeff who had the real fun. Sometimes while poor Teackle was wrestling with the Aeneid, Jeff was studying a work no less important, the wholesale catalogue of Butler Brothers, the great Chesapeake jobbers with whom Doc Wicker placed his orders. This was indeed a bible of western commerce, where goods are so varied and so cheap at wholesale. He discovered it in the proper way, out in the backhouse behind the store, among a thicket of sunflowers and a buzz of big blue flies.

But Sandy Hole comes first. Even in the picturesque geography of Jeffland there had been nothing like this; mentally he sprinkled a number of mountain streams across the map of imagination. The map itself, since Teackle was a little scornful of that sort of game, remained rolled up in Aunt Bee's trunk. He was immersed in the wonders of actuality; and immersed is the right word: at least three times a day the boys were in and out of that rocky basin. Six feet down a white sandy bottom shifts slowly with the coil of circling water. In the clean pothole the stony walls are polished smooth at the edges, the fine grains churned by steady spin into a soft mound at the middle. Like a clapper in an inverted bell lay the great round boulder which perhaps had helped to rotate the hollow. The fall of the stream from the rift above was only about eight feet but it came with strong cold push down an unusual deep fissure. The engineers in the cabin, many years before, had tinkered with Sandy Hole for their own amusement. They chipped a ledge across the wall of rock so one could walk warily to the edge of the sluice where the creek jetted through. The opening was almost like a nozzle that widened upstream into a cavern of astonishing echoes. No wonder they call the defile Blowing Gap; down that crooked elbow comes a steady draught from Appalachian forests. The breeze moves with the tumble of water and keeps the foliage above in a twinkling flutter. "What a place to let loose a load of bonnet boxes," Jeff said. "Even the trains are always blowing." Twice a day they heard the catamountain scream of the express, and more often the arduous rumble of some freight. Any sound at large in that groove of hills seemed to float in overtone to Sandy Hole.

Teackle, braced on a knob under the lip of the fall, could stand in the very cascade, his head projected from a ruffling cloak of foam, but at average flow the stream was too strong for Jeff. He struggled to hold himself firm under the sluice but always, with a glorious cold wriggle, he would be tossed into the basin of golden rock. Of course he boasted about it: he said it taught him to dive. After a good many stinging belly-whackers it did. Above the waterfall was a narrow rocky channel which could be groped through except after heavy rainfall. Teackle called it by its local name, the Slut, which Uncle Dan interpreted as a variation of "slit." The Yankees, he said, would call it a flume.

"I like flume better, it sounds like Latin."

"Aw, go sit on a tack," said Teackle, and got even by scrambling up the steep chimney of rock that overhung the bend of the ravine. This was too sheer for Jeff; after several struggles he stayed below and nicknamed it the Funnybone.

"Ain't a funnybone, it's a wishbone," jeered Teackle from above. "Don't you wish you could climb it! I can see the bridge from here, that's the bridge my father built." After sliding perilously down he confided with an air of scandal, "People round here call that bridge Tiddyhigh Trestle. They were just

303

starting to build it and they had a flood, washed it all away, the water came down the valley tiddy high. Wait till I show you, Major scratched the name on one of the piers. It says *Tiddy-high, H. W., 1870.* I don't think that's decent, my father's an ornery old man. You know how he limps on one leg, he likes to let on he got wounded in the war, but he got that limp when the flood washed him into the Slut."

Humiliations of the morning on the tutoring balcony were requited at Sandy Hole in the afternoon. Wedged among the boulders beside the pool was a large slippery log naked with erosion. Two carefully peeled sticks were kept here for dueling. These fencing bouts, in which the loser fell into the stream, were associated with the universal penalty of youth which Teackle now approached. Uncle Dan deplored it as much as anyone, but he knew it had to be done. The climax of the summer's discipline was to write an essay on "Coffee Houses in the Reign of Queen Anne." This seemed to Teackle to present a psychic blockade more unscalable than Chimney Rock. "Aw, shucks, Mr. Barton, there must be a million ole essays on those Coffee Houses. I don't care for coffee anyway. Why couldn't we use one that somebody else wrote?" But Uncle Dan was strict, he had to be. Teackle's only retaliation was to cry as they approached Sandy Hole, "Come on, fall to with rapiers, you're Addison and I'm Steele." And as would have happened in real life, it was always Sir Richard who remained on the log.

"I'm glad we got up here before the Fourth of July," said Uncle Dan. "Independence Day is the only time when I really feel sorry to be an American." Those who remember the national fête as celebrated in early 1900's will sympathize. Chesapeake, always rather proud of its juvenile ruffianism, was on that day a panorama of frightened horses, weeping girls, punk-burns and tetanus. The exact tin-boom of old kitchenware soaring upward over bursting cannon crackers still tingles the ear of any old Oriole Boy. Perhaps the only sound still more endeared was the screech of the female child when a torpedo went off between her feet, or the glorious clatter of a runaway horse on cobbles.

"They have the Fourth up here, too," said Teackle, "but golly, this time I'm gonna climb that greased pole. I reckon I can do it too, if Miz Bee will help me."

"I don't think I'd be very good at that," said Aunt Bee. "They always used to have one at Wilford Regatta. It was a mast between two yachts, why, I remember Dan and Harry Bredfield fencing with each other sitting on it. They both fell in, like you boys at Sandy Hole."

Jeff was a little startled to think that old people ever had so much gumption, but he kept quiet. The defeats of dueling on the log were humiliating.

"This kind of a pole stands up on end," Teackle explained. "They have a greased shoat too. They let it loose on the Fair Grounds and everybody chases it. Whoever can hang onto it can take it home. I wouldn't be surprised Jeff might catch it, he's such an active little squirt. It was funny as—I mean it was funny, one time the pig ran right into the Lutheran minister. He fell on it and grabbed it inside his long black coat. They have big doings, the Catoctin Mountain Band parades through town and all the old veterans turn out, both the Blue and the Gray."

"No cannon crackers, I hope?" said Aunt Bee.

"Country kids don't have much money to spend on firecrackers," said Teackle, "so you don't need to worry. Anyhow they're all shot off before parade time. The parade's really slick because the G.A.R. and the C.S.A. both try to see who can turn out the most veterans. Of course the Blues always have it, but they get along together right well because they both sit back and laugh at the Spanish War boys. There's usually a fight when one of the old codgers asks them were they wounded by Spaniards or canned willie."

Some of this was mysterious to Aunt Bee but her instinct always was to wait and see if things would explain themselves without questions asked. "You see we're only a few miles from the Mason and Dixon Line," said Uncle Dan.

We're practically living in history, thought Jeff. "Then we're right in the middle of America?" he said.

"You're in the middle of it up and down, but not sideways," said Uncle Dan.

"Oh, that ole Dixie line don't cut any ice," said Teackle. "But the Major's right comical about it. We were up here one time and he wouldn't go with us to Blue Ridge Summit because he said it was foreign country. You see, Ma'am, it's plumb on the boundary. Mother wanted him to be social because there's important diplomats goes for their vacation at the hotel. Major said they *better* be diplomats, living right there. That's how come they went there first, in the Secession War, they had to be tackful."

Uncle Dan doubted that Aunt Bee would wish to attend the Fourth of July celebration but to his surprise even before Doc Wicker hitched up the rig she was out on the farmhouse porch wearing the hat with wings. Jeff had on his oldest clothes in the faint hope of embracing the coursing pig; Teackle surprised them by wearing his slicker. He said he was sure there would be the usual Fourth of July downpour. He said he could hear it coming, though Doc Wicker believed that far-muted rumor was only the Hagerstown freight. It was often difficult to know—just as some of those in the parade might in their time have mistaken for distant thunder what had been the guns of Antietam or Gettysburg. Far up the valley of Hunting Creek, like a notch in an organ-pipe, is the cleft of Thunder Gap. Riding with wind and water on heavy afternoons comes the murmur of the West. Like sounding-boards the hillsides echo and confuse it. Sometimes it *is* the Hagerstown freight, but just about as often it is tempest, both blue and gray.

Evidently Teackle had made a previous attempt at the greased pole for he remarked, "I hope this time they'll play fair. When

I tried it before nobody could make it because they stood it up-side down, the butt end at the top. I got as high as any of 'em, though. The kids round here call me Greasy because I got the tallow all over my face. They think I'm citified, I'll show 'em." He aimed an imaginary rifle at a soaring buzzard and clicked synchronized tongue and fingers. "Bing!" he said. "Right through the eye."

"You-all are feeling your oats," said Jeff enviously.

"Listen, I've told you forty-leven times you don't say you-all when it's only one person. Bet your neck I'm feeling my oats and they ain't Quaker Oats neither. Spit in your eye and blind you.—You'll pardon me, Ma'am, but Fourth of July I'm always rarin' to go."

Jeff was amazed: he saw Teackle and Aunt Bee wink at each other.

The triumphant climax was, Teackle did climb the pole. Jeff, who had tried to galvanize his own powers by imagining the pig as a wild boar in the Forest of Arden, did not even see the creature. But after cream soda (which had no glass marble in the bottle) and fireworks and innumerable drums and brasses (*A Hot Time in the Old Town, Mr. Dooley, Dolly Gray*, &c.), they gathered for the return drive. "I'm so covered with smear I better put that slicker back on," said Teackle, grinning. "Look, I got a .22 rifle for first prize. Gosh, and the Major wouldn't let me bring my gun with me, said we might danger ourselves."

"And now you can, isn't that splendid," said Aunt Bee, who seemed in superb spirits. "Dan, give the boy his mackintosh, he'll get the carriage dirty."

Dan did so, but he had already noticed something.

"What was it you said about fair play?" he asked.

Aunt Bee had sewn sheets of emery-cloth on the inside of Teackle's overall pants.

52. *The Trestle*

Memory too is a greased pole for climbing. Long afterward Jeff sometimes got almost to the top of the mast, hugging with tightest knees and elbows. Just one reach—if he could free an arm he would cap the pole, see and smell and hear and feel. But loose that arm and down you go; literally, as they said then, stung.

"At least have the decency to get out of sight," muttered Teackle. He only whispered because he and Uncle Dan were still striving with Virgil on the balcony. Jeff as usual had finished his task earlier, had been unsquirmed from a chair and sent off. But Teackle looking under a tented elbow gave him such a glare that he went uphill behind the house in search of entertainment.

"*Quadrupedante putrem sonitu quatit ungula campum,*" Uncle Dan was saying. "That's a very famous line. Don't try to translate it until you get the sound." He said it again rapidly. "You see how clever that is, it gives the actual rhythm of a horse trotting."

"Unh-unh," contradicted Teackle. "No siree, that's not trotting, that's galloping." He illustrated by clapping his hands together and onto his knee in rapid sequence. "If you'll let me go out to the barn I'll get old Clara and show you—if she can still gallop," he said doubtfully.

There's something very interesting, Jeff was thinking, about living on the side of a hill. He had noticed among the other boarders that as soon as they came off the front porch they teetered instinctively down toward the creek. Stout Mrs. Mister, for instance, found herself far down the sloping meadow without quite knowing how she got there. Then she puffed and complained when the dinner bell rang—that far-bruiting brass which echoed back from several mountainsides. "Like half a dozen dinners at once," said the voracious boys. "And all the others probably better than the one we'll get," suggested ungrateful Uncle Dan, who found meat three times a day excessive.

They ought to enjoy it more on the way down if they make such a fuss coming back, Jeff thought. In spite of the natural pull of the creek—and he had now learned to distinguish a creek, a branch, and a run—the uphill pasture behind the barn had allures of its own. First the farmyard, all buzz and chuckle in forenoon sun, was a level pause between the exertions of up or down. In the narrow shade of the simmering woodpile Shep the veteran collie languidly fanned a courteous brush but averted his eyes lest Southern courtesy compel him to stand up. Jeff thought, He ain't no mo' shif'less than I am. Jeff himself had come up behind the house on purpose for fear Mrs. Mister would catch his eye and ask, "Honey, were you aiming to go to the post office?" That had embarrassed him since the first time he made the trip to the Slabtown store to ask innocently, "Is there any mail for Mister?"

It was just upon lunch time and the elderly postmaster was sharp set for grub. He looked out impatiently. "Mister who?" he grumbled.

"Mr. Mister."

"You're too fresh," said the postmaster and ran the window down with a slam.

"Mr. and Mrs. Mister! it's really names," cried Jeff through the pigeonholed partition. Nothing could appease Mrs. Mister's appetite for mail; it may be that Mr. Mister, who only came up at week-ends, had not sent her the promised allowance. "I would certainly suspect him of duplicity," was Uncle Dan's little joke.

A blue morning-glory was tickling Shep's ear and this rather than courtesy moved him from siesta. Once up he made his dash at Buster, the old tomcat who was assessing the probabilities of lunch through the screen of the summer kitchen. But even this gallantry (it took courage to assail Buster, a tortoise-shell of mighty thews) was only a gesture. It's their hot Southren blood,

Jeff said to himself; he heard much about this fluid from Teackle. Buster made his usual jump to the top of the rain barrel, curving himself in the attitude Jeff called Buster's Last Stand, but he did it half-heartedly. You could almost hear both animals say Aw Shucks.

"If you're going up through the field keep an eye open for eggs," said Mrs. Wicker, a massive and fuzzy outline through the rusty screen. "I think your favorite Happy Hen is laying up there." The christening of the individual fowls had been stimulated by Aunt Bee's observation that where everything else in the world was different from the Thorofare, fowls were just the same. The comic opera of barnyard poultry is universal.

It was neither the orchard nor the sun-blazed field that drew him uphill. Under the hump of Roundtop, like a tight collar round the rocky scarp, was the bend of the railroad. There was only one track on this line, and how much more romantic is the single way. You know, without ever pausing to analyze, that where there's only one pair of rails someone has to do a lot of planning. The metals themselves danced over by curlicues of dazzle seemed to have caught the color of the mountains. What Teackle called the bobwire fence was there to discourage cattle. It might once have been horse high, bull strong and pig tight but it was no barrier for a boy. To wriggle under, choosing perhaps the very spot where some cow had eased herself, and stumble up the rough among grasshoppers for a view round the curve, was best done alone. On the porches of distance one wants no company. Looking toward that thinning swerve of rails, the hover of burning air, the intimation of yonder is knowable and unsaid. At a particular spot marked by a raspy clump of black-eyed Susan he felt the trestle beginning to begin. He couldn't see it from there, the loom of the hillside still hid the view, but he knew that just a few steps further and the hollow of Blowing Gap would open. A painted post said W so he knew that anything would whistle before thundering round the bend. A huge boulder said B. M. 1066 so it really was over a thousand feet up. B. M., Teackle said, meant bench mark, but there was no bench. But when solitary the rail itself could serve though it took hardihood to sit on it until one had cooled it down. "Ouch, ouch, ouch!" he cried, jiggling up and down on the burning steel, but determined to allay it by the repeated application of humanity's best conductor of heat. There was a phrase of satisfaction often uttered by Teackle which he presently uttered, perhaps without realizing how appropriate: Gee, this is all to the mustard.

Yet there is a kind of traffic that doesn't whistle. In that long curving groove, like the ʃ-hole of a violin, vibrated all the music of the day: from shrilling insects to the moody grumbles of Thunder Gap, the meridian wail of the Piedmont Creamery, the reproachful bark of Shep, who had sense enough to stay inside the bobwire. The hot rails like strings carried tremolo and stir. He felt them tickle before he heard the soft increasing hum. As Teackle had taught him he laid his ear on the grape-colored rail, now cooled for contact. Surely there was something coming; molecules jigged and sang. With terrifying suddenness it swelled to a tinkling rattle—it must be crossing the trestle—he leapt aside and saw his first handcar come rocketing down the curve.

Pumping at the flying handles two men leaped up and down, bowing to each other in alternating frenzy. Like Alphonse and Gaston gone crazy; but they grinned and waved as they spun by so everything must be all right. I declare, everybody is certainly friendly, he thought. He decided that would be an excellent way for the President to make his inspection trips on the Great Eastern & Western of Jeffland. But Teackle was less impressed when he described it. "Major used to make trips to inspect roadbed setting right on the pilot of the engine, wrapped up in a bearskin sleigh robe. They sure had sport in those days. If I ever get quit of this ole Virgil Princeton chore I'm going to get me a job as train butcher and work up."

One of Teackle's first remarks when they got to the farm

was, "We better hurry up and walk across the trestle before Uncle Dan says not to." So before Uncle Dan had even seen this lofty scaffold the boys had made the transit. It was simple enough if one kept to the middle of the track though even there the empty downwards between the hot-smelling ties might be disturbing. Creosote exhaling from the wood smelled like bandages, Jeff said. Teackle, whom no elevation ever daunted, would pigeon-toe on the rail, or even stand out on one of the cross-pieces which projected at the sides. Fortunately Aunt Bee, who was not good at rugged walking, never saw the bridge except safely from below, but there was a lively argument on ethics when Uncle Dan learned of these exploits. "The smell of bandages sounds reasonable enough," he said. "If anything happens the bandages would be yours but the responsibility is mine."

"We always listen to the rail to be sure nothing's coming," said Teackle. They admitted however that they had exceeded prudence and each member of the conference had a word for it. Teackle said, I guess it wasn't square. Jeff said it wasn't straight. Dan: It wasn't cricket. Aunt Bee: It wasn't right. She added, even Shep knows better. She remarked privately to her brother, "I dessay you might make a study of the neighborhood and find out what they oughtn't to do before you go away. Boys that age don't like taking orders from women." But she was touched when she noticed in one of Teackle's textbooks that he had written—though probably long before—

> Teackle Warren, his hand and pen
> He will be good but God knows when.

The effect of this however was a little spoiled by Jeff's mischievous editing. After the word "good" he had inserted "student."

It took Aunt Bee a little time to adjust herself to this quite new sort of living. At first it was incomprehensible that she had nothing special to do. She rather yearned to show Mrs. Wicker a few kitcheneering wrinkles—sausage rolls, for instance—but realized that this would be an error. Dan, who had been spoiled on Carroll Street, sometimes remarked sadly, "It is really astonishing when you think, there are millions of people who have never in their lives had what you might call an interesting meal." Aunt Bee unconsciously made small chewing movements and looked exactly like Grandma.

But as soon as she could get her overworked conscience under control Bee was learning to enjoy. Perhaps she was happiest when she sat in a niche by the stream watching them bathe. Teackle had gallantly dragged a log of convenient shape into the angle of some rocks commanding the pool. It was surrounded by moist clumps of green and christened the Valley of Fern. Aunt Bee, however, who sat there with a lap full of masculine mending, called it more realistically Pants and Socks. "Or Susquehanna," said Uncle Dan. "That was a pantisocracy."

The boys groaned. "Penalty!" they exclaimed, and Aunt Bee concurred. Any allusion, during bathing hours, to what were considered Lessons, or any specially vile pun, had to be paid for by a forfeit. This was to be blindfolded and pushed off backward from the dueling log.

53. Tuition at Sandy Hole

"Don't forget your sand-shoes. You'll need them in bathing," Aunt Bee called from the balcony.

Jeff turned and held one foot high in air to show he had them on. "They're not sand-shoes they're sneakers," he shouted, "and I've told you forty-leven times it's not bathing, it's *swimming*."

"Teackle must have hurt his leg, he's limping so," said Uncle Dan, who was patiently editing the essay on coffee houses.

Aunt Bee had already suspected the reason for Teackle's sudden disability. They hadn't been forbidden to take the .22 rifle down to the stream, but Teackle thought the less publicity about it the better. He had it inside the leg of his overalls. Even to Uncle Dan's unwatchful disposition the limp seemed unduly obvious and severe; he opened his mouth to say something but Aunt Bee laid a hand on his arm.

"You go and take your forty-leven winks," she suggested.

"You're a wise old girl, aren't you?" he said. "We mustn't always be nay-sayers."

One would have thought from the sagging outline of Uncle Dan in the faded hammock between two apple trees that he was having his nap, and that was what he pretended. But like many people, he could never sleep lying on his back, and he was thinking.

Remarkable indeed how Bee had conquered their inherited preoccupation with morals in decisions where really no morals were involved. The card games, for instance. Doctrine on the Thorofare had it that cards were probably wicked if they bore pips and faces; those were gambling cards; the only kind allowable to virtuous people would show birds or flags or flowers, or Mr. Bones the Butcher and the other tradesmen families. But Teackle had brought in his trunk a pack of gambling cards, fresh in his passion for a new game called Five Hundred. Reluctant but unwilling to offend, Aunt Bee was cajoled to take a hand. In concession to her feelings they altered "I bid" to "I affirm." Bee affirmed to such purpose that she won the first round handsomely. Dan, a trifle maliciously, asked her how she felt. "Dessay I don't feel any wickeder than before," she admitted.

And what about firearms? Dan wondered. The .22 would probably cause woe soon or late but after all, human beings must take risks. He saw the boys going downhill, with an increasing air of prowess as they decided they had outwitted him. Perhaps it was a little too comical to be devoting so much spirit to thinking about Wordsworth or the *Spectator* when there were young and living imaginations so close to hand. Even Teackle, active and gay on the dueling log or the precipice of Chimney Rock, was closer to Dick Steele than the most learned footnote. Here indeed was tuition in full measure; as Dan watched and listened he could see Jeff grow. Why cannot everyone learn what the boy was learning: how water flows and fire burns (leaning against the wind when properly sheltered); they waded in the creek hunting waterfalls (Wordsworth did it too, he remembered), if they didn't find them they built them, hoisting slippery rocks in peril of their toes and calling Aunt Bee to award the prize for the best-constructed cascade. When Jeff at last built a fireplace which drew, he shouted with glory: "Gee whiz, a fire is only a stream that flows upward!" From endless and varying resource the creek provided them power, the woods smelled different daily and in different hours of the day, tin pails flashed in upland sunshine and they learned that only the first few blackberries make that tingle in the bucket. Life was hard for many crawfishes and even an occasional trout, but the four-pound bass whose outline had been left on the cabin wall by Major Warren's engineers must have been sterile. Evidently he had no progeny. After many hours in the old punt on the millpond, where earthworms turned from pink to black in the warm bilge, Teackle found a consoling theory. There was some kind of acid from the excelsior mill that turned the water to beer, and the bass, if any, were sleeping it off. When boys begin to have theories you know they are practically men.

"It's about all them apple trees is good for I reckon," said young Wicker who passed through the orchard just then with a kerosene-soaked corncob on a fishing pole; he was burning off caterpillar nests. "I mean they're only fitten for to swing hammocks—by gorry, even the caterpillars use 'em that way. We got a second crop of the buggers this year, likely it's the only second crop of anything on the Hump. Yes sir, it's hardscrablin up here. No wonder Doc leaves me work the farm while he sits by the cracker barl down to the store."

Uncle Dan was somewhat ashamed: lying there in a gentle to-and-fro he had only noticed what bright-colored birds rubricated the orchard. He made the frequent resolution of self-centered men: I must learn to be more observant. It was Jeff who had first remarked the paintbox plumage of the birds. When both red and yellow were in an apple tree at once, and Aunt Bee admired, Jeff said, "No wonder: it's a cardinal and an oriole. Bet there's no such birds in England." "England isn't so bad," said Uncle Dan mildly. "Over there every cardinal has an ordinal."—"Penalty!" grumbled Teackle. "You promised not to talk school after lunch."

The mountainside might be ordeal for apples but even Joel Wicker passing like a flamen under the arches of trees couldn't spoil it for hammock musing. "Why should this happen to *me?*" Uncle Dan brooded, resenting certain ironies in his own condition; then realized that whenever one says "It *would* be like that, it *would* happen to *me*," one makes instinctive admission of the contriving art-spirit of the world. What a gruesome thing consciousness is, he thought, and yet without it no art can be. The boys perhaps had the blessedness of animals who can never be artists since they bear no burdens intentionally. My God, he thought, did I have to come to this hardscrabbling hillside to get a glimmering of some things old Daddy Wordsworth had in mind in his wise passiveness? Is it only my own private pains that make this country seem so enormous and so strange? From Teackle's copy-book exercise on the sophistry of coffee houses I look off into a ravine of sun and gale. Blanche wrote me she couldn't go back to Shropshire this summer and what a homesickness she had for rectory gardens and seedcake and a parlor-maid bringing in cucumber and watercress sandwiches for tea. I thought I had it too. . . . He looked across the great trough of hills toward Thunder Gap where the stifled electricity of the afternoon was murmuring unease. High beyond the pinnacle of Chimney Rock floated some great bird, he hoped it was an eagle, not a buzzard—or even Mark Twain's *oesophagus*. From the rectory garden standpoint the scene was wild and shabby and shiftless and forlorn, and yet he didn't want to leave it.

A smoke of frizzling caterpillars drifted across the hammock; it seemed pleasanter to go and share the art-spirit at Sandy Hole instead of mazing himself with words. A green apple fell on his forehead with a thump and startled him up. "Guess I'll go down to the sounding cataract," he decided. "Dessay the arts won't bear thinking about."

He stumbled happily down the wooded path, across black and white stripes of dazzle. In surprising release the feelings that would not come by demand now enchanted him unbidden. Oh be aware, he said to himself, that every creature capable of nerves and senses is proved by the very anxieties most sure to reach his quick. Those are his differentia: the difference to him! See the shape of these trees, or the pour and ruffle of the creek, the slow streaming coil of sand grains in the goblet of the pool—all flawless, triumphant in composition. Why with such examples should man resent taking pattern under pressure?

Aunt Bee was sitting on the log in her mimic Valley of Fern. She motioned him to silence until the bird she was watching flew away. It looked like President Beinbrink at Commencement, with a tuft of nervous hair and academic hood barred blue and white. "A kingfisher," she said. "I've mended your bathing drawers."

"Please call them trunks."

"The person who does the mending has a right to call them what she chooses."

He plunged, swam under water, felt the current tug at his beard, wondered in that cold splendor why one should ever be grieved. He floated gently with the circling eddy of the basin and (like a good observer, he reminded himself) verified the mound of loose sand piled on the rocky bottom. He noticed a certain sharpness in Bee's watching attitude. Too bad that Wilford girls in her generation were not taught to swim. Sometimes they "waded," in a great humped bustle of tucked up skirts, but they never "went in." Probably they were frightened off by that horrible name Bathing Drawers. . . . He wondered where

317

the boys were. He was looking forward to the peaceful palaver they enjoyed after their swim. They usually sat basking on a modestly screened flat boulder. Uncle Dan, draped in his favorite Wilford bath towel (as big as a blanket), blew pipe-smoke at dragon-flies and cherished his toes. "Shucks, Americans don't need towels that size to get dry," said Teackle. "I bet you had to have them in England to wipe off the fog."

"I have a special way of drying my toes," Jeff might announce. "I put ferns between them. It attracts the sunshine and makes me smell very sweet." Dan reflected that while it's probably unimportant to the universe just how any individual dries his toes, yet there's a moment in living when it's enormously urgent to the individual to emphasize himself as unique—and if important to the individual then it *is* important to the sum total? Such idle thoughts are the bliss of after-swimming. Consciousness itself is a pothole in a running stream, and gathers a little mound of bright sand in the turn of the eddy.

He crawled out, dried his hands, picked up his pipe (waiting already filled in a crevice of rock) and sat near Bee.

"What do you think about when you sit looking like that?" she asked.

"Less than nothing," he said.

"You can't think less than nothing."

"Oh yes you can. Anything that's less than nothing is on its way to being something in the opposite direction. Minus quantities are just as real as plus quantities. I learned that from Blanche."

He was on the point of saying more when the boys appeared coming upstream from the direction of Slabtown. Teackle was carrying the gun and seemed to be arguing with Jeff, but the younger boy broke away and ran toward Aunt Bee. His face looked strangely out of shape and he shocked them by bursting into a choking sob.

"What on earth's the matter?" asked Aunt Bee.

"It's awful silly," said Teackle, "he's got me so upset I'd like to cry too but you can't really cry after your voice is changed. I think it was mostly accident but he shot a frog. Doc Wicker said if we got a mess of frogs' legs, those big bullfrogs down in the swamp, we could sell them to the hotel in Piedmont. I let Jeff have first shot, he must have a good eye, he drilled him right through the back."

"I shot a frog," howled Jeff, "and he looked at me with such dismay."

54. A Letter to Blanche

"Possum isn't ill, is she?" asked Jeff after bringing up the mail from Slabtown. He had read one of the terse postal cards which were Blanche Bristol's only communication when beset with work.

"I know it's bad manners to read other people's mail," he continued, "but her handwriting's very temptatious. I thought at first it had taken three months for it to get here, she better learn the American way of writing dates. Look, she puts 4/7/03, that ought to mean Fourth Month Seventh, April Seven. Some day that might get her into a serious predicament."

"The English way is much more logical," said Uncle Dan. "First the day, then the month, then the year, in the natural order."

"Aw shucks, if the English had been logical people they'd never come to this country anyhow. America's too exciting to be logical."

"I expect you could work out some sort of algebra to prove what time of year that way of writing the date would make the greatest misunderstanding. You might try it on Mr. Bolton."

"Aw cheese it," said Teackle. "Have a heart!"

But Jeff was interested in the problem. "Suppose she wrote and said *Come to dinner on 12/1,* she meant the Twelfth of January, but you wouldn't go till the 1st of December; she'd never ask you again."

"For goodness' sake let me read it," said Aunt Bee. "What makes you think she's ill?"

"She says she's worried about her Functions," said Jeff, surrendering the card reluctantly.

"She means a mathematical paper she has to read at a meeting in Chicago," said Uncle Dan. "Something about the Theory of Functions. She's been working on it a long time and it's very important for her."

There may also have been a little guile in Miss Bristol's limiting herself to such brevities; it is a fact that a series of postcards at one end of a correspondence often elicits a long letter from the other. While Aunt Bee and the boys were down at the creek Dan settled himself on the balcony with pen and paper.

c/o Wicker
Sandy Hole Farm
12 July '03

DEAREST BLANCHE,

I hope the combination of Chicago and Mathematics in midsummer won't be too trying. I know it must be a grief not to have your annual trip home, but I quite agree that the Chicago meeting must take precedence. I sail in a fortnight, I'm going second cabin in one of the fast ships from New York. It won't be as comfortable and certainly not as romantic as our old "10-day boat" but I've pledged myself to be back in God's Country in time for my birthday. I'm wondering already what Jeff will discover this year that he specially needs to give me as my present. Very likely a fishing rod; Teackle brought up a jointed steel rod which is Jeff's particular envy at the moment. I admit I don't care so much for it myself in this region of terrific thunderstorms. Lightning always follows the streams and to walk up the bed of the creek holding a steel rod seems to me giving a dare to Jove himself. Another thing Jeff hankers for is a back-pedaling brake. His oblique diplomacy was amusing: he remarked that in Jeffland the President and all the members of the Cabinet had New Departures, viz., back-pedaling brakes. "Something every statesman should have," I said—I think T. R. could use one sometimes. U.S. naval bases in Cuba sound pretty imperialistic.

I have a horrid feeling that you are getting much better work done than I am, but I suppose mathematics grants a more blissful abstraction than my poor line of country. The English Romantics, as we pedants have to call them, have such a damnable way of knotting themselves up with one's own qualms. I dare say it's absurd to have been low-spirited because the two boys are as amusing as a Punch and Judy show. I wish I could describe for you—it might mitigate the heat of your Mathematical Congress—the miniature canyon, smooth flanks of panther-colored rock through which the cold stream sluices down over a ledge into Sandy Hole. It can be quite dangerous in a freshet but when the water isn't too high we clamber through this stone groove building miniature waterfalls. It has most curious acoustic effects, one of the boys' best games is to set Bee and me as audience down by the bathing pool while they sing or recite at us from the Slut (as the flume is called here). Jeff's favorite is "Oh dry those tears," which he has never forgotten since Mrs. Bannister rendered it. It would make even Martin Luther laugh to hear "Life was not meant for so-ho-ho-ho-row" booming down this resonating gut. But we were startled when the boys appeared in a wrestle on the very brow of the cascade which falls seven or eight feet into the pool. Teackle braced himself against a boulder and gave Jeff a shove so that he came arms and legs flying a sousing plunge into the eddy. He might have been hurt but was only surprised. You couldn't possibly guess the cause of Teackle's ire. Jeff, trying the acoustic splendors of various sounds, had been chanting *Marching Through Georgia*, which Teackle has learned from the good old Major is an "o'nery song." But the explanation, when Jeff had finished coughing and regurgitating, was surprising. The Civil War is only a name to Jeff but he loves that song specially because of

321

two lines which have their own meaning to him—"So we made a thorofare for freedom and her train, Sixty miles in latitude, three hundred to the main." Jeff loves to hum this to himself and I think he visualizes some very special feature of Jeffland topography. I'm sorry to say that Teackle insists that if he sings that tune he must use a ribald small-boy version about "Georgia was a Southren gal, she came to New Jerzee," and a mosquito and a flea who go "marching through Georgia."

I suppose I ought to feel superior because I'm getting the trip across and you aren't—my first in five years. I should be elated, but the errand is a depressing one. My dear, you can believe that I understand your own family problem well enough since mine too has no easy solution. Of course I agree that you can't move your old people at their time of life and with your brother so far away I can well realize your feeling of responsibility, obligation, or whatever the word may be. But I'm also glad that you decided to give your summer to those ineffable "Functions" because that proves you understand your equal responsibility to your professional career. Of course I've thought a great deal—usually in the hammock up in the orchard, when I was supposed to be asleep with W. W. Jacobs or Sherlock Holmes—about our private ironies—certainly an example of "high iron" as Major Warren calls the main line of his railway. In this matter of "Stepping Westward" I dare say (I guess) it's particularly hard on the generation that makes the first jump: they get homesick in both directions. All spring I was so excited about the idea of going "home"—even the saddening nature of the errand, the final disruption of an old solidity, could not altogether spoil my sentimental delight. Even just a few days on a pushbike among Suffolk villages, and the bells of Cambridge in the Long, even a few flanneled fools at the wicket, would be something to make my heart leap up. Now as the time approaches, I actually dread it. Even the induced nostalgia of Kipling's new book which I have just been reading—"God gave all men all earth to love, But since man's heart

322

is small, Ordained to each one spot should prove Beloved over all," &c.—doesn't obscure something that has happened to me, particularly in this ragged landscape.

The boys sleep down in the old cabin by the creek. This has been a new experience for Jeff and at first the night-noises rather agitated him. This region is a real concerto of sounds from the faraway thunders and railway whistles of the Blue Ridge to the crickets and katydids of the field, and even an occasional wildcat on the mountainside and the double-bass of the bullfrog. But the first night Jeff camped out he heard a sound so eerie that he wanted to wake up Teackle. He felt very jubious and indeed it is the voice of the banshee. It was what Teackle calls a "squinch owl" and if you've ever heard one in the woods at night you know how *fin de siècle* it is. But I was quite touched when Jeff said he calmed his terrors (rectified his perturbations, as Burton would say) by thinking of the night-light at the head of the stairs in his childhood on the Thorofare. I guess we all remember those candle stubs set in a saucer of water; my mother always had one in the upstairs hall at Wilford "in case anyone was ill in the night." I was thinking that in spite of all it means, the idea of England to me now is only a kind of Night-Light.

Perhaps I could strike out the adverb "only"?

As our colored maid Moxie said, after a visit to some doctor, "he diogenes my condition." I dare say you diogenes mine. It's characteristic of an English prof to deal so liberally in quotation but I can't resist closing with the admirable phrase of one Skinny Granger, who in a letter to Jeff subscribed himself

"Your lovingest freind,"

D. B.

55. *Truly Rural*

After so much forehand preparation it was rather absurd that Uncle Dan (in Aunt Bee's phrase) only just "saved the train." Perhaps it was partly the boys' fault: they had wanted to do something that would show they were sorry he was going away. So after long muddy wading in the steaming marsh near the millpond they put leeches in his bed. "He's always talking about some ole leech-gatherer," said Jeff, "he'll be pleased. If they suck hard they'll act as a kind of back-pedaling brake. It's what you call a vacuum."

Aunt Bee, by old Wilford custom, preferred not to go to the station; the boys drove Uncle Dan to Piedmont in the surrey. The Blue Mountain express came down the grade in all its glory, and seasonable too—just the opposite of a Wilford train, since the cars were painted blue and not the engine. They had to switch old Clara into a matronly trot when they heard the whistle wail for Tiddyhigh. "It always sounds mo' tragical when somebody you know is leavin'," said Teackle.

"Teackle often surprises me," Jeff said. "Sometimes he's quite observant."

"Aw get the hook. Challenge you to a duel with rapiers when we get back."

"That means Jeff will have a good splash," said Uncle Dan with resolute cheerfulness. "I envy him." It's difficult for the traveler when people who stay behind allude to things that will happen after he's gone.

Beside the train Jeff reflected that if you say good-by properly you don't have a real chance to study the locomotive. But the conductor (the extra-splendid one who always wore a wing-collar) was looking at his watch. The greatest folk-cry in the world resounded: All ABOOOOARD! and farewells were cut short by the usual thunder-squall that had followed the train through the Gap.

"You ride the whirlwind and direct the storm," said Teackle proudly as the first gust swept the platform and Uncle Dan climbed into the smoker. Evidently the duels of Addison and Steele had their literary value.

"Send me a picture postcard of the *St. Louis*," said Jeff.

324

"Take good care of Aunt Bee," called Uncle Dan, and they watched the train winding down from Piedmont.

"Hot dog! No more tutoring," was Teackle's envoi.

"I forgot to remind him to keep to the left when he gets over there," said Jeff. "He's terribly absent-minded. Why, that's crazy, imagine! Keep to the left. That's certainly punko. It's parochial."

They took shelter in the freight-house until the squall was over; they were to bring back some boxes for Doc Wicker. In the glitter of new-washed air they loafed among the delights of the siding: the weedy grass growing among cinders, drenched clumps of goldenrod, the blistered sides of box-cars with names of summons: Hocking Valley, Chesapeake & Ohio, Big Four.

"Ma & Pa would be embarrassed up here with these big trains," Jeff said.

"There's a new one, Nickel Plate," Teackle noticed. "Say, I haven't been to church all summer."

The rusty rails of the freight yard led to the blue streaks of the main track, through fascinating tongues and flanges of a switch. Another line went to the coal depot, where Teackle thought it was mighty cute for the same dealer to sell the opposites, Coal and Ice. "He gets you both going and coming. I think maybe I'll be a doctor. He does that too." Jeff was pleased by the sign LUMBER AND TRIM. "It sounds like a fat man and a thin man."

They studied the workings of the switch. "You can understand it when you look at it but it's hard to think about."

"I bet everything's like that."

"Those signals look funny to me," Jeff observed, looking down the main line. "Semaphores. They're turned the other way, different from Wilford."

"Sure they are, they do everything backwards in England. I bet they even get out of bed the wrong side, like Dan did this morning. He was certainly peeved about those leeches. All the same we're going to miss the ole skeezicks."

325

"I know what let's do," said Jeff. "Let's write a newspaper, 'The Sandy Hole *Cascade*.' There are times when I just feel like writing an editorial. When Uncle Dan gets back he'll know what happened."

"Charge everybody five cents apiece to read it."

It was an excellent idea. Teackle rashly volunteered to write a serial story, *The Adventures of a Crawfish, in Ten Shells,* but the chapters ran shorter and shorter. Jeff's editorial against animal bloodshed turned out different from his intention, its conclusion startled Aunt Bee. "I don't think I should mind killing people," wrote the editor, "but I'm never going to kill any more animals."

This did not mean that all animals led thereafter a completely peaceful life. The chickens served on Mrs. Wicker's table were exceptionally sinewy: it occurred to the boys that if these fowls could be subjected to some form of suspended animation they might not be so tough. "We could hypnotize them," Teackle suggested, and showed Jeff a trick. A hen held down on the floor, with a chalk line drawn straight out from her beak, thinks she is tethered and lies a few minutes in a sort of cross-eyed trance. Whether this hiatus actually delayed the hardening of the fowl's muscular tissue was never proved but it caused much amusement. There was a day when they had just laid out half a dozen powerful Plymouth Rocks on the front porch, each hopelessly gazing along its deceptive life-line. Just then a familiar figure came up the meadow path under a green parasol. "It's Miss Beamish!" exclaimed Jeff in horror. "She looks like the Ghostly Demon under that sunshade."

"Good luck there's no piano in the house," said Teackle. "I've had my bellyful of lessons for one summer."

No one else was on the porch and the boys hastily got out of sight on the balcony above. Lying flat and peering cautiously over they saw Miss Beamish approach, look somewhat puzzled at the prostrate hens, and sit on the front steps to draw breath after the climb from town. She always looked rather henlike herself with her sharp little nose and brightly querulous eyes.

"If we could hypnotize *her*," said Jeff, "she wouldn't start asking about the nobility." Just at this moment the chickens began to revive from their swoon. Their behavior was always the same: the most intelligent, probably Happy Hen, would make a tentative flap, discover that she was not really in bond, and then rush off with a cackle of scandalized embarrassment. She was followed in succession by all the rest, like a string of firecrackers. With a sudden flutter and scream of outrage the whole covey flopped past Miss Beamish, who also leapt up and fluttered and squeaked. The boys could not control themselves and burst into yells of delight. Fortunately Aunt Bee, who had been sitting in the lawn swing under the maples, appeared just then and was able to soothe the visitor.

"Looks like you're gwineter have chicken for dinner," said Miss Beamish, unconsciously quoting Brer Rabbit. This almost set the boys off again but Aunt Bee cautioned Jeff with an esoteric allusion. "Geoffrey, remember T. E. T. and that letter of apology." Jeff remembered: T. E. T. was a private mnemonic for Temper, Excitement and Tongue, and the famous letter was one that had to be written to Mr. Rhodes after he and Skinny had laughed themselves into hysterics in the classroom. "Why didn't Caesar cross the Rhine in a boat?" asked Mr. Rhodes. "He said it was beneath his dignity," Jeff answered. "George Washington wasn't so particular," said Skinny. "Maybe Americans aren't as dignified as Romans," Jeff retorted. "Washington showed his pride by standing up in the boat," suggested Mr. Rhodes. "He knew the redcoats couldn't hit him," said Star, and the class exploded. Skinny's cartoon of Caesar disdaining the humility of a rowboat was much admired.

Miss Beamish who was staying in the village had walked two miles uphill in mere kindness, as she thought, to suggest there might be a chance to continue music during vacation. The boys, returned to courtesy, explained politely that the acoustics of Sandy Hole gave them all the harmony they needed. "As a

matter and fact," said Teackle, "we're getting up a Canyon
Chorale to surprise Major when he comes up. You should hear
us holler, it's like being inside a tunnel, and I'm going to surprise the old man with his favorite song."

"And what is that?" said Miss Beamish with natural interest.

"I don't think I better tell you, Ma'am," said Teackle, and
the boys choked again.

If Major Warren had planned his trip to Sandy Hole in the
fear that the trio might be left at a loose end in Uncle Dan's
absence his kind solicitude was exaggerated. With no morning
lessons the boys found themselves in constant activity. The first
and probably the most unselfish project was building a bench
halfway up the hill, for Teackle had noticed how Aunt Bee
suffered when climbing back to the farm in midday heat. The
bench was designed to be what Teackle called truly rural; this
involved the loan of Doc Wicker's axe and some vigorous work
with saw and hammer. The completed work was indeed so rustic
that it was spiky with knots and the green wood perspired with
resin. But after all Aunt Bee could sit on a newspaper and
Geoffrey explained that the gum was useful as a fly-catcher.
Then the boy of all work at Wicker's store cut his foot badly
on the blade of a reaper and Teackle and Jeff took turns helping at Slabtown. This involved driving the wagon over to the
freight depot to collect cases of goods. Probably there was never
a stronger feeling of identity with the life-stream than the first
time Jeff was able to set off alone behind leisurely old Clara,
rattling down the Sandy Hole road with one hand on the rusty
brake lever. Everything was done, he flattered himself, in perfect timing and manner. He allowed Clara to make her usual
detour to the old watering trough where a cold spring flowed
through the hollowed log, and he knew enough to prevent her
from drinking her fill. His farm-boy hat had the proper hole
through which sprouted a tuft of sun-burned hair; his overalls
had the stains and rips of the countryside and when he could

back the wagon across to the open door of a box-car on the siding to receive packing cases from Butler Brothers, he felt that
even the freight agent would recognize one who belonged. All
the way down Main Street he was practicing just the right in-
tonation. How he would say—so offhand a blend of the respect
due a freight agent with easy Blue Ridge tone—"Hi, Jake. Got
a way-bill for Wicker's?" Way-bill should have been right?
He had seen it printed on the forms and yet old Jake peering
over his spectacles and wearing those wonderful pale striped
overalls that are railroad and not hick said "Bill of Goods?
Sure. Summer boarder, hey?"

And Jeff could even see, when he stopped to do errands in
the town, that native boys rather resented these invasions of
their privilege. He secretly gave the overalls an extra soaking
and bleaching down by the creek because he felt they were too
freshly blue. Aunt Bee wondered how the "aubergines" aged so
rapidly. (Aubergines was their family name for them since Aunt
Bee had astonished Mrs. Wicker by that name for eggplant.)
He toughened bare feet on hay-stubble, went with Shep to drive
the cows home (watching Shep for hints), and practiced a chew
of plug tobacco. "Got to let it melt a bit first," said Doc Wicker,
amused by his struggle. Teackle boasted: "Major won't know
us from regular hayseeds," but Jeff was aware of a little too
much consciousness in their performance.

Before Major Warren arrived something quite remarkable
happened. Probably it would not have been achieved except
that the boys were so much away on their own adventures. Aunt
Bee would have been far too bashful if anyone had known or
watched, but she had made up her mind to teach herself to
swim. Unsuspected she walked down to Piedmont and bought
a bathing suit, the usual frock and bloomers of braided bombazine, and black cotton stockings. It was difficult to conceal
this sinister purchase from Mrs. Mister who accompanied her,
but somehow she smuggled it back to the farm and when the
boys were absent she made secret visits to Sandy Hole. The

next problem was to find a tutor, and Uncle Dan when he heard about this later, would have given much for a glimpse of his sister in pursuit of instruction. By scrambling and plunging on the edges of the marsh she finally sprang forward and seized her teacher. It was an unsuspecting frog who had not yet heard of Jeff's marksmanship. He squirmed and looked suspicious, but firmly she carried him to Sandy Hole, placed him in a convenient pool and watched attentively. Then she waded gallantly into the cold basin and imitated his calisthenics. She had been studying Teackle without his knowing it, and the even more perfect co-ordination of the frog suggested the simple and terrifying art. She struck out bravely into the bubbling eddy, would gulp, struggle and founder, then scramble sneezing to shore, stir up her model and again contemplate his action. The chief difficulty was to conceal the wet bathing suit from observation on the farm clothesline, but Aunt Bee discovered in herself a talent for strategy she had never suspected. Like Jeff's aubergines the bombazine bathing dress aged rapidly: it had to dry under her bed and got mildewed. Great was the excitement and homage of the boys when they returned from Catoctin (where they had heard tempting rumor of a rattlesnake den) and found Aunt Bee actually swimming across the rotating currents of Sandy Hole. "Hot dog," cried Jeff, "I never knew aunts could swim. Teack, you be Scylla and I'm Charybdis and she'll navigate between us."

Some of the best times were breakfasts down by the cabin. The boys took bacon and eggs and milk with them in the evening and Teackle even ventured on oatmeal patties cooked on a slab of slate, and hoecake which in spite of much practice was always heavily cindered. It was quite a while before Doc Wicker discovered what had become of his best hoe but Teackle said the cakes weren't legal without the proper implement. Young Warren had the true zeal of a cook, the most endearing of all traits in any companion, and Jeff, who was a slow waker, came to morning consciousness with the snapping of the skillet in his ears. He had taught Teackle the magic word *Hurrp*. When that was shouted Jeff sprang from his bunk and there was just time for one plunge of ecstasy while the eggs matured, then "Bunker Hill!" Teackle would cry. "Don't fire till you see the whites of their eggs." They scrambled from the frigid pothole and ate as they dried in the sun.

"Gee it's great to be crazy," Jeff remarked. "It's nice to be down here without any consanguinity. You can talk with your mouth full."

"You are certainly the damnedest kid," said Teackle. "You can even say a word like that when your mouth's loaded. You can't do a back flip down the falls, anyhow. Watch me, ole stick-in-the-mud!"

There was plenty to talk about. The bunks in the cabin reminded Jeff of his ocean voyage. With improving acquaintance he did not hesitate to suggest to Teackle some of the institutions of Jeffland. The meeting with Miss Beamish had involved that lady's frequent allusion to the D.A.R. which puzzled Jeff. It was confused in his mind with the G.A.R., but Teackle explained. "That's a grand idea," said Jeff, "all the original settlers in my country came over in the *Westernland*. I'm going to have a patent of nobility, people who are Daughters of the Westernland."

"You better be strict," said Teackle. "I bet in just a few generations there'll be forty-leven thousand impostors and carpetbaggers claiming to come in. You gotta be awful careful about bastards. They're terrible buttinskys. Of co'se if you are just making up a country it simplifies things if you have all the people one color."

"You'd need to have a few Uncle Remuses, though, to tell stories," Jeff submitted.

"I wonder who are the smartest people anyhow," Teackle meditated. "I don't think the English are so smart, the Major took me over to Great Britain one summer, of course I was just

331

a poor little squirt, but it made a bad impression on me. Look at those ole thatch roofs. Gee, they grow those cottage flower gardens so you won't look at the roof and see where moss grows on it. I bet they'd put a thatch roof on Westminster Abbey if they weren't afraid the tourists would criticize. The Major is so crazy about ole-fashioned habits he dragged me all around the darnedest places. My God, we went to a school where the kids wear silk hats and if they're pleased about anything they all say *Hear, hear!*—They got some mighty pretty hosses over there though. I remember those cavalry guards, they sit so firm you couldn't tell where hoss leaves off and man begins. I stood in front of one and I declare even when I winked at him he didn't wink back."

"I dare say they don't do so much winking in England," said Jeff. "Perhaps he thought you were just a nervous breakdown. I guess I don't remember very well. I've been through such a lot since then." One of Uncle Dan's phrases came to his mind—"It's rather like a dream than an assurance"—but he didn't say it aloud. "Uncle Dan says probly the smartest people are the French because they put a mark on the tail of the 7 so it doesn't get mixed up with a 5 or a 1, and when they add up the bill they don't ever cheat themselves."

"I guess those ole Addison and Steele were pretty smart," Teackle admitted. "Aw shucks, let's not get educational. Juba killed a yellow cat, To make his wife a Sunday hat, Niggah, what you think of that? Juba, Juba!" He broke into a shuffle, using the frying-pan to imitate a banjo.

"Say, we better rehearse the Canyon Chorale," said Jeff. "You said Major will be here tomorrow."

In the manner of older brothers, Teackle was rather contemptuous when the Major alighted from the train accompanied by the nursemaid and child. With the extreme dignity of six years old, Serena Lavinia accepted the porter's hand and stepped to the yellow stool. She showed stains of travel and emotion, but must have been newly exhorted with the Major's best pretty-please, her only comment was, "Is this a nice place?"

"Aw cheeze," Teackle confided in Jeff's ear, "here's ole Baby Trundle and black Mammy. A little more soot and you wouldn't know 'em apart. What's the idea of us being all cluttered up with an infant?—Howdy, Major, Ah hope you had a right pretty scenery ride?"

"None of your juvenile ironies at me, you limb of Satan," said the Major. "I declare, we're all tuckered out. We'll have to get some new screens in that parlor car."

"She could take some new wheels, too," said Teackle. "She sound flatfooted to me. I might loan you some of Jeff's oatmeal patties but what would you do while she's in the shop?"

"Behave like a gentleman if you can and be sociable to your sister, she's right fretful. Been so hot your Ma figured she'd send along Baby Trundle and Hessie to refreshen their spirits. I got her an all-day sucker but I opine they exaggerate some. She had it chawed up befo' we made Union Bridge. You-all got the surrey here? Let's get up the hill and cool off."

Teackle and Jeff toted the bags. "He's an all-day sucker himself, the ole idiot," said irreverent Teackle. "He's plumb uxorious, going travelin' with babies and nursing maids."

"This is something like," said the Major as Clara pulled hard on the upgrade, lathering under the harness. He noticed with approval that the boys jumped down to lighten the load as they came to the rocky ledges. "You young rips don't look like you grieve yourselves studyin'. Teackle, have you accomplished any Virgil or you been all-time swimmin' *in gurgite vasto?*"

"Ain't done so bad," said Teackle. "I got a laugh out of Uncle Dan. I figured that ole Aeneas might be Jewish, the way he's always tending up his palms to heaven."

"I can almost milk a cow," boasted Jeff. "Trundle will be amused, the Wickers have a big cat called Buster, he comes

333

under the cow and opens his mouth, Joel squirts the milk right in."

"Appears to me I like this place," said Trundle.

56. *The Canyon Chorale*

Aunt Bee and the Major attended by Trundle and Hessie seated themselves comfortably to enjoy the Sandy Hole Canyon Chorale. Even Shep must have guessed something special for he followed them down the hill. Then also Miss Beamish appeared, perspiring but full of zeal. "I just couldn't resist," she said. "The boys told me about it. I suppose they're going to sing some of those lovely old English glees."

"Very pleased to greet you, Ma'am," said the Major. He unobtrusively estimated her requirements and led her to a conformable boulder. Meanwhile the boys in their bathing suits had scrambled up into the rocky cleft above the cascade. Their voices could be heard consulting, with occasional squalls of mirth.

"Such a lovely setting," said Miss Beamish. "It always makes me think of Up the airy mountain, Down the rushy glen, do you know that? Green jacket, red cap, And white owl's feather!"

The Major, a little uneasy for some anticlimax, refrained from saying that the red caps always reminded him of railroad porters.

"Reckon it's fo'tunate the creek's low," he remarked. "I've seen this here gully after a cloudburst when you couldn't hear yourself talk. Blowin' Gap was always quick-tempered and there's right queer sound effects. That fork in the stream up beyond the trestle, we used to call that the tunin' fork. You could hear a kind of rumble far away when they had a freshet in the hills. I'd like right well to be a boy moseyin' round here again and bunk out in the cabin. Sho' is scenic the way that water comes spurtin' out and then stirs around the pothole. Always puts me in mind of a good highball. All respects to you ladies, I think I'll brighten up for the concert."

He drew a well-worn flask from his hip and looked judgingly at the gauge slit in the leather cover. "Best combination in the world," he apologized. "Good Bourbon at body temperature and cold mountain water to wash it down."

"I was a bit 'mazed by men's hip-pockets when I first came over here," said Aunt Bee. "I couldn't imagine everybody would carry two revolvers, now I know what the other one's for." The familiar chewing movement of her lips, which the observant old Major noticed, was partly his fault. When she listened to his talk Aunt Bee always felt the most curious warming and softening inside her mouth; like a bolus of honey and cotton wool. It was not easy to keep her oral muscles in the traditional East Anglian rigor. To conceal her self-consciousness she passed round the box of candy the Major had brought her. "That's the first time anyone ever gave me sweets in a box," she said. "Always before they were in a paper bag."

"Well, Ma'am, I think your Suffolk gentry mighty deficient in cavalierin'."

"If I can't have another candy," said Trundle, "can I walk across the waterfall?"

"Now, Sugar, you hush," said the Major. "I'm trustful she ain't goin' to make herself burdensome, she's a mighty demandin' little tike. I can't figure how so much frivol and tantrum accumulate, I'd a thought the ladies in her species worked it all off." Reckon it was because her parents lay fallow quite a spell, he reflected. "It's good-natured in Jeff to let her traipse round after him. She's sure took a fancy to his company. I'd be flattered if she was more considerin', but she's young to take a hint."

"When I'm down at the branch I wear my khaki bloomers," Trundle stated, "and I don't aim to behave."

The clangor of the farmhouse dinner bell which Teackle had borrowed called them to attention. Magnified by the rocky

335

reredos it sounded almost like the good-by of a locomotive. "Oyez, oyez, oyez," warbled Jeff, standing wedged against a flange of boulder at the mouth of the Slut. Shep was puzzled by these sounds and looked expectant. "The Sandy Hole Canyon Chorale will begin with a double aquarium somersault performed by Teackle Warren, Esq., not related to the nobility."

Jeff stood aside. Teackle appeared in the fissure and tried a balancing bow to acknowledge their cheers. But the push of water and the mossy slime underfoot were difficult. He felt himself going too soon, seized Jeff by the leg, and both boys went down the cascade in a whirl of unrehearsed attitudes. The dinner bell flew high and fell into the pool with a clanking gulp. The act was probably more effective than the projected exhibition. Shep barked with joy and plunged in to join the mellay. Trundle was enviously impressed. "Daddy, can I do that?" she asked.

"That's what comes of trying to be polite," said Teackle as they scrambled out. "Hessie, you hang onto this ole dog." But his humiliation was more than atoned by a perfect dive from the dueling log to retrieve the foundered bell.

"I've got a crick in my neck," said Jeff gaily, "also my neck in the crick."

"Don't you take on," said the Major, "there's many a fine performance been blemished by being too attentive to the audience."

"I think it's a very good way to begin a concert," said Aunt Bee. "Isn't there a play or something called 'The Sunken Bell'?"

"By God, Ma'am, you're right," said the Major admiringly. "I declare, Miz Bee, you have a resourceful mind. If you ladies will indulge yo'selves with another tidbit I'll recruit a little more Sandy Hole toddy. This here festival may be an ordeal befo' we get through."

It proved more so than the good-humored Major expected. Teackle had mischievously chosen for the recital three of his

336

father's favorite songs, but one of them had always been reserved by the Major for very informal rendition. Before these, however, by Jeff's insistence, came his solo performance of *Oh Dry Those Tears*. The acoustic powers of Sandy Hole were such that even backstage whispers were audible; between verses the artist was heard saying, "Cheese it, Teack, you'll make me laugh and spoil the effect."

"He certainly sings better than he plays the piano," admitted Miss Beamish.

"He never got over that song. Someone sang it on board the *Westernland*," explained Aunt Bee. "Funny boy, I don't think he ever forgets anything that amuses him."

"A very lucky faculty," said the Major.

Then followed duets. Jeff had discovered "If you sing a little different from the tune it sounds sort of good, but you've got to keep just the right distance away from the tune. Sometimes I don't." His boyish alto and Teackle's new-found bass, resonated by the funnel of the Slut, were pleasantly effective in *John Peel*. "That's what I call music," approved the Major. "I declare that's the best song in the world. Uncle Hartley took me up to Troutbeck one time, that's where John Peel lived." He was so pleased he threw two bright coins into the pool which the artists dove for.

We'll All Go a-Hunting Today was equally well received. But then, after more bell-ringing and oyezing and announcing, the Major was alarmed to hear—magnified with calculated practice—the realistic chantey of *The Old Sow*. Since hearing it long ago in some cockney music hall he had often sung it himself in moments of hilarity round the dining table at Greenaway, but in more bohemian and convivial company. Teackle and Jeff, who had located just the right focal point for projecting sound waves, put their heads together and the verses came booming across the pool. Teackle had evidently tutored his companion with care, the barnyard interruptions were well synchronized, the word *sow* followed in turn by a grunt, a raspberry, and a whistle:

"Oh there was an old man and he had an old sow (*grunt*)
Sow (*razz*), sow (*whistle*), shandiddle-ow;
There was an old man and he had an old sow,
Lillibu bu-le-ro, O-o-o-oh,
The Major's a funny old man,
(*Grunt*) Man, (*razz*) man, (*whistle*) man,
The Major's a funny old man!"

The boys looked out from the brow of the waterfall to see how the audience was taking it. There was no question about Trundle's enthusiasm, she was already trying to imitate, though surpassed by Shep's staccato of excitement. The Major took another small potion of Sandy Hole and said, "Young ruffians. They need a pint of strap-oil."

The second verse issued from the flume with even more brio:

"Now this old sow had nine little pigs (*grunt*)
Pigs (*razz*), pigs (*whistle*), shandiddle-igs;
Now this old sow had nine little pigs,
Lillibu bu-le-ro, O-o-o-oh,
The Major's a funny old man,
(*Grunt*) Man, (*razz*) man, (*whistle*) man,
The Major's a funny old man!"

But the third stanza was an artistic bathos: the performers collapsed in laughter and could not enunciate. Weakened by their own amusement they slipped and once more came foaming and jangling down into the pool.

"Just a couple of young hawbucks," said the Major, hiding a grin behind his confederate mustache. He had to admit to himself that the ballad was appropriate for Blowing Gap.

"It ain't scandalous, Miz Bee, it's literary," Teackle defended. "It's in Virgil, what Uncle Dan calls onomatopoeia."

"You never told me that one," Jeff reproached him.

338

"Horse-petals, you don't know everything. You ain't even had Cicero yet."

"Don' do dat, honey," Hessie begged her small tyrant. "Poop yo' mouf all out o' shape."

"Reckon you-all better start some other game quick," said the Major. "Try to put this here ornery tapoeia out of Trundle's mind."

The boys gallantly volunteered to escort Miss Beamish as far as Slabtown on her return way. "An ole lady like that can't stand these incessant shocks," said Jeff. (Miss Beamish was probably about fifty, the age of Aunt Bee.) They made polite conversation. "These mountains are very old," Teackle said, "they're prehistoric. Major says there's dinosaur tracks in the sandstone up on Buckskin Mountain."

"There's some up by the college at Emmitsburg, too," said Jeff, "Joel told me. He said we could see 'em on our way to Gettysburg."

"Major says there's always dinosaur tracks near gals' colleges."

Miss Beamish, a little shaken, parted from them at the Slabtown store, and the boys brought home the mail. "What do you think," Jeff exclaimed, "there's two letters from Possum, one for you and one for Uncle Dan."

"Oh, that's hard lines, poor Dan missed his steamer letter."

"One's fat and one's thin, like Lumber and Trim. Which will you have?"

"Reckon mine's the thin one," said Aunt Bee.

57. Society Notes

The Sandy Hole *Cascade*—like its namesake, it was most fluent on rainy days—passed through the customary phases of holiday journalism. The nickel exacted from subscribers for reading each issue (in manuscript) was in very modest proportion to the effort exerted by the editors. During its brief run the *Cascade* exhibited the familiar frenzy of diarists struggling to keep their chronicles abreast of fleeting Now. For a few days Teackle and Jeff never left the balcony without holding a column open for Society Notes and Stop-press so that on their return they could fill in history right up to the dinner bell. Old Clara was scarcely unhitched before Jeff would rush to the work table to make entry:

"Mr. Geoffrey Barton was seen hauling freight from the R.R. Depot this morning."

Jeff showed special relish in his miscellaneous paragraphs called *Bubbles:*

Messrs. Teackle Warren and G. Barton plan to accompany Mr. Joel Wicker on a picnic to Gettysburg, Pa. Mr. Warren says this will be the first time a member of his family has crossed the frontier since Major H. Warren visited Illinoise unexpectedly in 1864. Mr. T. Warren threatens to make a G-burg Speech.

Scores in Sandy Hole 500 League:—

	W.	L.	P.C.
Miss B. Barton	30	10	.750
Mr. T. Warren	25	20	.555
Mr. G. Barton	20	25	.444
Mrs. G. W. Mister . .	10	30	.250

Literary Notes: As suggested by Prof. Barton before his departure, the editors took turns in reading aloud *The Wrong Box* to Miss B. Barton while she was doing her sewing. For a time they were somewhat bafled but Mr. T. Warren exclaimed, "I bet this is intended to be funny," after which better progress was made.

Doings Behind the Barn: Mrs. Happy Hen, interviewed by our uphill correspondent, says she is fixing to set and is not fooled by Mr. J. Wicker's ingenious china egg. This is more truth than poultry.

Sporting News: Messrs. T. Warren and G. Barton were not seen cutting willow switches for hurling crabapples, but these were so successful that Mr. T. Warren threw a crab completely across the Mill Pond. No one caught it. Mrs. D. Wicker is still hoping to make crabapple jelly.

Visitors arrived from Chesapeake: Mr. Geo. W. Mister, Major Hartley Warren, C.S.A., Miss "Trundle" Warren and maid Hessie Pinckney.

First foreign mail ever received at Slabtown P. O.: one letter from Prof. D. Barton, now traveling abroad. Mr. Cy Shanks, post-master, asked to keep the stamp, saying that King Edward VII looks real democratic.

Correspondence from readers: Dear Sir, When did Virgil die, and if not why not? Yours, T. W.

Science Note: Mr. T. Warren cut his foot on a rusty nail but his Hot Southren Blood at once dominated all germs.

N. B. to Our Patrons— ☞ The price of this paper is 5¢ to read at the dinner table, TEN CENTS when done if delivered by carrier. Patrons are requested to read individually, Reading Aloud is NOT ALLOWED.

"I reckon it's worth the extra price," said the Major as the latest issue was handed to him in the lawn swing. "Yo' Stop-press department runs even-Stephen with events. The editor says 'Major H. Warren and Miss B. Barton were seen taking their ease in the garden swing. The subject of their conversation was—' Why, we ain't fixed on any subjects and topics yet awhile," he protested. "We're just conversin' casual. Miz Bee was tellin' me she feels herself some guilty up here while populace-people is all colickin' with hotspell. I tell her she surely earns a breath of this climate."

"You've got to finish reading the paper now," said the editors. "The other customers are waiting."

"Jeff and I have to raise fo'ty cents befo' sundown. We're going down to Slabtown to see that medicine show."

"Well, you-all vamoose," said the Major. "If I can't read my paper in peace I'll catch up later."

Shadows of late afternoon moved down the long slopes. It was the fortunate interval after supper when interruption takes a holiday. Baby Trundle and Hessie, Happy Hen, Shep, Mrs. Mister, were all elsewhere on their own concerns. Under the canopy of maple trees the swing commanded a far prospect of Monocacy Valley.

"You're right, Miz Bee, it's a pity that sundown shadow don't reach clear to the city. There's a lot of folks in Chezpeake could use the shady side of a mountain."

"I had a terrible shock before we came away," Aunt Bee said. "Our colored girl sent a message she was ill and I went down to see her where she lives. It was really dreadful. A little hovel in a hot squalid alley, about a dozen of them living in two rooms behind somebody's stable and a pile of manure buzzing with flies. Of course I got there at a bad time. Moxie wasn't really ill, they'd had a party that ended up in a razor fight. I couldn't see at first because it was dark after the sunlight outside. Moxie said, 'Mighty Gawd, Miz Bee, you better step round dat hemridge—' and I saw the whole place was a mixture of blood and deviled crabs. There was a darky in the corner groaning and his head tied up in a filthy apron. A policeman got there just then and I thought I'd have to go to court. I was sorry afterward that I didn't. I could have said my opinion about such conditions. It's pretty ghastly when you see anything like that but I believe the city's full of it. I shall never forget that smear of blood and broken crabs on the floor. —I'm afraid you thought I was rude because I didn't eat crab salad when we had supper at Greenaway."

The Major unconsciously rocked the swing gently to and fro; Aunt Bee felt a curious faint reminder of the *Westernland*. "I'm powerful fond of soft crabs," he said, "but that kind of dressing's unsavory."

"I declare," said Aunt Bee, "maybe it's that queer little Miss Beamish who started me thinking. She turned up here the other day with her usual question."

"You mean 'Is you-all kin to nobility?'" asked the Major.

"Yes, she doesn't intend anything by it. It's just an automatic remark, but what I mean, it just came over me lately, in this country I feel related to everybody. It's so different from England where you find yourself in one special class and unless you're very Christian like my sister Alice the things that happen outside that class are none of your affair. I dessay I don't say things very well but it troubles me like a Concern. This country has been wonderfully good to the Bartons and I feel related to everything that goes on whether it's those poor darkies in the alley or that wonderful conductor on the express. I dessay that's how you get to be nobility in America. You've got relations everywhere."

She sat silent a few moments, then added briskly, "But I don't think enough people in Chesapeake feel like that. Dan had a friend from England who came to visit, and I found I was ashamed for fear he would see too much. Dan pretends it's amusing because it's like the eighteenth century but I could get along better with less culture and better drainage. Sometimes I don't wonder the boys are so tough, raised on cobblestone streets."

The Major did not answer directly. He guessed from a certain tightening of Miss Barton's lips that she did not enjoy the motion of the swing, so he let the old cat die. "If we sit here till dark," he said, "we'll see some of them persid meteors. I'd admire to get a glimpse of 'em before I go back to town."

"Why don't you light your cigar?" said Aunt Bee. "It keeps off the midges."

"Miz Beamish ain't the only one that had nobility on her mind," said the Major presently. "I recall when I stood up for Dan down at the Co'thouse." It always took Bee a moment to realize what the Major meant by "Coathouse"; she had a puzzling vision of a cloakroom full of garments.

"When he took unto himself a country," explained the Major, "become a citizen. I recollect very clear because back of the judge's bench there was a mural wall-picture of Co'nwallis's surrender at Yorktown, he had a locum tenens in a lobster

343

coat hand over his sword for him. I was hoping Dan wouldn't notice the picture, it seemed to me misfo'tunate. But bless gracious, Dan was so busy worrying about his moral character he took note of nothing else. He was real concerned somebody would pop up and forbid the banns. He had to renounce hereditary titles and emoluments and when they called on me to testify, I had a right smart little speech thought up tracing his ethical and spiritual titles of nobility but I declare they acted so impatient I never did do it justice. Yes, Ma'am, it's a right substantial matter when a fella takes up a new nationality, and they hadn't ought to let it be too info'mal. Howsoever, it was a steamin' hot day and gov'ment always kinda let down when you get Confed'rate weather. It's remarkable, come to think of it, how those fellas put over a Declaration of Independence in Philadelphia in July. The way I feel this time of year I don't even fret if the Blue Mountain Express ain't exactly on time. Of co'se Philadelphia's a hotter town than Chezpeake," he added, faithful to one of his city's most cherished beliefs.

With a rolling trill of salute Buster leapt into the seat with Aunt Bee. She and Jeff had noticed with approval that Buster made the same kind of burrp that old Jue had done. With the massive cat by her side the swing balanced better.

"First thing I said to Dan when he commenced citizen was I reckon you could relish a julep. We went round to the Chezpeake Club and by the time I introduced him to all the members as a new taxpayer we was as high as Uncle Hartley. Higher maybe. I recollect Judge Paca, the same one that had set on the bench, come in about Bourbon time. He said if he'd known we was such rounders he'd never signed Dan's documents. Of co'se, Ma'am, that was just his jocularity. We soon softened him up till he was chipper as a bee in a rhododendrum. The old Judge, his heart's in the right place and it ain't on his sleeve neither. His sleeve's empty since '63. He studied in a hard college same as I did, the War of Secession, and a lot of them students didn't live to graduate. He knows this country can use a lot of new citizens of the right sort, that can git there fust with the mostest ideas. I put it to him that the thing lackin' in our public life was stern daughter of the voice of God. He said Wordsworth had been dead quite some time an' we argued about that; I says no one ain't dead so long as people is still thinkin' his thoughts. One of the boys at the bar wanted to spout Lucy Gray, about the footprints in the snow, because he learned it in school. You know how the footprints goes half-way across the torrent and further there were none. Old Tullius Teackle used to read that to me and I always had to blub."

"I know," said Aunt Bee. "Jeff used to read it to me until I had to ask him not to."

"That was a right eventual evenin' to look back on. Dan took Judge Paca and me back to his bo'din' house to look up some argument. Dan said Wordsworth wrote a poem about Nutting, an' the old Judge says lots of his poems were about that. Then we got to reading 'Kubla Khan' aloud but the Judge give it so much delivery the landlady ask him to leave. He was fit to jostle a constable, his footprints wandered off like Lucy in the blizzard."

The very slight tremor of the swing might have been due to Aunt Bee's amusement, or to what Jeff called Buster's stentorian purr, a sound which blended perfectly with the humming of summer dusk. "I declare," said the Major, "that cat looks big as a quadruped. Maybe he had lion blood into his forebears. It would take considerable spunk to twist his tail. Makes me think, Uncle Sam ain't always so good about acceptin' criticism. Anybody twist *his* tail he sure hollers. I was always irked by that fool piece in the newspaper about Uncle Dan, the one about English professor chides American education. That make me rare up among my bristles. It's impo'tant you-all and we-all keep our sense of humor.—I reckon I'm tirin' you with too much of my chatter."

"Please go on," said Aunt Bee. "I haven't had a good talk all summer. Dan's been so moody and anxious about his trip."

345

"Bein' a teacher takes a lot out of you, I reckon," said the Major. "You think folks have been kind to Dan. I can retaliate that boy has done a powerful lot for us-all. This Union of States is a queer kind of a three-ring-circus, Miz Bee. Sometimes I figure this country puts a sensitive person under heavier pressure than anywhere else. It crushes a plenty of 'em, like Edgar Poe, but it makes a few of 'em bid for trumps."

He paused a while and the glow of the brightening cigar shone pink on his small white chin-whisker.

"Appears to me like Dan's got things on his mind; well, that's what a mind's for, ain't it? I don't believe any of 'em's as difficult as he is prone to think but that's the hell-and-all of bein' grown-up adult. You can make things as tough for yo'self as you please. Anyhow I can do projeckin' too, I'm an old hand at a blueprint. Dan don't know this and I don't intend he should yet-awhile. When I heard he got turned down on that job at the University I said to myself there's a nigger in the woodpile. One day I step around to Patapsco College and sneak in to hear Dan lecture. One of the special talks in the big meetin' room, so I can sit under the overhang and he don't know I'm there. All the time he's educatin', Ole Major sits in the shadow and what goes over the gals' heads falls right in my lap. If that scholarship ain't good enough for University then I says we'll keep it right here in the cat's cradle. What I'm tellin' you now, Miz Bee, is just between us two. It ain't no sociable information like Sandy Hole Bubbles. My mind runs clear back to old Tullius Teackle and what some of those Britons did for him. By God, Ma'am, there ain't no way to figure tit for tat but I'd be mighty tickled to scheme for it. The kind of talk Dan give those gals sure aimed to put in their heads a respect for the intellects and maybe loosen up their hold on frivolity. I hear Dr. Beinbrink tell how Dan is one short in his lecture schedule, some spiel he forgot to turn up, well, I'm all congested too with a speech I had no chance to deliver. I ain't got no solution for colored folks in alleys. I

346

ain't got no eckonomical solution for anything, but I'll stick to what's close to my nose. I ain't ready for pronouncements but I'm fixin' to sell off some of that old plantation land and if I get anywhere near real estate money we'll likely have some funds. I got it all set up in my head, the Tullius Teackle Lectureship in Poetry, not Lake Country poetry, and not Confed'rate poetry, just God-all poetry, excusin' the phrase.—We can keep this like privy counsel, Miz Bee, and don't let anything faze you. The human mind's right fidgety stuff."

On the other side of the farmhouse a game was being played, they could hear the cry "Red Rover, Red Rover, Let Trundle come over," and above the rising darkness of the valley a spark slid down-sky with smooth cosmic speed. "That's another kind of Red Rover," said the Major. "I read in the *Sun-Paper* they fizzle out fifty miles from earth. I reckon they sort of burn up in our coarse atmosphere. It's like mighty poets in their misery dead, though I declare I don't know if poets' misery is any more painful than rat-catchers' or railroadmen's. Miz Bee, did you ever see a med'cine show? What say we hitch up and go down with the boys? Before I go back to Chezpeake let's make a night of it. Doggone, I'll buy you some rattlesnake oil shampoo."

58. *The Hair-ribbon*

"Trundle sounds a good name for riding in the swing," Jeff said. He was acting as engineer, with Trundle and Buster and a doll as Pullman passengers. Both the child and the cat had a strong fancy for the measured squeak and slide of the suspended platform. It was considered good for digestion and also gave the devoted Hessie an opportunity to relax over her own meal. She needed it, for Baby Trundle was a fatiguing charge. "That chile am sho' movable, she scoot round something perilous. I don' darse let her out my sight. If tain't climb a tree it's

347

play pattycake with hoss's hoofs. 'Clare to Gawd only time she set quiet is if Marse Jeff ride her in de swing."

"My name isn't Trundle after supper," the child was saying. "I don't mind wearing bloomers and sunbonnet all day and playing with you-all down at the creek, but come supper time I tell Hessie, 'You fix me pretty. I'm Serena Lavinia Warren.' Hessie says quality fuss up with a hair-ribbon for supper and then sets around to be entertained. Hair-ribbons is a nuisance but it's worth it."

There was a whole battery of these adornments. Hessie ironed them in the warm dusk of the summer-kitchen after Serena Lavinia had been wheedled to bed. Perhaps the flamboyant hair-ribbon was an emblem of that age, the badge of a mysterious empire. At a corrosive game of croquet on the bumpy lawn the huge tilted bow glimmered to and fro in twilight like a pale mothmiller, accompanied by shrill assertions of foul play. "She's sassy as a moggin colt, you don't have to swallow her smoke," said her brother. Yet Jeff, suddenly observing female humors in their candid prime, found himself often watching her. There was some new charm in her constant trotting scamper, her attitudes of diminutive assertion or despair, her delicately stitched and tended clothes. But most of all the hair-ribbon: he could condone anything for the strange glamour of that symbol. A boy who has never had sisters brings peculiar freshness of astonishment to his first conscious glimpse of girls' adjoining world. How could he help suspecting that unnecessary and adorable flop of satin was the banner of a mustering army? Its varying toss and pattern, its conscious coquettish display, are like a trial balloon between the two great instincts—the two supreme cross-purposes, the wishing to make a work of art and the wishing to *be* one.

"I think you were mighty mean to go down to that med'cine show and not take me," said the passenger. "You can give me a nice long ride to make up."

"We brought you some Soapity-Soap," said Jeff. "It was

very amusing, there were two men on a wagon dressed up like colored people. They had washing powder they invented from the soothing balm of nature's forests and they made a song about it."

"Sing it to me," commanded Serena Lavinia.

"It's not very good unless you keep time with your feet. Something like this: 'Ladies need not give up hope: Is your wash a trial? Nope! Girls it's marvelous, Soapity-Soap!' Then they turned a somersault and washed the black off their hands with it."

"That's not a very good song," she objected. "I'll try Soap-ity-Soap on Lulabelle but I bettn't use it myself. Hessie allows my skin is very sensible. I aim to keep it that way," she added, screwing herself more comfortably on the seat. "Buster, quit encroachin' on my ruffles. He's certainly a most selfish cat."

"He likes it when the swing goes very slowly," said Jeff. "I expect that's why they say Let the old cat die."

"Well, who-all's bein' entertained, me or that ole tomcat? Besides he makes me sneeze and it's bad for me."

Buster may have heard some of the barnyard mice at evening prayer, at any rate he departed with an air of just having remembered something.

"Now we can be comfortable. He was annoying Lulabelle." She brushed the seat and placed the doll in the corner, austerely smoothing its skirt. "I'm not being very much entertained, I think you better sing the Pig Song."

"I'll sing Monocacy Railroad," amended the engineer.

The swing at these times became an imaginary train. When Jeff sat there alone he had sometimes accomplished the whole run from Westernland to Sprunt City, making all the scheduled stops and visualizing a notable variety of scenery ride. But for Trundle's benefit the line became the Monocacy Valley Railroad, routed through stations she had viewed with complacence on her own journey. If the oscillation of the vehicle was timed just right the anthem composed by Uncle Dan (to

349

amuse Buster) synchronized in cadence. "All abo-o-o-A-RD!" Jeff recited. "Monocacy Valley accommodation train, making all station stops to Blue Ridge Mountings and the Far Far West. From Rocky Ridge to Union Bridge with never a failure or stop, For all the aristocracy, they ride on the Monocacy, And even the nobility are treated with civility, Aboard the old Mo-nocacy, the M-O-N-O-Ockacy Rail—Road."

"But you *do* make stops," said the critical passenger.

"Songs don't have to be accurate."

"Hey, Jeff!" sounded Teackle's voice beyond the house. "Commere.—Something doing. Hessie's got a bat in her wool."

Loud screams from Hessie and barks from Shep testified melodrama.

"You'll have to excuse me," said Jeff, and ran. "It looks like a black hair-ribbon," he remarked as Hessie struggled to disentangle the creature. The bat squeaked.

"It won't hurt you," said Teackle, "it's only a mouse with wings."

"He scratch me wid his hooks," moaned Hessie. "Pry him loose, Marse Teack, bats is bad conjur, dey puts an omen on yo'."

59. *Emotion in Tranquility*

Thorofare, 18/8/03

DEAR BEE:

I'm glad you didn't come. It's all been fairly painful but the worst's over now. A lot was done before I got here. Mother and Allie have been wonderful. Thank goodness none of us let ourselves go though I admit that when Allie and I went up to Em's old gazebo to make a clearance of those dreadful stuffed pets I had to swallow hard. It was that abominable mixture of pathos and absurdity which sticks in the throat. We found a tin box half full of poor old Em's peppermints, you remember how she used to retreat up there and grind her teeth on them when she found the Family too trying. I was going to be sentimental

350

but good granite Allie saved me. With her noble grimness she said, "Don't taste them. They may be poisoned. Em liked the mint but she saved the pepper for the rest of us."

Everything's packed, or earmarked for the sale, and I'm shipping a few of the old treasures to Chesapeake to be held in bond until I get back. I shan't tell you what. It'll be a surprise for you. There was something unreal in going through all this during Regatta Week, the River full of yachts and the town gay with flags. One afternoon Harry took me for a sail in the *Scandal* (tell Geoff she's had a coat of paint!) and we got becalmed in Troublesome. The swans on the River glided about and sneered at us. You'll be relieved to know that Mother and Allie are going to be very comfortable in the cottage. It even has a garden not much smaller than our yard at 1910 with a sort of rockery of ferns which Mother already calls The Wilderness. Speaking of that, the stone deer were more like white elephants. I wished I could have had one crated for the Major. It would have been amusing at Greenaway. That reminds me of Miss Debbidge (the big glassy eyes, I dare say); tell Geoff she's married, so his earliest romance is blighted. But she wouldn't accept her faithful swain (a good solid farmer from Dallinghoo) until the old business closed; and her bridegroom bought a whole nuptial set of bedroom china from the shop at regular prices, disdaining to wait for the auction when he could have got them for almost nothing.

This is the last letter from the old house. I'm sitting in the dining-room, but not in my usual place; I had to turn my back on the glass door of the counting room so as not to see the ghost of dear vixen Em at the naked cash drawer. It's queer how one misses bad-tempered people the most of all! I made a final tour round the garden this afternoon. The meadow as you know has been rented out as a hay field and crossing the stubble damned if I didn't almost shatter my ankle on one of the old croquet hoops well rusted in. The wasps are still there and send you their remembrances—as Lizzie Batts might have

351

said, nothing like a Wilford wapse. They keep their dander up very heartily. Most of the news will have to wait until I see you, I'm just letting my mind run. Now that the break is actually come we all feel better. The whole family was here for Mother's birthday. We had a photo taken in the garden and I think that spot on the plate is one of the wapses looking for the Birthmark. We drank your health in stone ginger. Mother is now very keen to get into the new quarters, and her spirits are really marvelous. It's a wonderful record. She came to this house as a bride of twenty and leaves it, more cheerful maybe, as an old lady of eighty. The Wilford *Reporter* had a polite and respectful little note about the closing of the old shop. I'll save it for your scrapbook. Mother produced from her famous Mystery Chest the old Barton scrapbook with all its autograph letters; I'd forgotten what a lot of exciting things in it including the letter from C. Lamb. She wants me to bring it back with me for safe keeping, and it's just as remarkable in its way as the Major's album at Greenaway. It seems to include practically all the old Quaker Worthies and Wilford Wits except E. F. G., and that amuses me: I believe they still think he was a bad man because he praised wine that wasn't home-made—to say nothing of the Persian women and song. But wasn't it just as wicked for us to sell him the decanters he drank it from? What shocks *me* is taken quite calmly by Wilford, viz.: Bloxsome's advertisement in the *Reporter*, probably unconscious: *Bloxsome's Trousers Are Down Again*. Geoff might use that in the Sandy Hole *Cascade*.

The packing and sorting took longer than I expected, partly because we excavated so many forgotten things from the box-room and Mother got delightfully reminiscent about many of them. Why aren't more historians old ladies, they seem to remember all the really interesting things? She swears (I means affirms) the story is true of Old Fitz walking through the quickset hedge while absorbed in reading, and going on, though lacerated, without losing his place in the text; but she admits that the legend of his boiling his watch and timing it with an egg is probably invented. Myself I should think the probabilities might be reversed. How I wish I had just one of the copies of the *Rubaiyat* pamphlet that Wilford Friends burned in the kitchen grates because it was carnal. One of the masters at the schoolhouse has Fitz's copy of the *Odyssey* that he was reading when he fell overboard. It's still stained with salt water and a generous tinge of Deben mud. Some day I shall risk Dr. Beinbrink's ire and give the girls a lecture about E. F. G. on the general idea that after *The Ancient Mariner* maybe the *Rubaiyat* are the most effective (I don't say *greatest*) poem in English. The best artifice, the way a musician would conduct a symphony. Harry Bredfield and I walked out to the little church to see Fitz's grave, the Persian rose looks rather sadly. Then we played bowls and had beer; some of Omar's precepts Harry practices almost too faithfully.

I tried hard to give Mother and Allie some idea of Sandy Hole but I'm sure it's hopeless; they're convinced you're somewhere in the Rockies. A few days ago I had dinner with our friends at Martlesham (wonderful lobster curry) and met a lady who would have pleased Miss Beamish. She was related to the nobility, and really top-hole, priceless. I explained I came from Chesapeake; she asked, "Is that right out in the country?" I said No, it's a big city, half a million people. Evidently she didn't believe this, her enigmatic remark was, "Did it spring up very suddenly?" No, I said patiently, as a matter of fact it's rather an old city, one of the most historic in the States. The well-meaning creature, groping for bearings of some sort, then said, "What is it near?" I tried to be helpful. I said it's near Washington, that's the Capital. This was too much for her, the very idea of the U.S. having a capital threw her into confusion; she feebly fell back on the immortal *"Really?"* I almost lost my temper and blurted out, "You know, Americans take a lot of trouble trying to understand the English. Don't you think they might do the same about us?" She said,

"Surely you're not an American, your voice is so natural!—You know what I mean. Do they talk like that on purpose?"

But I must control myself because as soon as Mother is settled I shall bike to Cambridge and have a few days in the old digs. Cambridge in its Olympian calm—which makes even Oxford seem parvenu—also adopts the *How very quaint!* attitude toward any innocent remarks I let slip about our American doings. Patapsco University, as they always call it, they probably visualize as a collection of tepees or adobe huts; I can foresee their malicious chuckles at the amusing idea of Oxford soon having to receive wild men from the plantations on the Rhodes bequest. But you know how I love the place which has its own special meanings for me; I try to be patient with it and I think the attitude is mutual. I want to have a few dinners in college, watch the port go round "with the sun," and look up some books. My trouble is really the same as Wordsworth's when he was walking with his friend Jones: I crossed the mountains without knowing it. I've got a rather jolly idea for a paper— Wordsworth said his poetry came from emotion recollected in tranquility. I shall point out that the tranquility was William's but the emotion was often Dorothy's. You know you yourself are often a bit of a Dorothy?

The days are going so fast, I wish I *could* boil my watch and time this interlude with a conservative Wilford egg, then I remember your saying, "You can do anything if the time is short enough." I'll be back before you and Geoff realize I'm away— tell Geoff I'll bring him something from Miss Hoo's for my birthday. This is a long letter but at least it's not crossed like so many of those in the old autograph book—how did they ever read them? You know how much love and happy memories come to you from the Thorofare. Mother encloses too—

Yr affte bro:

DAN

60. *Thunder Weather*

"It certainly do swelter," Teackle complained. "No wonder Joel called off the Gettysburg picnic, he says the weather ain't bearable for old Clara. You can tell how rotten it is, even the bugs keeps crawlin' in corners like they got something on their minds." He captured a large praying mantis which was supplicating in a corner of the balcony and showed it to Aunt Bee. "This here's a dinosaur's bedbug. He holds up his hands to heaven like ole Aeneas. He likes you, Miz Bee. He crosses his heart and hope to die."

"Please remove him," said Aunt Bee. "And if you must allude to parasites I wish you'd call them norfolk-howards. I thought you boys were editing your paper."

In that abominably sultry noon all forms of amusement had palled. Teackle particularly was restless, he had sniffed through his Virginia-smelling collection of cigarette picture-cards and then tried rather feebly to untangle a snarl of fishing line. "I feel slow as molasses in January. I sho' feel unworthwhile."

"Don't be so darn lackadaisical," said Jeff (it was a reproach often used by Aunt Bee). "You ought to be writing the Adventures of a Crustacean. You've only done a lick and a promise. There's six more inches to fill."

"Aw shuckety-shucks, ole Simon Legree. Don't give me none o' your slack. There ain't really much account in the life of a crawfish. He might as well make tracks to the quicksand. I been all over my mind with a fine-tooth comb, I declare I don't notion a thing."

Even Jeff suddenly felt languid and contemplated the endless toil of a handwritten newspaper.

"I was listenin' to hear the ice-cream freezer," said Teackle, "but I bet ole Joel's too shiftless to grind the crank. I can't abide any hot dinner today. Tell you what we might do, Miz Wicker can give us sandwiches and we'll go hunt those dino-

355

saur tracks back of Tiddyhigh. Major said there's a ledge up there where they walked in something soft."

"That's a good idea," said Aunt Bee, who was writing at a sewing table just inside the window. "But please remember you promised to keep off the trestle."

"Looks like Aunt Bee's writing a newspaper herself," Jeff yawned.

"I'm writing to Blanche Bristol."

"Gee, you must have a lot to tell her. Why don't you write some of that for the Sandy Hole *Cascade,* then we could sell it?"

Aunt Bee evaded this. "You've been so busy, I haven't told you what Blanche said in her letter. What do you think? She and Aunt Kilda were on a train to Chicago and in the dining-car they met Mr. Snead."

"Well, wouldn't that jar you! Dinosaurs in dining-car," said Jeff. "Anyway he always did turn up for meals." He explained to Teackle, "Mr. Buckingham L. Snead, that was a funny old gambler who wore diamonds in his cuffs. He made speeches at concerts. I bet he'd have been crazy about the pig song."

"I dessay he knew it but he had sense enough not to sing it," said Aunt Bee. "Blanche says he sat at the table behind them but he recognized Kilda even before he turned around."

"Ha-haugh! Fishwives!" shouted Jeff, mimicking so exactly that Aunt Bee was startled.

"Why didn't you do that at the Chorale?" said Teackle with admiration.

"Did she make her speech about those ole Functions?"

"I'll read you what she says: 'It was most amusing. I was afraid Kilda might be bored while I was at the Math meetings but Mr. Snead was very attentive and took her to a prize fight. Mark of admiration. He told her he had a lot of money to spend because he had sued some casualty insurance company. They sent him a pocket calendar made of celluloid and it caught fire from a box of vestas and burned him badly. He said they paid up to keep him quiet. Very likely they were wise. But I wish I could have seen him and Kilda together at the boxing match.' "

"That's an idea," said Teackle, "we'll take a box of vestas with us and we can light a fire and toast our sandwiches."

"I should think you could get along without a fire a day like this," said Aunt Bee. "If you're going round by the post you can drop these letters. Blanche's ought to go off to Uncle Dan. I haven't forwarded it yet."

"Aw shuckety-shucks, it's too hot to go way down there," Jeff protested. "There's no hurry. Joel's probly going down to the store. Give it to him. Gosh, this weather bulges my ears in. It's like somebody whispering a long way off."

Not a bad description of the murmurs of Thunder Gap, Aunt Bee thought after the boys had gone to consult Mrs. Wicker. She reflected with amusement that scrambling for dinosaur vestiges on Buckskin Mountain would be a lot warmer than a visit to the post office with its usual bottles of cream soda from the box of ice under Doc Wicker's counter. But probably Jeff was right, there might be no hurry about forwarding that letter to Dan. It was a fat letter (after so many postcards), and when people knew each other as well as Dan and Blanche a fat letter somehow looks dangerous? Even the envelope's careful Pallas Athene script suggested that Blanche, like Dan, was one of those quixotic self-deniers who can ravage themselves with the pure acids of idealism.

Poor Dan: how many things brought him to mind in absence. Even habits annoying enough in practice were lovable in separation. His indolent reluctance to tie his bootlaces—Bee would *not* call them shoestrings—until he reached the halfway seat now called Bootlace Bench. His vague way of polishing the bowl of his pipe on the corner of one nostril when puzzled about anything; the inevitable and maddening remark "Poor Parsons came a nasty cropper" when anyone stumbled or fell.

357

The flat rock was still there where he sunned himself on a saddle of moss, the dead tree above Sandy Hole where the kingfisher looked like Dr. Beinbrink, the pipe dottles scattered on the path, the binder of his lecture notes he had left behind— how much he did for them all, how little he ever asked in return. These were the feelings that had prompted her letter; not an easy one for her to write, but she also had her theory of life's functions. She reviewed it from the beginning. "Dear Blanche, I've had something on my mind. . . ."

"No, honey, yo' caint tag along after the boys," she heard from below, and a querulous treble from Trundle. You couldn't blame anyone for being fretful on so heavy a day. She called down to Hessie: "Tell her if she's a good girl we'll take her down for a bathe later on."

"Well, if I can't go no more can Shep," shrilled Trundle. "Somebody has to stay at home and entertain me, don't they?"

"Well, Shep isn't going either," shouted Teackle. "Ole fool dog, he'll have a heat stroke the way he's panting."

"Besides he might get stepped on by a dinosaur," said Jeff. "Go back, Shep, behave yourself."

Shep seemed singularly obstinate. He flattened himself on the ground, rolled his eyes and gaped sideways to evade direct look from the boys, and showed every intention of following them. Aunt Bee watching from the balcony wondered if the persuasive aroma of roasting mutton might be partly responsible for the irritability of the household. Mrs. Wicker as usual was celebrating the summer's hottest day by a torrid meal of meat and potatoes.

"Damn that purp," Teackle growled. "If anybody wanted him to go he wouldn't budge. He's worse than a sumptuary mule. I never saw him act up so. I bet he's got hydrophobia. Stay away, Trundle, he might tear out your juggler vein."

"I bet you can't trust collies," said Jeff. "I read about them in *Bob Son of Battle*. They get blood lust from sheep and spring at you in the moonlight."

"That's no joke neither," said Teackle. "Think of that ole Hound of the Baskervilles. Get away from here, you crazy dog. Twenty-three, back to the woodpile. Put that in your pipe an' smoke it." He gave Shep a smart stroke with his crabapple switch. They had planned to cajole themselves on hike by flinging the small apples ahead of them.

Trundle burst into yells of reproach. "You're wicked, you're disgusting. You're mean to dumb animals. Look how he beat that poor dog. Here, Shep, here, Shep. Come here to Missy."

Shep was in distress. No mean observer of the social network, he understood that the child had some special relation to his old friend the Major and her clear peremptory voice was one to be heeded. The nickname "She Who Must Be Obeyed" (quoted by Jeff from Rider Haggard) was one he might have understood. In the despair of that hot Southren blood flowing two ways at once he simply lay flat and gazed in a neutral direction. Trundle knew now that she was very angry. "You can always tell who's kind to animals," she yelled. "Shep, you come right here to Serena Lavinia. You come right here, you sweet old dog. Damn, hell.—He's stickin' out his tongue at me," she screamed, and tried to drag the animal by force. He looked apologetic and made himself immovably heavy.

"You quit blasphemin', you ole sister of mercy," shouted Teackle, glad of an excuse to explode. "You better say you're sorry, you'll go perdition. Want to see who-all that dog respects? You get twenty feet one side and we'll stand twenty feet the other and you can call first and you'll see how he acts."

"Now honey, don' go frettin' in this heat," pleaded Hessie, coming to aid. "Yo' pretty face is all over prespiration. Now don' you to'ment yo'self with those ole boys, you'll sicken."

Shep twitched an ear at this provocative word but remained disconsolate between the competitors.

"Leggo of me, Hessie. Damn, hell. Here, Shep, here, Shep. Come and give me a big hug."

"She thinks he'll mind her and the po' lil squirt can't even whistle," said Teackle contemptuously.

"He looks very dismayed," said Jeff. "I don't think he'll go anywhere. I bet he's got a nervous breakdown."

Teackle and Jeff both whistled. The strain of conflict in the dog's mind was shown only by the courteous deprecating flutter of his brush.

"That ain' no way to treat a dawg," mumbled Hessie. "You-all givin' him a mizry and he don' like thunder weather." But Aunt Bee, who had come downstairs, was watching from the porch. "Shep, come here," she called, and the dog, released from his sorry dilemma, ran to her. The boys, pretending not to notice, went off past the orchard and Hessie scooped up the infuriated child and carried her howling and kicking toward the house.

"Take her clothes off and put her under the pump," said Aunt Bee. "She's fair dunted by this weather."

"Ole fool dog," Teackle grumbled as they trudged up the valley. "That kid got him so worked up he didn't know Gee from Haw. That's the kind of things girls do when they get associating round."

"He wanted to come with *us* but he knew he darsn't after you switched him."

"It ain't right to take animals out in weather like this. He's got nothing to sweat with excepting his tongue. You and I can do it all over," said Teackle, amply illustrating the fact. "Gee, it's too hot even to throw crabs. Let's set down in the water and eat the sandwiches, then we won't have to carry them."

"This is more like, this is bully," Jeff said as they sat up to the waist in a pool below the trestle. "I bet it was no cinch being a dinosaur in summer. Do you suppose they could only sweat with their tongues?"

The subject of dinosaurs' tongues, were they long and flickery like lizards', led naturally to further speculation: the size of their eggs, did they hide out in the hills in a setting mania like Happy Hen, and other theorizings agreeable to young scientists. "Major said their leavings is way up on those ledges," Teackle remarked. "Seems quite a skirmish to get up there. I bet they were about as big as Ma & Pa."

"Looks like quite a skirmish for us, too." Jeff was less enthusiastic about rock-climbing. "Maybe they had a nest down here in the valley. Some of them might have been lackadaisical."

"Probly wasn't any valley then," said Teackle. "I allow things must of looked different. I bet ole Hunting Crick flowed way up there. It took a lot of history to work itself down here. Even that ole Slut must be forty-leven million years old." He was privately a little relieved at Jeff's suggestion because in the shimmer of afternoon the sandstone cliffs of Buckskin Mountain looked uncomfortable. "There's kind of a toolshed up the other end of Tiddyhigh, where they keep stuff for repairs. I found it unlocked one time, there was a box of track torpedoes. Those things they signal with. I bet they're just as interesting as dinosaur eggs. We might mosey up there and take a look. I got a notion we might better not hike too far, there's awful big thunderheads upstream."

"It's funny today," Jeff said, encouraged that Teackle had an eye on the weather. "It sounds all the time as if a train was coming."

"Ain't no trains this time of afternoon. We used to tease ole Major about that. He figgered out the schedule on this road, and he didn't fancy any trains racketing across the trestle while he took his afternoon snooze. Mother said it must be fun to figger out a railroad so's not to interfere with yo' personal sensuality."

That was one of the advantages of the Great Eastern & Western of Jeffland, thought the President, but there was not energy available for conversation as they clambered up the ravine. He held to one thought, however, and waited until they reached the toolshed blistering on a flat of cinders. Beyond it the track sliced through a rocky spur and followed round the contour of the hills. They sat puffing on a stack of spare sleepers which were stickier than they expected.

"In England they call it shedule, imagine."

"I wonder why they go out of their way to do things so comical over there?"

"I used to wonder about that too," said Jeff. "I guess everything's comical if it's far enough away. Uncle Dan said Boxing Day isn't really any funnier than Decoration Day."

"Decoration Day ain't so funny either. Confed'rate Memorial Day comes ahead of it."

They discovered that the toolshed was locked. "Well anyhow, there's something this ole road does on schedule," Teackle said. "Less go study along the cut. I bet it's hot enough to bring out the copperheads."

61. *The Gold Thimble*

After lunch Bee retired to a hard bench at one end of the veranda, behind the trumpet vine where occasional humming birds whirred like very small electric fans. Mrs. Mister suggested a rocking chair but Miss Barton could never be persuaded to try them. "It's only babies that have to be rocked all the time," she thought. She was always amazed to see George W. Mister, when he came up for the week-end, pass most of his time quite silent in a rocker alongside his oscillating wife; a long thin man smoking a long thin cigar. His brown shoes were long and thin and always beautifully shiny; Jeff remarked that even his hair was getting thin. The Misters always offered perplexities; after the first oddity of their name was accepted there was still another. Jeff had asked if the middle W. stood for Washington? No, Mr. Mister was heard to say, "It stands for Y." This fresh anomaly "bafled" both Jeff and Teackle into chokes of mirth, but presumably poor Mr. Mister was accustomed to misunderstandings for he pro-

362

duced his visiting card. It read: Mr. George Wye Mister. "Wye," he said proudly, "that's a mighty honored name on the Eastern Sho'." Mrs. Mister confided to Aunt Bee that in the good old days her husband's ancestors had "Owned near a thousand niggers. They say God won't let any man own a thousand, but old Chancellor Wye he had nine hundred ninety-nine. If they bred too liberal he raffled 'em off."

Looking out through a chink in the vines Aunt Bee could see Trundle bullying Hessie on the croquet ground. The child insisted she must have practice, and was swiping balls around for her nurse to chase and bring back. She had refused to wear her sunbonnet and good-natured Hessie was pursuing her charge with an umbrella, in a vain attempt to shield her sensible skin. As the colored woman trudged patiently to and fro Aunt Bee was struck by an optical illusion. Under the dark shadow of the umbrella the nurse's black face disappeared, she walked like a headless figure above her white apron. It was quite weird. "I wish you'd come out of the sun, Hessie," she called. "Walking under that umbrella you look like a ghost."

"Mighty black ghost," said Hessie cheerfully. "Sun don't stricken me none, Miz Bee. I reckon it's best to let Baby Trundle just run herself out. It's too hot upstairs to take her nap."

Too hot even to think, Aunt Bee admitted. She had given Joel Wicker her letter to mail but was still withholding the other one to be forwarded to Dan. She tried to concentrate on knitting the egg-cozy she had promised the Major. This was a result of discussion at meals. Jeff had been greatly taken by a white china dish, in the shape of a hen sitting on a nest, in which Mrs. Wicker served boiled eggs to keep them hot. Aunt Bee maintained that the Wilford method, putting a woolen jacket on each egg, was more efficient. The Major said he had never had an egg-cozy and Aunt Bee offered to make him one. But the skein of wool felt hot in her hands, and the steady creak of Mrs. Mister's chair teased her nerves. The lowering weather made her head ache; Shep's head seemed to bother him too, he kept pestering as she sat on the front stoop, pushing up against her and laying his chin on her knee. When Trundle came bothering also, insisting on the promised walk to Sandy Hole, Aunt Bee gave in.

"I'll bring my fancy work," she said to Hessie. "I don't feel like mending." She got out a tea-cloth she was embroidering and took the gold thimble as a talisman. It was the one Grandma gave her when she left home; she had admired it from childhood, sewing with it always brought back something of those long memories, tranquilized by time. She remembered the golden tip flashing to and fro in the lamplight, shining above Grandma's black silk, moving across and across the First Day frill of lace. On First Days one never did practical sewing (if you did, it had to be taken out with one's nose in the future life) but works of art were allowed.

"It's right peevish weather," said Hessie as they went down the stony path through the woods. "Miz Wicker fill me up so wid hot mutton I kin sca'cely keep my eyes open. I'm puffy in my bowels too, feel mahself rumble like dat Thundrin' Gap."

"I told you Shep would rather come with us," Trundle boasted. "He don't like those ole boys. They're mean to him. I've got my overhauls on, I can walk right into the waterfall the way Jeff does."

The collie certainly seemed cheered by being with them. He lay on a rim of sand at the edge of the pool, his long tongue running in and out over the humps of his teeth, while Trundle splashed in the shallows.

"Oh dear, I forgot to bring my field glasses," said Aunt Bee. "I wanted to watch the birds. They'll all be down for a drink this afternoon." Uncle Dan had brought from Carroll Street an old pair of binoculars and Aunt Bee found bird-study a new and thrilling pleasure.

"I'll go back for them, Miz Bahton," said Hessie, but the colored woman was stout and unhappy on her feet and Aunt

Bee refused the offer. She had a sort of obstinacy in repairing her own mistakes, also she felt that the walk alone would be a respite; Hessie was talkative. "No, it's my own fault, I'll get them. It won't hurt me if I take my time."

"You leave yo' fancy-piece wid me. Maybe I cud put a few stitches into it while you'se gone. I'd admire to use dat gole thimble."

Aunt Bee had a curious reluctance to allow anyone else to work on her treasure, which she was slowly ornamenting with American autumn foliage in colored silks; intended as a Christmas gift to Wilford. But there was no way of denial without hurting Hessie's feelings.

"Gole thimbles is sure enough quality," said Hessie. "It look mighty pretty on black. I'll put it on lil finger, others too big. I always did crave to use one o' these. Ole Miss say nothin' like gole thimble fo' infants to cut their teeth on, she run it along their gooms. Baby Trundle done cut her lil toofies on gole thimble, dat bring highbo'n luck."

Aunt Bee was leisurely on the way back. She rested a while on the halfway bench. Perhaps the walk was wasted effort, for she noticed in the woods that the birds seemed unusually silent. But the uneasiness in the thunder-charged air made movement a relief. At the farmhouse no one was stirring—except Mrs. Wicker's rocker which was still swaying feebly by itself. Evidently even Mrs. Wicker felt disinclined for society and had retreated when she saw Miss Barton coming.

She took the field glasses from her room and set off slowly to return to the creek. There were constant bumps and roulades beyond the hills, but still the needed storm was withheld. Spasms of wind tossed the tree-tops, and again the woods were dull with silence. At the bench she paused once more, studied the bark of trees through the glasses, noticed Teackle and Jeff's initials heavily incised. Jeff's carving was rather sketchy, but G and B are difficult letters. She remembered Dan's story about Coleridge having cut his initials in a stone on the way from

Keswick; and when William and Dorothy Wordsworth found it later, William was not satisfied with Coleridge's workmanship. (S. T. C. were not easy to do either.) William took out his knife and began improving the S, and Dorothy suddenly struck the blade from his hand. Dan said Dorothy bent and kissed the clumsy letters.

There were times, Dan added, when William had the soul of a proofreader. . . . Aunt Bee was thinking of other initials, D. B., B. B.—Anyway I sent off my letter to Blanche; dessay he'd be very angry if he knew. But I certainly won't let him give up his whole life to looking after his sisters. . . . Suddenly she was frightened by a louder rush of wind pouring overhead. A draught of chill sifted through the glade. She heard Shep barking, barking, barking.

The boys found it a disappointing sort of day; the hike was labor, the listless air took the impulse out of everything. Rolling weights of sound kept jarring loosely from ridge to ridge higher up the valley but seemed to lack the energy to come their way. Then there was a change in colors, the sun was a hazy yellow, the red embankments and green river bottoms shone vividly bright. "That ole Thunder Gap is sure livin' up to its name," said Teackle. He pointed to purple blackness in the far notch of hills, veined with wriggles of pure hurry. They agreed, maybe that was what a dinosaur's tongue looked like.

"I wouldn't be surprised somebody might think we better go home," said Jeff, but Teackle didn't take the hint. They had practiced walking on the rails and were now waiting near the same toolshed to enjoy the afternoon freight. Miscellaneous small articles were carefully balanced on the hot iron to be flattened by the wheels: two copper pennies, two horseshoe nails neatly crossed, a piece of copper wire, and the crust of one of Mrs. Wicker's sandwiches. These were all gummed to the rail with oozings of tar from the pile of railroad ties, so they would not shake off. The sandwich, Teackle affected to believe, might give the engineer a noticeable bump.

"It's funny how you see things without intending to," Jeff remarked. "There's that clump of black-eye Susans the other side of the trestle, just at the bend of the track, see how it stands out in this light. I always notice that when I go up through the orchard. It's the very beginning of the Tiddyhigh curve."

"Looks like somebody crazy with the heat," said Teackle.

With their eyes on the clump of flowers they saw a man running round the bend. He stumbled urgently on, with jogging step measured to the ties of the roadbed. Without altering his steady gait, watching his footing shrewdly, he came across the dizzy framework of the trestle.

"Cheese, that's something to do," Teackle admitted. "Acts like he's run so far he don't know how to stop. Say, it's Bill Kruger. He's the track-man on Slabtown section. Hey, Bill, what's doin'?"

Kruger's face was streaming scarlet. He closed his eyes a moment, put his hand to his side, and leaned against the shed. Then he pulled out a key and tried to insert it in the padlock, but his hand shook.

"Unlock," he gasped. "I'm beat. They phoned, been a cloudburst up Left Fork. Searing's dam broke loose, flood coming down. Might shake up this ole trussel. Aim to put torpedoes on the track, stop that freight."

He snatched off the opened lock, stumbled into the shed, then turned panting.

"Better light out for home. If anybody's down to the crick, get 'em out of there." He seized the torpedoes and hurried off up the track. They wondered if he noticed the objects they had set out on the rail.

"I bet Aunt Bee and Trundle's down at Sandy Hole," said Jeff. "Holy Gee," was all Teackle said. In a horrid flash Jeff realized he had known all day something abominable was going to happen. To scramble down the ravine and follow the bed of the creek would be endless. But Teackle was already running and Jeff followed. The trestle was the shortest way, and there was no time to remember promises.

Even Teackle had to slow down on that high scaffold where every stride was across emptiness, for perspiration blinded them at once. The thunder, heard all day until disregarded, now sounded like immediate warning of horror; yet looking down between the ties they saw the innocent shining of the stream below, glittering over smooth brown slabs and grassy edges. Jeff's stomach felt upside down, his feet in sneakers heavier than boots of K. Careful, careful, step and step, slow and slow, while sluggish disbelief held the mind in retard across each depth of nothing. It was like a nightmare: why do they always happen just when one least wants to wake up? It would be tempting to slip through the open beams, plunge far down to the cool water. There was the very hollow where they had sat in soak. Surely the creek, their playmate of every day, would not trick them now? By the time Jeff was across the bridge Teackle had already vaulted the bobwire and was shortcutting across the hillside below the orchard. Jeff squirmed through the wire with a long stinging gash and pounded gasping after. They slid through the hedge into the dusty road and so to the wooded path, with a distant glimpse of Mrs. Mister rocking on the porch and keeping time with a palm-leaf fan. She rose from her chair, a grotesque of staring amazement, but they were too far to shout. "Probly thinks we found a dinosaur," Jeff supposed, and wanted to laugh even in his anxiety. The rumble of thunder kept following and pushing from behind, and without hearing wind they could see the tree-tops toil and bristle. But as they neared the stream one sound broke through above others; it was Shep barking, barking, barking.

"At least it *sound* cool down here," said Hessie, sitting in the Valley of Fern. "I like the way that crick say *hushgush*."

If no one else was available she was easily resigned to her own company and talked to herself. "Sho' kind in Miz Bahton to loan me the use of her gole thimble. She ain't snooty about her belongins like some folks. She take her time, I kin finish dis piece o' folage befo' she come. Don' think she find de birds show off none just now, dey don' savor dis prodigal weather. Right queer how dat storm roll roun' de edges an' never loosen up. Air today feel like somebody breathe it already, suck out all de good. Mighty drowsy-makin', even Baby Trundle seem to take herse'f mo' peaceable."

Shep lay studious with head on paws, the child was digging and squatting round the pool. "It doesn't matter if I get good and dirty," she announced, "because you'll have to wash me up anyway."

"Dat's all right, honey," said Hessie placidly. "Dat's all right, pleasure yo'self fo' once. I'm sewin a right proud seam wid dis gole thimble." Must be nice to be white folks, she thought dimly, such handsome fixings and nice places to keep them—even if ole Hessie had a gole thimble she wouldn't know where at to keep it—her hands relaxed in her broad lap, her head bent toward them, she was asleep.

It was the first time Trundle had been at Sandy Hole with any real freedom of maneuver. She made passes at an imaginary opponent on the dueling log but fortunately fell off on the shallow side. Experiments in the hospitality of mud proved satisfying: it was always deeper than it looked. She launched chips of bark as toy boats into the circling eddy, exclaiming (as she had heard the boys do), "A letter for the government!" as they floated away downstream. This phrase had originated from Teackle's explanation to Jeff that the water of Hunting Creek, flowing into the Monocacy and thence to the Potomac, finally entered politics at Washington, D.C. The boys would have been amused to hear her utter this innocent ejaculation; in confidential moments they had adapted the phrase for private reinforcements of the stream. Then a persistent horse-fly attacked her; she yelled "Damn! Go to hell, ole fly!" and awaited enjoyable shock from Hessie who had remarked lately, "There's too damn much cussin' in dis famly." But Hessie said nothing, and peeping round a boulder Trundle saw the nurse was asleep.

The ledge across the deep end of the pool was Trundle's ambition. She saw the boys use it constantly, and said to herself, "I reckon I can do whatever those ole boys can." Her confidence was justifiable; Major Warren and his engineers a generation before had cut the shelf sloping inward. It was sure enough footing for nimble feet. Probably easier for her than for a larger passenger. One had to be careful stepping over a great shiny root from the dead tree that still stood silver-brittle on the chine of elephant rock. The boys always walked gaily across the ledge to dive down the waterfall, to listen to echoes in the flume. At the end one could stand on moss at the very fringe of the cascade where it poured through the granite notch and spread in lacy sweep. She did so, carefully, and jiggled a little with triumph. She wanted to try the echo, but it might wake Hessie. Then she started, a cold nose touched her bare leg. Shep had followed her. He growled softly and took the slack of her khaki bloomers in his teeth.

"Naughty ole dog, go back. Shep, you quit chasin' me, it's none of your beeswax." She gave his face a smart slap. "You leave me be, Shep, I'm mad at you. Go back, darn you. Damn!"

The collie retreated a few inches and crouched watchful. He made a low strange yowl.

"You lay there like that, how can I get back anyway? You hush, ole fool dog, you've got hyderobia. I'm listenin' to the water."

She had no idea it would sound so loud close to. Hunting Creek was running slender after several days of drouth, but behind the crisping splash of the little fall and the hiss of its widening bubble-and-suds was a deep booming sough in the narrow Slut. Under the shade of cliff and trees the air was darker and there were windy sounds above. Suddenly she screamed "I'm frightened." Shep began barking.

Hessie started up at the cry of the dog. Above their sheltered hollow the tree-tops were thrashing in a stress of wind, but now a rush of water came pouring through the narrow sluice of the fall, carrying a blast of cold air and the dull grind of loose boulders swept down the channel. Trundle cowered back against the shelter of the rock. She might have fallen, from mere fright at the bursting jet of water sweeping past, but she slipped on wet slime and huddled safe on the ledge.

Hessie gave one panic cry of disaster. She knew she could not manage the narrow path below the overhang of cliff. The basin was already wild with a churn of muddy foam, but she waded in, deep as she could fight against the push of water. "Jump, honey, jump," she shouted. "Jump in de watah. Mammy ketch you." She knew she was not heard. She waved and beckoned. Fortunately the child was too terrified to move. At first Trundle may have thought the dog was attacking her and tried feebly to push him away. Shep whined and hackled, he shook with chill, but only shifted his grip and held her fast.

The water was rising. Hessie saw there was no chance for her to reach the child across the pool. A surge of mounting current almost bore her off her feet. Could she find a long pole to stretch from the shore? "Hole on, Mammy comin'," she cried, but wind and water covered all other sound. She turned clumsily, wallowing in the spate, to grope her way out. At that moment the great skeleton tree above, long dried and weatherbeaten, broke from its rotted hold. It fell like the arm of a derrick or the slow sweep of a great scythe. Slanted over the granite wall the naked trunk made a barrier which would prevent Trundle from falling, but the jagged fork of limbs crashed full on Hessie, struck her down, crushed and held her under.

The water was rising. Backed up at the farther end of the Slut it spread sideways, began to seep over the broad sunbath rock above the fall, trickled in spray over the roof of the pool.

371

The child lay still on the narrow bench of stone. Shep sniffed her anxiously, then wrestled a moment with a branch of the fallen tree that blocked their return. He went on barking, barking.

At first Aunt Bee could see nothing but the gray sprawl of the fallen tree, the brown seethe of water foaming through ragged branches, the ooze and sprinkle flooding above and bringing down clods of soil and shrub. Through lashing wind and water she could hear Shep's incessant high-pitched bark. Then he sprang up for a moment teetering on the slanted wreck of tree, as if to catch her eye, and jumped back again. Under the angle of dripping trunk she saw his long snout go down to snuff something on the rock; she saw the wet gleam of the child's leg. The roar in the cavernous groove above them sounded as though the whole hillside was blasting down, but she felt her way along the greasy ledge. Once she faltered but the natural veer of her gait, which Dan and Jeff had always smiled about, tilted her inward. After a few perilous steps she was able to seize a spike of the dead wood. It was slick with mud, but it held. Then she saw Trundle lying in a palsy of fright between a sliver of tree and the rock. The child looked at her with large almost senseless eyes. Somehow Aunt Bee managed to scramble over the angle of trunk, seized the child in a savage grip and sat panting on the edge of the shelf. Trundle wailed at her: "You're hurting me. Why don't Mammy come?" The water was almost at the level where they huddled; Aunt Bee wondered how soon it would lap over.

As soon as she had hold of Trundle the dog sprang past her face, onto the tilted bole, and ran down it as if it was a gangplank. With incredible skill he balanced where the water foamed through the broken fork of timber, and then Bee saw the rag of dress and apron flapping under water. She saw why Hessie did not come. Even as she realized what had happened there was a grinding slither, the splintered tree jolted farther down, clear of the vertical rock. She saw the dog tossed into the cataract, his gallant plume pitifully snaky in the flood. It waved helpless as he rolled over with striving paws; he disappeared over the next rocky terrace. In the next instant a projecting elbow in the root-mass shoveled both her and Trundle into the stream.

Swimming was impossible, but at least her ventures in Sandy Hole had taught her some confidence. The tree could not move far, jammed against boulders just below. With Trundle in clutch she was whirled gasping into the tangle of wood. There was nothing to do but hold on. She felt an agony in her right wrist, as she tried to hoist the child a little higher in her arms. "Good thing I wrote that letter when I did," she muttered to herself. She was still holding grimly when the boys got there. Joel Wicker and the hired man, called by Mrs. Mister, were only a few minutes later.

From the plateau beyond Tiddyhigh, where Bill Kruger and the crew of the freight train watched, it did not look a very serious washout. They could see the brown swirl of water rush down the trough of the valley, rising high enough round the piers of the trestle to justify its nickname, caving banks of the creek, undermining trees and heaving boulders. But there was enough overflow to hurl a three-foot wave at the bottleneck of the Slut, where it poured through like an avalanche, piling up as it went. Then the torrent subsided. The marsh and spillway by the millpond were able to absorb the floodwater, the surge of wind down Blowing Gap blew the sky clear like miracle, and by the time Joel and other men had chopped away the wreck they carried Hessie uphill in one of the Blue Ridge's most serene sunsets. It was Teackle and Jeff who finally found Shep and did the same for him.

Aunt Bee was able to dominate the pain in her broken wrist by consoling Trundle and getting her to bed. The child was bruised and scraped but undamaged. "Is Hessie and Shep both dead?" she asked presently.

373

"Yes, dear, I'm afraid so," said Aunt Bee. "Now you say a prayer for them and go to sleep."

"Did the Lord their soultotake?"

"I dare say He did," said Aunt Bee, wincing as she adjusted the mosquito net over the bed. "Now don't think about it just for a little while and go to rest like a good child."

"Sho', that's too bad," said Trundle. "They'll have to get me a new nurse."

It was quite late that evening before the village undertaker could do his duty by Hessie. He came politely to give Miss Barton a small bright object. "Miz Wicker says this is yourn. It was squeeze so tight on her finger I could scarce get it loose."

Aunt Bee felt her mouth bothering her and had to speak quickly. "Please put it back. I want her to keep it."

He saw she meant it and was too much a mountaineer to argue. So Hessie took the gold thimble with her, a badge of quality.

62. Dan Writes a Postal Card

The Major sent old Lightfoot up to Sandy Hole to bring Hessie home to Greenaway. He telegraphed Teackle to come down with them as a mark of family respect, and to escort his sister. Lightfoot rode most of the way in the baggage car with the coffin, "to keep Hessie company," he said; "she was kind of a fraidcat about travelin'." Teackle did his best to keep Trundle amused, but he missed his usual visit with the candy butcher in the baggage car.

The funeral service was held in the big house, as was Greenaway custom. Hessie's son Mutual was much assuaged by the dignity of keeping the big fan twirling. A fine old colored preacher came out from town to officiate and say the words of consolation in accents of dark and flowing charm. Resurrection certainly sounds more probable when pledged in the Negro voice; perhaps because those much-tried brethren have more right to it. The Major wore one of his tropical linen suits, because he knew they would expect it of him; it looked incredibly white in that setting. After the preacher had finished jubilizing the Major said a few words and found himself breaking down. Lightfoot hurried him to the library and produced a julep already in frost. "I had a notion it might be needful," he said, "I done wring out fresh yarbs befo' de ceremonials, jus' in case. Now don' you take on, Major, you done everything mighty seemly. You set right there an' drowse yo'self. I'll bring dat Reverend in here after de interment, he like to pay his mite of respect."

The Major obeyed. He could hear them singing a spiritual,

> "An' befo' Ah'll be a slave
> Ah'll be buried in mah grave
> An' go home to my Lawd an' be free."

Then the white folks withdrew and Hessie was carried out to the little colored burying ground behind the old slave quarters.

It must have been about the same time that Uncle Dan was composing in his mind a letter to the Major; with that felicitous fullness of letters that don't get themselves put down on paper.

My dear old friend (Dan was thinking, and with the coasting joy of mind that moves without the dull backpedaling brakes of grammatical connectives): How I've been wishing you might be here; such a different Lake Country from the one you know. I think you only got as far as Yarmouth? If I had a scratch-block (scribbling pad!) on my knee I could set down a pleasing address: Aboard the *Bittern*, River Ant, near Barton Broad, Norfolk. This was all a surprise. Harry Bredfield said he simply must have a holiday; if he stayed "a-tome" any longer he'd go balmy. We took train to the immortal town of Norwich, went out to have a look at Mousehold Heath (remember *Lavengro*) and then on to Wroxham. There I hung around the old stone bridge while Harry who knows all the ropes found the somewhat battered 26-foot sloop *Bittern* (Teackle will think that sounds very Baskerville) available for three days of "ditchcrawling," viz.: sailing the little rivers and lagoons of the Norfolk Broads. Few outlanders ever see this unique region. Imagine the streams winding in corkscrew loops and twists through grassy marsh and meadow and past little rising copses (cheese it, the copse! we cry if in danger of running afoul of shrubbery). Here and there a windmill, or its spiritual equivalent, a lovely old parish church, with an obsidian sparkle of squared flints. There's been no becalming in Troublesome, for the east wind blows and blows, stinging with Frisian salt; great mapscapes of blue shadow coast across the green flats and shivering bulrushes. Even your grandfather and his 1812 privateer might admire Harry in his minuscule navigation where you go surging on a racing tack for maybe 200 feet into the armpit of the breeze and then luff like lightning for another foaming rush of 40 yards. Across the field you see someone else's sail skimming like a butterfly in the opposite direction; or a windmill waving parson's sleeves at you, and sometimes a waterside inn bright with flowers. Unless we're on one of the Broads themselves I let Harry handle the tiller, after I didn't come about nippy enough on a sticky turn and mired us deep in a lee swamp among bulrushes and marshmallows (not the kind the boys toast at Sandy Hole). It took some hellish pushing with the quant (sort of punt-pole) to shove off. Harry boomed like a bittern with indignation—but I haven't heard the bittern boom; he only makes his loud bassoon, Harry says, in the mating season. My credit fell like Lucifer, or Admiral Dewey. But we're even-Stephen because Harry walked off a dyke after an evening pub and came a cropper in a bed of nettles.

It takes quick dodging to avoid the great wherries (sailing barges, the trippers' char-a-banc of this region) that come rippling along under huge brown sail reaching out high, wide and handsome almost across the whole stream. The gaff towers high enough to catch some wind when trees overhang on the bank. They're sheered so deep they practically dip their midriff under. They're full of trippers on camp stools and probably someone playing a piano or accordion. If you moor near one for the night you'll hear *Soldiers of the Queen* and the *Bedouin Love Song* and *Mandalay* and *Daisy Bell* until you really *are* half-crazy. I heard one cockney sportsman singing *The Banks of the Wabash* and I dare say he supposes the Wabash is one of the rivers of Norfolk. Sorry we had to be here at the height of the holiday season. Some of the favorite reaches get pretty noisy with their pianos and picnic parties; imagine what it will be like if Mr. Edison's gramophone ever gets popular. We made up a verse:

> Three rivers are the trippers' cure,
> The Yare, the Waveney and the Bure,
> But smaller streams are still extant:
> The Thurne, the Muckfleet, and the Ant.

Muckfleet, mud flow, gorgeous word! With the east wind on our cheeks, we slid up the tiny Ant, thou sluggard, where Harry thought I should have a look at Barton Broad and the hamlet of Barton Turf, which I like to imagine ancestral. We've been out all day in unusual sunshine, almost warm, had a bathe very different from Sandy Hole, and you can tell Teackle that I caught a roach eight inches long—but it's a fish. Walked along a dyke to Stalham to replenish supplies and had Norfolk cider in a fisherman's pub. Now we're moored for the night alongside a staith, if you know what that is: a little landing stage along the bank; a word that I dare say came over with the Angles themselves. We met a pleasant chap when we were taking our swim: he was bathing from a boat near by, we got into talk and I couldn't help noticing two puckered scars on his body. A bullet went right through him at Paardeberg,—sideways, missing all essentials. He said cavalry make a wonderful target and I thought of you. Harry remarked, that sort

of thing makes a war more real than reading about it in newspapers. He's smoking his pipe against midges in the little cockpit. I came below to stow our stores and found myself thinking
this letter.

Anyway I've been successful in throwing off my fit of black
dog, what Bee calls grumping. I had a lonely crossing in the
St. Louis, didn't find anyone very congenial in the second cabin,
and had leisure for solitary communing and made some decisions about my work and my duties. Then at Wilford, getting
family affairs settled I was too busy to mope. Harry's suggestion of this little jaunt was an inspiration. Poor fellow, he
booms like a bittern himself when he blurts out his own problems and observations: the snobbery or stupidity of the upper
classes, etc. "I've stuck it too long ever to get out now," he
says somberly. "Dan, you don't know how lucky you were: the
President of the Immortals had the lines all laid for you to
run respectful in the groove and end up just a provincial clark
or a shopman like me. How did you slip your mooring? Some
of this sharp old east wind of ours got on your tail and blew
you out of it? Listen to those bloody fools downstream playing
the accordion and letting off squibs. They've forgotten all about
the Boer War already." I was rather glad if they had, but I
don't interrupt Harry when he wants to run on. There's a
wonderful avenue of huge trees in Wroxham where we took
shelter in a shower, we saw a superb old ruddy parson in his
black straw hat creeping along on a tricycle. When Harry
sees anything that he thinks symbolizes Toryism he nudges me
and says "Great and Little Snoring!" Those are two adjoining
parishes somewhere in Norfolk whose names he noticed on my
road-map. The clerical ancient trundling along annoyed him
while to me of course he was utterly charming; I thought what
a decent life to be vicar of Great (or Little) Snoring and ride
round the country churches taking rubbings of memorial brasses
—aren't they man's best attempt to make a long story short? I
was saying that I wished Jeff could have been with me to see

378

some of all this, but Harry burst out, "By God I envy him, he can start from scratch without having to swallow all the horse-nuggets some of us do. Dessay the blue rails of your Major's High Iron will mean to him what the River does to us. Please to remember a Thorofare don't fare through if you squat in the same spot all your life."

In spite of his grumblings that the Old Country's done for (which it isn't, by any means) Harry's one of the most useful citizens anywhere. Never having seen "The States" he idealizes them as much as the Lady Collamore crowd undervalue them. Myself I've been away long enough to quit *comparing* one country with another and just relish them each by each. You know how startled I was in that old newspaper episode to discover how much latent hostility against Britain there is in some quarters in the U.S., due in great part to the famous condescension Lowell wrote about. Yet Americans can be condescending too, I've noticed: e.g., their deliberate damnable insistence on finding everything over here *quaint;* surely just as irritating as the English determination to find U.S. doings *crude.* Those are two labels I highly resolve to forswear forever. I admit it's jolly trying when you overhear some touring blighters patronizing as amusingly picturesque some poor and ancient simplicity which had its origin in a thousand years of dour human struggle. If a thatched roof is "quaint" by God so is an Indian tepee, and I don't see why the corduroy trews of a Suffolk yokel are any "funnier" than our American blue jeans? I get very hot when people sneer at beauty who never knew it anyway. I've been away from all this sort of thing so long that now I get all the joys and humors of a loving stranger. Harry laughed at me when we laid in our grub at Wroxham, where they have a sort of Sears, Roebuck supply house for yachtsmen—they call it "the world's largest village store," surely an American sort of touch?—I insisted on choosing all the stuff with names that amused me and reminded me of auld lang syne, things poor Bee has foraged for in vain round the marts of Chesapeake.

Listen to them, Major: I take the names right from our larder: lemon curd, Oxford brawn, prawns in aspic, bloater paste, "desiccated soup," custard powder, galantine of game, pressed fowl, bramble jelly, cherry brandy (a great specific in these parts)—how's that for a Full Dinner Pail? Happen it sounds a bit like the delicatessen scene in "The Eve of St. Agnes"—and here's a grieving thought: happen like Keats it's mostly the names I'm enjoying: I have a lurking nostalgia for a barbecue down by your old cabin at Sandy Hole, and ears of Wicker's corn right off the stalk into the embers. Or huckleberry pie, and the tankle-tonk of cowbells on that stony hillside, or some hot exploding thunderstorm down the Gap instead of this flesh-goosing Easterly. But damn it, I wouldn't *compare* all these things any more'n I'd compare the moon in its first and third quarters. I saw a lovely waning moon when I got up early this morning and went on deck to write a letter to the government (needn't quote me to Teackle, because I reproached the boys for doing it). And it struck me it's just as lovely as the young moon, only they're just bitten into the other way round.

I'll be going over to Cambridge, where I enter a different atmosphere entirely and become momentarily (and I fear a little hypocritically?) upper-class: a don, if you please! And I go in good spirits, thinking of myself in Daddy's words:

> The village schoolmaster was he
> With hair of glittering gray,
> As blithe a man as you could see
> On summer holiday.

By the bye, I posted Mrs. Warren a parcel of sausage rolls from Wilford, but I fear they're bound to deteriorate in transit. . . .

At this point Harry came below. "I say," he remarked, "what on earth are you doing, sitting there in the dark? Haven't you got those groceries stowed away yet? I'm about ready for a cherry brandy and some Great and Little Snoring."

It was a pity the Major never received the unwritten letter, it would have pleased him and given warrant for some conspiracies of his own. But when the *Bittern* had been brought back to her own boatyard Dan did send the Major a picture postcard of Wroxham Bridge. It said, "Had three days' boating with H. Bredfield. Great fun, must tell you all about it."

63. The Fire

There are experiences one does not attempt to describe until an adequate interval has passed. It was cold and blowing February before Uncle Dan got any sort of picture in his mind of the tragedy at Sandy Hole. The narration might not have happened then except for a casual remark by Jeff. He had brought home from the Blue Ridge a mongrel puppy given him by Doc Wicker, who said every boy ought to have a dog. The Doc further averred, and one may suppose his testimony accurate, that the pup Sandy was sired by Shep. Sandy MacShep, or sometimes Sandy FitzShep, were his full entitles, and when Uncle Dan and Jeff set off for an afternoon walk that First Day (Aunt Bee pleaded headache) the boy said, "I don't know what's the matter with Sandy, he acts just like Shep did the day of the flood."

There was another reason too (how many more reasons there are for everything than one suspects) why Jeff was suddenly and copiously reminiscent. At lunch Uncle Dan accused him for the first time of being Grown Up, and though Jeff felt with relief that this was not really so, yet it created a subtle feeling of companionship and assurance. The reason for the impeachment was that Uncle Dan had discovered that with his Christmas money Jeff had gone downtown to Strauss's and bought for himself (it should stand in capitals in any biography) His First Book. It cost 19¢ in the January clearance sale at Strauss's and Uncle Dan was rather thrilled when he noticed it, *Rubaiyat of Omar Khayyam*—and written on the flyleaf in a labored youthful script, *Ex Libris Geoffrey Barton*. Dan wondered where on earth the boy had picked up the "ex libris," a tag which he himself had outgrown.

But this precocious accident, and perhaps the fact that Aunt Bee was not with them, led to unusually candid talk. As they went up Key Street Avenue Extended and through the chinquapin grove Jeff was finishing the account of the tragedy at Sandy Hole.

"It's funny the way things happen," he reflected. "There was so much to do, with chopping out poor old Hessie and sending word to the Major, and then part of the excelsior mill was flooded and fell down, gosh, it was like Caesar; you know, everything had to be done by Caesar *eodem tempore*, at the same time."

"I know how it is," said Uncle Dan.

"Anyhow it was all hunky-dory because two days later when we drove Teack and Trundle down to the train Aunt Bee said 'Cheese, I forgot to forward Dan's letter.'"

"I can't imagine her saying that," said Uncle Dan, "but go on."

"That very minute a boy comes out from the telegraph office with that telegram for Aunt Bee."

"What telegram was that?" Uncle Dan asked.

Jeff realized he had gone farther than he intended, but he couldn't pull back now. "Why, the telegram from Possum. Gosh, maybe—aw shucks, you know, about the letter you didn't get—"

"I haven't the faintest idea what you're talking about."

"Well, you can imagine that with everything happening like it was I didn't have a Chinaman's chance to go forwarding letters and especially when it would take about ten cents extra postage for foreign mail. Aunt Bee's wrist was broken, I didn't like to ask her to go fumbling in her purse. And a good thing too, Aunt Bee said when she got the telegram."

"For heaven's sake, what did the telegram say?"

"Well, I guess as man to man, if you don't know you better

382

had. It was from Chicago and it said 'Do not forward letter to your brother, please destroy it.' Ten words, I bet mathematicians know their decimal system. Signed 'Blanche Bristol.' "

Uncle Dan mumbled something to himself which Jeff pretended not to hear. "Did she destroy it?" he asked.

"It's a cinch Aunt Bee never destroys anything. She's too smart. She was right busy until the undertaker got poor old Hessie fixed up. Teack and I were busy too. We were burying Shep back of the barn. I bet there's no dog in America ever had a better-looking sepulcher. You know how he always loved to chivvy the cows around. Well, we buried him out there by Doc Wicker's old bathtub where the cows drink. If Doc Wicker had cared about taking baths they wouldn't have put that tub out in the pasture for the cows' drinking fountain, and if Aunt Bee had been able to take a regular bath she wouldn't have taught herself not to be scared in the water. I swear I don't know why Sandy behaves this way. He doesn't seem to enjoy his walk. I hope we're not going to have any more calamities."

But Uncle Dan, with perhaps forgivable egotism, was putting together a jigsaw puzzle of his own. "She didn't destroy it? You mean she kept it?"

"No sirree, she had me put it in a new envelope and she mailed it back to Blanche herself. Registered Mail, too. I was with her and Cy Banks had to look up in his book how you register letters. He said they hadn't done it at Slabtown in a coon's age."

At the far side of Carroll Woods they sat down to rest on a fallen trunk of chestnut. Uncle Dan rooted thoughtfully in the ground with the ferrule of his stick. Jeff practiced owl whistles through his cupped hands, but was not yet up to Teackle's skill. Sandy did not seem happy, instead of scouting about as usual, he stayed close and sniffed the air. "Jeff, it's queer you should tell me all this just now," Uncle Dan said presently. "I wondered why I never got that steamer letter, but it didn't matter because when I came back I got one that more than made up for it. It's funny, though, Aunt Bee never said anything to me about it."

"Aunt Bee's like that," said Jeff, in this new mastery of human motives tentatively labeled Grown Up. "If she thinks you don't need to know anything she certainly keeps her mouth shut."

"There's something you need to know," said Uncle Dan in a tone that made Jeff feel as though he himself were the uncle. "There's going to be a vacancy in the math department at Patapsco. They've offered it to Blanche, and after college gets out this spring she's coming to live with us."

Dan need not have been so bashful, for Jeff immediately reverted from the unfamiliar and difficult role of adult. "Hot dog, that's slick—but where will she sleep? Will I have to move out of the good ole cave?—Or no, I suppose you'll sleep in your study all the time."

"Maybe not—you see—well, I mean—damn it all, she's going to marry me."

"Gosh. Well anyway, we'll always know when Easter is."

"Gee whiz, somebody certainly spilled the beans in the frying pan," said Jeff as they came out of the woods on their way home. "I bet that's why Sandy acts queer."

South of them the whole of downtown Chesapeake was covered by rolling billows of smoke; even though the strong northwest wind was blowing it away from their quarter they imagined they could smell burning. There was a distant thud and a pale waft of flame lit the curls of black and yellow reek. "Explosions, too," said Jeff exultantly. "Gee, Uncle Dan, it looks like the Chesapeake colors, orange and black. Good thing there's no school today, the boys would be saying those ole British have landed on Fort McHenry."

Across Division Street people were out in the vacant lot watching the sky. "Lucky the wind's blowing like it is," said

384

someone. "They say the whole of downtown's burning. Explosion in some warehouse down on German Street."

"I heard the watchman took time off to go to church, while he was saying his prayers the wind scattered sparks all over town."

Aw shucks, I bet that's just a story, Jeff thought. Probly watchmen don't go to church.

Star and Bert came racing from the bluff by Sassafras House. "Hear the news?" they shouted. "The whole town's on fire. There's engines coming from Washington already. Gee, even from Philadelphia."

"My father's goin' down to his office in a few minutes," said Star, "try to save his papers. I bet a lot of those ole clients would rather they'd burn up but he says it's professional duty. I'm goin' with him to help. He's got to get a whole mess of last will and testaments out of tin boxes. Carrying papers from a burning building!" he exclaimed proudly.

"I'm going over to the pospital with Hop," cried Bert, unconsciously transposing in excitement. "He's got some ole patient over there in the G.U. ward, he says she might get burned up. Wanta come along, Jeff? You can help carry 'em out."

"Gee, can I?" Jeff begged.

"Sorry, old boy, but if it's as serious as it looks it's no place for youngsters. You'd only be in the way."

Jeff was aghast. "You mean to say you'd let the whole damn town burn up and not let me have a hand in it?" Even the admitted supremacy of his Museum of Relics, collected later from what Chesapeake so long knew as the Burned District, never quite atoned. Other boys whose families had business downtown helped in the race against flame and dynamite. But Uncle Dan was only a prof.

Ingram Sylvester Duffle was a comfort: he also was forbidden to go downtown. They left the anxious Sandy shut in the cellar and spent most of two days and nights watching from North Avenue Bridge. Sometimes a change of wind blew burning scraps and cinders in their direction and Ingram was elated to chase and stamp them out. No citizen has ever forgotten the great fog of smoke and burning that lasted so long. "It smells worse than Friends' Meeting," said Ingram, almost relieved that his own errors were forgotten in larger woe. The flames were so alive, so terrifying, it was hard not to think them conscious with malevolence. "The big fiends," Ingram muttered, standing in his long overcoat against the railing of the bridge.

Aunt Bee agreed. "It really looks like hell-fire," she said. "I dessay it's a judgment." In the panorama of rioting flame stood momentary outlines of shattered masonry, jagged and black against fury beyond. That same Sunday other fiery news had been ticking in (from Port Arthur), but the Chesapeake papers, printed out of town, had no room for it. It looked indeed like the end of their world, and long later Jeff remembered how his boyhood closed with a curtain of red light.

THOROFARE

64. *The Foxhole*

The Fuchshoehle or Foxhole, a modest German rathskeller much favored by Chesapeake students, was on the yonder side of Lexington Market. Indeed it was almost opposite the shop where Jeff and Skinny used to buy the dividend-bearing chocolate mice and contrive a glimpse of Nick Carter. It was a pity, Skinny said one time, that their reading of Nick Carter and Old Sleuth had to be so "surreptious." Why parents were prohibitory about these pamphlets no one has ever known: their melodrama was no more ferocious than Captain Mayne Reid and their prose style not much more grievous than that of Mr. Bowser.

But one would not have reminded the T.S.O. 4 of these juvenilia just now. It was the spring vacation of senior year, already most of the routine class-work was over and they felt themselves on the brow of a hilltop of assurance. From there they would coast in a glory of awareness and alarm toward Finals. Though classmates, they had followed different sports and studies; this last of college breathing-spells gave them opportunity for a small reunion with tankards.

Fortunately for human composure no one has ever recap-

387

tured the rich complacent gravity of that mood. It would be unbearable, for everything subsequent in life would seem flat. "Bliss was it in that dawn to be alive": perhaps old Daddy came as close to it as anyone. Jeff defined it one time, quite by accident. A complicated telephone call had to be transmitted to Uncle Dan, who was at that moment in the bathtub. "Come in," said the bather, "the door isn't locked. Just a moment. I can't hear you." Jeff was astonished to see Uncle Dan, sprawled in the old tin tub, raise his left foot and turn off the pouring faucet with his toes. "Gee whiz," said Jeff, "I didn't know anyone else ever did that. I thought I invented it."

The T.S.O. 4 thought they invented the kind of feelings they were enjoying. Young men have their first love among taverns as in anything else. The Fuchshoehle was their Mermaid, their Cheshire Cheese, their Salutation & Cat. It would be an abominable liberty for Mr. Sprunt or any other philosophic observer who saw them on the way to their innocent Bohemia to embarrass them by recognizing the universal pattern. They were gloriously unconscious of padded shoulders and sharp-cut lapels, of pompadour haircuts, pegtop trousers and pointed wide-welt shoes. Derby hats and waisted overcoats, tall starched collars and narrow knitted neckties, might be comedians' fortune long enough later, but were then the natural protective coloring of their kind. The derby hat was no less proud an emblem than a young warrior's helmet. Only in the historian's morbid trade do man's blessed taken-for-granteds become falsely grotesque.

They were so absorbed in conversation, at their favorite corner table, they forgot to snap down the pewter lids and Fritz had already brought another round of beer. Skinny volunteered to pay for this one because he was on his way to sell some old textbooks. He produced several from under his chair as evidence. "*All-Night Algebra*," he said. (Hall & Knight's austere treatise was always so called.) "Thank God I won't need that any more." He opened to a flyleaf covered with somber notations and assignments. "Gosh, I was certainly proud when I wrote my name in there; that was the first time I wrote *C. W. Granger, '11.*"

They passed the book round the table with luxurious sentimentalism. "We were mighty young then, weren't we?" said Star. "Look at poor Skinny's freshman handwriting."

"When I first wrote *G. Barton, '11* I didn't suppose 1911 would ever really come. Living at 1910 somehow I figured that was as far as anything went."

"Suppose you were one of the kids taking entrance exams this spring," said Bert. "They'll be class of 1915. My God, imagine! Come to think of it, though, I'll be '15 at medical school. It's terrible, the century will be age of puberty, most anything might happen."

"What makes me feel old," said Star, "I don't see Skinny weep any more. I've got to hand it to you, Skinny. I bet you haven't cried in public since Freshman Algebra."

"He wears spectacles now," said Bert. "It's toughened those lachrymal ducts."

"Aaah nuts," Skinny retorted. "I've had enough beer to do it now if you insist." To his horror he felt his eyelids grow warm but the worst that happened was a fog on his lenses. The light was dim in their corner and no one noticed.

"Maybe the English idea is better," Jeff suggested. "Uncle Dan says at Cambridge and Oxford they don't reckon by dates that way, so when you're an old man out of college maybe five or ten years you're not embarrassed by always having your numerals tagged onto you."

"You were pretty proud of yours, G-offrey, when you made Freshman football team. Jesus, we used to think you probably slept in that sweater the way you wore it everywhere."

"Remember, you big bum, you're still an alien," said Bert. "If you go around allowing the Limey way is better, we'll turn up at the cohthouse when you apply for citizenship and say you ain't loyal."

"Spheroids, pillules, vesicles," said Jeff.

"Nobody needs a dictionary of synonyms if they trail around with G. Barton, '11," said Skinny. "I thought this meeting was called to celebrate his birthday. It's about time we drank his health." This involved a scuffle of backpounding and mugclinking but there was always plenty of noise in the Fuchshoehle and no one paid any attention.

"Have you handed in your thesis?" asked Skinny.

"Yes, and I wish I hadn't," Jeff answered. "As soon as I dropped it in the box I began to think of things I hadn't covered."

"Ain't it a hell of a note," said Star. "I was writing about Constitutional Dilemmas in the Missouri Compromise, and I just saved myself from putting 54-40 when I meant 36-30. That would have been Alaska instead of Louisiana."

"Remember the time at school when Bill Shawbuck got the Missouri Compromise mixed up with the Mississippi Bubble."

"What's your thesis on, Jeff?" asked Bert. "About junior year every fellow gets interested in his own line and loses touch with the others. I've been so busy in biology lab I scarcely know what you-all are up to, except of course I know Jeff's one of the literary fellers. They tell me you've written a grand piece for the yearbook in the style of Sir Roger de Coverley."

"I'm not offensively literary," said Jeff. "I guess my uncle was surprised but I changed over to major in economics."

"*E*economics?" jibed Star. "What was the matter with *eck*onomics?"

"Nothing, except that I looked up the etymology of the word," said Jeff good-humoredly. "I expect Chesapeake is the only college in America where they pronounce it right."

"Well, if you're going to be so all-fired meticulous," said Skinny, "you better call it *oi*conomics. It comes from the Greek *oikos*." Skinny was still their classical authority.

"Three long rays for scaly-assed Scholiast Granger, '11," shouted Star, the cheer was given and stein-lids left open for Fritz's attention.

Jeff resumed: "I got to feeling that literature was too much fun to be a good specialty, if you know what I mean."

"I certainly don't," said Bert. "Maybe this Pilsener will help, though."

Jeff struggled to explain. "Too remote, too Olympian sort of, like those gods in Tennyson's poem reclining on the mountain and looking down on struggling humanity. Seeing things through other people's emotions instead of having emotions of your own."

"If it's the Greek gods you're talking about," said Skinny, "they weren't very remote and standoffish. Appears to me they must have been bored by being gods, for they took every possible opportunity of mixing with human beings. Mostly with the ladies."

"Bet there was a Nobody Home sign on Olympus most of the time," Star suggested. "While they were all out fussing."

"I want to enjoy literature, not pick it to pieces," Jeff insisted.

"I'll admit one thing," Skinny said, gazing blandly through his glasses, in an intellectual ecstasy. "In literature everything has been said already, and said perfectly. But the oiconomists express themselves so badly, you must feel encouraged."

"Piffle! Take Veblen, for instance. His book about the Leisure Class is enchanting; why, it's more amusing than Mark Twain. I read some of it aloud at home and even Aunt Bee laughed."

"The British sense of humor was always mysterious," Bert observed.

"No kidding, there's something tremendously actual about the laws of economics."

"Hold on, wait a minute, old top," cried Star. "That's a horse of another horse. What do you mean, the *laws* of economics? Those aren't laws, those are just statistics."

"I reiterate, piffle," Jeff exclaimed. They were all leaning forward over their mugs. "Preserve old Star from wrong," burlesqued Skinny. "Through him the most ancient fallacies are fresh and strong."

Jeff was full of zeal: "They're every bit as much laws as your poor little judicial statutes and sanctions. What is a law anyhow? It's something that's just got to happen, invariably. Behind those statistics you can damn well see something looking at you, like the Great Stone Face."

"The army of unalterable law," said Skinny solemnly. "Ever read any Meredith?"

"Jeff skids over an argument like Sliding Billy Watson," said Bert, a faithful student of the burlesque wheel. "Meanwhile you haven't answered my question. What's your thesis about?"

"I've got a grand subject: The Social Effects of a Municipal Disaster."

"What was that, the time we persuaded Ingram to go swimming with the sea-lions? Poor old Ingram, no wonder he had those fits. Let's drink his health." They did so with the appropriate ejaculation, "You big fiends!"

"I mean the Fire, of course, how the town thought it was licked, insurance companies busted, even the mayor committed suicide. And then look how it started new streets and sewers and wiped out a lot of those old alleys and mosquitoes and typhoid fever. Why, this is getting to be almost a modern city."

"You always were excited about the Fire," said Star. "How sore you were because you couldn't go downtown with the rest of us."

"I remember Professor Barton dragging him away from North Avenue Bridge one night and Jeff looking back at the fire over his shoulder—it was like Aeneas and Ascanius at the burning of Troy."

"Well, it was some conflagration, believe you me," said Star, "but fen we lay off theses. I've been giving my days and nights to the study of Blackstone and I'd like to forget about work a while. What are you-all going to do this summer?"

Skinny and Jeff looked at each other. "Shall we tell them?"

"We've been keeping it a secret," Jeff said, "but Skinny and I had a great idea. We're going to work our way over to England on one of the cattle-boats and we'll have a couple of weeks over there to see what things look like. I want to see Wilford again. I haven't been there since I was eight years old. I bet it's a comical little place."

"I tell him he better not like it too much," said Skinny, "or he may regret becoming an American citizen."

"Seems a funny idea," said Bert, "the minute you get to be an American you want to see the Old Country again. But you always were kind of ridiculous. I hope you'll be good and sea-sick."

"You better get some tips from Mr. Sprunt on how to make friends with cattle," said Star. "Those steers can be right ornery when you have to make their beds for them. Don't get foot-and-mouth disease."

"Speakin' of mouth disease," said Bert, "you've just gotten over that English accent you used to have. For God's sake don't revive it." He declaimed a muffled falsetto which he fondly be-lieved was English undefiled: "I say, Sandringham old chap, cry tallyho to the parlormaid. I'm perishing for a blighter.—Or is it a bloater?" he queried.

"Did you hear about that English poet that lectured here a few weeks ago?" Skinny asked. "First he said he'd been in a Pullman all night and was jolly well knocked up; the students all laughed like fools and he couldn't imagine why. Then he went on to talk about Tennyson's 'Iddles of the King.' I thought I'd pass out."

"Americans have to have an English lecturer to play with every once and so often," said Bert. "Look at the way they car-ried on about Oscar Wilde, poor bloater."

"If you go over there be sure to take your umbrella," Star advised. "And you better take your tuck, viz.: dinner jacket. In case old squire invites you for a cut off the joint at Little Orse-manure, Scrag End, Slopshire. What, what?" He screwed an imaginary monocle into his eye and gaped with lowered jaw.

"Don't forget, if they offer you a small Bass it's a drink, not a fish."

"The worst thing that ever happened for the English was the invention of the dinner jacket," Bert exclaimed. "What's the only kind of clothes America ever invented: good old hard-working overalls."

"Well, there's one thing you got to hand them," said Star. "When other nationalities get your goat at least you know they did it a-purpose. The English do it unconsciously."

Jeff was well inured to this sort of chaff. Perhaps his even humor was one quality of what they were criticizing. Poor English, he thought; how they get it in the neck—even from themselves. He decided this was not the moment to enlarge on his private feelings about the projected voyage. A quite different thought came to his mind. "There was something in *Grimm's Fairy Tales* that used to tickle me," he said presently. "When the old man dies and his sons set out to seek their fortunes, they start along the road and come to a place where it splits several ways. They stop at the signpost and argue and then each one takes a different road. That always seemed to me the most exciting moment in the whole story. One of them gets to a castle with a malevolent sorcerer in it, and another to a cottage with a pretty girl hanging her goldilocks hair out of the window, and another one meets an old woman whose keg of beer has sprung a leak, or maybe it's a maidservant with red heels or climbing the beanstalk or whatever, all those old fables —but just for a minute the boys are all there by the signpost and nobody knows what's what. That's what I call drama, it makes me feel monstrous full of fleas."

"Well, we can take a ballot right here if we like," said Star. "Sentimental G-offrey I suppose would vote for the blonde flapper. I hope she's a pippin. I'm for the beer keg with a leak in it. Fritz, *nun noch ein mehr.*"

Jeff's parable, though casual and not specially eloquent, emphasized to them all how satisfying was the romance of their lot. When did any table of plain wood look so clean-scrubbed or smell so malty? In what shadowy corner of the world's many taverns were such lovable and masculine adventurers gathered together? What Gothic rafters more stained with smoke or seasoned with good cheer? Where—not even in fabled Heidelberg, they felt sure—could there be more handsome an array of giant mugs and staghorns? The symbolic fox's mask over the archway twinkled at them with glassy eyes—a gaze more than once returned by patrons equally glassy.

"One thing I like about this place," said Star, "is its Akademische Freiheit."

"Bummeljahr!" ejaculated Jeff. He and Star had taken a beginners' course in German with the distressing result that after a few steins of beer they felt a bohemian necessity to practice the few phrases they had acquired. They believed perhaps they were doing the good Saxon Fritz a benevolence by ventilating these echoes of his mother larynx. In fact Jeff had even been heard to criticize Fritz's pronunciation, which he said was barbarous German, not the true Hanoverian. Fritz's tact, however, was never so strained as when Star asked him if their talking German made him homesick.

"Academic freedom," Star insisted blithely, "the way students and profs and musicians and everybody get together in here on equal terms, just good humor and good fellowship and talk about things that really amount to something. Look at that bunch of funny ole fossils over there in the corner. They only take about two beers and a sandwich the whole evening but they have a grand time and sing songs. You see people in here who are really great artists—excuse me," he added, shaken by a gust of malt in his windpipe. "It was the Mississippi Bubble."

"Three long rays for F. S. K. Lanvale, '11," Jeff proposed.

"Thank you, gentlemen, thank you. I will rejoin you shortly, I want to see a man about a dog. Tell Fritz the next round's on me."

The usually moderate Skinny found his glasses humid with

fellowship and good cheer. "Hitch my flagon to a Star," he ejaculated. "Bright Star, would I were steadfast as thou art."

F. S. K. Lanvale paused for their united attention. He stated solemnly: "All puns are detestable, but learned puns are worst."

In the interim of Star's absence each of them thought what a marvelous time they were having. How unkind it would have been to tell them that even their bold japes and ribaldries were really the young man's shy defense against experience. Fritz brought another round of beer.

"This disproves the oiconomists," Skinny glimmered round the flap of his seidel. "The law of diminishing returns doesn't operate."

"Even Wordsworth got pickled once," Jeff admitted.

"How about Economic Man?" inquired Bert. "Isn't he in a constant judicious equipoise among marginal utilities?"

"Economic Man is only an intellectual fragment," declared Jeff. "I mean figment. Intellectual figment."

"He's an enigma in the woodpile," cried Skinny triumphantly.

"Well, you better not say so until you've passed Finals," Bert advised. "You know the proverb, call the bear Uncle until you get across the bridge."

They saw Star weaving his way back, past the table where the older patrons were making merry. He was greeting the professors with gracious and encouraging gestures, and waving time to the accordion Fritz had brought out.

"Star ain't as steadfast as we thought," said Bert.

"You know what Fritz calls that thing?" Star reported. "He says when he was a steward in the North German Lloyd they called it Nordseeklavier. North Sea piano. That's a very fine figure of speech. Jeff, is that a trope or a metaphor?"

"It's a semaphore," said Skinny. "If you ask me, I think those old men are very infra dig. Old profs like that drinking and singing and clowning themselves. They ought to be more teleological, at their age. Don't they know what Dr. Osler said?"

"He never said it," objected Bert. "My father says he was brutally misquoted in the papers."

"It got into the vulgate, and when anything gets into the vulgate you've got to accept it as a folk-saying. Useless to contradict a Volkssage. Look at that ole Dr. Friedeck. He ought to be home working on his Sanskrit philology or something."

"Is Friedeck there?" asked Jeff. "I didn't see him behind that other fellow's beard. He's probably dividing Languedoc by Languedoil."

"I bet the beer's too strong for him," said Bert. "The top of that noble porcelain bean is quite pink."

"Akademische Freiheit," Star repeated. "Bert, don't talk premedical shop. Just because you been writing thesis on blood pressure you see spigmometers everywhere—I guess I mean sphygmometers."

"If you mean anything, which I doubt, you mean sphygmomanometers. Anyway a little more blood pressure won't do us any harm. Here's to Jeff, the big fiend."

"I don't care if his head's pink or not," said Jeff. "I wish I knew as much as he's got inside of it." Solemnly all four leaned sideways and peered admiringly at the egglike pate of the Indo-European scholar. It was one of the last unconscious gestures of their undergraduate life: how often the stricken student contemplates some professorial skull wishing its contents might be painlessly transfused. Fortunately the learned Doctor was absorbed in edging his tenor into the harmony of *Am Schwarzen Walfisch zu Askalon*. He and other Teuton colleagues always met on Saturday afternoon at the Fuchshoehle and usually floated into the madrigals of their youth.

"I took one of his courses," said Skinny. "I thought it would give me some background. He told me I was wasting my time with Latin and Greek, they're practically modern slang compared to Sanskrit. He's a great scholar but he's got a mighty bad temper."

"Let's not have a bad temper," said Star. "What I like about good old T.S.O. 4 is we've all impuggened each other so long we don't mind. No use getting het up like that gal Jeff used to talk about, what was her name?" His voice was lost in the hollow of his mug. It sounded like "Sophie Pitkin."

"Sufi Pipkin, waxing hot," Skinny quoted, winking at Jeff. This was a password of their own from the *Rubaiyat*.

"That's her, Sophie Pitkin," asserted Star. "Jeff took her out to the ballgame one day. I saw them. Boy, she's a lulu. Kind of young, though."

"I like them young and fugitive," Skinny said. "Like Horace's Hinnuleo. Odes I, 23."

"Twenty-three yourself," said Jeff. "It's very bad manners to discuss a lady in a public place."

"Wasn't discussing, just mentioning," Star apologized. "I thought this was Akademische Freiheit. If a man can't discuss at his ease in his inn, what can he? Want to do something to celebrate Jeff's toga virilis. If those old men in the corner can sing, why can't we? We got rudiments of a glee club right here at this table. Fritz, give my compliments to those old minnesingers. Tell them to hush up a minute and we'll sing them some rudiments." Without further preface he warbled *Hallelujah I'm a Bum*, and his companions loyally supported him. "Hallelujah, give us a handout to revive us again," they sang with barber-shop enthusiasm which was applauded, ironically perhaps, by patrons at other tables.

It was a mistake to encourage Star in any musical escapade. His taste was indeed rudimentary and always declined toward *Sweet Adeline* and *The Old Millstream*. Fearing this Jeff and Skinny tried to divert the argument and the Teuton gleemen began another of their choruses. But the song they chose was provocative, it included (after enough beer) a North Sea piano suggestion of a bugle call. Star was captivated.

"Say, that's out of sight," he exclaimed. "I want to learn that song. Fritz, you write down the words for me."

"I remember that," said Jeff. "I heard old Dr. Friedeck play it years ago on board ship. Something about morning red, to-morrow morning I'll be dead."

"A very pretty song," said Fritz.

> *"Ach wie bald, ach wie bald*
> *Schwindet Schoenheit und Gestalt!"*

"Write it down for me," insisted Star. Fritz did so labori-ously. Star examined the Gothic script and cackled. "Oh how bald, Oh how bald," he mistranslated. "It's certainly the right song for those old geezers. Yumping Yiminy, the words are wonderful:

> *Prahlst du gleich mit deinen Wangen*
> *Die wie Milch und Purpur prangen,*
> *Ach die Rosen welken bald!*

Milk and purple, just what old Friedeck looks like. I'll put it into English for you. I can write poetry too. Jeff, what's a rhyme for bald?"

"Caterwauled," Jeff suggested.

"The very word."

Star wrote busily on a menu card. "All together, boys," he commanded, "How's this?" He lilted his own version of tune and words:

> "Oh how ba-ald, Oh how ba-ald,
> Swindled beauty caterwauled.
> Though your cheeks are sleek and shi-iny,
> Glittering and milk-and-wi-iny,
> Youth can never be recalled.

Not bad! Now if Fritz will give us the accompaniment—"

But Fritz was playing another song for the rival table. The boys joined the infectious rhythm, beating mugs on the board at the end of each line:

> *"Der Sultan lebt in Saus und Schmaus,*
> *Saus und Schmaus!*
> *Er wohnt in einem grossen Haus,*
> *Grossen Haus!*
> *Voll wunderschoener Maegdelein*
> *O Maegdelein!*
> *Ich moechte doch auch Sultan sein."*

"Prachtvoll!" Star applauded, with an appropriate Mississippi bubble. "That's literature! Saus und Schmaus! How do you translate Saus?"

"Look in the mirror."

"Right back at them; come on, Fritz, give us the music." And Star burst into "H, A, Double R, I, G, A, N spells Harrigan."

Perhaps no feelings would have suffered except that Kapellmeister Friedeck decided he was hungry and called for the menu. It was too bad that the one Fritz brought had been scribbled over with Star's version of Dr. Friedeck's most nostalgic song. He read it and was purple rather than milk. He strode over to their table and took the young men by surprise. They stood up, wavering but courteous; Jeff was eager to pay respects to the old fellow after so many years.

"Do you remember me, Professor?" he said politely. "Geoffrey Barton." Then, in the fumes of hilarity and from some buried nucleus of memory he exclaimed: *"Hast du Eier gerne frisch? Setz das Huhn gleich auf den Tisch."*

The remark was ill chosen; and Star made it worse by waving an arm to introduce their quartet and ejaculating *"Frisch, frei, froh, fromm!"* This he had been told in class was the motto of German student clubs. And poor Skinny, now a trifle stupored, made the unfortunate echo: "Fee, fi, fo, fum."

"Frisch is the word well chosen," said the angry professor. "You are exceedingly impudent disgusting young men. And you, Barton; no, I have not forgotten. I was going to ask you for a gentleman's apology."

"Akademische Freiheit, Professor," babbled Star, wagging a reproachful finger.

"I see you are still the same." Dr. Friedeck glared at Jeff. "Evidently you set your irresponsible companions on to ridicule your elders and betters. I don't even dignify you by asking you should behave as a gentleman. Pfui!"

The T.S.O. 4 were grieved and sobered by this unpleasant interruption. "Why the ole Sophie Pitkin," said Star.

"You ought to have known better," said Bert. "Germans can't stand kidding."

"Listen, you can't indict a nation," said Jeff, feeling rather miserable.

Skinny roused from his swoon. "Hell's bells," he said, "sometimes they force you to.—Le's order some schnitzel, not going pious Unitarian home like this. Jeff, you please telephone my mother souse, accidental contraction, my mother's house."

"One more seidel," said Jeff. "To drown the memory of that insolence. Prosimus!"

65. *Economic Man*

Thursday, when Moxie's destroying grasp was absent from the kitchen "zink," was the day for High Tea; and really high, for Aunt Blanche had brought apostle spoons (from the old rectory near Much Wenlock) as part of her dowry. These were balanced on the other side of the house by the Wilford egg cozies, the best Thorofare china, and the Sheffield steel knives— now worn thin as stilettos by Moxie's abrasive hand. Thursday tea, spread on the dining-room table, with sausage rolls and boiled eggs, plenty of thin bread and peanut butter and if possible both gooseberry and damson jams, was Jeff's idea of the top of the week. On Sunday tea had to be in the drawing-room, for there were likely to be callers. But Thursdays were just for themselves. Any outsider who came then would have thought the Bartons were all bickering, but it was only the most ancient

Anglo-Saxon rite of mutual contradiction. Aunt Bee, who presided over the silver teapot and huge earthenware jug of hot water, said less than the others but was always an acute arbiter. Sandy scoured the outskirts for bits of sausage roll; and even the alley cat Ampersand, whom Aunt Bee had salved from some feline camorra, knew when it was Thursday and came scratching at the dining-room window. She had only three and a half legs and Jeff noticed that when she sat to her toilet raising her stump she had the profile of the symbol &; hence her name.

"I know why Uncle Dan married Possum," said Jeff. "He knew she had some apostle spoons. That really makes it Much Wedlock. It's a good thing we have tea in the dining-room, so Possum can smoke. If Dr. Beinbrink knew about it she'd be fired. Have a Fa*tima*?"

"I'll have a *Fat*ima, please," said Blanche.

Jeff's approaching Americanism had specially sensitized him to pronunciations. "It's amusing how the English always put the accent as near the front as possible," he said. "Look how they say *de*tails, *de*corous, *all*ies, *app*licable, *hos*pitable."

"How about *lab*oratory?" asked Dan. "In Cambridge they like to say la*bor*atry. And ca*pit*alist."

"Exception proves the rule," said Jeff. "Yes, yes," he hurried to add, "I know; *proves* the rule means *tests* the rule. Skeat, page 78."

"American pronunciation, when left to itself, is Elizabethan," said Uncle Dan. "If Oliver Twist lived in Chesapeake he wouldn't ask for more, he'd ask for moe—like Shakespeare."

"Americans speak slower than English," said Blanche. "They don't make up their minds how they'll pronounce a word until they've already started it. That's why they delay the accent."

"Why be so snobbish about pronunciation?" said Aunt Bee. "It's not a matter of right or wrong, it's just what's customary."

"Of course right and wrong exist only in mathematical problems," Uncle Dan suggested sadly.

"Nuts vobiscum," cried Jeff. "What a time Skinny and I

402

are going to have learning the language on our trip this summer. I've been rehearsing him. When we get to London should we checkwee in at an Otel, or go to a block of flats? And ask for the lift?"

"What will you do without your monkeynut-butter?" asked Aunt Bee ironically.

"Literature's more perplexing than mathematics," continued Uncle Dan, "because you can't always tell what's right or wrong. I was correcting papers this afternoon and look what I found: 'Though Shelley fell into unfortunate creeds he had unquestionably a soul.' How would you assess that statement?"

"Put a note of admiration in the margin," said Blanche.

"The girl's living in a sleeping-bag," said Jeff.

"Literary criticism is only butter in a lordly dish," Blanche teased. "Of course it's all mush because the symbols are different to each individual. There are four different symbolisms in that poor child's statement: Shelley, fortune, creed, and soul. How can you possibly guess what they mean to her—she probably doesn't know herself."

"Mathematics must be very grim," said Dan. "When you make a mistake it isn't even amusing; it's simply wrong."

"At least in math you have a chance to see students learning to reason; not just feel, or suspect, or adumbrate—"

"*Adum*brate!" Jeff interrupted.

"Perhaps you get better students in math," said Dan. "Or if not actually better, in a better frame of mind. At least they come to class resolved to try to use their deductive faculties. What you don't realize is, English is supposed to be a snap course."

"Ghastly phrase," said Blanche.

"A leadpipe cinch, if you prefer," Jeff offered. "That's what I'm telling you, Uncle Dan's too easy on these girls. No wonder they vote him their favorite prof, he just encourages their vile sirupy sentimentality."

Dan finished his sausage roll before attempting to reply.

"Dessay it all looks fairly simple at twenty-one," he said, wiping crumbs of pastry. "But I cry out, hoping not to be quoted, that a certain amount of wholesome sentiment is all most of 'em are fit for. They're doomed already by obdurate—ob*dur*ate—frivolity or extreme poverty of mind. My dear Jeff, to encourage their timid leanings toward satire or reasoning power would only frighten away the earnest young men—like you—who will have to support them."

Jeff was appalled. "Why, you darned old cynic!"

Uncle Dan cackled cheerfully. "I was telling one of my classes about Queen Elizabeth having a levee in her bedchamber. Professor, said one of the girls, what was that for, to keep the river out?"

"I have my troubles too," said Blanche. "After chapel the other day I thought I'd give my freshmen a problem that my old father used to worry his curates with. The board in the chapel where Miss Beamish puts up the numbers of the hymns has four grooves. Suppose there are 700 hymns in the hymnal—"

"Goodness, are there as many as that?" Jeff exclaimed.

"Well, including canticles and plainsong I expect there are."

"It's just as well Aunt Bee sticks to Quaker Meeting," said Jeff. "Did you ever hear her sing? Excuse me, Possum, I didn't go to be rude."

"I'm sorry to be so liturgical in a Quaker household," said Blanche. "Anyway, the problem is, what's the smallest number of cards, each carrying one digit, Miss Beamish must keep in stock so that the numbers of any four different hymns can be posted on the board?"

"Jeez—I mean phew; that's worse than Seager on Marginal Utility."

"Can a 9 upside down be used for a 6 and vice versa?" asked Aunt Bee.

"You're very acute," said Blanche. "It makes a difference in the parish budget."

404

"Don't make it worse," cried Jeff, holding his head in caricature of anguish. "I wouldn't know how to begin. I bet you'd need a couple of hundred cards."

"You'll never make an economist," said Blanche. "The answer's eighty-one. But the point is that one of the girls came up to me afterward and said the problem was sacrilegious."

"I expect she said sacreligious," said Dan.

"She did. They're nice enough girls, quick-witted and high-spirited and very anxious to please, but not much of what we used to call *nous*."

"Known round here as using the old bean," said Jeff.

"I've learned to tone down the strong poison of mathematics to suit their capacity; but it doesn't dilute easily. They're extraordinarily feminine, aren't they? I don't wonder they all get soft on Dan."

Blanche still looked very girlish herself, with her cropped curly hair and small figure. Dan went round to her side of the table and leaned over to give her a consoling hug. "I never should have lured you away from Radnor," he said. "I suppose the students there were all perfect Pi."

"Uncle loves Auntie," said Jeff, sneaking the last slice of cake. "Possum, you're his musical snuffbox. Reference to John Stuart Mill, chapter on Demand and Supply. Mill quotes it from De Quincey, but I expect it's in one of the volumes Uncle Dan didn't get. You're Economic Man in a steamboat on Lake Superior on your way to the wilds of the far far West. One of your fellow passengers has a musical snuffbox and you conceive a vehement desire to own it. It has a strange magic to lull your agitated mind. You've simply got to have it to soothe you in the wilderness. At last, after some De Quinceyan purple passages, you pay sixty guineas for it, though you could have bought one in London for six. This proves that Difficulty of Attainment plays the deuce with Intrinsic Value."

"You're suggesting Dan paid more for me than I'm worth?"

Jeff winked at her. "Just a parable," he said.

"Perhaps Miss Hoo will have a musical snuffbox."

"I doubt it," said Uncle Dan, "but Grandma still has the old Swiss thing, you can play *The Blue Bells of Scotland*."

"I'd be afraid to," said Jeff, "music has been ruined for me by listening to you do *The North Wind Doth Blow*." It was a sad fact that in ten years Uncle Dan had never progressed beyond this exercise.

"If you're going to take Skinny to Wilford with you," said Aunt Bee, "break him in gently. It's sometimes quite a shock to young Americans to find England so much more comfortable than this go-ahead country."

"Be sure to have a game of bowls with Harry Bredfield. He'll beat you with his left hand but that will please him."

"I hope the old white horse is still pulling the freight cars," said Jeff.

"Goods wagons," amended Aunt Bee.

"I shall buy Skinny a pair of sand-shoes, bathing drawers, a toy yacht with an anchor, some cocoanut ice, sponge cake with hundreds and thousands, lemon soda with a marble in it, a copy of *Books for the Bairns*, a night-light, K-boots, and three hapence worth of Edinburgh Rock. We will put them all in a luncheon hamper with some bread-and-dripping and go down the Rope Walk to the jetty at high tide."

"Happen it won't be high," said Aunt Bee.

"Nonsense," said Uncle Dan. "That's because you don't smell very well. Any Wilford boy can tell without looking when it's high tide by the sniff of the air."

"Or by the skip of the minnows?" said Jeff. "I'm really glad I've been away from there so long, everything will be as good as new."

"Or as good as old," Aunt Bee said.

"Aren't you forgetting one thing?" Blanche said. "The shrimps. At least that's something we didn't have to contend with in Shropshire."

"Well, don't coach me too much," said Jeff. "I want to get

my own impressions. Too much advice from the sidelines gets a fellow bewildered. You remember how we lost that game with Washington and Lee because the coach just wouldn't let us alone and play football. But I shall have Skinny's virgin intellect to examine. What do you suppose he'll think when he finds nothing but obits on the front page of the newspapers. Imagine!"

"A little imagining won't do either of you any harm," said Blanche. "And a reasonably accurate obituary is worth more on the front page than that headline the other day." Her exact mind had been outraged by one of Chesapeake's characteristic journalisms: PRICELESS PAINTING WORTH HALF A MILLION.

"Oh shucks," said Jeff, "if you're going to be an American you better learn not to take the papers seriously. How about the famous English headline: TERRIBLE GALE IN CHANNEL, CONTINENT ISOLATED."

"I must go and do a little work," said Uncle Dan. "I'm having a good time with my lecture for the Southern Orthoëpists on Given Names as a Social and Cultural Index. I don't suppose there's another college where the girls are so ingeniously baptized. One of my students now is called Rhea May Birst. I look at her with apprehension."

"Sometimes you really shock me," said Jeff. "My chore is less amusing. I've got to review the whole of Laissez Faire and the Physiocrats, before Finals. I get so devilish discouraged. There's an awful lot of Economics to learn and it's hard to visualize the ideal consumer they're always talking about. Anyway I've got all the diagrams memorized. I hope old Prof. Holabird isn't going to make monkeys out of us in the exam by asking us something we've never been told."

"Now don't be emotional," said Aunt Bee. "Americans are so excessive."

"I hope nothing will ever happen to make monkeys out of the economists," said Blanche. "I'm jubious about applying the mathematical spirit to such uncertain material."

"I can give you the laws of economics in one proverb," said Uncle Dan. "One leg under and one leg over, brought the little dog to Dover."

"All policemen have big feet," said Jeff. "I'm going to commune with my virgin intelligence; come on, Sandy," and they thumped upstairs.

"I must revise my lecture on Choice and Chance," said Blanche. "If I use any more problems involving cards, dice, and dominoes, the girls will think I'm encouraging gambling."

Meanwhile Bee was washing the dishes.

66. *The Pilot-house*

Jeff was in his cubicle on the roof, running a woolly cleaner through the bowl of his proud curve-stem briar, a present from Skinny. But it was curve-stem no longer; in his desire to prove to Aunt Bee that a pipe need not be as foul as Uncle Dan's he dropped it to purge in boiling water, and to his dismay the bent rubber straightened itself. Consequently the implement had a peculiar tilt, the bowl retorted toward his nose in almost scorching proximity. He wondered secretly whether this would be bad for the mustache he hoped to raise during the voyage to England.

The peaceful act of pipe-cleaning seems to clean the mind also. He was considering (a little jubiously, though he wouldn't have admitted it to Uncle Dan) the peculiar jargon used by political economists. He had read more than once Professor Seager's statement: *The general law in reference to demand is that the quantity of any good that will be purchased varies directly with changes in the intensities of the desires for the good of purchasers.* He presently observed that what Seager really meant was not *desires for the good of purchasers* but *desires of purchasers for the good;* and marked the transposition with a strong pencil swirl. He added *Katydid!* in the margin, which was shorthand for "Thou say'st an undisputed thing In such a solemn way." But the notation was half-hearted; he didn't even bother to scrawl *Write English!* as he sometimes did to poor Mr. Mill. His mind was elsewhere—

Life really has more plot than you think, he reflected. It's like Cheese Into but not Onto. . . .

This was a reminiscence of the days when Aunt Blanche first came to live at 1910. Her arrival caused various domestic readjustments; among them a discussion of tastes in food. Aunt Bee remembered that the bride differed from Dan in at least one gastronomy. "You can't expect everyone to enjoy your weird pleasures," she said. "Blanche likes cheese cooked all through the dish, not just baked on top of it."

Dan put up a feeble defense of his preference, and made some learned reference to smearcase, a wonderful word he had learned from Dr. Huffenbutz. Bee was firm and thereafter cheese became an ingredient, not a top-dressing. But she had some difficulty in expounding the distinction to Moxie, who finally said what became a family apothegm: "She likes Cheese Into but not Onto." The picturesque villages of Cheese Into and Cheese Onto were at once added to the map of Jeffland; they gave the President as much speculative pleasure as Uncle Dan got from the two Snorings.

Yes, sir, Jeff was telling himself, the pattern or wood-grain of living seems to go clear through; not just something baked on. A game of consequences, by golly. A river flows as a whole, not just a skim of movement on the surface. Didn't good ole William James say something to that effect in his chapter on The Stream of Consciousness? He was tempted to pull out his much-marked copy of *Psychology, Briefer Course,* but refrained. Better not mix up psychology and economics. He and Skinny had once imagined a nightmare, in which a muddled student got the diagrams confused in an exam. Instead of what they called vulgarly the Bedpan Picture (Seager's diagram of capitalistic production in equilibrium) he drew James's plan of a Stream of Consciousness nourishing a "half-warmed fish" (so the lecturer had spoonerized the half-formed wish).

There was a half-warmed fish in Jeff's mind at this moment; something simple and slippery he wanted to think about, but he wasn't ready to approach it yet. He had other things to think about first. Yes, sir, plot or sequence seems to be part of the whole works. It must be so because it shows itself in such trivial matters. When I slept down below, in Mowgli's cave, the boxroom, I was always looking up through the skylight and imagining myself on the roof. And now I am. If there were only some pigeons it might be Aunt Em's old cupola on the Thorofare. Sandy would do for a stuffed animal.

Sandy, slowly heaving in repose on the steamer rug on Jeff's bed, must have felt the thought; he sighed, and then ingratiated with his tail.

"You'd look quite handsome stuffed, with bright glass eyes, ole fool dog."

Sandy expanded, blew earnestly through his adenoids, flickered his eyelids but decided not to open them. He deflated himself into a pretense of sleep. He knew when he was being teased, and to feign unconsciousness was easier than having to take up an attitude. In spite of their annoying habits, dogs are wonderful cushions for the moods of their curators.

For Jeff was pretending too; talking to Sandy to reassure his own morale. He was ashamed. If I could only go back a couple of sentences and start again from there. Things that hurt begin so suddenly. I hadn't the slightest intention of saying what I did; it came like a flash, just when I was feeling so happy. That's a terribly dangerous feeling. . . .

He had been on his way upstairs, whistling *Yankee Doodle*, and suddenly ran down again to quote something that came into his head. "Aunt Bee, what's the difference between an American, a rooster, and an old maid? The American says Yankee Doodle Doo, the rooster says Cock-a-doodle-doo, and the old maid says Any old dude'll do."

This was not received with any marked favor, and he apologized by saying, "It's a wheeze Bert and I heard at the Bon Ton Burlesquers."

"If you're going in for burlesque," said Dan, "it's just as well you gave up the study of literature."

(Yes, that was a snotty sort of thing for Uncle Dan to say, but I needn't have lost my temper?)

"Oh, for goodness' sake," Jeff exclaimed. "It's absolutely Elizabethan; I bet it's a pretty slick way to study the vulgate."

(Of course the leg-show, in days when the bend of a knee was practically Ultima Thule, had nothing to do with it. But why didn't he stop right there; not at the knee, at that bend in the argument?)

"Gee whiz, you don't have to be always sailing on Lake Superior. Gosh-all-hemlock, Uncle Dan, let's cut out that top-heavy patronizing. What do you and Possum think you are, a kind of intellectual Salvation Army over here to convert the barbarians? Jeeze, sometimes I don't give—I mean I get awful impatient with English people."

Uncle Dan looked really angry. They must both have had their private sore spots to be so fast on the trigger.

"What is this, a nest-fouling expedition?" said Dan with pedantic irony. "You might try to be patient with them as long as you're still one of them."

It was so painfully true that poor Jeff went overboard with all three T's. "You're being priggish," he cried. *"Tom Jones!"*

This was practically an oath. When Jeff had discovered *Tom Jones* he burst into guileless praise of it as the greatest novel ever written. Dan remarked that he kept the Patapsco College copy in the locked case. "The girls won't have to associate with stable-boys in life," he said, "and I don't want them to in literature." Jeff, in the now-everything-is-solved assurance of senior year, rebuked this as disgusting prudery.

Aunt Bee was shocked by the sudden irrational argument. Perhaps she was less well inspired than usual. She started to quote a verse she had clipped from the evening paper and pasted in her scrapbook. "Live in a house by the side of the road," she said, "and be a friend to man."

"Oh tarradiddle," Jeff retorted. "Live in a house by the side of the road and take everybody's dust." He was further enraged when Aunt Blanche blew a smoke ring at him; a better one than he could do himself. He stumped off upstairs, more noisily than the first time, and closed the trapdoor of the pilot-house with a bang.

(But what a way for a man of twenty-one to behave, he grieved. Jesus One, he had supposed that after that apocalyptic birthday everything would just naturally be mature, rational, controlled, philosophical, kindly and wise, William-James-like; like the calculable entrepreneur or Economic Man. It was tough though, at college always being horsed for being English; at home horsed for being American. Jesus Two, Dan's actually an American, he oughtn't to keep throwing dornicks. Always making irritating comments, such as "An Englishman's home is his castle, an American's home is everybody else's castle." If Dan was honest-to-God American he'd have said "everybody's else castle." Jesus Three, I guess I sholy am getting to be a regular American. I can't take the least little bit of criticism—why does one accept these things so well from outsiders and get so sore when they're said at home?)

He could hear Uncle Dan moving around in the box-room below. He opened the trap and called down, "I'm frightfully sorry."

"Cheer-ho," said Uncle Dan. "It was my fault."

Jeff winced at the "Cheer-ho"; a gruesome word for an American citizen to use; but persevered in tolerance. "No, it was my hot Southren blood, inflamed by sausage rolls."

Jeff's pilot-house, a cabin or belvedere on the roof, had been added, after much commerce with the landlord, while Dan and Blanche were on their wedding trip. (They called it so, Uncle

412

Dan said it was absurd to talk of a man with a beard having a honeymoon. Jeff, always argumentative, said that since Blanche's hair was cropped the total of their coiffures was less than average. Dan said this was a quibble-springe.)

The pilot-house was disastrously extreme in temperatures. Jeff sometimes remembered a remark of the old Major in the garden at Greenaway: "Everything is confoundedly circumstantial. There's a kind of a day if you get it in March you say it's warm, the same weather in September you say it's chilly, and likely it's the same Fahrenheit both times, maybe 60 degrees." But this crow's nest was the only third story on the ridge of Carroll Street, and had a broad command of outlook. The vacant lot was no longer vacant, Sassafras House was now somebody's backyard and alumni of the T.S.O. 4 wondered in whose cellar the quicksand of the Pogeypond bubbled its skeletons and quagmires. Many landmarks of the T.S.O. 4 era were visible from this eyrie: deceptively large steam cumulus from Ma & Pa, the rising profiles of new skyscrapers downtown, and a younger generation of Orioles and Mount Royals on their way to Druid Hill spring. There was even a new coronation toward: could it be that life goes round in circles?

"In cycles," said Aunt Blanche. "Circles have no direction, cycles do."

"Lots of nice things do go round in circles," said Jeff and dusted off the old toy steam engine (still known as the *Westernland*) for a nostalgic run from Sprunt City to Port Remus. Uncle Dan, who had unselfishly moved his own study to the cave, so that Blanche could use the back room for mathematics, was surprised to hear the toy whistle blow for the S curve and level crossing at Much Wedlock. It's a very selfish whistle, Jeff had remarked long ago, it absolutely saps the flywheel.

Uncle Dan said he could work perfectly well in the old box-room; as a matter of fact, he averred, literature has to be studied by artificial light. But he did insist on Jeff removing to the pilot-house his extensive Museum of Relics of the Great Fire. These lumps of melted glass, broken bricks and charred wood in velveteen texture made him feel and smell like Polly Flinders.

Perhaps the young exemplar of economics hardly realized what a suggestive *lab*oratory his pilot-house was. Unconsciously arranged in sequence were the exponents of his progress—like the chambers of the nautilus, or shells of crawfish. If the subtitle of any true history of men might be "They took it as it came," here were serial chapters, from the small china yanimals of Miss Hoo, passing through the Zouave barracks, the stamp album, the nose-guard, the cardboard ship-models, the 19¢ *Rubaiyat*, the *All-Night Algebra*, the cobblestone graphs. What idiot called economics the dismal science? As the young statistician looked about his pensive citadel each trophy or furnishing led into economic stuff—the old plaid blanket (disregarding Sandy's deciduous coat) meant ocean traffic; the toy engine, which could not advertise itself and also make the grade to Wedlock Edge, was that not a fiscal parable? Even that distant company of small boys rumbling their express wagon over Cotton Duck bridge, even they unwitting were a social fossil—for the Fire had brought new water supply and artesian pocket-money was doomed. His eye fell on a tattered volume loosened from its binding, *The Boys' Own Handy Book*. It still opened to that noble chapter "How to Build a Model Steam Engine." The marks of grimy thumbs—all ten of them, he reflected sadly—were over the pages, memorial of days in the cellar when he struggled at that impossible project. Yet there in diagrams was the glorious thing, imagined empress of the Great Eastern and Western of Jeffland. But neither the President nor Uncle Dan was handy enough and the model locomotive remained only a picture. Was not *The Boys' Own Handy Book* as accurate a symbol of the hopeful impossible dream as John Stuart Mill or Seager's *Introduction to Economics?*

✦

Jeff and Skinny were up in the pilot-house; there was just room for two if Skinny pushed Sandy off the bed. They had been going over Uncle Dan's old pocket Atlas considering how they could best utilize their brief visit to England. "You're certainly crazy about maps, aren't you?" said Skinny, looking at the faded chart of Jeffland pinned to the wall.

"I got that from Uncle Dan. He always says that an Atlas is the best textbook of literature."

"The trouble is," said thoughtful Skinny, "things sometimes look so much better on the map than they do when you get there."

"I guess that's a chance you take when you get born," Jeff admitted. "I keep that survey map of the Susquehanna to remind me of Uncle Dan's disappointment. He had himself all hopped up with a notion of that earthly paradise Coleridge used to dream about. But poor old Dan, when he and Dr. Huffy got there, what with heat and mosquitoes and hayfever and Pennsylvania Dutch farmers setting the dogs on them, they were painfully disillusioned. Uncle Dan felt mighty sadly, but he saw the comic side of it, though. He remembered that one thing Coleridge worried about was, how would the colonists take care of their teeth in the wilderness? Dan said, 'We didn't have any trouble with our teeth. It was the dogs' teeth that bothered us.' He said he'd give me the map to remind me not to be too much of an idealist."

He looked at the sheet tacked up on his limited wall space. Across a pale network of brown contour lines like old tawny lace, ran the great blue diagonal of the river in bends and bulges. "Bert thought it was a map of a varicose vein," said Jeff. "It's funny, when anyone says anything vulgar enough you never forget it."

"Well, if we're still idealists after all these years with Bert and Star," said Skinny, "I guess there may be something in it. *Vilia miretur vulgus, mihi Castaliae aquae.*" Jeff was always abashed to notice how far Skinny's classics had gone beyond his own and defensively resumed his own topic.

"Uncle Dan said it's a lesson, you can't live in anyone else's paradise. You've got to go about inventing your own. But anyway it's a wonderful map. Just look at those names, it's the whole history of America: Baumgardner, Slackwater, Mount Nebo, Bald Eagle Creek, Brogueville, Chanceford, Conestoga—how's that for a big name?—West Lampeter, Shank's Ferry,—no wonder Walt Whitman wrote in catalogues. How else would you get everything in?—I bet that's where Butler Brothers and Sears, Roebuck got the idea."

Skinny's eyes, brightened by so much irrigation and Greek text and the new spectacles, were sharp. "Not Shank's Ferry," he said, "Shenk's Ferry."

"What a pity," Jeff grieved. "Well, maybe that's where the Mandrake Pills came from."

"Still the idealist," said Skinny. "We had some damn good names in Jeffland and LaGrange. Here's one I always envied you, the town of Happenstance. I said I was going to have a fortified town and you invented a fortuitous town. Say," he added, looking at the antique map, "you've added some places that didn't use to be there. I don't remember the twin cities of Languedoc and Languedoyle."

Jeff was a little embarrassed. "I found it was a good way to remember things when I was studying. I put 'em on the map where they'd sort of visualize in my head."

"Boy, that's a slick idea. Why, you old master of mnemonics. Now I know how you got that A in Victorian poetry. I see you've got a beach resort called 'Matthewarnold.' But what does that dotted track mean? I think Matthewarnold ought to be on the main line. He had a really classical mind."

"It's a bridle path," said Jeff. "The main line goes the other way, through Tennyson Junction and Keats Regis."

"Maybe it's taking an unfair advantage to have so much

fun in your studies," Skinny suggested. "What's this Three R's line, it looks like a new development?"

"Oh shucks, that's just some old memo. Look over here, I wanted to show you something. Remember how we used to draw little figures on the margins of the book, when you'd spin the pages over they came alive? We were really inventing Doyle's Dancing Men." He shuffled Skinny away from the map of Jeffland. He had remembered just in time that the RRR (Railroad of Romance) recently acquired a new terminus.

Before Skinny left, Jeff made him recite his exercise for translation. This was a paradigm of casual sayings Jeff had been subconsciously overhearing for many years; he had bullied his friend into believing they were prerequisite for any intercourse with the island race. Obediently poor Skinny recited:

"Whilst I've got on my bowler and mack I'll do the errands. At Boots' Cash Chemist I'll get pastilles for my relaxed throat. I need some bootlaces for my K-boots. To the Left Luggage Office for my Gladstone bag. To the Enquiry Agent to engage a cook-general and a char. I'll post the letter and be jolly well sure there's plenty of gum on the envelope. If I can't find it in Bradshaw I must ask the booking clark how much for a third single to Saffron Walden. The Bespoke Tailor is making me a lounge suit but he needn't put buttons on the bags, I never wear braces. A thrippenny bit, a tanner, a bob, a florin, half a crown, a thick 'un, I must keep a note of my exes. Don't stumble over the tramway setts and before you step off the kerb, mind the lefthand traffic; don't get run down by a pantechnicon. To-night we'll go to a music hall. Gin-and-French, Miss. Steady, the Buffs! Guinness, what a time we'll have."

"Hear, hear," said Geoffrey. "Skinny, you're good, you ought to get along all right even if we're separated."

"My God, I hope I don't say any of it before we get over there," said Skinny. "I'd be terribly ashamed if Star or Bert overheard me. They're such wisenheimers. But won't it be slick to have a holiday after we get through with those damn steers.

417

Think of being in a foreign country where at least you can understand some of the language, and go along the street watching people, just to see how they behave. I always wonder about that, suppose you could study someone all day long, know what he was thinking about, why he looks that way, why he puts on those particular socks or where did he get that hat. What's in his mind when he ties his shoestrings—bootlaces."

"You feel that way too? I thought it was just me being morbid. Well, I bet if we buy some British tweeds we could be almost unrecognizable."

"Most people are when they wear them," said Skinny.

"If you don't talk too much we won't be suspected. We'll take the whole human landscape by surprise—we might even see an Economic Man—but I mustn't be what Aunt Bee calls 'excessive.'—Remember, never say 'Thank you,' that gives you away as a bloody foreigner. Just say ' 'Kyou.' "

"I can hardly wait till we get on the boat—sorry, I mean ship. We'll surely get some time off to cool our fevered brows?"

"It's going to seem queer," Jeff said. "Like going backwards somehow. I always think of ships sailing the other way."

Jeff found it another proof of Cheese Into that he owed much of the pleasure of his watch-tower to two elderly ladies. Here for the first time he was relieved from the Cyclopean eye of Mrs. Maggots; and in faint memory of Aunt Em he realized what her dovecote may have meant. "I feel eccentric," he used to say when he felt like climbing to his solitude. The eccentricity was normal enough and went round circles (or cycles) that have never been improved. If the evening involved concentration upon Seager he would put aside on the pillow beyond Sandy some literary lifebuoy which would later float him asleep. It might be Keats, it might be Captain Kettle, and no offense to either. Looking up from Seager's analysis of Railroad Problems ("As the volume of traffic grows, the earnings of old, established railroads should show a marked tendency upward") it

418

was good to see the easier volume waiting. And no offense to the hopeful and humane Seager; Dan had suggested that Jeff's devotion to that textbook was really a subconscious memory of the old Ipswich potted meats. A good analogy too, Jeff said; nourishing pemmican in a modest package.

It doesn't really matter so much what a young man is reading; whether it's Blackstone or Keats or Conan Doyle he'll find plenty in it to bring him back to his own splendors of egoism. Like Cheese Into, the rich tang of Me runs through the pudding. Or let's be younger and more shiny: the auroras of self ripple in luminous fringes across the dark northwards of the mind. Just a chance phrase can do it. He made a coded pencil tick, with meanings of its own, against Seager's cool passage: "In studying the principles of economics, passion is out of place."

And now he was ready to think about that simple evasive sweetness. He wished Skinny hadn't made the allusion to Horace's *hinnuleo*. He remembered the line perfectly: *Vitas hinnuleo me similis, Chloe.* "You shun me, Chloe, like a fawn" someone translated it. She did, she was: soft brown eyes with sparks of topaz, slender ankles and baby hands, quick watchfulness and quick retreat. The tender forming of her shape, and Oh her honey-slurring voice! At last he had got over those years of agonized clumsiness when to speak to any girl whoever meant rehearsal and resolve. Now, he felt, he could almost imitate the offhand chaff and ease of Teackle or Star—and now, when he was bursting with social grace unuttered, all sorts of witty entente cordiale, she herself had become suddenly shy or mocking.

Well, for God's sake; Jesus One, he enumerated, how would you expect a fellow who never knew any females at all except Aunt Bee and Possum and Miss Beamish to be able to meet a lovely creature like that on equal terms? And Jesus Two, isn't it incredible, the little baby-child that was so fascinatingly annoying and so selfish and impudent, what *happens* to anyone to make her all of a sudden so exquisite? But I knew it all along

(Jesus Three), just the look of her clean crispy clothes, she always looked as if she just came straight blue and starch from the mangle (is that what they call those things, rubber rollers, smell of ammonia, soapstone washtubs, blunt steamy push of hot sad-irons—sad? *glad*-irons!—crimping lacy cake-frosting frills; like the outward-teasing layers of a Valentine). You couldn't even walk alongside of her without smelling her clean sweetness and thinking about the silky back of her neck under the snood of dark hair curling up at the ends; and a tortoise-shell barrette—

Oh Serena Serena, Lavinia Lavinia, Serena Lavinia Warren! I knew it from the first time I saw those hair-ribbons like moth-millers in the dusk; I couldn't take my eyes off her, the little minx, sitting so pleased with herself in the swing; just a vain comical Trundle-doll; and all of a sudden I see her walking across the lawn at Greenaway and I can't even ask her if she'd like to go to a baseball game (by God, we beat Virginia, too) without having to practice my tone of voice so my throat wouldn't choke on me. She said, "I'd love it." She used the word *love*; anybody so perfect ought to be careful how she uses a word; people might misunderstand it; how does a girl feel when she uses a word like that?

What if she *is* young? Anybody says flapper I'll beat his teeth in. She's not any younger than Juliet and how is that for high? Why when Swift fell in love with Stella she was only a baby. Serena's practically fifteen, isn't she? When I'm twenty-six she'll be almost twenty, and I bet that's a lovely age.—Her eyebrows will be wonderfully emphatic by then; they look surprised at themselves already.—Bet you could comb them with a very small comb.

People just don't appreciate how special a person can be, everything about them is so exciting. Gosh, even her own family don't appreciate her. Teackle still calls her that disgusting nick-name. She was so dignified and sweet when I took her to the game, I remember just how she said, "I declare, I must have been terribly spoiled in those days," and I said, "You were awfully cunning when you were a kid." That was a gauche remark, it sounded as though she wasn't cunning any more. I could feel my cheeks getting shamefaced and just then somebody hit a pop foul right into the stand. I caught it lefthanded practically in front of her nose. What a stroke of luck, and she was so bright about it. "You certainly saved my face that time." "It's mighty well worth saving," I said, and that's the only what you might call intimate thing I've ever said. I stuck the ball in my pocket and gave it to her after, as a souvenir. But I simply couldn't say what I wanted to; she might think it was silly, I dare say it's pretty damn sentimental for a college senior and Economic Man—

There's nothing to be ashamed of in being fourteen, is there? There's only fourteen lines in a sonnet and it's the finest poetry there is. It could be written with two rhymes at the end, sort of tied up in a couplet like a bow of ribbon; sort of reminiscent:

> The long years fade and you again are there,
> A laughing child, with ribbon in your hair—

He rather liked that, though a little suspicious of it because it came so easily. He reverently sharpened his pencil and wrote the lines at the bottom of the page so there would be room to work down to them from above.

What he really wanted was to ask Serena if he might have one of her old hair-ribbons, to use as a marker in his Keats.

67. *Motto for a Sun-dial*

Jeff found the Major kneeling on a cushion as he weeded the gravel path round the sun-dial. The veteran was wearing an ancient panama jaundiced with sun and what he called his gardening trousers. He was chewing a stub cigar and murmuring to himself in good humor. "Geoffrey Crayon!" he said. "A pleasant surprise. You find me in poverty, idleness, an' the pride of literature, like they said about Doctor Johnson."

Jeff was always amused by the Major's insistence on his poverty. It was his only snobbishness.

"I'm sorry to burst in on you, sir, but I came out to beg a favor. I've got to show up right soon for my citizenship hearing and I thought maybe you'd be a character witness for me, the way you did for Uncle Dan. I've got some instructions here that give all the dope."

"Put the papers on the sun-dial," said the Major. "Ain't that what your favorite Sherlock Holmes always says? Glad you come, my boy. I was just honin' fo' an excuse to spell myself with a fresh cigar. Lend me a hand to rear up. Reckon I didn't do enough genuflectin' when I was your age, that's why my kneebones is so stiff."

Jeff gave the Major an arm to hobble across to one of the weatherstained benches under the box-hedge. "It's hot," the old gentleman continued, loosening the neck of his shirt. "Ease your fumin' collar, like it says in the Georgics. *Fumantia solvere colla.* I been rereading my Virgil, do it every spring."

"What's the dinner bell doing on the sun-dial?" Jeff asked.

"Ring it an' yo'll see.—Not so ladylike, give it a real good tocsin. *Donnez un peu plus de volée à vos cloches.* Likely you ain't familiar with that smutty line from Balzac. Dr. Gildersleeve quotes it to us oldtimers. I still read his *Journal of Philology* to see what little jokes he works into it. It's a fine thing to be a bit of a scholar, you meet up with some mighty underhand witticisms."

"The boys had a copy of *Droll Tales* they passed round at the frat house," Jeff admitted. "But I'm afraid it was a translation. Still, I think I recognize the allusion."

"You may reckonize it. I hope it'll be a long while befo' you appreciate it."

"The old sun-dial always makes me think of Hazlitt's essay. Did I tell you Uncle Dan gave me a set of Hazlitt for my birthday? I told him it was probably one of those purposeful presents, the kind I gave him as a kid. When you give something you really want for yourself."

"If so, it was a right smart one. It took me quite a while to get onto Hazlitt's curves, then I see he's really a test-case. Folks that don't care fo' Hazlitt just don't care fo' what I call literature. It's nice to have a way of knowin' the sheep from the shoats."

"It's such a lovely thing, that piece about the sun-dial," Jeff said happily. "I noticed it was first published in October, that was so absolutely right, when the sun's going away and you appreciate it more."

"Remember who yo' talkin' to," said the Major, pretending to be severe. "None of these here autumnal sentiments. That was a right clever motto Hazlitt talked about, *Horas non numero nisi serenas*. It used to make me jealous because we didn't have any inscription on our sun-dial, but my old Tullius Teackle said there was ne'er a motto slick enough to keep up with Father Time. Once I had a mind to carve on it that thing they put in contracks, *Time is of the essence*. But it sound so whoreson legal. There's an epitaph I saw at a plantation house in South Ca'lina, *It is later than you think*, but the mo' I considered about that the mo' it griped me. There's a line I come up with readin' my Georgics, *Soles et aperta serena prospicere*, lookin' on sunshine and cheerful spaces, that would be a pleasin' sentiment."

"It would please Serena," said Jeff. "How is she?"

"Just fine. She'll be back from school bimebye. She's shapin' up right cute. I wish she could do better with her Latin. I told her it wasn't right fo' me to be construin' it fo' her, and I found her tryin' to get Lightfoot to help."

Lightfoot himself arrived just then with the decanter of Madeira. "Howdy, Mist' Jeff. You ain't been so frequent lately. Mutual see you comin' up the drive, he hopin' you an' him go swimmin' together after he meet Miss Trundle."

"You tell Mutual keep his mind on his work," said the Major. "We got matters to talk. I see you bring out an extra glass, just in case."

"Yassuh, my ole han's gettin' shaky, I might spill."

"All right, pour yo'self one, you ole reprobate. *Cras ingens iterabimus aequor*, tomorrow we'll travel on water."

"Yassuh. *Absit omen*." The old Negro poured a very small libation in the third glass and drank it with a respectful roll of his yellow eyeballs.

"You go an' pull the wool over yo' eyes, it's time for yo' siesta.—I surely do spoil that ole nigger, but I been doin' it half a century. He's ten year older than I am, he's the only critter round here makes me feel young."

They drank the Northeast Trades, the Major gave a small relaxing belch and smoothed his bruised knees. Jeff was trying to visualize half a century, which was just the interval between the old gentleman and himself. Fortunately it can't be done— at either end.

"This is the wine Ben Franklin wanted to be coopered up in," the Major said. "Said he'd like to be preserved in a barrel of Madeira and come back a century later to see what the Yewnited States looked like. He wouldn't been as surprised as some of 'em. I swear he'd be tickled to see young G-offrey Barton rais- in' his hand to take citizenship. Makes me think o' that feller Clough I've told you about, the one who had a chance to make a scholar out of me an' missed it. I bought a book of his writin' one time, to see what sort of things he'd have tutored me, and I see he suggested citizenship might be made interchangeable between Britain and the U.S.A."

"I don't think that would work," said Jeff. "I think it's bet- ter if it's a privilege, both ways."

"You're right, sir, you're right." Jeff was enormously thrilled, it was the first time the Major ever called him "sir." "Of co'se I'll be proud to be a character witness. Who's the other one?"

"Dr. Beinbrink was kind enough to say he'd testify for me."

"That's good, he's a solid godfearin' man. He don't appreciate liquor the way I'd like him to, but he's a right perseverin' conspirator. Him an' me pulled some wires together one time, touchin' on an' appertainin' to the fortunes of your Uncle Dan. Reckon maybe I did most of the pullin' but Dr. Beinbrink ain't had no cause to regret it."

Jeff was about to say, "You mean about that vacancy in the mathematics department?" but he reflected that the Major was always capable of saying what he meant if he intended it to be said. So he sat silent, and the Major was pleased.

"It'll be right satisfyin' to see that mural wall-picture of Lord Co'nwallis again. I hope it's toned down a bit since it afflicted Uncle Dan. I presume you've renounced your association with the nobility and cetra."

"I made my declaration of intention three years ago," said Jeff. "When I was eighteen."

"You let me study the instruction an' I'll write a letter of affidavit, an' when they fix the date I'll be on hand for the hearin'. I think we should have a jubilee afterward, like we did for Dan. Tell you what, we'll have a Comin'-In party. Miz Warren is already talkin' about what we'll do for Serena Lavinia when she has to come out but that ain't yet-awhile, thank goodness. We'll have a Comin'-In celebration for the new citizen. Now tell me some mo' about this education you been gettin'."

Jeff was dismayed; there can hardly be any more unanswerable request. If one stopped to think, what *had* he learned in those four happy years? Diverse memories ran through his mind: the joyous discovery of Chaucer and reading it aloud to himself with phonetics of his own—William James's *Psychology*, a kind of bible for his generation—hot showers in the gym after football—the delight of his careful graphs of the rise of paving blocks replacing cobblestones—but he was embarrassed to speak to the Major about his special study. He could imagine his comment, "Why, they ain't even sure how to pronounce it."

The Major noticed the young man's hesitation. "I ought to ask your pardon for such an unmannerly request. Nobody knows what he's learned until he's called on to exercise it. I recollect one time Dan asked me to invite his nymphs and wenches out here to have tea and see the Apery. He said he wanted them to get a notion what a gentleman's liberry looked like."

"He also said he wanted them to see what a gentleman looked like."

"Go along with you, none of your blarney. They wouldn't require to go outside Dan's classroom to see that. Anyhow we had a real cultural lotus-eatin' afternoon an' then Dan got mischievious, he says I must make them a speech. One of your little soliloquies, he says—to me, sir, that usually don't get a chance to shove a word in slantwise. So I told them about Uncle Hartley and the Lake Poets, and the Album, and some of my idle chatter. Of co'se it was impudence for me, just an old cavalry soldier and railroad engineer, to be openin' my face on topics of bell letters. I says the best kind of a college is where you can sometimes hear what you never expected to from people who got no business to say it. Folks who got no vested interest in their ideas. If you hear a literary teacher say Wordsworth is a great poet, well sho'ly, that's his business. But if you hear a brokendown old railroader say it, you begin to prickle up your ears.—Then of co'se I apologize, like I always have to when I say anythin' good. I allow I didn't go to be so pontifical. Dan says, 'Major Warren's an old bridge-builder, he's got a perfect right to pontificate, that's what the word means.' Then the gals all laugh an' clap and sing me one of their glee-club spirituals about *She'll Be Comin' Round the Mountain*. Good thing they don't know the way the railroad boys sing it in the caboose."

The Major puffed to enliven his fading cigar, and poured himself more wine. "I can quote you clear from your native heath," he said. "The grape that can with logic absolute The two and seventy jarring sects confute."

"As a matter of fact, sir," Jeff ventured, "I think maybe it was the *Rubaiyat* that made me change over in my studies. I dare say I told you before, in my sophomore year I chose Fitz-Gerald as subject for a term-paper. You see that was 1909, the year of his centennial. I guess Omar is sort of a phase all the fellows go through. The profs push a lot of philosophy at you and you write down labels in your notebook, pragmatism, hedonism, agnosticism, rationalism, transcendentalism—"

"Just a minute, go easy on old Master Shallow. That's right savory, Jeff, that-all's what I always hankered for and never had. Say that again."

"It don't mean a thing, sir. I'm sorry to say it was just a sequence Skinny Granger made up to memorize, because the initials suggested a vulgar word.—Like the old Pig-poop song, I'm afraid."

The Major experimented until he grasped the acrostic. "Jemmun!" he said. "Now you ain't goin' to disillusion me about a university education?"

"Not a bit, sir. You get a marvelous thrill out of that sort of thing because you think you've really got the terrapin by the tail, then all of a sudden he dives out of sight, kerblinkety blunk, and the Omar Khayyam feeling is about all that seems left. That's when the Fuchshoehle makes a good thing out of the fellows, while they're in that Wine-Bread-and-Thou period. Myself when young did eagerly frequent Doctor and Saint and heard great argument, and cetra. Then you kind of bounce back again, at least I did; you realize college is half over and you want to get hold of something a bit more solid. You call it utilitarianism in your notebook, but what you really mean is, you want somehow to be useful."

Jeff found himself embarrassed by his confession. "That's how I switched over to—to eckonomics," he said gallantly, giving it the pronunciation the Major would approve.

The Major blew a long whiff of blue smoke into the bright spring air. "There has been times when I thought myself that bell letters was maybe a superfluity, unless you could teach it like Dan does. Then I recollect that puttin' the right word in the right place is a sure-enough technical achievement, same as Tiddyhigh Trestle. Likely yo' right, eckonomics is goin' to overhaul us somewheres along the line, we might as well clear a track fo' it. Sometimes it rise up an' smite. I keep a brick on my desk at the depot to remind me of the railroad strike in '77. That's when eckonomics drew a graph on the side of my head. The Dismal Science of throwin' bricks."

The Major scratched a scar under his white hair. Jeff was quite content in a listening mood.

"I reckon eckonomics took kind of a trial trip in '61-'65," the Major reflected. "A little mo' Dismal Science ridin' hoss-back with General Lee and destiny might show up a different manifest. Would have been a pity, too. But I had somethin' on the tip o' my tongue, I interrupted myself— Yes, I wanted to say, I hope you ain't gone through college without writin' any poetry. I declare I don't think a man's educated if he ain't been taken short with a sonnet."

Jeff colored slightly; he admitted he had written a sonnet. The Major misconceived the reason for the blush; he would have been surprised to know the subject of the verses.

"Ain't no call to flush up, my boy, there's no law compellin' a man to put his rhymes in print. It's good exercise for the romantical feelin's. Likely your style get mo' compact as time goes on. Didn't work that way with me, I fear. But I wouldn't expect a man to write his best poetry so young, like that Yankee bard Mr. Bryant. It's a mighty tragical thing fo' a poet to write his best piece at eighteen. He was a right sweet old bard, though; I recollect Tullius Teackle got somethin' out of him for the Album. The old gentleman wrote about Truth crushed to earth will rise again. I ain't so sure on that point. I've seen times when Truth crushed to earth just burrows out of sight."

Like Uncle Remus's crawfishes, Jeff thought, but felt no

428

impulse to interrupt the Major's flow. He can do that quite well for himself.

"One thing I envied Mr. Bryant, his knowledge of Greek. You didn't study any Greek in these bright college years?"

"I'm afraid I didn't."

"I've been thinkin' some about takin' it up in my eighth decade. I got my Virgil pretty well digested, but I always hanker to know if Greek is really as wonderful as it looks in print. If it raise folks like Dr. Gildersleeve and your friend Miss Shaugraun, there must be somethin' to it."

"I feel that way too," said Jeff, "but I had to choose between Greek and Chaucer."

"Now there you are," the Major exclaimed. "That's the way it is. Man's got to be the choosinest animal. That's what makes it all so damn disconcertin'. Why can't a man live to be a hundred? I ain't got around to Chaucer neither, doggone it; I sneaked a look a few times but I took a scunner to that simplified spellin'. I couldn't even pick out the scandalous bits. They tell me he's no slouch when he's in the mood."

"Oh, he's everything," Jeff blurted, feeling painfully inadequate. "You sort of think of him on a spring day like this. The air, the sunlight, flowers coming up out of good clean dirt, everything with a twinkle in it, or a driving rainstorm too—he's just like *weather*."

"You don't think he'd be mo' difficult than Greek?" said the Major anxiously. "Maybe I'll have a try at him yet. I recollect Dan tellin' me one time, it seems Chaucer wrote a piece for his boy to explain about a sun-dial or a sextant or something."

"Yes, a letter to 'Little Lewis, My Son,' about the astrolabe."

"That's it. Dan was tellin' me that Chaucer writes to Little Lewis he won't try to tell him all about the Astrolabe but 'just sufficient for our horizon.' I says to myself that ain't a bad motto. These here choosin's an' dead reckonin's you got to make, the best you can do is a judgment sufficient for your own horizon. Like I says to Dan, when he allows he was lucky in makin'

429

friends, it's because first-off he made friends with himself. You got to figure out what-all kind of a person you is yo'self and act accordin'. Some folks never does know and of co'se they're always bitched-bothered-and-bewildered.—But I wasn't intendin' to make baccalaureate speeches. Let's walk back to the house, we might consult Miz Beuly about that Comin'-In party. That'll be sufficient fo' our horizon at present. Then I'd like you to take home some of these lielocks to Miz Bee. Tell you one thing, they ain't never goin' to make an American citizen out of *her*."

"I told you I'm going over to England on a cattle-boat this summer," said Jeff as they walked along the box alleys. "Some of the fellows were teasing me, they think it's a bit comical to go back to England right after I get to be an American citizen. I couldn't seem to tell them what I had in mind, but I can tell you—there are some things I still remember and I'd like to see them again, see if they're anything like my impressions. There was an old brick wall in the garden at Wilford, the place has been sold but I could go and look at it; and I remember flying kites on the chalk downs with my cousin, I never had such a sense of space anywhere; and there was fizzy lemonade with a glass ball in the neck of the bottle. It's not silly to be excited by things like that, is it?"

The Major turned on him quite sternly. "My boy, if I thought you commencin' citizen meant you should turn your back on your own vitals I'd never be a witness to it. No sir, if you don't keep in touch with your native childhood you'll never be a poet, nor anythin' else of consequence. I got a right to speak, by God I have, ain't I lived mo'n half the lifetime of these Re-yewnited States."

The Major took Jeff by the lapel and looked up earnestly at the tall youth.

"I wish I could go along with you an' yo' friend Skinny, but I calculate I'm too old for gaddin'. By God, sir, you're just the right age to recuperate yo'self with a little of what's beautiful.

When I think of Uncle Dan movin' over from those colleges of Cambridge to come an' work in the warehouses of Patapsco— it's really shockin'.—I've seen English folks that got me deterrèd in my temper, but there's one sure thing, they got their country in their guts, they love the look and feel and smell of it. There's too many people in these Yewnited States that ain't ever learned to love anything at all. No sir, you go and take a look at that old brick wall, I wouldn't be surprised you'll find it's got nosegays growin' on it. You can bring me back a slice of that thin brown-bread-an'-butter an' a cup of black-strong tea. Yes sir, an' some Yo'kshire puddin' an' kidneys with mustard. You listen to me, the world has spent a lot of time an' trouble in educatin' the English an' we ain't goin' to waste it because they talk off a different part of their palate. You go an' take a good look at the Yarmouth Express and see how they handle their traffic. Then you might come back an' work for the rail-road downtown. That's as good a place as any to study eckonomics: yes sir, you'll get a bellyful."

There was a crescendo of pulsations along the winding drive and a Ford runabout pulled up under the portico. Serena jumped out gaily with an armful of schoolbooks. "Goodness, Daddy," she called, "what are you laying down the law about? I could see you being terribly severe about something. Are you bullying Jeff?"

"We been havin' a real good conversation," said the Major. "It's the most civilized form of art known to man, an' one you don't know nothin' about. You been drivin' that explosion-buggy again?"

"Mutual let me, just from the station. Oh, I'm glad Jeff's here, he can help me with my Latin."

Jeff was thinking how surprised she would be to know he had thought of a Latin title for his sonnet. It came right out of the birthday Hazlitt with just an apostrophe added: *Horas non numero nisi Serena's.*

431

68. *The Coming-In Party*

The Major had chosen the Fourth of July for the Comin'-In party. Teackle drove to 1910 in the Ford runabout to give Jeff a ride to Greenaway; the others were coming a little later on the Ma & Pa. Teackle's grip tightened on the wheel as an Oriole boy threw a firecracker to explode under the car. "Guess I'm still ole-fashioned," he said, "I always think she's going to shy if anything scares her. You know, in some ways these things is really better than a hoss—except of course on a hill," he added, as they chuffed gradually up the long slope of Key Street Extended. "Gee, I wish I was going with you and Skinny on that cattle-boat. I got to work in the freight office all summer, terrible drudgery. I guess it was a mistake for me ever to graduate out of Princeton, even if Woodrow Wilson made me take five years to do it. That man's pretty near ruined the place fo' a lot of nice Southren boys."

"The Major says I can go to work for the road when I get back," said Jeff.

"You can have my job anytime. All those tariff differentials is drivin' me dotty. It ain't as much fun as being a train-butcher like we figured on. Boy, we certainly are shooting around scads of freight until the Interstate Commerce Commission makes up its mind."

"Seager says railroad earnings ought to go on climbing," said Jeff, but with the humility of the theorist speaking to the practical man.

"Bushwa, those economists make me tired," grumbled Teackle. "They don' know what trouble is. I bet on a long haul they'd be no more use than a yard-goat."

After thunder in the night, summer was at her most superb. They ran the gauntlet of York Road's constant crackle of gunpowder for Teackle to buy cigarettes, then through rain-fresh byways approached the Warren demesne. The Ford slithered down a pink shaly slope and crossed the branch on the rattling timbers of an old manure-smelling covered bridge. They rolled gently through, striped by ripples of shadow, toward the gilded opening. "I sho' do relish this ole shed-bridge," said Teackle. "Zebra Bridge, Major calls it. He says it was the first place he ever kissed a gal, the ole libertine."

It's like a tunnel; really a thorofare, Jeff thought. "I bet the stone bridges in England aren't any more beautiful than this," he said.

"When I get through that bridge I always figure I'm really *there*," Teackle said. "You'll have to be on your behaviors today, old top. Citizen and all, by Godfrey. Major has wrastled up all kinds of a shindig. Last night he shut himself in the Apery with a jug of Bourbon to prepare himself a speech. He had Lightfoot in to rehearse him, Trundle an' I went to listen under the window, he was carrying on about blood bein' thicker than water. Liquor's thicker still. When he didn't come to bed Mother went in search. Him an' the ole coot was blooie. You can always tell, when Major starts to sing 'Come up Whitefoot, come up Lightfoot. Come up to the milkin' shed.' "

"Did you give Serena my note?" Jeff asked.

"I didn't exactly give it to her, she was off gallivantin' somewheres, but I reckon she got it. I put it the only place I knew she'd surely see it, on her mirror."

The Major had curry-combed Greenaway from end to end for the celebration. When Jeff and Teackle arrived he was toddling about the box-garden pointing out chores with an old bamboo cane, faster than the perspiring Mutual could obey. He had stuck a fallen oriole feather in the ribbon of his panama. He had Mutual so rattled that the young colored man even started to brush the morning cobwebs off the box-hedges.

"Don' do that, don' do that, you numbwit, that's gauze kerchiefs from the queen of night. That's luck omens, don't you touch a one of 'em. Here, give me that besom befo' you lash

433

into any mo' scenery. You get to hell down to the springhouse, rustle up that mint befo' the sun take the virginity off it."

"Gauze!" muttered Mutual as he fled, "ole Major sho' is workin' up a storm."

"Well, Major, you look right pert," said Teackle after Jeff had been thoroughly greeted. "Ain't been tidin' yo'self over?"

"You're an irreverent scamp," said the Major. "No suh, tide rise too soon it overflow the jetty. We'll have juleps on the swordblade of noon, sir, and not befo'. I been out and around since milkin' time doin' a little surveillance. If you don't he'p along them no-account boys the old place look like Aceldama. Jeff, we had quite a little disturbance in the welkin last night and things got cluttered up. 'Like a foul bombard that would shed his liquor.'"

"You mean you and Lightfoot?" said Teackle. "I declare, it's scandalous the way you drag that saintly ole nigger down to your level."

The Major saw he was being chaffed and was too acute to be drawn.

"My leg been pulled by better men than you," he said. "No suh, I'm quotin' Shakespeare. It's cleared off right scenic. Cobweb handkerchers on the hedge and the Chezpeake oriole shucks a feather, it means a pretty day. Like what a new citizen deserves. As a matter and fact I ain't had nothin' this mornin' but Capn Emerson water. We might set in the po'tico and take some coffee pendin' the other folks get there. Just an old-time family party, Jeff, and we bid Dr. and Miz Beinbrink too, seein' he's your only real reputable sponsor."

A fusillade of firecrackers went off behind the house as they were drinking coffee. "Reckon that's Trundle," said the Major. "She hanker to set off some squibs. I said she could go down and touch 'em off with the colored boys if she'd wear overhauls. She hone to be Baby Trundle just for one day instead of Serena Lavinia. She look right fetching in overhauls, it don't surprise me them young sprigs from the Valley has started makin' sheep-eyes. She don't scarcely ever have to carry her schoolbooks home. It's like Virgil said, *Vires acquirit eundo,* she snatch up the men just by walkin' around."

A louder detonation sounded and perhaps Teackle felt a nostalgia for the music of a cannon cracker under a tin can. "Jeff and I better go down and see what they're doing. They might frighten the hosses."

"I brought along my Brownie," said Jeff. "I thought it would be a good chance to take some snapshots."

Between the stable and the springhouse was an old relic of which the Major was very fond, an ancient high bicycle he had ridden in the '80's as a pioneer member of the Green Spring Valley Velocipedes (afterward a branch of the League of American Wheelmen). The rusty old bone-shaker had been discarded a generation ago, but since the Major would not have it removed, Mrs. Warren screened it by planting morning-glory vines. Now on sunny forenoons it was draped with riotous goblets of blue and the Major often insisted it was the prettiest ornament on the place. Jeff and Teackle were amused to find Serena sitting gaily on the lofty iron saddle conducting an orchestra of colored boys with explosives. They approached from behind and Jeff sighted his small camera. What a pity it won't come out in colors, he thought. That would certainly be a picture: blue flowers, blue jeans, black kids and red firecrackers.

"Don't you dare take my picture in these old pants," cried Serena when she saw them sneaking to a point of vantage. At that moment one of the pickaninnies, showing off with enthusiasm, threw a lighted firecracker toward the bicycle. It burst close to her, she startled and squawked, almost losing balance. The shutter clicked at the same time.

"I think you're an old prune to take it just then," she said.

"You brute, hissed the countess!" mimicked Teackle, quoting his favorite *Graustark*. "I hope it comes out, you don't know how comical you looked. Jeff said he got the Brownie to take pictures of the cows on board ship; Jeff, you better mark the film or you won't know which is which."

"Take *our* pictures!" cried the colored youngsters, swarming round the celestial bicycle.

"You he'p me down offa here," said Serena, scrambling off the wheel with some damage both to flowers and overalls. "I've got a good mind not to give you what you asked for."

"What was that," said Teackle, "old Trundle on a trundle-bike?"

Jeff had not expected the sacred topic to become public like this, but he noticed as she slithered down among the morning-glories there was a roll of ribbon stuffed in the hip-pocket of the jeans.

On the swordblade of noon, as the Major had said, the break-fast party assembled. The host watched Mutual with a hawk's eye as the young man carried in the tray of juleps steaming with chill. It was the first time Mutual had been promoted to this dignity; the salver was too heavy for Lightfoot. The old darky tottered alongside muttering counsel and handed the frosted, green-topped glasses. But the Major, who had evi-dently spent much thought on ceremonial, served Jeff him-self. He cunningly kept the julep out of sight until he placed it in front of the guest of honor. It was served in a silver mug and among the leaves of mint stood a small American flag. All applauded and Jeff was properly abashed.

"Ladies and gentlemen," said the Major, "kindly be seated according to your respective qualifications. Jeff, you at Miz Beuly's right; Miz Beinbrink an' Miz Bee down here along-side me. Miz Blanche you betwixt Jeff an' Pres'dent Beinbrink. I promised Miz Beuly I wouldn't start speechifyin' until the sausage rolls are consumed; she says we should eat them before they deteriate. We serve them hot now, Miz Bee, which I know ain't canonical. What I got in mind is mo' than a relation for a breakfast, like the Bard said, but before we stultify ourselves

436

with vittles we better have a pre-prandial pull at this here specialized julep. The new citizen!"

It was the first time that Aunt Bee had ever imbibed the Major's most honored elixir. At first she did not quite know how to get at it, but finally parted the foliage and inhaled a few drops. Privately she thought that the fame of this potion was exaggerated; it seemed only an eskimo version of the peppermint water of her childhood.

"I should remark," said the Major to her, "that when the frosting subsides Jeff will find writing on his mug. It's sort of a christenin' cup for a new-born citizen."

Jeff had already wondered why his julep was the only one served in silver and presently found the tankard engraved "Geoffrey Barton, July 4, 1911," and under it the emblem of the rabbit worried by the dog. "That reminds me of the first time I came to Greenaway. I noticed the crest and I said I thought life was very hard on rabbits."

"You're right, sir," said the Major, "and I remember what I said, which is what nobody else ever does."

"*I* remember what you said," remarked Aunt Bee.

"Well, good for you, Ma'am. Miz Bee was always a lady I could pay court to."

"I remember, because I didn't understand it. You said, 'There are two sides to every story. Perhaps you never saw rabbits in a truck garden.' I never did know what a truck garden was until I asked Mr. Sprunt."

The conversation went to and fro, in the intervals of the hot sausage rolls, long since mastered by the Greenaway kitchen, and cocooned in a pastry more fragile than even Aunt Bee had ever accomplished—and waffles with honey, and corn bread and pickled watermelon rind (to which Aunt Bee had now accustomed herself). Even President Beinbrink, so far from his college campus, did not hesitate to suck cautiously at his julep. "Young man, if you make as good a citizen as your uncle," he said, "your sponsors will have no regrets."

437

"But I can remember a time," prattled Mrs. Beinbrink, elevated to chirping by a few bubbles of Bourbon, "I remember a time when Pres'dent Beinbrink didn't think Professor Barton would be such a good citizen. He was doubtful about the way he held his pipe in his mouth."

"Jeff always holds his pipe the same way," said Serena, "I noticed it since he's gotten so grown up."

"You startle me, Mrs. Beinbrink," said Dan. "This is something I didn't know about."

Dr. Beinbrink, on the opposite side of the table from his wife, tried to reach her with a flash of discretion, but the good lady having captured everyone's attention was too flattered to pause.

"It's something about the way an Englishman holds his pipe in his teeth," she said, "it looks obstinate, don't you think? I mean determined, like if he got his teeth on anything he'd never let go. Of course he didn't do it around college, because it's against rules, but I used to see him coming from our sitting-room window, and he'd knock out his pipe on the last corner before he came onto the campus."

"Reluctantly," suggested Blanche. She could see that Mrs. Beinbrink had now received the impact of the President's gaze and was flushed with anxiety.

"I kind of liked that about Uncle Dan," said Teackle, "the way he'd put his pipe in his mouth and just go off and leave it there. I bet when an Englishman comes down on anything he comes down on it hard. You ain't never heard of an Englishman wearing rubber heels, did you?"

"Of course we haven't got any Englishmen here so we can be perfectly frank, can't we?" said Mrs. Warren, with gentle but not ineffective rebuke.

"There's no harm done," said the Major. "Here's Miz Blanche, is a citizen by marriage, and Miz Bee, who's a citizen of the world, and they don't mind if we fight some of our favorite battles over again. Of co'se Jeff is seeing everything now in a new perspective."

438

"Like when you put the pillow the other end of the bed," said Aunt Bee. Her decisive twang cut humorously through the softer tones of the others.

"And a mighty conformable thing to do," said the Major. "Excepting you try to get out of the bed the wrong side in the morning. I declare, Miz Bee, I think you said the last word on the subject. It's the same bed but Americans and British sleep at different ends. Lightfoot, I don't see any obstacles to a little reinforcement."

"No thank you," said Dr. Beinbrink, "no more, there's a very pleasant residue in my tumbler, ha-ha, quite sufficient. To tell the truth, the only time I ever felt dissatisfied with Professor Barton was when he went off somewhere with his pipe and forgot that Shakespeare lecture which I was anticipating with a deal of interest. He left me, so to speak, waiting at the church. I had some considerable difficulty in exculpating us both. The class were waiting—"

"Do you say *were* waiting or *was* waiting?" inquired Serena, who always found Dr. Beinbrink tiresome. "Collective nouns are hell on earth."

"Serena, *please*," said Mrs. Warren.

"A good political epigram," said Aunt Blanche.

"I guess either is right," the new citizen encouraged Serena, admiring such vivacious candor. "Uncle Dan said something awfully good one time, Syntax was made for man and not man for syntax."

"Well, ha-ha, since we are off campus," said Dr. Beinbrink, "it's surely permissible to relax. I was only suggesting that I always wanted to hear that lecture Professor Barton was going to deliver. When Dr. Outward recovered of his mizry he resumed the Bard where he left off, but the class was, or were, defrauded on that lesson. If I recollect, Professor, you had prepared an exordium on *The Tempest*. I think we've still got it coming to us."

439

"That's a right cultural idea," said Mrs. Beinbrink, eager to atone.

"We can all assemble in the Apery," suggested Mrs. Warren. "Dan might shine up our minds with a little—what is that you called it, President?"

"Accordion," suggested Serena, winking at Blanche.

"Every college ought to have some kind of a stop-gap exordium on hand," said Teackle. "I mean a lecture that would be good for any old class, no matter what, when the Prof takes sick."

Jeff liked the idea. "You could put it on one of those phonograph cylinders and just roll it in."

"It could have a little preserved literature, some of ole geezer-Caesar's armavirumquecano—and a little math too, at the bottom of the cylinder," Teackle added.

"Very elementary, I suppose," said Blanche.

"I'm afraid that's just the kind of talk I was going to give," said Uncle Dan. "But I dare say, *pace* Dr. Beinbrink, it was good luck it never got delivered. What I had in mind is better not to talk about because people need to figure it out for themselves. If I had English IX, perhaps I wouldn't even mention *The Tempest*; that might make the students curious and they'd look it up in private."

"Gosh, is it that kind of a story?" exclaimed Serena. "I bet I'll read it right away. Daddy, have you got a copy?"

"I always wondered why they put it first in the book," said Teackle, "but it wasn't required when I took English."

"You-all not only humiliatin' yourselves, you're humiliatin' yo' sire. I declare, I don't see how anybody with sentiments could hep readin' if he just noticed the stage direction? *A ship at sea, and afterwards an island*, why, there ain't anything in the world except maybe a railroad locomotive that's mo' suggestible an' romantic."

"I don't think ships are so romantic," said Mrs. Warren. "I

think they're very uncomfortable, and likely Miz Bee thinks so too."

"I bet Jeff will agree when he gets on that ole cattle-boat," said Teackle. "Pugh!" He pretended to shield his nose.

"You're missing the whole point," said Uncle Dan, rousing to his favorite theme. "In *The Tempest* that's not a real ship, any more than the model in the picture of Old Highboy Zeb up there. You haven't even begun to think if you suppose everything means only what it says. I could give you an example—" but he restrained himself.

"Bravo," said the Major. "Dan's expressing my ideas exactly. Nobody ever gave me credit for the wide expanse between my notions and my statements."

"Major's mind runs such riot, it don't leave no gray matter for the next generation," said Teackle. "Here's Serena Lavinia and me, intellectual paupers."

"You let Uncle Dan proceed with his parables," said the Major. "It look to me like he had a queen bee in his bonnet."

Whether by strategy or tactics, just then Mutual handed Uncle Dan a fresh-rimed tumbler. Dan sniffed the pungent leaves and felt encouraged to continue. "I'm glad the Major mentioned locomotives. Jeff and I tried to build a toy engine one time, but we weren't clever enough."

"We had just the right shade of blue all mixed up for it," said Jeff.

"I was so ashamed of our clumsiness," Dan said, "I had to do something to re-establish myself in Jeff's esteem. So I figured out a way to make ship models with sheets of cardboard. After a bit of experimenting I found you could cut patterns in the flat, paint the sections and then glue them together. We made some pretty fine ships, if I do say so; especially one we called the *Waesland*."

"Because she had a figurehead!" exclaimed Jeff.

"Or maybe because while we were looking at the real *Waesland* I first held Aunt Blanche's hand," said Uncle Dan mildly.

"Why, you old hypocrite," said Jeff, "you never told me that."

"She foundered soon afterward," said Aunt Bee.

"Who did?" asked Serena.

"Kindly hush up, whether citizens or aliens," said the Major, "let Uncle Dan speak his piece."

Across his nosegay of mint Uncle Dan met the particular kind of look from Blanche which they called among themselves The Square Root of Minus One. She knew—with the double apprehension of a woman and a mathematician—what he was groping to say; and she knew it was probably better unsaid. Alertly he switched a whole train of thought onto a siding and said, "I was only remembering a limerick Blanche told me on the *Westernland—*

> There was an old fellow of Trinity
> Who solved the square root of Infinity;
>   But it gave him such fidgets
>   To count up the digits,
> He chucked Math and took up Divinity."

"I'm relieved," said the Major. "You had me frightened, so few limericks end up with divinity."

Not a train of thought, Uncle Dan remembered; a ship of thought. The consequence of evenings making cardboard models with Jeff. The fancy had come to him that long-ago Thursday; that, we dessay, was how he forgot the Shakespeare lecture. Shakespeare would have forgotten too.

He was on a sunlit deck, paneled between white rails was such sparkling blue as points the wet brush before it dabs on paper. Along the washed passage of the promenade he saw the chairs in row, an end of untucked blanket fluttering its fringe, the steward tilting a tray as he rocked on practiced heels, and from within, below, the hum and grumble of her steadfast going. Weather had lately changed, he could feel it by the sting of air and light; comfortably assured the passengers lay in doze or talk. Solid and serene she rode the embracing curves, sparks of sunshine kindled the brasswork, the strong black hull was cleaving bubble and hiss. In awful prudence he raised himself delicately from the chair and tiptoed to the rail. Warily he watched the long white sheer of deck. All went on as usual and he alone knew the ship was cardboard. He had built her himself. The least alarm, the most trifling shock, she would collapse, dissolve. He could almost feel the paper footing, so cunningly contrived with scissors and glue, sink beneath his tread. Great chain-links on her focsle, strong rigging thick with tar—impossible gear for this brittle shell of dream.

But steady rumble and hum came through her fabric: what marvelous illusion. Surely first of all he must warn them down below where danger was most near. He tiptoed over the brass-bound sill, down creaking stairs and corridors, past stateroom curtains that floated in a bulge of air. Down the slippery rungs, ladders plunging deep, to the tremendous fever of her work. A solitary oiler with a foolscap of sacking on his head watched like a gnome under circling knuckles of slogging steel. In the very bends of her bottom he laid a hand against the plates as she rolled, his hand went through. The sea poured in—almost relief, the terror and tension past—he tried vainly to shout alarm, and as he looked up the glinting ladders, steep to the sooted skylights, he saw Blanche coming down. Her dresses fluttered in the warm draught. . . . There's no harm done.

Of course Blanche was right; his dream of the cardboard ship could not be told in full; it was of body as well as mind; no less important to him than Shakespeare's vessel cast away in brainstorm. What else, he thought with his nose still in the mint, are all the arts: cardboard hulls with seams of glue and thread—built in eclipse and rigged with curses dark—yet they must seem real enough for the voyage. Perhaps the most valuable passengers were those prudent to say little—like that fellow Francisco who had only one speech that mattered. He could tell them that: "There's a fellow in *The Tempest* called Francisco," he started, but the table were (or was) already thinking of something else. He was ironically amused, they supposed the ancient limerick was all he had intended. It was his stop-gap exordium.

"Before we go any further with these obsequies," Teackle was saying, "I think we should have a speech from the new citizen."

Jeff tried to beg off, but the Major insisted. "I scarcely know which is mo' excitin'," he said, "Jeff getting to be a citizen, or his goin' over to see the Old Country again. I hope at least he'll send us a postcard like Uncle Dan always does."

"With one of those crazy addresses on it," said Teackle.

"That gives me an idea," Jeff said. "I won't make a speech but I can recite something. When we were all at Sandy Hole Uncle Dan left us a poem to remind us to write to him. It's a parody of those funny English names Teackle and I used to kid him about. He was trying to teach us some English geography."

"I thought you'd forgotten that long ago," Blanche said.

"Not a chance," said Jeff. "I always thought it was a humdinger. It's called *The Postman's Lot Is Not a Happy One,* we published it in the Sandy Hole *Cascade.*" He looked up toward the fan, which was barely moving, perhaps to ease himself of Serena's humorous gaze:

> "Remember, when you're at your desk,
> My name is Daniel Barton, Esq.
>
> In sending letters to Great Britain
> The addresses must be written
>
> From a careful memorandum,
> For you'll never understand 'em.
>
> The English postman's far from happy:
> It's hard for him to make it snappy.
>
> First he diligently pants
> To Upshott, Steep, Old Worldham, Hants.

He raps the knocker, hoping drinks,
At Buttery Hatch, Yeast Rising, Lincs.

Through the mire he goes on stilts
To Little Quag, Wrung Withers, Wilts.

He probably remarks Oh shucks,
At Spital Green, Great Horseleech, Bucks.

With British pluck and dogged spurts
He finds The Yews, Monks Bottom, Herts.

And there are other queer-named spots
In Glos. and Beds. and Yorks. and Notts.

In Old England you can date your
Letters with weird nomenclature:

It would send my spirits soaring
To write to Great or Little Snoring,

But to this one, postman, gallop—
The Priory, Nuns Veiling, Salop."

"I think that's real cute," said Mrs. Warren.

"Uncle Dan wanted to mention his real address, Barton House, The Thorofare, Wilford," said Jeff, "but there's no rhyme for Suffolk."

"We'll have out the Album," said the Major, much pleased. "You must write it in, and you and Dan both sign it."

"I certainly won't write to you if it's as difficult as all that," said Serena.

"I didn't plan to have any centerpiece on the table," said Mrs. Warren to Dan and Jeff who sat either side of her. "I usually aim to see if the Major starts slippin'. I suspect he had Lightfoot set that big bundle of posies right plumb in the way so's to cut communication."

"You better get a purchase on him now, Mother," said Serena. "He'll be good until the bottom of the third julep."

"Geoffrey, you catch him right by the eye," whispered Mrs. Warren. "Hold up your mug at him. He'll ne'er forgive me if I let him spoil himself, he's all set up for his elocution."

Jeff raised the new silver tankard. "Major, may I drink your health?"

"We'll all drink it," said Uncle Dan. "And health to Greenaway, the home of all lost causes."

The Major fell happily into the trap. He rose to his feet. "Miz Beuly an' friends," he said, "I toast it right back at you. This here tumbler is practically a lost cause, nothin' but driblets. I'll have to eke it out with a full po'tion of good feelins. Howsomever, it's too late now for strategy, I'll have to fall back on tattics. I'm glad you give me the high ball while I'm still *compos oris*. I aim to make my spiel without too much doctifications.—Mutual, liven up that boy with the fan, appears to me the temperature is risin'.—I address myself first to our new citizen. Jeff, we-all been lookin' to this day fo' some time. As my ole friend Virgil might say, *Tantae molis erat Americanum condere civem*. I look around an' I see other citizens who become so under my auspices. Not only you, Dan, I'm thinkin' of Lightfoot."

"Yassuh, yassuh," Lightfoot said dimly, rallying himself in the easy chair that had been set for him in the corner behind the Major. But he got his cue mixed. "Yassuh; *navigat aequor?*"

"Not just now," said the Major. "Do our speechifyin' first. Ain't goin' to be all quotations neither, but I made up my mind I'd quote either Virgil or Daddy Wordsworth. I hope Dan ain't goin' to be offended. This time I reckon to pull through without quoting the old burgher of Skiddaw."

"Twenty-three Skiddaw," whispered Teackle across the table to Jeff.

The rickety fan stirred lazily overhead, strips of noonday

barred the windows of the dim-shining room; it was like a fortress whose walls were only summer. How often Jeff wished afterward he could have remembered sharper, or had the wit of shorthand, man's subtlest art to salt the birdwing moment. He tingled with julep but with something else too. On the swordblade of the hour the old Major was more than just a garrulous comedian. There was sunlight on the hour's edge but under it was well-worn steel.

"Only one mo' quotation," said the Major, "an' I blame that on Uncle Dan. He showed me a piece by a poet with right pleasin' initials, William Watson. It's a poem addressed to the Invincible Republic, where he says

> When Fate
> Was at thy makin', and endowed thy soul
> With many gifts an' costly, she forgot
> To mix with these a genius for repose.

Mr. Watson goes on an' says plenty mo' good things I disremember, about the fell Delilah Luxury he doubts might be sappin' American guts and so forth. I stipulate I got as good a taste fo' repose as any man anywheres but I don't see much of it in store fo' the Invincible Republic. I opine that bein' a citizen of these Yewnited States is goin' to be mo'n a picnic. I catch the bright eye of Mr. Teackle Warren who surely inherited a goodly proportion of his father's love of repose—"

Laughter interrupted the Major and gave Teackle an opportunity to retort. "Now, Major, no fair. You ain't addressing yourself to me. Leave the family out of it. You know I been wantin' to get a real hot-diggety job down on the Panama Canal."

"Well, that Panama job comforts me some. If we pick on a piece of engineering that size we ain't altogether succumbed to fell Delilah. As a matter and fact, Jeff, the Canal's a Thorofare too, ain't it; an' they tell me they haul their traffic to leftwards because the colored workboys from Jamaica don't understand

447

nothin' else. Did you know we got a railroad that runs on the left-hand track? It's the Chicago Northwestern if I rec'llect. It was built with British capital and they took up the left-hand rule as a compliment to the pound sterling. When I took Teackle to England he was too likely to think everything was comical. I had to remind him, Son, don't laugh too quick. There's other things too that keeps on the left-hand side; you got one inside of you.

"Howsomever I'm gettin' distracted from my topics. Don't let me go barkin' up the wrong tree, I'm likely to get left on a limbo. I had occasion to watch Uncle Dan a good many years and I know it ain't easy when your patriotism gets divided up. Sometimes you get too noticing of what's measly on both sides. Nationality can get to be right cussed. I don't forget when my own was tore in two."

The Major explored his tumbler to see if any more sweetness had melted down. He often said that his ideal in drinking was like the right-of-way whistle—two longs and two shorts. But it was really his mind he was dipping into, rather than the julep.

"Of co'se it would be mannerly to say I'd admire to change places with the new citizen. I ain't so sure. It's right pleasurable to be seventy-one. You don't particularly hanker for nothin'. You still got sense an' sensibility, and it's like when you set outside at sundown an' watch the colors drain out of the flower-garden. Like Hazlitt says, numberin' only the sunny hours. You've had seventy years as per contrack, an' a little unearned increment for thinking. I had to do my schoolmasterin' for myself mostly, but I can see I never got very far without somebody took me by the hand an' showed me the way.

"Now I'm addressin' myself mostly to President Beinbrink, because the real topic is education. As a matter and fact, and like Uncle Dan would say, *pace* the ladies, it's female education that's mo' on my mind. The boys get a certain amount of learnin' hammered in anyhow, but gals sort of got to pick it out for themselves. Seems like a young woman is so swarmed over by her own personal identity she feels a natural resentment for printed matter. Maybe I wouldn't even tally that idea Uncle Dan derived, the way to educate a gal is to put her on a desert island with a philosopher and a savage—"

"I say," protested Dan, "what a way to travesty my innocent suggestion."

The Major winked and proceeded. "I hope President Beinbrink still has a few of those residues in his glass, I'm shortly going to propose a toast. Mr. President, you ain't as far off yo' campus as you thought. You-all heard me grumbling a long while about being land-poor, them old tobacco fields and pastures being no good to anybody. I figured there's another kind of crops they might help to raise and that's the young women of Patapsco. We talked already about the Tullius Teackle Warren professorship, now there's another side to it. I sold off some acreage for suburban developings an' I got more'n I ever expected. But there's a right pretty piece left, woods and hills and fields, and a stretch of crick for a swimmin' hole. I never did like the look of them brick warehouses of yours on Patapsco Street. Mr. President, if yo' trustees and alumnae can raise an endowment for the buildin's the land's yours for the new campus. It's free and clear, with a name on it an' a deed of gift, and the legal documents awaits yo' attention.—Mutual, wake up old Lightfoot and tell him fetch me those papers he knows about; an' you can bring us a relay of juleps.

"I'm goin' to quit before I talk too much. You-all can study that landscape drawin' while those that's so disposed has their customary forty-leven winks. There's an old farmin' road runs through the territory, I figured we could build along that and maybe I could start the ball rolling with a little small gateway in mem'ry of Tullius Teackle. When a man's my age it's funny how he gets to feel like his own father. Anyways that gate an' that road would be our main artery. I can imagine the gals going along it to their classes and all blowin' steam about some-

449

thin'. I stipulate that if a fair propo'tion of 'em is good-lookin'
it won't do no harm.

"Miz Beuly, President Beinbrink, ladies and gentlemen, on
this birthday of the Invincible Republic I ask you to join with
me and drink healthy mem'ry— And by God, just a moment, I
forgot one thing. Miz Bee, if you cast your eye on that map
you'll see that road across the middle's got a name onto it. I
hope it ain't takin' too much liberty. A healthy mem'ry to Tullius Teackle, on the Thorofare."

There's one thing about all that shrubbery on top of the glass,
Bee thought: it hides one's mouth if there's any quivering.

69. *The Bookmark*

"Major thinks he's playin' chess," said Serena as her father
made a knight's gambit across the black-and-white marble
checker of the hall. Aunt Bee had the familiar sensation that
all this had happened before: the heavy sunlight pressing in,
the ancient panama hat cast on a polished wooden chest, the
tall hoarse clock in the shadow—not unlike the one at Wilford
for which Geoff had recommended a troche. Why are those
grandfather timepieces always set in the hollow of the house,
their difficult midnight asthma comes to a child's ear at midnight like punishment treading upstairs? The thought was canceled by Teackle and Jeff who slid down the shining banisters
from above.

"You see we still use the same furniture polish," said Mrs.
Warren.

"It works better than it did," said Teackle, rubbing. "I reckon
the bigger you get the hotter you slide. I'm going out in the
garden and play me a tune; what-say, Jeff, let's harmonize."

"Jeff's comin' in the Apery with Dan and me," said the Major. "He's got a job to do."

Mrs. Warren escorted the ladies upstairs. Dr. Beinbrink asked
permission to sit in the drawing-room to study the architect's

plan. The Major led the way down the corridor past the sporting relics of Uncle Randy. In the passage Dan noticed a table with a pile of books. "Major, don't tell me literature is creeping in here?"

"Just an idea of mine," said the Major. "I put some of the new stuff here to ripen a bit while I make up my mind do it get promoted to the Apery. If I was to give some of the old books away I'd be needin' to fill up the gaps."

The Album was ready on the Major's desk. "I set out a nice clean page," he said. "What you might call the sonnet's scanty plot of ground. Uncle Dan wrote one fo' the book, likely it's yo' turn now."

Jeff begged to do Uncle Dan's postman verses instead.

"You write what you feel fo'," agreed the Major. "Sonnets is like sausage rolls, they better be handled just so. They can be right indigestible if you take 'em out of the oven too quick. It'll be coffee today instead of Madeira. We won't let anything compete with what we had. Lightfoot don't bring it in till it's the same color he is."

The stable-boys had squandered all their fireworks by this time and even Teackle's college mandolin somewhere in the garden was comfortably faint. He imparted conscientious wistfulness to *Working on the Railroad*, which he found consoling after hours in the freight office.

"This is what I call sedentary quo," said the Major. "Take the weight off your brain, Dan; I reckon that chair knows yo' shape by now. The ladies is gone to Bedfordshire. We can indulge. Fo' me, po' man, my liberry is dukedom large enough. . . . Of temp'ral royalties he thinks me now incapable. . . . Confed'rates. . . ."

For a few moments Jeff's fountain pen moved steadily across the slippery page, but his mind went over the edge. He was thinking this was an adventure for that hard-working nib which had experimented so many slopes of doctrine, from Chaucer to Seager—"What comes after Wrung Withers, Wilts?" he asked.

There was a peculiar quality in the silence, then a small china clink; he turned and saw Uncle Dan hold up a finger. The Major had again performed his most admired achievement, falling asleep in the very action of laying down his cup. At that moment running feet were swift in the passage. The words came through with the opening door: "Can I borrow *The Tempest?*"

"I'm awfully sorry, Daddy," she said. "I didn't know you were asleep." She perched on the arm of the Major's chair and gently tweaked his beard. Again Jeff lost his way among the English shires. How much better than overalls: the white dress, and her hair braided round her head—there must be plenty of rhymes for crown?

"Who, me? Man of my age don't go to sleep, he just thinks with his eyes shut."

"I only wanted to borrow *The Tempest* and I'll get right out of the dormitory."

"A likely excuse, you got yo' own copy of Shakespeare, ain't you? I give you one when you put yo' hair up."

"I didn't know it was by Shakespeare," she said. "It sounds too exciting. You and Uncle Dan is just cozenin' me to make me read literature."

"It's over on the desk," the Major said. "I been readin' after it myself."

"Reach it to me, Jeff," suggested Serena, observing that the young man was still trying to concentrate on the Album.

"Kitty Swerrock where she sat, Come reach me this and reach me that," the Major said. "Reach it yo'self, you minx."

Serena stayed where she was, one foot swinging.

"Folks don' get things like that reached to 'em," said the Major. "They got to purvey fo' themselves." But the old gentleman was smart enough to know this was only an epigram. Even an eavesdropping bee, falling heat-struck from the honeysuckle in his heavy woolen reefer, uttered a derisive buzz.

"Thank you," she said as Jeff brought the book. "I'll run away and you-all can enjoy yo' naps."

"Start at the second scene," the Major advised, "the beginning won't interest you much."

"If it's literature maybe I'll need some tutorin'," she said and was gone.

Jeff continued the postman's route and then looked through the pages of the Album. He felt better about his own sonnet after reading some of the entries. He was amused to find a recipe, annotated as hearsay from Uncle Hartley: Nether Stowey Flip (as drunk in the lime-tree bower). Now he knew where Uncle Dan had discovered that dark concoction he once boiled in a saucepan and spilled on Aunt Bee's rug. He was about to mention this discovery in triumph, but looking round saw they were both asleep.

Serena, in the warm-smelling shade of a quickset alcove, heard steps along the gravel but did not look up. She was honestly trying to concentrate; besides, a suggestion of absence is becoming in a woman of letters. "I'm poring over my book, I'm so *distrait*," she said to herself. So she pretended surprise when he sat beside her.

"Goodness, I thought you were takin' a nap. I'm reading after Miranda but she keeps goin' asleep. I been droopy myself."

"Major and Uncle Dan dozed off," said Jeff, "so I tippytoed out."

"I didn't aim to bust in thataway. I declare I'm always doin' the wrong thing. I bet I get it from Major. He shames us-all the way he misbehaves. He soliloquize to everybody."

"I thought maybe you'd let me take your picture, by the sundial."

"Ye gods, you took one this morning, just to be provokin'."

"I'll throw it away if you let me get a good one."

She laid Shakespeare open on the weathered pedestal. "Don't be all day about it," she said. "It's blazin' here."

"I was just wondering if you have that ribbon, maybe you could put it on, it would be, well, you know, like a trophy."

"A trophy?" she exclaimed. "Trophy of what?"

He wondered what makes words go wrong when you're talking to girls. "I don't mean a trophy," he said. "Sort of a souvenir, a keepsake."

"Yes, I've got it," she admitted, producing it from inside her short sleeve, "but I can't wear it. You don't wear ribbons when you've got yo' hair braided up like this. I stipulate you don't know much about women's clothes."

"I dare say not," he said. "Well, we could put it as a bookmark in Shakespeare. That's what I'm going to use it for."

"It'll look like the Bible," but she spread the strip of silk across the pages. The thin leaves were curling upward as if alive in the brilliant dry air. The little camera clicked, and they returned to the shaded seat.

"That's certainly an important ribbon," he said, folding it carefully. "There's only one other I ever saved, the one that was tied round my diploma.—I can see the least little crinkle right where it was tied in a bow."

"I should think you'd be glad to forget all that nonsense."

The subject of the ribbon did not seem to lead anywhere, though he had imagined it looped into endless fancy. "How do you like *The Tempest?*" he asked.

"It sure is a queer kind of a story. I was so humiliated, not to know it was by Shakespeare. I guess I'm awfully ignorant."

Serena had discovered it was rather fun to criticize herself, it seemed to lead young men to swift contradiction.

"I'm a bit rusty on it too. Uncle Dan had me read it but I've sort of forgotten. Probably I was too young."

"I'm disconsolate bein' told I'm too young fo' this an' that. People don't feel as young as other people keep tellin' them. I suppose you're right set up, bein' citizenized."

454

"Monstrous full o' fleas," Jeff agreed.

There was a silence while she smoothed the pages of the book in her lap. The sunny space before them, roomed in by hedges, was like an island of light, or the golden pool of study under a green lamp. Flower beds too: like the colored lights of the gas-stove, warm gules on the pilot-house floor, snug evenings when Jeff was alone with Keats. Everything was like something else, the wariest way of being itself? But Keats was out of luck, he thought; the marker was going to be used for Shakespeare. . . . Teackle's distant mandolin faintly pursued its dulcet repertoire: *The Old Apple Tree, Juanita, The Spanish Cavalier, The Yama Man.* These required no thought, they were Cheese Onto; under their harmonic simplicities Teackle's mind was happily shoveling the Culebra Cut or recuperating from yellow fever under the cherishing hand of a Spanish-tinted nurse.

"It's nice to have music outdoors," Jeff said, then felt vaguely that someone somewhere might have had the thought before. "I mean, a garden like this is sort of like music somehow, everything has been composed together, everything is there instead of something else that might have been there. The Major had to make up his mind and choose whether he'd put roses or peonies or what-all, I mean shrubs and borders, or hardy perennials? I guess roses *are* perennials, aren't they?"

He wasn't much interested in gardens except as picturesque background, and wondered how on earth he got into such a topic. Serena disregarded it:

"I sort of got interested in Miranda because I reckoned she's same age I am, but goodness she starts right off and says *stinkin'*, that's a word Major wouldn't tolerate fo' me to say. I bet those old plays weren't intended to be put in books, people were all too illit'rate to read, weren't they? But when anybody sees a thing on the stage they got a chance to appreciate it, and if there's a lot of folks around you can't afford to be embarrassed. Like Romeo and Juliet. When they enacted a play like that I really thought it was excellent."

455

Serena was quite astonished at herself. This sounded so literary she would have liked to say it again.

"I always think if you can't go to the theater it's almost as good to read it aloud and take parts. I used to read a lot of Shakespeare to Aunt Bee, but it wasn't so good having her do the part of Juliet. You know how she talks, through her nose. The first person you hear read anything, somehow you never quite get over it."

"You could read some of this to me. I think I'd get the hang of it better."

Jeff looked over the pages. "Let's both read. Yes, there's only the two of them for quite a bit. Prospero talks a lot more than Miranda."

"I guess that's why she comes over drowsy. I declare, it's true to life."

"We haven't any Ariel."

"Pretend Teackle's Ariel, makin' that crazy ole music."

"Say, you know what would be fun, some day we could get everybody to take parts and give a regular open-air performance right here in the garden."

"I bet Teackle would love to be that ornery Caliban."

Jeff, refreshing his memories of the play, thought how wonderful Ingram Sylvester Duffle would have been as Caliban. With the instinct of a stage director he could hear him cry: "I shall be pinched . . . the big fiends!"

"Is there a part for you?" Serena asked.

"Oh, I guess so. I could do Ferdinand; he doesn't come in yet."

"Shall we turn over to his part?"

"You better get the plot first. Let's begin with Miranda and I'll be Prospero."

"Maybe we ought to have another book."

"I guess one'll do if we both hold it."

They began to read. After a little shyness Serena gathered spirit; always afterward (rather like a dream than an assuhance)

Jeff heard *The Tempest* in the soft accents of Chesapeake. And why not, he thought. Isn't it a Southren fable?

The Major, strolling the garden with newspaper and cigar, heard their voices. Mutual and Lightfoot were carrying tea-things toward the box-garden; he motioned them to halt and himself approached quietly along the grass border. He was amused to see, beyond the hedge, the two heads earnestly together.

"Wherefo' did they not that hour destroy us?" asked Serena.

"Well demanded, wench," replied Jeff. The Major cocked an ear and grinned sideways from the cigar. He enjoyed the two young voices: one so deliberately spaced, the other with its soft tonguebound slur. They were too absorbed to suspect his nearness; and after all, he thought, Shakespeare likes to end a scene with a couplet.

"So, of his gentleness, knowing I loved my books," Jeff continued. This was a cue the Major could pick up: he chimed in "He fuhnished me, from mine own liberry, with volumes that I prize."

"Would I might see that man!" laughed Serena, reading the next line— "Major, yo' ole reprobate!"

"Enter strange shapes, bringin' in a banquet," said the Major. "Sorry to interrupt, you'd have been broke off in a moment anyhow. Lightfoot an' Mutual's totin' out tables and things."

"There's no harm done," said Jeff. "Say, I was so surprised to find that very phrase, what you and Uncle Dan are always saying, 'There's no harm done.' I didn't know you were quoting."

"It's really fun," Serena exclaimed. "We were thinking we could have a party some time and give the play out of doors."

"There's a right scenic little holler on the new campus," said the Major, "sort of a dingly-dell they could lay out fo' an open-air theater. Dr. Beinbrink an' Dan has gone walkin' through the brush to look over the grounds. As a matter and fact, Jeff, all this here schemin' is partly yo' fault. Do you rec'llect tellin' me that game of imaginary countries and imaginary colleges you an' Dan used to play Sunday afternoons? Reckon mebbe that's what put notions in my mind. Now if you-all is goin' swimmin' befo' tea you better make tracks."

"Nix on swimmin'," said Serena. "Let's go look at that dingly-dell. Daddy, if I learn it this summer, could I be Miranda when Jeff gets back?"

"Po' worm, thou art infected," the Major quoted. "Miz Beuly an' I goin' to take the ladies walkin' down by the briar patch."

"Major," said Jeff, "could I ask you one special favor for my Coming-In? There's one thing I've never heard read aloud the way it ought to be, and you're the only one who could. Would you do it, after tea?"

"What's that? Yo' mean Prospero? I please myself I could spout Prospero like a barn on fire." Waving his cigar he did so: "The cloud-capped towehs, the go'geous palaces, The solemn temples, the great globe itse'f, Yea all which it inhehit, shall dissolve—leavin' no rack behind."

Jeff blurted what had been on his mind for some time. "I was wondering if you'd read us one of the stories from Uncle Remus."

The Major was piqued. Uncle Remus seemed a comedown when he was thinking of Shakespeare; it was too close to home to be literature.

"Well, mebbe so, mebbe so. I'm goin' to sit down an' read my *Sun-Paper*. You-all scamper along an' catch up with those Professors. Tell 'em No'theast Trades blows at five o'clock."

A peaceful eddy of smoke rose from behind the newspaper as he sat reading, the volume of Shakespeare on the bench beside him with Serena's handkerchief crumpled inside. He found plenty of interest. German gunboat *Panther* sent to Agadir in Morocco. Germany Awaits France's Action. United States Holding Aloof. The German minister has notified the Moorish gov-

458

ernment that Germany has decided to occupy Agadir and the hinterland.

Othello's occupation's gone, thought the Major.

70. So Long Ho!

Jeff was up and doing in the pilot-house before sunrise. He and Skinny were to report aboard ship many hours before sailing time. Skinny was coming to 1910 at 6:30 and Aunt Bee had promised them a real Wilford breakfast before starting. As he packed his suitcase Jeff was noticing things by the dawn's early light. The tree-tops of Druid Hill were filtered with pinks and greens; the Backs of Schier Street brightened; and in the valley Ma clanked a morning crosshead and shrilled a steamy *hurrp* to her consort Pa. She sounded as if she got out of the roundhouse the wrong side.

You see things first of all just in outline, he thought; color fills in gradually. I must watch that on the *Minnewatha* (we'll have to get up at 4 o'clock to water the cattle). It might be an idea for a sonnet: Opus 2. I certainly will be an experienced person when I get back to this pilot-house. Uncle Dan says the *Minnewatha* is a comical ship, she carries cattle on one deck and college professors on another. I bet some of those profs have daughters with them. When they look down onto the farmyard deck they'll never guess those two fellows in overalls are Chesapeake graduates, one of them going to Harvard to study Ph.D. and the other practically started on his second sonnet.

Aunt Bee was early too. Sausage rolls were in the oven, and she got out the Wilford eggcups and cozies instead of the dish called Happy Hen. And there was Cooper's bitter Oxford marmalade—the only Oxonian product to which Uncle Dan would grant supremacy—and oatmeal and cream with Demerara sugar. Aunt Bee and Jeff had conspired together to astound Skinny. This trip is going to be a great education for him, Jeff prophesied. And by gosh, things are certainly looking up. I've graduated; I've got a job; I'm going to Europe with my best friend; and I guess I'm in love—anyway I've written a sonnet.—Serena had given him a leather diary called *My Trip Abroad*; it was tucked inside the flap of the suitcase with a slice of The Ribbon as marker.

Waiting for breakfast Jeff sat down at the piano and played *The North Wind Doth Blow*, to rouse Uncle Dan. "Good lack!" said Aunt Bee, a mysterious ejaculation which Jeff never entirely understood. "That's not a very good tune for today. It's going to be plaguy hot. Dessay we'll have that traction engine roaring in front of us all day."

"It's not a traction engine, it's a steam roller," said Jeff. "You ought to be pleased Carroll Street's being paved at last. I bet the rollers in Wilford were never as big as that."

"I wouldn't remember," said Aunt Bee. "The Thorofare was paved about 1840."

Jeff got even with her by playing *Chopsticks*, which she detested. "I like coffee, I like tea," he warbled, "I like girls when girls like me. Wish my Uncle'd hold his tongue, he liked girls when he was young." Skinny arrived and they made it a duet, until Uncle Dan shouted for mercy. He came downstairs in his dressing-gown looking very mage-like with his beard bent sideways from sleep.

"You'll wake Mrs. Maggots," he warned. "You don't want The Eye watching you all the way to the corner. It'll put a hex on you."

"I've got it all figured out with Possum. When we leave she's going out in the backyard and do something crazy. Poor old Maggots will get rattled, not knowing which way to look."

Aunt Bee was a bit grim. "Don't footle, sit down and eat."

"This is certainly some breakfast," said Skinny admiringly.

"Ampersand's purr fills the cave with thunder," said Jeff, sharing scraps with the animals.

"I hope it'll be high tide when you see the River," said Aunt Bee to Skinny, watching Jeff play the Oatmeal Game.

460

"We'll get out of our third-class carriage at Ipswich and tele-phone—I mean ring through—to Harry Bredfield to find out how the tide is," said Jeff. "That'll shake him up some; if he has a phone?"

"Don't be too stern with the poor English," said Dan. "They've been through a good deal since Hengist and Horsa."

"Hengist was a Horsa's Horse," Jeff whispered to Skinny.

"At least I'll have the use of some socks and handkerchiefs while you're away," said Uncle Dan. "Pass the mustard."

"I'm going to hear Skinny his conversation exercises every night on the *Minnewatha*."

The well-mannered Skinny felt that Jeff was almost too T.S.O. 4 in mood. "Are you-all going away somewhere for a trip?" he asked politely.

"We're going to explore New England," said Uncle Dan. "I've taken a little cottage on Cape Cod. Aunt Blanche and I have work to do and Aunt Bee's going bathing."

"I've always been curious about Massachusetts," said Aunt Bee. "There are so many East Anglian names of places."

"They talk the same way too," said Jeff. "Aunt Bee's nose will feel quite at home."

"Kilda always says the Yankee accent is really chronic ca-tarrh," Blanche observed. "They've had it in New England for three centuries."

"We've had it in Wilford for a thousand years," Aunt Bee said proudly.

"They probably forgot to bring any handkerchiefs in the *Mayflower*," Jeff suggested.

Aunt Bee had sat late in her cozy corner the night before; after finishing some mending she went through a cache of old treasures. Now she brought out a sheet of juvenile script. "Geof-frey is feeling so sprightly, happen this might amuse him. Do you remember the History of Jeffland you started one time?"

"Gosh, did you save that all these years? Read it aloud!"

"You read it," she said. "Such beautiful writing, I might give it a nasal twang."

"History of Jeffland in the Twentieth Century," read the President emeritus. "Jeffland, a modern republic, was founded by pilgrims from Wilford who were looking for something unusual. They heard there was a great deal of prosperity with maple sugar and peanut butter. They waited until they found a ship with two funnels, called the *Westernland*. This name was used for one of the important provinces. They came very fast but there was time to get aclimated to hot cakes and their hair cut before landing. In Jeffland there were a great many Vacant Lots. After the tin cans had been cleared away the President built a stately pleasure dome for the capital. The motto they adopted was Large and Clean and New, there were some rather incessant wars with the neighboring country of LaGrange. After the Battle of Martello an indemity of 1 million lucres plus 50,000 demi-reps was paid to the Rajah of LaGrange. Among other pests were feirce animals and insects, and not much drainage, but the President invented a large wire fence to shut in buffaloes and a small wire fence to bafle the moskitoes. The people were sometimes too pugnacious and manners not always good, especially among schoolboys, instead of inherited nobility they got along with Daughters of the Westernland. Some people called it God's Country but that was only their joke."

This was received with applause. "The historian wasn't overly generous to LaGrange," said Skinny.

"I've warned you about *overly*," Jeff rebuked him. "They don't say that in England."

"I'll study my exercises *whilst* we're on the ship," Skinny said. "I swear I won't *drop any bricks*, you'll be *fearfully bucked*."

They all laughed at Skinny's earnest docility. "Don't you let Jeff bully you," said Uncle Dan. "He doesn't really know any more about it than you do."

"My father says he's sorry we don't land at Liverpool," said

Skinny. "Then we could go straight to Chester and Stratford-on-Avon and Oxford."

"Pooh, that's what all the American tourists do," Jeff asserted. He already felt superior to such gullible unfortunates. "We'll see plenty going up the Channel and landing at London. I bet we'll see Eddystone Light, and Dover Castle, and London Bridge."

"I thought that fell down," said Skinny.

"Do we go to Euston? I've never forgotten that gateway with the smoky light—it was like the pillars of Hercules."

"I'm so eager to see Paddington," said Skinny. "That's where Sherlock Holmes was always taking the train. Or do I mean Waterloo?"

"You'll go to Liverpool Street," said Uncle Dan. "You'll see Stratford-atte-Bow, which is much more genuine than Stratford-on-Avon." He felt a little envious. What castles or cathedrals are as thrilling as the old Victorian railway stations? He thought of the boys' young excitements, equally glorious going and coming back; and for Geoffrey the strange tart flavor of forgotten recognitions. A ship at sea, and afterwards—an ancient smoky terminal, porters in corduroys, a bookstall with newspapers that smell pungent as primroses. He understood that Jeff's high spirits this morning were really to conceal queer feelings underneath.

"What do we do after we get to Liverpool Street, Uncle Dan? Tell a buttons to call a hansom?"

"Wait and see. If I were you I'd go to the Refreshment Room and have a grilled whiting, with a spot of Worcestershire. And a cup of strong tea. Avoid their coffee as you would the devil."

"If it was me," said Aunt Bee, "I'd go somewhere and have a bath. You'll need it after eleven days with those bullocks."

"I suppose it's some kind of symbolism," Jeff considered, "bringing them their roast beef of Old England all the way from Sprunt City."

463

"The steamship company gives us a free trip home from Antwerp," said Skinny. "That ought to be jolly interesting?" he added experimentally. "We go over from Harwich—"

"Pronounced Harridge," Jeff interrupted.

"Oh blimey," said poor Skinny. "There's another one. Anyway, it's where Dr. Johnson saw Boswell off for the Continent. Imagine!"

"Have some more marmalade," Aunt Bee offered.

"Thank you, Miz Bee, I'm a-plenty. I feel like my sister Nixie used to say, You can lift me down, Mother, but don't bend me."

"I'm sorry you won't see some of the other parts of England," said Blanche. "Don't forget the old story: when the Angles first landed the acute Angles went north and west, the obtuse Angles stayed in Norfolk and Suffolk."

"Skinny mustn't mind the way we-all chip at each other," Jeff said.

"I'm beginning to get wise," said Skinny. "England and America always have a special kind of Family Joke—each other."

"Time's getting on, G-offrey," said Uncle Dan. "I can hear that road-roller putting on its vast thick pants."

"I'll go out in the backyard and wave a red rag for Mrs. Maggots," said Blanche. "I'll smoke a cigarette and toss my short hair."

Aunt Bee's mind was on the good-by corner, as they always called the bend at Carroll and 19th where anyone departing went downhill out of sight. How many times through the years she had austerely watched Dan or Jeff as far as that along the vista of brick pavement and marble steps. She drew Jeff aside a moment and hugged him with unusual force. "Good luck, dear boy. Here's something for you I've been saving a long time. Spend it on the Thorofare." Wrapped in tissue paper was a golden sovereign.

"Jeemineezer!" he exclaimed. "A pound sterling? Dollars

four-point-eighty-six-and-two-thirds! Why, Aunt Bee, I could buy an *Ellen Arkins* at Miss Hoo's."

"Have a good time, old man," said Uncle Dan. "See you after Labor Day. Tell Harry Bredfield we're still looking for his visit."

Aunt Bee was munching resolutely. "After you've gone I think I'll ask Uncle Dan to read me a chapter of Mayne Reid."

"Take good care of Sandy while I'm away. He's so sentimental."

"We'll give him a whole sausage roll as anaesthetic," said Uncle Dan.

"Oh dear, why didn't I think to make up a parcel of them," Aunt Bee reproached herself. "They could eat them on the ship."

Skinny looked anxious. "Listen, we're full to the muzzle," Jeff said. "We must beat it, we'll miss the train."

"Bring back some hundreds and thousands for Dan's birthday!" cried Aunt Bee and ran upstairs to watch them a little farther from the busybody window.

Jeff had been afraid Uncle Dan might embarrass him in front of Skinny by saying "Cheer-ho!" To his relief Dan used the phrase they had evolved as a substitute: "So long ho!"

The boys picked up their suitcases and now the worst was over. They would walk to the Key Street trolley. Already workmen were cooking a great caldron of tar, the ancient cobbles were being carted away. A few early Oriole boys gaped at the operations. Carroll Street would never be the same.

Uncle Dan in his famous old bathrobe stood on the marble stoop for a final salute. "Good luck, both of you. Keep an eye open for some subtleties of the isle."

"Right-O," said Skinny.

"O.K.," said Geoffrey.

71. Thorofare Extended

"Let's have another cup of coffee," Dan said. He was at a loose end: too late to go back to bed and too early to start the day. "I'm glad we can get away, now Jeff's gone. I'll go downtown and see about the baggage transfer."

There was a sudden slosh of water in the brick runway next door. "It's going to be hot," said Blanche. "You can always tell, when Mrs. Maggots takes a bath in the morning. Keep on the shady side of the street."

"Some shun sunshine, some shun shade," he quoted the family tongue-twister Jeff had invented. "Let's hope the boys won't have a downpour for their sailing."

"The milk bottles were oozing," said Bee. She had learned that the new cardboard bottle-tops were useful as a barometer. When the milk bubbled round the edge she took her umbrella with her to market.

"I'm going to pack," Blanche said. "Please put out the books you want to take so they can go in the bottom of the trunk."

They heard the squeak of the backyard gate and Moxie arrived under a hat of purple straw. Bee firmly ushered the animals into the cellar and began carrying dishes to the kitchen.

Dan visualized the cottage on Cape Cod, wide blue air and beaten sands. There he could concentrate on his writing. No carnelians or amber, but he might find Hazlitt's shoe-buckle. He lit his pipe and wandered vaguely upstairs. A rising eddy of tobacco followed him up to Jeff's pilot-house. Intending to choose a volume of the Hazlitt birthday-set he looked round.

There was the usual betraying evidence of both order and forgetfulness. Dan had a troubled sense of taking advantage of another's sanctum; the pain love feels in seeing a place just left. He had been almost peevish at Jeff's going off in such high spirits; now he reproached himself. Here were the boy's treasures, and things say more than words. The old steam engine with the selfish whistle was carefully covered against dust, but a shirt and socks lay on the floor. Bedclothes eagerly flung off had upset the saucer of water for Sandy if he was thirsty in the night. On the bookcase a roll of tissue paper guarded the new Diploma. On the desk was Shakespeare with a ribbon in it, and a calendar with today's date ringed in colored pencil. "Ring Around a Saturday" they used to chaff Jeff's habit of marking T.S.O. 4 junkets far ahead. In a pile of notebooks labeled for lecture subjects was one conspicuously marked G. B. PRIVATE! Uncle Dan slipped it out of sight in the desk drawer. On the wall was the snapshot of Miss Debbidge caressing a stone deer; the map of Jeffland showing various gradations of skill; the survey sheet of Susquehanna.

A row of large textbooks were so neatly shelved they looked already memorial; earlier books, on lower levels, were less prim, less mortuary-looking. Straightening them he noticed the little school text of *The Ancient Mariner*, the one with the famous error. This misprint had always pleased him, for he had once thought of preparing a new edition of the poem himself and a rival teacher had been more enterprising. He opened the book and observed some classroom jocularities written in the margins, then reread familiar lines in small print:

In his loneliness he yearneth towards the journeying Moon and the stars that still sojourn, yet still move onward . . . the blue sky is their appointed rest, and their native country and their own natural homes. . . .

Often, in his homesick years, he had been moved by that noble passage. He thought with love and envy of the young Traveling Barton who would also find natural homes at both ends. How quickly Jeff had fallen into the characteristic bravura of his adopted country; yet that was the way of youth, annotating life's ancient text with confident green japes. The careful notes in the new Hazlitt set were different. He could see by paper markers where the enthusiast had been reading: those clarion

titles that ring like hunting horns in the deep woods of print—
On the Feeling of Immortality in Youth; On the Ignorance of
the Learned; My First Acquaintance with Poets—

He chose one of the volumes, and considered that the cattle-
men's berths of the *Minnewatha* would be a contrast to this
light and intimate cabin on the roof. The boys, on their way to
Philadelphia, would soon be crossing the Susquehanna; he wondered if Jeff would recall its associations. But one cannot meddle
with anyone else's living and thinking.

Now the boy was off on his own; he must form his own
idea of the two countries, sometimes tragically alike, often humorously different. Perhaps Americans were sometimes forget-
ful of the love and hope of so many who had helped to build
the vast immoderate land. Even some who had never seen her
had strengthened the young republic with their dreams. Americans were quick to take credit to themselves for happy-go-lucky
fortune.

It was growing warm in the pilot-house as the sun rose above
the stone tumors of Patapsco College. The new Patapsco, he
thought happily, would be his Susquehanna; his New Atlantis;
his Jeffland. His mind was already busy with a fresh course of
lectures for fall. He looked again at Jeff's map. It had under-
gone many revisions through the years but some features remained unchanged. Approaching the coast was the dotted line
marked *Voyage of the Pilgrims;* it was zigzagged to represent
a romantic gale off Cape Bredfield and Cape Hoo. There was
still the great highway named Thorofare Extended. It had no
Roman directness but wound here and there to visit the most
flourishing towns, the handsomest mountains, ingeniously shaped
lakes and famous battlefields. Dan remembered what one of the
strong-minded Paston women had written in Norfolk centuries
ago: "This world is but a thoroughfare—"

Bee's voice came up from the box-room. "Hurrp!" she called.
"Take your bath so Moxie can clean."

"Bee and I are going shopping," said Blanche. "I can't do mathematics against that steam roller."

"I rather like it," Dan said.

A long road, he thought, and not always well-paved; but a road for good men's feet.